A Rogue in Moonlight

The Whisky Rogues, Book 3
Originally published as The Highland Groom / Avon
And also as Laird of Secrets

Susan King

ARE YOU SIGNED UP FOR DRAGONBLADE'S BLOG?

You'll get the latest news and information on exclusive giveaways, exclusive excerpts, coming releases, sales, free books, cover reveals and more.

Check out our complete list of authors, too!

No spam, no junk. That's a promise!

Sign Up Here

www.dragonbladepublishing.com

Dearest Reader;

Thank you for your support of a small press. At Dragonblade Publishing, we strive to bring you the highest quality Historical Romance from some of the best authors in the business. Without your support, there is no 'us', so we sincerely hope you adore these stories and find some new favorite authors along the way.

Happy Reading!

CEO, Dragonblade Publishing

Additional Dragonblade books by
Author Susan King

The Whisky Rogues Series
A Rogue in Firelight (Book 1)
A Rogue in Twilight (Book 2)
A Rogue in Moonlight (Book 3)

Highland Secrets Series
The Scottish Bride (Book 1)
The Forest Bride (Book 2)
The Guardian's Bride (Book 3)

Celtic Hearts Series
The Hawk Laird (Book 1)
The Falcon Laird (Book 2)
The Swan Laird (Book 3)

The Lyon's Den Series
Lyon of Scotland

For Jeremy and Jason, brewmeisters extraordinaire,
Thank you for the inspiration (and commotion) while I wrote this book.
So wondrous wild, the whole might seem
The scenery of a fairy dream.
—Sir Walter Scott, "The Lady of the Lake"

Prologue

Scotland, the Highlands
May, 1807

JUST BEFORE DAWN on his thirteenth birthday, Dougal MacGregor climbed a hill behind his father, whose steps were long and sure. Tall for his age, Dougal kept pace and glanced around in the half darkness, where surrounding mist obscured the trees and rocks on the hillside. Even in daylight, the climb was risky, but his father knew every step and misstep over these hills. Born in Glen Kinloch, John MacGregor was the glen's laird, a farmer, and a clever smuggler.

Dougal was proud to be Kinloch's son and eager to be the newest keeper of the family secret, which his father had promised to reveal to him that very morning.

Where hill met mountain, the way grew steep, but Dougal and his father had the strong legs and good lungs of Highlanders used to long miles. His late mother, Anna MacIan, had often said that her son was even more handsome than his brawny, dark-haired father. Dougal wanted to be as fine a man as John MacGregor of Kinloch one day, and watch over the people of Glen Kinloch with the same fairness his father showed.

He wanted to be a smuggler like John, too. The free trade put coin in poor Highland pockets, though the new laws and regulations had made the enterprise more dangerous. But Dougal would rather run whisky over the hills and outwit the revenue men than go to school. Books and learning were not half as enjoyable as leading gaugers on a merry chase by moonlight, and reaching the shore of the great loch, where sloops waited to take whisky kegs along to the river, and out of Scotland entirely. Dougal had gone with his father and uncles on a few runs, and they had declared that a swift and clever lad was a boon to the work.

John MacGregor did not want that life for his son. He was adamant that Dougal would have an education; he wanted books and cravats in his son's future, not illicit exporting. He had saved every spare penny and a modest inheritance to ensure that one day his son would attend university in Glasgow and become a lawyer. Education and personal wealth were the best ways to save Glen Kinloch, John insisted. If the laird was able to assure the well-being of the people of the glen, they could remain in their own homes, tending their livestock, and brewing whisky for their use with no need to smuggle.

He knew that over the past two generations, Highlanders had been forced from their homes due to the greed of wealthy men who bought acreage to stock the hills with wool-producing sheep, or to turn land into shooting preserves. Clan chiefs with funds could save their lands, but Glen Kinloch was a small, poor lairdship. So the laird had turned to smuggling for better coin.

And he had decided that books and neckcloths would be part of his son's future. In a few short years, he would send Dougal to university and away from the glen and all he loved. Until then, the boy attended the little glen school whenever there was a dominie to teach there. Currently, that was a sour-faced man that Kinloch paid personally. Though quick and clever at learning, Dougal preferred to tend the herds and fields with his father. Even more, he liked the excitement of the smuggling runs.

Climbing the hill behind his father that morning, Dougal was eager to learn the Kinloch secret, so closely guarded by each laird that Dougal knew only part of the story. Something to do with a fairy promise and the gift of a recipe for a magical whisky made only at Kinloch. Finally, he would learn the whole of it.

"Come ahead, lad," John whispered, leading Dougal to the

top of the steep slope, where trees crowned the ridge. Far above, the peak of the mountain loomed through a ring of mist. "Look for the markings that show the way." He gestured at the ground.

Dougal looked at thick clusters of heather spreading over earth and rock, newly green but not yet blooming. "What marks?" he asked.

"Fairy footprints. See, just there." John pointed.

Then Dougal saw marks on the rock like tiny feet all in a row, marching up the mountain. He blinked in awe. "The Fey came by here?"

"The fairies leave their mark where they walk or dance. And their footprints show the way to fairy places. But only a few can see the marks."

"I see them."

"The MacGregors of Kinloch have the gift, and we know the secret of this place. Come ahead." John led the way upward.

The sky was lighter now. A wall of sheer rock rose to one side, while below, the vast glen looked like a bowl of mist. Dougal looked around. "Da, can the revenue men find us up here?"

"Not in this fog. The gaugers rarely come up this high, most of them being Lowlanders not fit for the climb."

"I feel as if someone is watching us," he said uneasily.

"Could be the mountain fairies. They will not harm us. Come up to me," his father said, offering a hand as he helped his son climb up over a cluster of boulders.

Something glinted on the ground, and Dougal stooped to pick up a small, shining stone. It was a crystal of the sort called cairngorm, its peaty color glowing in the dawn light. He dropped it into his jacket pocket and walked on. "Da, tell me again about the Kinloch gift."

"Aye then. Long ago, the first laird of Kinloch and his wife were walking on this very mountainside, when they came upon an ailing fairy woman about to give birth. They delivered her babe and gave her a dram of whisky made in their own still, thus saving her life, and they were thanked by the woman's husband. The next night, he knocked on the door of their home and gave them a gift—the secret of making a magical brew."

"Fairy whisky," Dougal said. "A magical brew that men would kill for."

John huffed. "Your uncles have been going on again. True, Kinloch *uisge beatha* is legendary, and the secret of the brew is guarded closely by the laird of Kinloch and his family. Some covet our whisky and would like the recipe. But Kinloch's fairy brew must never be sold for coin. Only sharing it freely keeps our luck with the Fey. Remember that always, when you are laird."

Dougal nodded. "I will. It must never be sold, only given away. And I will guard the secret with my life."

"We hope it never comes to that. Remember, too, that riches may come if the fairy whisky is sold, but consequences will follow. So be warned. Besides," John said, "our Glen Kinloch brew is excellent stuff, and earns us enough coin to live by. So we need never sell the fairy brew."

Though young, Dougal had occasionally tasted Glen Kinloch whisky, *uisge-beatha ghleann ceann loch*. But he had never tasted the fairy brew, which his father called *uisge-beatha sìthiche an ceann loch:* the fairy whisky of Kinloch. "What is so different about the fairy sort of *uisge-beatha?*"

"That sort has powerful magic and must be prepared and taken with care. Not all are affected by the magic. Some consider it simply a good whisky. And we never let on." His father winked. "Now look there."

Following John MacGregor's gesture, Dougal saw a small birch glade on a ledge along the slope. The light of dawn slanted through mist and trees as Dougal and his father approached, their footfalls crushing grass. He heard the keen cry of a hawk overhead.

There in the pale light, Dougal saw a blue haze. Thousands of bluebells were scattered along the ground in a dense carpet beneath the birch trees, delicate bells drooping gracefully on slender stalks. As he and his father walked through, dewdrops shed over his legs and kilt hem. He had seen wildflowers in profusion, but not like this.

John MacGregor took a small silver flask from inside the folds of his plaid. Handing it to Dougal, he withdrew two more flasks. "Here, at dawn, we collect the fairy dew, and we thank the fairies for the blessing. The dew and our gratitude give the whisky its special magic. We will fill the three flasks and add them to the brew later. It will pour out as if the bottles are bottomless, though it will suddenly disappear when it is time to make it again."

Dougal looked around dubiously. "Collect dew from wee bluebells? That is impossible. It is a task that lassies might like, not men," he added with disdain.

John laughed. "Not the dew from flower petals, lad. Come this way." He waded through the bluebells toward a cluster of birches, pushing aside flower stalks with his boot to expose a natural well in the ground. "No one knows this place is here. The fairies guard it."

The opening in the earth was only as wide as an ordinary kettle, its edge obscured by stones, flowers, and grass. Dougal peered down to see a dark reflection of water. Natural springs were common enough. He frowned, doubtful.

His father circled the well three times, murmuring in Gaelic. Then he looked at Dougal. "Walk thrice round the well, ask politely for your dearest wish, and thank the fairies. They will grant your wish to you."

"Did all your wishes come true, Da?"

"I wed my dearest love and I have a fine son." John smiled. "Now it is your turn."

Carefully, Dougal traced careful steps around the well. *I wish to be a brave smuggler like my father*, he thought.

"Now this. Pay attention, lad." John lifted his arms. "Mac-Gregor of Kinloch is here," he said to the trees, the air. "I ask your help in collecting the magical gift promised me and mine long ago. This is my son, who will one day be the keeper of this well in his turn."

Hearing the sound of rushing water, Dougal glanced down to see bubbles churning in the well. A spout shot upward, the water dancing with rainbows. In the mist rising from the well, small lights soared up, circling him. He stared in awe and delight, feeling delicious chills run all through him so that his hair and skin tickled.

"The lights!" He looked up as they flew in circles around him and his father, flitting and swirling like delicate motes of sunlight, though dawn had hardly bloomed yet.

"The Fey are showing us they are here. I am glad you have a chance to see them."

"I have seen lights like those before, but I thought it was a trick of sunlight."

"Sometimes it is just that, so we must look carefully to know it is the Fey." John dropped to one knee and began to fill his flask at the waterspout. Kneeling, Dougal did the same, tipping the second flask to allow the water to leap inside. When all three flasks were full, the bubbling spout subsided, and the tiny rainbow lights faded too.

John stood. Dougal rose too, as the carpet of flowers closed to cover the well.

"There," John said quietly. "Now you know the secret shared with our ancestor long ago. This is the source of the fairy water that we use to make *uisge beatha an Ceann Loch an sìthean*, Kinloch fairy whisky. No one knows it is here."

Dougal nodded. He felt reverent, almost like being in the kirk on Sundays. "Where are the fairies? I thought we might see them."

"They are here. The lights told us that. If they wanted us to see them, they would have appeared. Now listen, and remember. Circle the well three times, make your wish, then ask the Fey to bring up the water. Fill three silver flasks. And always leave a token of thanks." John plucked a silver button from his jacket and set it beside the little spring. Dougal noticed buttons, coins, ribbons, and stones scattered amid the profusion of bluebells. Some looked very old indeed.

The buttons on his jacket were wooden and not very special. Dougal reached into his pocket for the small cairngorm he had found on the slope and left it beside his father's silver button. John nodded approval.

They left the glade, walking down the steep hillside as the sun rose higher. Soon the mist burned away to reveal the long green glen with its meadow floor and a sparkling river like a silver ribbon. Cozy stone houses lay snug against the sides of the glen, and sheep wandered the meadows and slopes.

"What did you wish for, Da?" Dougal asked as they neared home. Kinloch House, the old stone tower where he lived with his father, his aunt, uncles, and younger sister Ellen, thrust up from a low bank of fog. The stone was crumbling in places, ivy softening the broken edges. Three hundred years old, the place always needed repairs, and Dougal often helped his father and uncles fix and shore up. Though it was old and shabby, he loved all its familiar, quirky flaws.

"My wish?" John MacGregor shrugged. "I asked that my son be Kinloch's finest and best laird someday so that he might save our glen from any harm to come."

"Will harm come? This is a peaceful place."

"The world beyond is not always peaceful, even if our glen is so."

"But Da, you are the finest and best laird the glen has ever known."

"I wish it were so, lad, I do. What was your wish?"

"To be like you," Dougal said.

John laughed. "Go on. Tell your Aunt Jean that we have returned with the fairy dew. Tell her to start baking and cooking, for we shall have a celebration. Tomorrow, we will spread fresh barley to sprout and begin your first batch of fairy brew."

A YEAR TO the day, John MacGregor was pistol-shot by revenue officers in the twilight and died at midnight. The laird of Kinloch had been carrying four kegs of whisky in panniers on the back of a pony when the excise men had found him. They gave him no chance to explain. MacGregor had not died defending his people, or even trading Kinloch's legitimate brew. Instead, he had traded his life for a few casks of peat-reek whisky. The kegs were not smuggled stuff. They were a gift meant for the manse and the reverend.

His father's unjust death troubled Dougal deeply, devastating him at night and hardening his heart during the day. He realized that his father's wish at the fairy well had come true: Now the son was laird of Kinloch, and far too soon.

In the years that followed, he knew that he could never be Kinloch's finest laird—John MacGregor had been that. Nor did he want to be the educated, wealthy gentleman and advocate of the law that his father had wished for him. Dougal found another way to honor his father as fiercely as the man deserved.

He became a smuggler the likes of which the hills had not seen for generations.

Chapter One

Loch Katrine
April, 1823

"Did you hear that?" Patrick MacCarran glanced up the long Highland slope as a gust of wind stirred the tail of his dark frock coat and sent a few loose pebbles scattering. "I thought I heard footsteps over the rocks up there."

Standing near her brother, Fiona looked up the steep hillside buttressing the towering mountain, with its limestone cliffs and dark scree and scrub. "Bogles," she said. "Haunts and fairies. Small stones shifting along the slopes."

"Or smugglers," Patrick muttered. "Had I known we would climb so far into these hills in search of wee rocks, I would have brought a firearm."

"Smugglers only come out at night."

"They're men, not bats," her brother drawled. He moved ahead, looking around as if he suspected criminals to leap out from behind the boulders and tall trees along the hillside.

Fiona smiled to herself, aware that Patrick only meant to protect her. Turning, she looked down, where the long slope swept toward Loch Katrine and Glen Kinloch. The hill might have more fossils hidden along its rocky incline—the area had already yielded nice examples, and she would have plenty of time to search, as she had agreed to stay in the glen until summer to teach in the glen school. Lifting a hand to her gray bonnet, she drew in a breath, admiring the vast Highland beauty spreading out below.

Though the hills were misty and the sky was gray, from her high vantage point, she could see the loch below, where fog drifted over the water and nudged the rugged foothills.

"This place has a wild beauty even in poor conditions," she said. "It would be spectacular in better weather."

Patrick looked about, nodding. Although Fiona wanted to explore more, her brother seemed impatient to return to the hotel at Auchnashee, where he was staying. He seemed uneasy, she thought, frowning a little.

For several months, her youngest brother had been serving as an excise officer at the southern end of Loch Katrine, and so seemed constantly on the alert for trouble wherever he went. The work had made him more somber, but she hoped he would soon regain his inherently cheerful nature.

"Did you hear that?" Patrick called again, walking toward her.

"Just the wind." She had heard something odd, but it did not worry her.

"Wind—or free traders on their way through the hills. Are you ready to go back now?" He stooped to pick up her canvas knapsack.

"Not quite. I found some excellent trilobites here today, and I am hoping there are more on this slope. And I want to make some sketches and notes before I go." A cool updraft lifted the ribbons of her bonnet and danced the skirt of her gray woolen gown over the tops of her sturdy leather boots. She brushed her gloved hands together, powdered with dirt and rock dust. The hillside was mostly rocks, earth, and scrub here, with a little spring green emerging among scraggly heather and gorse. But a wintry nip in the next gust made her shiver slightly. "This place is desolate, I know, but it is a perfect environment for finding trilobites and such."

"It is fairly remote, which makes it appealing to smugglers moving kegs through these hills to the loch and then down the river. Fiona, I have said it before, but I do wish you were not staying alone in this glen. We have had too many reports of rogues in this area lately."

"I agreed to teach here until summer, and I also intend to do my best to meet the conditions in Grandmother's will while I am here. Well, some of them. I hope you can do that too, and William as well."

"Grandmother Struan's will is a bane for all of us, though it proved a boon for James, who did find his fairy bride—or close enough to satisfy the conditions of the will," Patrick said. "I hope you can find a way to do that, too. As for me and William, I cannot imagine finding fairies anywhere. Do consider returning to Edinburgh, Fiona. You know Lord Eldin would lend his barouche if you decide to leave. He is fond of you, though he dislikes most everyone else."

"I do not want his charity or his barouche. I have promised to stay until summer with Mrs. MacIan, and I will keep my word."

"From what I could tell, Mary MacIan can barely hear, talks endlessly, and drinks whisky like a man. Months of that could drive even you mad, sweet and amiable though you are."

"I have not been sweet and amiable since I was three, but thank you. Mrs. MacIan is delightful and could use the company. Her grandson is the reverend, and he looks after her, but I am sure she will enjoy having someone in the house. And you know it is perfectly acceptable for Highland women to take a dram with the men or even on their own. I may even try it myself."

He laughed outright. "Beware of picking up her odd spinsterish habits! Truly, she is not a fit companion for walking about the hills, and I know you are stubborn enough to do that on your own. And stubborn enough to stay, I see."

"I did give my word."

"Your devotion to your word is admirable. Just promise that you will not go wandering the hills alone. There are too many rascals in this godforsaken place."

"An officer of the government suspects a smuggler around every corner."

"Not without reason. I am only concerned for your welfare," he added.

"As I am for yours. The work you do is far more dangerous than a little hillwalking. I know you were bored as a Signet clerk in the city and wanted this challenge. But pursuing smugglers is stressful work and risky. I worry about your welfare."

"I like the adventure of it, I admit, and I am careful. This region is rife with smugglers, though. Keep that in mind and be cautious." He frowned. "The loch is ten miles or so from its southern tip to this little glen, and more families are running private stills along its shores than we could count."

"Anyone can produce whisky, up to five hundred gallons. You said so."

"A small family distillery is fine. But what they do with the excess is a problem."

"Remember when we were small in Perthshire, and the home farm supplied the estate with whisky? Father very much liked their particular brew."

She glanced away, reminded too keenly of their father, who had died along with their mother when the four children had all been young. Twins Fiona and James, and siblings William and Patrick had been left to the care of their grandparents, Viscount and Lady Struan. Fiona and James had then gone into the well-meaning but overbearing guardianship of Lady Rankin, their great-aunt, while the younger boys stayed with their grandparents. Fiona still resided on Lady Rankin's estate just outside of Edinburgh, though James had become Viscount Struan and had recently married.

Much as she loved Aunt Rankin, temporary teaching positions in the Highlands—like the school in Glen Kinloch—had become a welcome escape.

"Home distilleries are not the issue," Patrick was saying. "But most owners of Highland stills manufacture far more whisky than their allotted amount, and never report the quantity to the excise men. Thousands of gallons a year are smuggled for export, thus avoiding taxes imposed by the Crown. So the government sends out excise officers to track the free traders. It is an unpleasant business, Fiona, both the smuggling and the search for smugglers. I do not say so lightly."

"I know. But free traders would hardly be interested in a glen teacher."

"If she wanders the hills and happens to witness their actions, they will be very interested. I will watch over you as much as I can, but I cannot be here all the time. You must be prudent in your wanderings."

"I will spend most of my days teaching in the glen, and I promise to be cautious whenever I go hillwalking. I will carry an umbrella as a weapon. How is that?" She drew herself to her full height, taller than most women, though not nearly as tall as her brother. "Truly, do not fret. I will be fine."

Patrick twisted his mouth awry. "Very well. But I want to hear from you often. The mail runs out of the glen village once a week, so a letter can reach me at the southern end by the next day, with luck. One cannot always count on the mail couriers out here."

"Reverend MacIan assures me the glen is quiet and safe, and most of the tenants are hardworking shepherds and drovers, the rest farming families. He says that smuggling occurs in other glens, but not in this one."

"Does he indeed?" Patrick huffed skeptically. "Farmers raise barley crops and make whisky from that. Did he mention that hardworking Highland farmers and shepherds by day are free traders by night, loading their pack ponies and carrying loaded pistols through these pretty and peaceable hills?"

"He did not." She walked up the slope, scanning the ground for interesting rock samples that might contain fossil imprints.

"Mrs. MacIan told me just today that they have a saying in this glen—'When the laird is on the mountainside, it is wise to step aside.'"

"Perhaps the laird of Glen Kinloch is a disagreeable sort."

"There is a notorious smuggler in these parts called the Laird," Patrick went on, walking beside her.

"I thought the Laird was apprehended a few months ago. In Perthshire, I believe."

"Ah, you must mean the Whisky Lairds, dubbed so by Sir Walter Scott, the ones brought down to Edinburgh after their arrest. They turned out to be very much more than mere whisky smugglers. Lords and such, I believe."

"Oh yes! I recall hearing something about it. One of them was presented to the king when he visited Scotland last summer."

"An interesting fellow," Patrick said. "I had the privilege of meeting him myself—the smuggler, not the king. But he is not the peat-reek laird who runs up and down Loch Katrine making excise officers miserable. That is another man. An elusive scoundrel."

"Do you mean the laird of Kinloch?"

"The laird of Kinloch is just a farmer and a herder of livestock. He lives in a ruined tower. This is a poor glen. The laird is called MacGregor. He raises cattle and sheep and makes only the legal allotment of whisky. At least, that is what he reports to the government. None of these Highlanders can be trusted where whisky is concerned. I expect you will meet the farmer laird since you will be teaching in the glen school. Fiona, you might help me out a bit while you are here," he said, stopping.

"How so?" She bent to scratch the dirt from the surface of a flat rock.

"Listen for any mention of this laird of peat reek, a rogue smuggler. We want to find that sly lad."

"Peat reek? Is that a poorer variety? The whisky we tasted at Mrs. MacIan's was very nice, I thought. Strong, but mellow."

"Excellent brew. The peaty flavor is admired in a good Highland whisky. But do keep your ears open and let me know if you hear anything I should know."

"I doubt I shall encounter any smugglers, but if I do, you shall be the first to know. Oh, look!" She knelt, dusting a bit of rock clean with a cloth pulled from a skirt pocket. "An ammonite fossil." She pointed to a curled shape impressed on the rock surface.

"A what?"

"Ammonite—an extinct marine mollusk, rather like a cephalopod. Oh, look, there are several here!" She rubbed at the rock with a gloved finger, exposing curled, striated forms as big as her thumbnail. "I believe there may be a massive limestone bed beneath this hill, with deposits of greywacke along with the Old Red Sandstone layer, and liberal evidence of a great ancient flood. I cannot wait to tell James about this!"

"Your geological babble is lost on me, dear lass, but your twin will love it. Fiona, come along now. I must get back soon. I have a dinner engagement at Auchnashee. You definitely must explore this hill with James once he returns to the Highlands."

"James and Elspeth will be in Edinburgh for another month or so." Her twin, James MacCarran, Viscount Struan, was an accomplished geologist and professor of natural sciences, while Fiona considered herself an amateur with a keen interest in fossils. "He must finish his lecture series for the university before he and Elspeth return to Struan House."

"Ah, true, Elspeth was insistent that their expected little one be born in the Highlands. Well, Struan House is just a few hours from here, so you will see them now and then once they are back—if you are still in the glen."

"I plan to be. And you, I imagine, will be too busy to visit any of us. Thank you for coming with me today, but please do not feel obligated to keep watch over me."

"Ah, you know I will if I can. For now, I have a good deal of work to do with the new tax laws in effect. Smuggling continues at full pace along this loch, despite the new regulations that locals want to deny."

"I thought the new laws might make your work easier." She stood, brushing her skirts.

"Not as much as I hoped," Patrick said. "Taxes were lowered to make it less tempting to smuggle whisky out of the Highlands. The government also recruited hundreds more revenue officers to catch offenders, and penalties are much stiffer. If a still is discovered and dismantled but no one claims it, the laird of that land is responsible, no matter what. But they continue, regardless."

"I suspect Highlanders enjoy the adventure of free trading too much to stop. Highlanders tend to ignore authority." She smiled, for she had always enjoyed the vein of rebellion that ran through Highland history and Highland character. "At any rate, you will be busy, and must not worry about me. I may visit you down the loch, though, since you are staying at Eldin's new hotel."

"He offered me a free room at Auchnashee, and invited me to dine with him and some Edinburgh businessmen tonight. Oh, did I mention Eldin has decided to become a revenue officer?"

"What!" Fiona stared, astonished. "Nicholas MacCarran, Earl of Eldin, stooping to regular work? I cannot imagine it. He is too concerned with his comfort, and too arrogant to care."

"I was surprised, I admit. He was not always that way, but after his family perished, he was never again the Cousin Nick we knew as children. But a law officer? That I did find hard to believe." He shrugged. "But it is a formal title only. He paid a fat sum for it, and will probably never ride out. He wants some authority here, and the Crown needs money, so he applied for the rank and paid the fee."

"It is another reminder not to trust the Earl of Eldin." Fiona sighed.

"I liked him well when we were children," Patrick said. "But if we cannot meet the conditions in Grandmother's will, then Eldin inherits the bulk of the estate, and we four will have next to nothing."

"We will find a way. Patrick, go on ahead. I want to gather a few more fossils along the hill before I go back to Mrs. MacIan's."

"MacDuff arranged to take me down the loch by boat so I should meet him soon." Patrick chuckled. "A gentleman who escorts a lady on a nature walk is rude to abandon her on a hillside."

"But a little brother can leave his big sister if she insists he go." Smiling, she waved him onward, then knelt on damp turf to brush dirt from a rock that looked promising.

"I doubt you will discover what you truly need here, Fiona."

"Fairies to satisfy the will? They are not thick upon the ground here, true." She laughed ruefully. "I wonder how I can ever fulfill Grandmother's requirement to sketch fairies from life—of all things!—for the book James is piecing together from her notes. She approved of my charitable teaching work, and I will continue that regardless. But finding fairies, along with her odd requirement that I marry a wealthy Highland husband, seems just mad." She sighed.

"I have been thinking," Patrick said. "We could contest the will—a mad old woman, however well-meaning, may have left a will in her dotage that is not coherent. I will speak with our solicitor about it."

"But if we do not satisfy the clauses, everything goes to Eldin. It is an extraordinary situation." Fiona stood again.

"We can manage without a fortune if we must," her brother said. "Easier than finding spouses with fairy blood, or sprites to sketch, and so on. Invent some fairy portraits and have done with it," he urged. "No one would ever know."

"I would know, so I have to try. You've said little about what the will asked of you, and William has not said much either."

"I have no intention of marrying a forest sprite, or whatever impossible creature my demented grandmother thought I should find," Patrick replied. "Do not frown so! I honor her memory, but it is not easy to agree with her will. Think of it. William is a physician. He could be labeled a quack if he went about collecting spells for fairy medicine, or whatever he was assigned."

"But James did manage to find a fairy bride. Was it a coincidence that he fell in love with a darling lass with a legend of fairy blood in her family? They say the MacCarrans have fairy blood too."

"Why look for more if it is already there? James thinks

Grandmother wanted us to refresh the fairy bloodline or some such lunacy. I mean to look into things to see if we can oppose the will and end this nonsense. First I must determine if we have a case, then everyone must agree. It would save you searching under rocks for fairies."

"I am searching under rocks no matter what for ammonites and trilobites, for extinct arthropods and plant forms. And I intend to stay in the glen to teach. The Edinburgh Ladies' Society is relying on me. No one else could take this assignment."

"No one else wanted it," he pointed out.

"I do not know why. It is such a lovely place," she said, glancing around.

"Steep, rugged terrain rife with smugglers and rascals. And rocks."

"But Patrick, if I stay in Edinburgh, I am just another spinster attending charity meetings and social events and finding dull ways to fill the time. The charitable work is interesting. It allows me to travel the Highlands to have some adventure in my life."

"You will never end a spinster, lass, I guarantee it," her brother said. "What does your group call itself—the Edinburgh Ladies' Society for the Betterment of the Gaels? Haughty as it sounds, you all do good work."

"The ladies are genuinely dedicated to helping Highlanders."

"And delighted to have an unattached lady fluent in Gaelic who is willing to climb into the remote hills to teach English, thus allowing the other ladies to stay home and find safer ways to pass the time."

"Some do what I do. The Deputy Lord Provost's daughter, for one. Miss Graham—well, not unattached now, since she found her Highlander. That same notorious smuggler you mentioned earlier." She smiled, thinking of her friend Ellison Graham, who had indeed made a good match to a fascinating, devastatingly handsome Highlander called Lord Darrach.

"That smuggler was a notorious lawyer, as I recall," Patrick said with a chuckle.

"She would never have met him if she had not spoken Gaelic, you know. Besides, Patrick—if not for the distraction of the charity work, I would have given in to grief after Archie's death."

"I know. But not you, lass. You are too strong."

"Am I?" Fiona shook her head. Very nearly a widow, in the end she was just a deeply bereaved third cousin. Yet Archie had been everything to her, and they had talked of marriage, even elopement. But she had been young, and now she was determined never to make the mistake again of loving someone so completely that she would give up her life for him, only to lose him suddenly. She should have learned to avoid hurt when her parents had died, leaving her and her brothers at such young ages.

Well, now she knew better and had steeled her heart against loving too deeply.

"Best go and meet your boat," she urged. "I promise to return to Edinburgh by summer, with or without fairy drawings."

"What about the required wealthy Highland husband?" Patrick lifted a brow. "Though that is a contradiction in terms."

"We will not find one in this poor glen, that is true. I can think of many qualities more desirable than wealth in a husband—but I may yet resign myself to spinsterhood."

"You are a lovely and intelligent lass. And you have rejected every suitor."

Not Archie, she thought, glancing away. "Most are only interested in what I might inherit from Grandmother. Ironically, we all lack a fortune until the conditions are met."

"Nonsense, however well-meant, is still nonsense."

A breeze stirred her bonnet ribbons. She looked around. "It is so beautiful and mystical here that I could believe any legend about this place."

"Not I, dear sister. How much longer will you be on this hillside?"

"A little while yet. It is a good area for fossils. They could help prove the new theory that a catastrophic flood brought primeval waters as high as these mountains."

"I cannot imagine." He groaned. "Ancient marine insects on mountaintops! But be careful, Fiona. Glen Kinloch is not all pretty legends. You need to be aware of that."

"I am, sir. Go!" She kissed his cheek, and he turned to descend, waving a hand.

Retrieving a small hammer and chisel from her canvas knapsack, Fiona knelt to angle the chisel point against a rock, smacking the handle with a hammer.

Her grandmother's intentions were not entirely demented, she thought as she wrapped the dislodged stone chunk in a cloth and tucked it in the canvas sack. She would be happy to marry a Highland man who possessed a title and fortune, provided he was a good man with a good heart.

Yet her grief over losing her fiancé and distant cousin lingered. Eight years earlier, Archibald MacCarran had died a hero on a bloody field at Quatre Bras, a day just before Waterloo. Her brother James had been injured in the same battle. In the aftermath, Fiona still carried the hidden scar of a broken heart.

But she had come to accept that she had lost a cherished dream of a husband, family, and home in the Highlands. Perhaps Grandmother had wanted Fiona to have happiness again, but no magical solution would bring that bliss back into her life. Love's magic was gone.

She hefted the hammer and chisel again, resuming her work. A little while later, she felt a strange prickling along the back of her neck, as if someone were watching her. She paused and heard a sound like a crisp footfall.

"Who's there?" She looked around. "Patrick?"

Her voice echoed. Shivers ran down her back. Though she dismissed such things in conversation, secretly she believed in the possibility of haunts, bogles, fairies, and the like. She was not always the practical, calm, capable, dull girl most thought her to be. Though she had tucked dreams and hopes away, she had an active imagination.

Suddenly the deserted hillside seemed eerie. Fiona shivered, recalling Patrick's stories of rascals in the hills. Seeing something glint among the rocks, she startled. But it was only a pretty white quartz crystal, common in limestone and sandstone deposits.

She had work to do. Lifting her knapsack, she walked up the slope.

Chapter Two

I N THE MIST, the woman moved like a dream, a fairy queen in a fog-colored gown. Just a glance told him she was beautifully made, graceful, and had a mysterious allure. With a woman like that, his days, nights too, might be filled with elusive happiness.

Enough, he told himself. Whoever she was, it was imperative he convince her to leave these hills and the glen quick as she could.

Dougal MacGregor, laird of Kinloch, leaned a shoulder against the cave entrance and watched the young woman. She climbed the slope steadily, closer to the surge of the great, dark mountain behind him. Inside, the cave held a valuable cache. Within arm's reach was a loaded pistol with which to protect it. He stood still, silent, wary.

The lass had come too far and too high into the foothills and was alone now. Odd that her companion had left her to go about on her own. What sort of fellow would leave a lady in the wild hills, where rogues even worse than the laird roamed day and night?

Perhaps she was a willful creature and had insisted. Dougal thought the young gentleman had asked her to go with him, but she had staunchly refused, and the lad had gone on his way. Strangely enough, the lady stayed to chip away at rocks. He did not know her, but the young man looked familiar.

"Damn. The new gauger," he muttered.

Recently, a new excise officer had been installed at the southern end of Loch Katrine. Dougal had seen him once or twice; they had not met yet, and he hoped that would never happen. But why would a government excise man escort a lady into these hills? Every customs officer in the region knew smuggling scoundrels lurked here. Was the lad so green that he was unaware of the danger and so took a lady on a jaunt?

As one of those scoundrels, Dougal frowned. Whatever brought the couple into these hills was not simple tourism.

With a charming disregard for her pretty skirts, the young woman sank to her knees, reached into her knapsack, and took out a small hammer. She struck hard at a rock, breaking off pieces efficiently. Chink, chink, *thunk.*

Dougal winced in silent amusement, seeing the pretty lass wield a hammer so smartly. Then he reminded himself she had no business here—especially if she knew a customs man.

He narrowed his eyes. She was no tourist admiring the scenery; she had a purpose and it had something to do with rocks. Now she examined the ground, then took a notebook from the knapsack and wrote or sketched. A map?

If she and the gauger were spies, that was concerning. With a decent map, excise officers could find caves and niches where goods were hidden.

Gaugers—and willful young ladies—must be prevented from sketching and exploring here. Dougal would have to dissuade her, and fast.

But when had she arrived in the glen? *Ah,* he thought. Could she be the teacher Reverend MacIan had hired for the glen school? But they were expecting an older woman. For years, the dominies who came to teach in Glen Kinloch were either male or middle-aged females. None of them had stayed long, and for good reason.

A tourist, then? She was climbing again, lifting skirt hems over sturdy boots. She had dressed pragmatically for hillwalking, he would give her that. But each step brought her closer to where he stood. He stepped into the shadow of the cave entrance, watching.

In her gray dress and bonnet, with her nimble grace, she seemed part of the mist and the rock. And his dreams. For a moment, he thought of the sylph-like fairy folk, the *Daoine Sith* said to inhabit the hills and hidden places in Scotland. If he still had a romantic nature, he might believe she was part of the magic of these hills. A sprite. A pixie. The very queen of fairies.

Years ago, he sometimes thought he glimpsed the ones who inhabited the hills; she was none of those. Earthly, she was, and beautiful. Then she removed her bonnet and looked up at the mountain.

Dougal sucked in his breath. That bit of haberdashery was unworthy of her. Oval face as serene as a Renaissance Madonna; delicate features; soft, large eyes under dark brows; the dark gleam of hair coiled in braids. He wanted to loosen that thick silk in his hands, cradle that exquisite face in his hands.

Time for her to go. Easing away from the cave, Dougal set out down the hill.

FIONA KNELT ON the ground, absorbed in the work, heedless of mud and ignoring the breeze that played her dark hair into loops. With her fingers and a small brush, she gently swept a cluster of stones, recognizing the preserved exoskeletons of tiny trilobites, sea creatures whose tracks were clear to a practiced eye—and evidence that the area had been covered in water a long time ago.

"James will be so pleased," she murmured, tapping the hammer around the edge of a bit of stone. Limestone was grainy and soft, as rock went, so the piece broke away easily and she tugged it free.

"Miss."

The male voice, deep and rich, startled her. She gasped and

looked up.

Wrapped in fog, a man stood on the rise above her, one booted foot propped on a rock, kilt draped over the powerful thigh. Leaping to her feet, nearly tripping, she gazed at him.

"Who—are you?" she asked breathlessly.

He stepped down and extended a hand toward her. "Come up to me," he said, fingers beckoning.

Fiona stared at the man who stood on the rocky slope. He seemed fierce, powerful, and wholly not of this earth. Tall and dark haired, in a kilt of muted dark tones with a brown wool jacket, he looked like a Highlander from long ago, as if he had stepped out of time. His legs were strong and muscled, swathed in thick stockings to flat knees. Chestnut brown hair sifted in waves to his shoulders, and the shadow of a dark beard dusted his jaw. His eyes, narrowed beneath a smudge of straight black brows, had a greenish hue. He glared at her, hand still extended.

"Come," he said.

"Who are you?" she asked, heart pounding. She had heard stories of the Sidhe, an ancient fairy race of tall, magnificent beings. They sometimes appeared to humans, even stole them away. James's wife Elspeth claimed that her grandfather and father had been taken by fairies. Elspeth was a charming storyteller, so Fiona did not entirely believe it.

But this handsome stranger appearing out of the mist made it seem very possible.

"Are you one of the Fey?" she asked in a hushed voice.

He beckoned again with long, nimble fingers. "Miss. Come up to me."

She stepped back, her gaze on his—somehow she could not look away. Then she whirled to run, stumbling on the rocky slope. The Highlander was instantly there, taking her arm to draw her toward him in a strong grip.

"Come with me, Miss," he said.

"No!" She pulled back. "You would steal me away!"

"What?" He looked down at her, like a giant on the steep

angle. "Who the devil do you think I am?"

"One of the—er, Sidhe." Then she realized how foolish it sounded.

He chuckled. "Not bluidy likely."

A hot blush rose in her cheeks. The man was real, and she was an idiot. "What was I to think when you appeared out of the mist looking like a ghost, or a mythical being?"

"I would credit you with more sense. You seem a practical woman. Have you never seen a Highlander wearing the plaid, walking the hills?"

"Of course! But you could have given me a warning before startling me like that."

"I beg your pardon." He inclined his head, dark hair sliding over his brow. He seemed amused. "Truly, I did not mean to startle you." He had the soft, elegant lilt of one who had spoken Gaelic before learning English. He released her arm.

Holding her bonnet tight against the wind, she stepped back. "I must go."

"I am thinking you will come with me." He reached out. She evaded him, snatching up her knapsack and hammer, and turned to run. Again he had her by the arm, his hold firm—and yet not threatening. It felt almost protective.

"My companions expect me. They are looking for me even now," she insisted.

"Aye so? Where are they?" He turned with her and walked across the shoulder of the slope. Fiona tried to break free, but his grip was strong as he took her along.

"Let go!" Clutching the hammer in her free hand, she struck his forearm with the bruising thunk of iron smacking thick wool and taut muscle.

"*A mhic Ifrinn!*" Son of hell, she understood. "Give me that thing," he barked, snatching the hammer. "I mean you no harm. I only want you gone from here for your wellbeing. These hills are not safe."

"I was quite safe until you accosted me," she pointed out,

trying to keep pace with his long, purposeful stride. Where was he taking her? "You have no right to handle me so, or to order me out of here."

"I do. This is my glen. I am Dougal MacGregor of Kinloch."

"Are you laird of this glen?" Laird of Kinloch—Patrick had warned her about him.

"I am Kinloch, for the glen is deeded to me, aye. Tourists are not allowed here."

"I am not a tourist, Mr. MacGregor. I am staying nearby."

"The terrain is treacherous here. Visitors do not know the safe paths through the hills. And rogues and smugglers are often about, night and day."

"Are you one of them?" She looked up at him. He had dropped her hammer into a pocket, but her bag held some hefty rocks that could serve as weapons.

"Give me that bag," he said, as if reading her thoughts. He took the knapsack off her shoulder and hoisted it to his own, its contents clunking. "What in the name of the devil is in here?"

"Rocks."

"From my glen?"

"I will put them back if it troubles you."

"Keep them. We have plenty of rocks. If it is gold or treasure you search for, there is none of that here. We would all be wealthy in this glen if so."

"I am not looking for gold. I am a fossilist."

"A what?"

"An amateur fossilist. I find and study rocks for imprints of ancient life forms."

"Rocks," he muttered, pulling along. "Come this way. It is a shorter distance to the road. Is there a carriage waiting to take you to Auchnashee?"

"Auchnashee? No." The man had the manners of a beast, she thought. "You claim to own this glen, Mr. MacGregor. Are you an earl or a viscount, to have so much land?"

"I do not own it outright. In Scotland, most of the land is

owned by the Crown and deeded back to the Scots. I hold the heritable rights to Glen Kinloch. But I have no fancy title if you are looking for such, being a Lowland lady."

"I am not looking for that at all. You are hurting me." She pulled against his grip. "How do you know I am Lowland?"

"Speech and manners," he said. "And you seem like a fine lady. Your father must be someone of note."

"My father and mother died when I was small. My grandfather was a Highland viscount, a title that went to my brother. Why do you care? We are not a family of note."

"It is enough, and your family is fortunate."

"I suppose we are," she admitted.

He looked at her keenly, head tilted. His irises were a clear hazel green, framed in thick lashes and straight black brows; striking, beautiful eyes for a man, especially a brusque and roguish one, she thought.

"An orphan, hey? My parents died when I was a lad. You have my sympathies."

"Thank you," she said, somewhat surprised, still stumbling along beside him.

"My father left me a lairdship with a house and some land. I am a farmer, like most of my tenants. Kinloch is a small glen far from anywhere. Earls and such—none of that sort would come out here. Rocks, hey?" He tilted at brow.

"Many appreciate the beauty of the Highlands. I know an earl who has purchased a hotel at Auchnashee." She did not add that Lord Eldin was her cousin.

"I know of him. He is one of those who buy up Scottish land to create shooting lodges and sheep runs, wanting to attract tourists who ride through to stare at our hills and homes. None of them belong here, and I will not sell my lands, so if you are exploring to tell your friend the earl about this glen so he can press me to sell, do not. Come ahead. Hurry."

"I do not intend to spy on your lands. Why the rush? Is someone after you?" She glanced back.

"Bogles, ghosts, and the Fey," he drawled. "Or perhaps smugglers."

"Your ilk, sir?" She dug in her heels, forcing him to stop. "Enough! Give me my things and I will go and trouble you no more." She pulled back, but he held her arm. "If there are rogues about, I suspect you are one of them."

"If I were, would I say? I would not. Do not fear. I mean only to warn you to leave this place for your safety. People, especially tourists, should not venture through my glen without reason."

"Why are you here, if it is not safe?"

"I have the right of it. And I keep others, like you, off my lands."

"I am not a tourist. I am searching for fossils, looking for the imprint of ancient flora and fauna left in masses of rock. They provide a geological record of Earth."

"Find your fossils elsewhere in Scotland. Not here, not now. Come."

Tugged by his strength, hurrying in his wake, Fiona concentrated on her footsteps on the rugged terrain. Drifts of mist obscured the way as they walked on.

MacGregor stopped short, fingers tightening on her wrist. Fiona stopped too. Hearing the clop of horse hooves and the rattle of a cart, she looked through the fog, trying to determine the direction of the sound.

"Is that a pony cart?" she asked.

"Aye, coming along the drover's track that runs to the road and the loch. This way." He pulled her along. Her booted toe hit a rock, and she stumbled.

MacGregor caught her around the waist, and she leaned against him, off balance. He felt so solid and sure that for a moment she stayed close, breathing hard. Then she straightened away. Once more, he drew with him over hillocks and stones.

Then he stopped quickly. Fiona bumped into his back. He put out a hand to keep her from tilting on the incline.

"Hush." He looked around warily as his hand found her

wrist. Sensing tension in the air, she stepped close to him, blinded in the deep fog on this part of the hill.

To the left, she heard the rumble of the cart, which came into view—a boxy wagon stacked with hay, pulled by a sturdy brown horse. Two men sat on the crossbench, one in a wrapped plaid, one in trousers, both in dark jackets and dark, flat bonnets. The driver in plaid was a lean young man, his passenger robust and older.

"Smugglers with a load of illicit spirits?" she asked softly.

"Farmers going home to supper," he murmured. "But hold."

"I hear that smugglers go about quite openly. And it is getting dark." She glanced at the fading light through the fog, wishing she had gone with Patrick after all. "Are they dangerous?"

He huffed. "They are my kinsmen. Not dangerous to me, or you. But those other fellows might be."

Now he was looking in the opposite direction. Fiona glanced there to see two men on foot emerging from the fog down by the loch road. They wore dark jackets, trousers, and brimmed hats. One had a pistol, the other a cudgel, she saw clearly as they moved.

"Smugglers!" she whispered, unconsciously edging closer to MacGregor. He exuded reliable strength; strangely, she felt safe near him, whoever he was.

"The two on the road? Gaugers."

"Revenue officers? Then we have nothing to worry about."

"Oh, not a thing," he drawled. Taking her arm in a fresh grip, he led her down the slope. Between the farmers approaching from one direction and the king's officers coming from the other, Fiona angled her steps toward the officers. They would know her brother and escort her to safety.

But MacGregor tugged her toward the cart. He gave a low whistle and half dragged Fiona with him, avoiding the gaugers.

With a sinking feeling, she knew then that the laird of Kinloch was not simply the farmer and landowner he claimed. He was the very smuggler that Patrick and Mrs. MacIan had warned her about.

When the Laird walks the mountainside, Mrs. MacIan had said, step aside.

Chapter Three

D OUGAL STOPPED SHORT, the lass bumped into his shoulder, and he set his hand firmly on her arm. He did not intend to let her go. Not yet.

Narrowing his eyes, he estimated the revenue men to be a half mile or so away along the loch road. From the slope's angle, they were clear enough, though distant. The drifting mist and the rocky angle of the slope would hide him and the girl for a bit. Nor would the man have seen the cart yet, though they might hear its creaking progress.

Taking the lass with him, Dougal ran down toward the approaching cart.

"Let go," the girl said. "The officers will take me to Mrs. MacIan's home."

"Mrs. MacIan? Is that where you belong?" Was she the teacher? That was different, then. "I will take you myself. You would not be safe with the gaugers."

"I am hardly safe with you," she pointed out.

He gave a low whistle, a soft trill like a curlew's call. The squeak of wheels slowed, for the driver knew the signal. Dougal hurried down the slope, towing the lass along.

"I do not need a ride, I can walk—"

"Hush," Dougal said, hurrying with her, hoping the curve along the base of the road would hide them from the gaugers.

The vehicle rolled to a halt, and Dougal waved, hauling the

girl with him. She was not eager to go. Not that he could blame her, but he had no time to explain.

"Miss, this is Ranald MacGregor and his son, Andrew. My uncle and cousin," he said. "Ranald, Andrew, this is—ah—" He did not know her name.

"Miss Fiona MacCarran." She gave his kinsmen such a warm smile that Dougal wished she had blessed him with a smile like that. But he had hardly earned it; in proof, she sent him a furious side glare.

"Miss MacCarran," he said. "Into the cart. Now," he added.

She blinked. He noticed then her eyes were the deep blue of a sparkling mountain loch. Something intangible within him shifted, a need, a craving. He frowned and offered his hand. She ignored it and gave his kinsmen another smile.

"Gentlemen, I am so pleased to meet you. I have come from Edinburgh to Glen Kinloch to teach at the glen school."

So she was the teacher they were expecting. She had not said so, Dougal thought with a scowl. But he had not asked, he reminded himself.

"Our new dominie! And such a bonny lass too. Not like the last one, hey." Ranald nudged the lad beside him on the cross-bench.

Andrew nodded. At fourteen, swathed in plaid like a High-lander and trousered like a Lowlander, the lad looked dumbstruck by the bonny lass. "We thought the teacher would be old and ugly," he said, blushing.

"Young or old, still a problem for us," Dougal snapped. He took the girl by the waist, his hands neatly fitting her slim, taut curves. "Up you go."

"No," she said as he dumped her over the side into the hay.

Dougal tossed her heavy knapsack after her, set a foot to the wheel hub, and leaped inside beside her. His kinsmen looked back. "Gaugers on the road," he explained. "Two coming this way. Hurry!"

"Och! Hide, then!" Ranald said. "Cover up in that old plaidie back there. If they see the new teacher in our cart, they will ask too much."

Dougal snatched a rumpled plaid lying in a corner of the cart and tossed it over the girl and himself. She gasped as he pushed her down beside him in the hay and pulled her close under the musty tartan covering.

She shoved at his chest. "What are you doing!"

"Hush. You are safer with us than with those gaugers."

"Even if one of them is my brother?" She pulled away.

"Ah, so your brother is the new gauger down the loch?"

"Aye, and you will regret holding me against my will." She shoved at him. Dougal caught both her hands in one of his, and peered out from under the blanket.

"Do either of you know the gaugers up ahead?" he hissed at his kinsmen.

"Too far to see who they are yet," Andrew answered. "Why?"

"Her brother is the new excise officer."

"Och, that's trouble then," Ranald growled.

"What sort of trouble?" the girl asked in Gaelic. Dougal and his kinsmen had used a quick, fluent mix of Gaelic and English. Dougal sighed. He should have known the dominie would understand everything they said.

"Hush," he said, "if you can." She shoved at him again.

"Hide, both of you," Ranald said. "I see them now. Andrew, take the reins." Dougal felt the cart lurch as the horse stepped forward.

Dougal snugged the blanket over his head and hers. "Hush," he repeated, his face close to hers in the shadow of the woven covering.

"I need not hide from my brother or his men." She struggled, and the blanket slipped.

Click. Hearing a gun latch, Dougal glanced up to see a glinting barrel poke through an opening in the folds of the plaid. Ranald, leaning over the back of the bench, held the pistol. "No word from you, lass. Do as the laird says."

"What the devil, Uncle," Dougal muttered.

"Mr. MacGregor," Miss MacCarran said crisply in Gaelic, "put that pistol away." She reminded Dougal of a teacher he once had: a handsome woman, strict but kind, whom he had unabashedly adored as a lad.

His big, beefy, fearless uncle hesitated. "Begging pardon, Miss, but you must do as the laird says, or we will all have trouble."

"I need not hide. Those officers are colleagues of my brother. And now I know you are all scoundrels," she snapped.

Dougal heard the indignation in her voice. Impressed with her ire as well as her deft command of Gaelic, he was not about to debate gaugers versus smugglers just now. Clearly she was disposed to favor one over the other. And his idiot uncle waving a pistol about did not help.

"Ranald, set that thing away," he snarled.

As he spoke, Miss MacCarran got hold of her knapsack and swung it hard enough to knock the weapon out of Ranald's hand. Snatching the bag, Dougal fell across her and held her down, losing the plaid in the process. Ranald was swearing a fair storm, shaking his hand. The horses sidestepped, and Andrew mastered the reins.

"Och, what an excellent lass!" Ranald crowed as he stretched back, grabbed the pistol, and stashed it under his jacket.

"You are mad, the both of you!" Dougal growled at his uncle and the girl both. He threw a leg over hers while she writhed beside him. Somehow he pulled the plaid high again, then flipped down an edge to glare at Ranald. "Uncle, what in hell was that?"

"Sorry, Kinloch. I thought to keep her quiet so she couldna make trouble."

"Yet she is. Stop it, you lass!" Dougal added as the girl pushed hard against him. "That pistol could have gone off and killed someone."

"Then he should not have pointed it at anyone. Get—off!" She shoved hard.

He shifted his weight a bit but kept his leg over hers, additionally pinning her down with an arm over her chest. Her breath heaved under his entrapment. He regretted using his strength and ought to apologize, but it could not be helped in the moment. He closed his eyes—she was soft, curvy, and fit. Damned distracting.

"Why would smugglers care if someone is killed?" she asked. "Kidnapping, murder, smuggling, breaking the king's law—it is nothing to such as you."

"Ruthless, we are," Dougal drawled. "Blackguards, we three."

"Wretches," she agreed. "Scoundrels."

"Och, we are not so bad as gaugers," Ranald said, leaning back to talk to her.

"I believe it is just the opposite," she rasped.

"Whisky smugglers are not all bad sorts," Dougal murmured. "Often they are decent men who simply correct bad governmental regulations."

"You mean blatantly ignore the law."

"Highland whisky makers have a right to do what they want with barley they grow on their land."

"The new regulations—"

"The Crown has no right to tax anything a Scotsman makes from his barley."

"You cannot argue with that, lassie," Ranald said as the cart rolled slowly on.

"Revenue men earn an honest living upholding the law," she answered.

"Hah!" Ranald grunted. "She seems a good Scottish lass, speaking the tongue of the Gaels, but she defends English law over Highlanders."

"I respect and appreciate Highlanders. I do," she added.

"If you do," Dougal said, "then know you are safe with Highland men of good character, and unsafe with gaugers who would kill a man just to snatch a keg of whisky."

"So you are smugglers," she said.

"I never said either way. But we are no friends of customs

men, those paid by the government to enforce limits on Highland whisky making and take the excess."

"My brother is a fine officer who is only interested in bringing criminals to justice."

"That says he is green and will soon learn that justice is often injustice here. If I were you, lass, I would not speak of your brother to Highland folk."

"I, for one, dinna want to hear about him again," Ranald said.

"Ranald, keep quiet or you will be heard," Dougal said.

"King's men just ahead," Andrew said.

"Lay still," Dougal told the girl, who struggled again. Tugging the blanket securely over both of them, he slid down to lie flat in the straw, pressing her tightly against him. Like lovers, he thought, bundled and courting. He scowled at the thought.

"Oof," she said. "Beast," she hissed in his ear.

"This is for your safety as well as ours," he murmured. "We must get past those men, and we cannot do that if they see you."

"I shall scream," she said fervently, and drew a breath.

He slipped a hand over her lips, over smooth, creamy cheeks, and leaned close. "Aye, do you dare?" he whispered.

She looked at him, eyes wide in the dim light filtering through the tartan weave and made a muffled squeak.

"Hush. Please," he whispered.

She bit his finger. He yelped, clamped his hand down again.

"Listen, my wee bonny lass," he hissed. "We will pass this road without incident. This is for the sake of many, not just us. Is it clear?"

She nodded. Dougal kept his hand over her mouth, though wary of her teeth. He wrapped her into his arms to discourage the writhing. A glimpse showed the fear in her eyes, and he felt such remorse he could barely look at her.

"I am sorry," he whispered.

"You there! Stop in the name of the king!" a man called out harshly.

The cart drew to a halt. Dougal lay still, holding the girl, feeling warmth generate between them under the plaid. His cheek rested against her hair, her hand curled on his chest, his arm and leg strapped her down. He felt her breaths, felt her tremble as they waited.

She smelled like rain and roses mixed with earth and rock dust. He closed his eyes for a moment. A long time had passed since he had held a woman in his arms. This one smelled like heaven and felt like a perfect fit, body and soul. If only he could have met her under better circumstances—

She jammed her elbow into his ribs, and he grunted. As her mouth moved, he did not want to be bitten again, and shifted his fingers. "Do not scream," he whispered.

"Let me go," she whispered. "I will not tell them you are smugglers. You have my word, I swear."

"A fairy's bargain," he said.

"A what?"

"A fairy's bargain is never to be trusted. Especially when it is offered by a stranger, a beautiful, charming lass who holds a man in her thrall." He moved his fingers over her mouth, but she managed to get a hand free to grab his hand.

"Thrall? Hah! What do you know of fairies?" she added.

"Some and not enough. Hush," he murmured, covering her mouth with his hand.

"Stop in the name of the king!" The shout echoed closer this time.

Dougal froze, felt Miss MacCarran do the same. He held her tight, improperly so, his leg wedged between hers, her skirts wadded between their bodies. He waited, sensed she did too. The plaid covered them well, but he rolled over her just enough to hide her, risking that his form might be noticed.

"Who are you? What is in the wagon?" one of the revenue men called out.

"MacGregors from north of the glen, sir," Andrew replied.

"Kin to the MacGregors who carry illicit whisky through these hills?"

"I do not know who you mean," Andrew said. He translated that to Ranald. "My father does not speak English. We are just farmers."

"We are looking for farmers, crofters, and smugglers. You are a slippery lot."

"There are many MacGregors in this glen, all around the loch," Andrew said.

"What are you doing out here?"

Ranald murmured to Andrew, who spoke again. "We are just bringing a kinsman to the healing woman in the hills above Drumcairn. Old Hector MacGregor from up the glen side is in the back. He is very ill, sir."

Dougal knew then he had better be a convincing Hector, an elderly and hearty cousin who lived at the far end of the glen. He groaned and coughed.

"Don't believe them," one revenue officer said to the other. "Rascals, the lot of them. Search the cart. You two sit there and do not move."

"I will have to explain this to my father," Andrew said, and began to speak Gaelic in a loud, distracting voice. What he said was not flattering to the gaugers.

Hearing footfalls, Dougal knew the revenue men had moved to the cart bed now, no doubt staring at the blanketed form in the hay. The girl tensed beneath him, and he lay motionless, his breath brushing the soft curls along her brow.

"There's a man there under the plaid," one of them said. "See his boot."

Dougal coughed, adding an ugly groan at the end.

"Sounds bad," the second man said. Dougal heard the rustling of straw as the gaugers reached over the cart side to pull at the plaid. Moaning again, he made a retching sound. Beneath him, the girl shuddered—tears? Panic?

"Ill, or drunk on his own peat reek," one of the men growled. "What else do you carry besides that old drunken rascal? Kegs of whisky to be confiscated?"

Ranald growled in Gaelic as Andrew translated. "My father says not everyone moves peat reek about, sir. He takes offense to be so accused."

"Insulted until we find crocks and kegs under the straw, eh?"

"We're carrying hay, and a very sick old man," Andrew answered. "Hector is not drunk. He's ill, and we need to get him to a healer who lives in these hills."

"They're all thieves and liars," one of the officers snarled. He thumped the cart bed so hard that the impact bounced through Dougal and the girl both. That sound came from a gun butt or a cudgel.

Dougal emitted another unearthly groan. One gauger cried out and both swore.

"I would not be touching Old Hector if I were you," Andrew answered.

"What's he got?" one officer asked.

"Fever, sir," Andrew translated.

"That's nothing. Get him up. Let's see him."

"*Tinneas-an-gradh-dubh,*" Ranald said quickly.

"Tinneen-groo-doo? What the devil is that?" an officer demanded.

"A terrible sickness," Andrew said. "He has had it for a while, and this is a bad spell. Do not touch him, sir," he added hastily. "You could catch it, and it is a horrible thing to bear."

Dougal coughed again, loudly, clutching the girl to him. Her arms slid around him, probably to ease her position. She was shaking again, convulsing, and he rubbed her shoulder in reassurance. Then he realized that she was laughing.

He huffed in her ear, a whisper of laughter. She relaxed a bit, softening against him. Her bonnet tipped askew, and his lips met the soft shell of her ear. She sighed.

Such a sultry movement, so close to him; a feeling rocketed through his body, eliciting a response that needed immediate suppression. He tilted away from her. She looked up at him in the darkness beneath the plaid. He caught that gaze and was lost.

For an instant, he forgot where they were, what they were doing. There was magic between them—where had it come from, so sudden, so sweet and tempting?

But he could not be distracted. He turned his head to fake another retch and an agonizing cough. The girl patted his shoulder in mock sympathy.

"Tinnie-what? I've never heard of it," one revenue man was saying to the other.

"A bad illness," Andrew said. "We hope to get him some help in time."

"They're lying so they can get illegal whisky past us. Search the cart!"

They had the authority to do whatever they wanted, he knew. Excise officers were deputies of the law, charged with apprehending smugglers, collecting illicit goods, and collecting additional fees to supplement their meager wages. Thus the incentive to find criminals in the Highland regions was strong, encouraged by the government. Dougal paused, waiting. Then he groaned.

"It does seem bad. Best keep away, Mr. MacIntyre," one man said to the other.

Dougal frowned. Tam MacIntyre was a tough, cruel law enforcer, lately promoted to chief revenue officer along the loch.

"*Tinneas-an-gradh-dubh,*" Ranald repeated. "Bad!"

"Bad, aye!" Andrew spoke hastily. "Mr. MacIntyre, sir, let us pass. Only the healing woman can help Hector in his suffering. We do not want to catch this."

"Go on, then," MacIntyre growled. "But if you see that rascal Dougal MacGregor, you tell him I am looking for him."

"I have not seen him for a while," Andrew said.

"He's likely crossing the hills with a load of peat reek," MacIntyre said.

"Kinloch has never been caught at such a thing," Andrew defended. "He is a fine laird, looking after his glen and his tenants, his cattle and his fields."

"And his barley brew? Tell him we discovered another whisky still up the glen side. We dismantled it, but we do not know whose it is. Any illegal stills found on a landowner's property are the fault of the landowner. The punishment and the fine will be Kinloch's to bear on this one."

Ranald murmured something and spat.

"In English, you old goat, I know you speak it," MacIntyre said.

"The reverend hired a teacher to come to Glen Kinloch to teach us English," Andrew said. "Perhaps my father can learn English from her."

"And you are a slick-tongued otter. I do not trust a word you say."

Dougal groaned and retched.

MacIntyre's companion swore. "Let them pass, sir. If the old man dies—"

"Go on," MacIntyre said. "But tell your kinsmen and friends we are watching them. We have more men now and new laws. Tell your free-trading kin they will not get away with crimes so easily as before."

"Good evening, Mr. MacIntyre," Andrew said, and snapped the reins.

As the cart lurched, Dougal kept his arms around the girl. His cheek was against hers under the cover of the musty old blanket. He felt her breath wisp over his ear. He heard Andrew and Ranald talking. Then Ranald laughed outright.

"Kinloch, did you hear it?" Ranald called back.

"I did," Dougal said. "Be quiet, you, until we are far away."

"*Tinneas-an-gradh-dubh,*" Andrew repeated, hooting. "The black lovesickness!"

"The black lovesickness is upon him," Ranald crowed. "He has it bad!"

"It will slay him for certain," Andrew added with gravity.

"Best see the lass home and save the laird from being sick with love," Ranald said.

"Enough!" Dougal called gruffly.

The girl was laughing softly beneath his covering hand, her lips tender against his palm. Sudden desire spiked hot through him. He lifted his hand away and wondered if it was safe to sit up yet. The air between them was heated with feelings he dared not explore.

"So *tinneas-an-gradh-dubh* is a plague in this glen," she said, laughing.

"Aye, if a bonny lass breaks the laird's heart, it is the black lovesickness for him!" Ranald crowed jovially.

"You all are enjoying this too much," Dougal said, and flipped the plaid down to let cool fresh air bathe his head and hers.

"Does the laird suffer this awful plague often?" she asked, eyes sparkling.

"Not too often," Ranald drawled. "So when he gets, it is bad indeed."

She laughed again. Dougal heard delight and a hint of reluctance, as if she did not want to be so much at ease with them. He smiled in the dark.

"Is it clear now, Uncle?" he called.

"The road looks empty ahead, but best keep under that plaidie for now."

Dougal ducked under the plaid again, pulling it high over the girl's head.

"Hector? Is that your name, not Dougal?" she teased.

"Hector MacGregor is my great-uncle, who is hearty but claims to be over a hundred years old."

"How does he manage good health at his age?"

He chuckled. "He says fairy magic keeps him young."

"Fairy magic?" She tipped her head in interest.

"They say the MacGregors of Kinloch know a few fairy secrets."

"Do you?" she asked intently.

He shrugged. "More than some, less than others."

"Fairy lore is so intriguing," she murmured.

She was intriguing, he thought. The feel of her in his arms, his body stretched over hers, the plaid cocooning them in strange intimacy, the tension of touch and politeness, of fear and amusement. His thoughts were not on fairies. Every jolt and lurch of the rolling cart brought him into contact with her, and he felt increasingly on fire.

He was no boy to be aroused without control, nor one to take advantage of a woman for the mere pleasure of it. But by God, he found it difficult to endure her warm, firm body under his, her sweet breath upon his cheek, her heartbeat thrumming under his fingers. He wanted to pull her closer, taste her, caress her, please her.

Stop it, he told himself. He forced himself to focus, her interest at the moment as odd as anything else that was happening. "What do you want to know about fairies?"

"Oh, legends and…sightings. Have you ever seen a fairy?"

Dougal raised his brows, surprised. "Seen them? I have heard that some kinsmen have seen them. My father—" He stopped.

"Your father has seen them?"

"He is no longer with us," he answered abruptly. "Strange questions. I would expect you to be complaining about smugglers, or even asking about the glen and the school, not about fairies."

"I would, but I am fascinated by fairy legends."

In the murky shadows beneath the plaid, her eyes glimmered like stars, her breath was soft as a breeze. "I am looking at a fairy creature just now," he murmured, "and she is the lovely queen of them all."

"That is silliness. I am serious."

So was he. Just when he should have pulled away, he felt her breath caress his cheek, his ear. A devastating plummet of desire went through him. The cart lurched then, pressing her body instantly to his, her cheek soft on his, her lips perilously close. Before he could draw back, he kissed her.

Her lips softened, her mouth surrendered for a moment. Just

for a moment. Then she pulled away. "Oh," she breathed, "oh—"

She touched her mouth to his again, of her own accord, surprising him wholly. He groaned low in his throat and gave in to that caress, her body warm and tight in his arms, pulsing, heating, while the cart rumbled onward. Only he and the girl knew what the blanket hid, or how that kiss tumbled full into another as if some magic spell had taken hold of both of them.

He could not account for it, could barely think. He was not drunk. He was his usual sober and wary self, yet this happened. He was fully capable in mind and judgment, yet he was kissing this girl as if he had known her all his life, as if he had loved her forever, as if he were drunk indeed with lovesickness.

It was like tasting fairy whisky, or seeing the first bright burst of dawn—unexpected, miraculous, to be savored, a thing that could change a man if he let it.

The kiss renewed between them. He touched his tongue to the soft, moist curve of her lip, and pressed his body to hers, hard and ready. He felt and heard her soft moan. She was not rejecting him—she was enjoying it. He would have pulled away, but she pressed closer with a little sound of passion and surprise.

"Aye?" he whispered. Sliding his hand along the curve of her hip and waist, sensing the heat of her body, he shaped her luscious curves with his palm. And then halted, fingers taut, waiting, a question.

Her hands slid over his shoulders to his neck, her fingers threaded into the thickness of his hair. She wanted this. He was surprised, sensed she was too. Her hand slipped over the width of his shoulder and down his arm, a slow advance—

The rumbling cart slowed, and Dougal pulled away, breathing fast, hard. She turned away, ducked her head, curling on her side.

"Oh dear," she said.

"Miss, I—" He was hardly sure what had happened. "Pardon."

She did not answer. He pulled the blanket aside and peered out.

And saw Ranald staring down at them from the bench. The air was fresh, foggy, dim. "Ready?" the old man asked.

"Ready," the lass said, and sat up. Hay bits were in her hair. Dougal sat up too.

"Mrs. MacIan's house is just there in the cove," his uncle said calmly. "We cannot take the cart down there in such a mist. But you can walk."

"Aye," Dougal said gruffly.

"Thank you, Mr. MacGregor." She straightened her bonnet, rose to her knees, brushing at her skirts. She did not look at Dougal.

Dougal came up and stepped over the side of the cart. He turned to reach up and help her down. Under his hands, her slim curves fit so neatly, felt so good that he just wanted to pull her close again. He slid her to the ground and they stepped apart quickly, looking away from each other.

"My knapsack," she said, reaching back.

Dougal grabbed the pack from the cart. Then he groped beneath the straw until he felt the hard shapes of the kegs hidden beneath thick straw. The revenue officers had nearly discovered those. He drew out one ceramic crock wrapped in straw and tied with string. Tucking it beneath his arm, slinging the knapsack over his shoulder, he turned.

"Let me escort you to the house." He gestured for her to precede him. The fog was thick here, so near the water, and the twilight turned it to a lavender mist. He could see the warm glow of brightly lit windows ahead.

She tilted her head in silence. He could still taste her lips, still felt his heart pounding, and wondered what she thought. Then she yanked the knapsack from his shoulder, swung it to her shoulder, nearly knocking herself over.

"No need to go with me," she said. "Thank you, Mr. Mac-Gregor, and Andrew," she told the two still gaping at them. "Farewell, Kinloch." She turned to walk along the road.

"Do not let her go, Kinloch," Ranald said. "She'll break an

ankle in this murk and mist on the path down to the cove, and Mary MacIan will be after us all for it."

"I need to bring the whisky I promised Mary MacIan." Dougal shouldered the keg and followed the girl. She was certainly not just another dull teacher from the city, afraid of everything. She was young and lovely. She was stubborn, independent, intelligent.

And she kissed like a fallen angel, seductive yet innocent. Even if he craved more of that, craved to know more about her, he could not trust her. Nor could he allow a woman in his life. Not now. Not yet.

Especially the sister of a gauger.

Chapter Four

THE MacIAN COTTAGE appeared through the fog, and ghostly mist drifted across the loch beyond the house. Walking toward it, Fiona glanced over her shoulder.

"I do not need an escort, Mr. MacGregor."

"Rogues about," he said, shifting the cask on his shoulder. "And the path to the cottage is uneven. You could slip and fall, carrying those rocks."

"You are carrying something too, and could stumble."

"Eh, I am fine. This is a gift for Mrs. MacIan and her grandson, Reverend MacIan." He caught up to her with long, sure strides.

"Was the cart full of illicit whisky, then?"

"I do not know. It was not my cart."

She sent him a sour glance. "I suppose you bribe people with whisky so they will look away from what you and your kinsmen do in the glen."

"Miss MacCarran, I am offended. It is tradition for the laird to give whisky to the manse. I share freely from the distillery on my estate."

"Free traders or sharing freely? But I will not say a word. It is your business."

"My business," he said curtly, "is a licensed distillery with my kinsmen. This cask holds legal brew. I bring some to the MacIans with each new batch."

"So the cart only held whisky that you share with others?"

"What else would it hold? Why would we smuggle it, with gaugers traipsing all about these hills?" He sounded amused.

She stopped. "Mr. MacGregor, let me suggest a bargain. I promise not to speak of what I have seen if you promise to never—"

"What? Never kiss you again?" He stopped too.

"That—should not happen again." She could not let him see how much his kisses had flustered her, weakened her resolve. "I apologize. It is not in my character to behave so. I cannot think what happened."

"Nor in my character. But I know what happened. The lovesickness." He grinned.

She wished he were not so devilishly attractive—that smile was everything in the moment, charm and humor, temptation and risk. She felt heat in her cheeks. "Your uncle said the lovesickness has plagued you before."

"Och, lassie, dinna believe Ranald MacGregor," he said with an exaggerated lilt.

"It could be true, since you stole a kiss from a woman you hardly know."

"I know her better than she thinks." MacGregor leaned forward, so close she could feel his nearness rush through her. "I was not the only one stealing the kisses."

She caught her breath. Something irresistible and magical had happened in that cart. Though she felt embarrassed now, part of her wanted to cherish it. MacGregor hovered near enough to kiss her again. Feeling her cheeks grow hot, she stepped away.

"About this bargain, Miss MacCarran. If you will keep the adventure in the cart to yourself, I will consider never kissing you again. Is that agreeable?"

"Oh," she said, flustered anew. That might be the poor end of the bargain, she thought; what if no one ever kissed her like that again? Blushing furiously, glad of the mist and lowering daylight, she turned toward the cottage. The door opened, golden light silhouetting a woman standing there. "Mrs. MacIan is waiting."

"And gone again," he said, as the door closed once more.

"No need to go farther, Mr. MacGregor. I can take the cask. It is not so big."

"Not large, but heavy."

"I am stronger than you think."

"I see that, for you are carrying that great sack of rocks of yours. Mary MacIan would have my head if I sent you there loaded like a packhorse. And if she knew the rest that happened," he added softly, "she would have my head for that, too. May it be a comfort to you."

"It is." She lifted her chin. "I will think about the agreement."

"So will I," he said, a little smile playing at his lips.

"Watch your step, the fog is that thick." He held out a hand, which Fiona ignored as she walked past him.

Two strides and he was ahead of her. Seeing his wide shoulders and the rhythmic swing of his plaid kilt above strong calves, she remembered those wanton kisses and the fervor she had felt—and felt her face, her body, grow hot with embarrassment and more. She had allowed those kisses, encouraged and shared them, but she could not it happen again. But her heartbeat quickened at the very thought.

"Mr. MacGregor," she called.

"Kinloch, if you please. Dougal, if it pleases you more."

"Kinloch," she said firmly. "Let us agree to forget what happened this evening."

"Every bit of it?" He turned and walked backward, the keg casually propped on his shoulder. "I will remember some of it always, Miss MacCarran."

So would she. "It was of no consequence. Just the moment, and the fear, I suppose. Sir, will you please stop?"

He did. "I may not forget it, but trust I will never say a word of it to another."

Relief went through her. "Let us keep our secret about—everything. And I promise not to tell the MacIans."

He shrugged his free shoulder. "Tell them or not, as you like. They are kin."

"Reverend MacIan would go to the authorities."

"You could try to convince him otherwise," he said.

"Is he involved in—what goes on in this glen?"

"He is a kinsman. That is enough."

"He is a man of God."

"Surely your brother, the important excise officer, told you that the free trade is common all through the Highlands. It occurs in Glen Kinloch now and then as well. Those who run it keep silent, and everyone else wisely looks away."

"So everyone in Glen Kinloch is either a smuggler or knows a smuggler?"

"We are hardly a nest of criminals, Miss. The people of this glen are fine, honest folk who do what they must to survive."

"Are you warning me to look away as well?"

He stepped closer, his gaze compelling in the gathering dark. "Take it as a warning if you like," he murmured. "Your brother sides with the law. That does not sit well here."

"One of my brothers is involved with revenue collection, true. But I do not know if he is assigned to this glen. He may be sent elsewhere."

"How many brothers do you have?"

"Three. A revenue officer, a physician in Edinburgh, and a professor who has an estate in this region. A cousin is nearby too. So I am less a stranger here than you might think. My twin is Viscount Struan. His estate is southeast of here."

"Struan! I know the name. I heard a Lowlander inherited it." He paused. "I heard he married the granddaughter of the weaver of Kilcrennan."

"Elspeth MacArthur of Kilcrennan, aye. Do you know her?"

"Her father is a distant cousin." He narrowed his eyes. "Twin brother, is it? You will be close, then. No doubt Struan will visit you here and you will tell him all."

"He is often in Edinburgh for months at a time. He is a lecturing professor there. And we do not tell each other everything." That was not quite true, but she could hold a secret well, though she was not sure yet what a bargain with Kinloch would mean.

"What of the cousin?"

"The Earl of Eldin. We are not close."

"Ah. Eldin purchased Auchnashee to make it into a hotel for tourists, I hear." He frowned. "You have lofty company among your kin."

"Not really. But I do have ties to the Highlands. I am not just a Lowlander."

He nodded thoughtfully. "The gentleman with you on the hill today. Who was he?"

"Patrick. The excise officer. I did not know you saw us earlier."

"I watch over my mountain and my glen. When Reverend MacIan invited you here to teach, did he know your brother was a revenue officer?"

"I did not know it then. Patrick was appointed to the post after I agreed to come here. But his jurisdiction is south of the loch, so he may not come here except to visit me and make sure I am safe." She wanted to make that clear.

"As the laird, I will guarantee your safety."

The Laird. Did he mean laird of the glen—or the smuggling laird Patrick mentioned? A yearning swirled in her, a hunger for adventure, excitement. She squared her shoulders against the feeling. "You may be the one in danger. The king's men are looking for the one called the Laird."

"I have heard that. They know where to find Kinloch if they want to talk to him. They suspect me, but I am innocent of all— except kissing a bonny lass in a moment of weakness. And for that, I apologize."

"No need," she murmured.

"As for what you saw tonight, the excise men are often after me. I am laird of a glen where free traders roam. It is not uncommon, and the laird is often to blame if the actual offenders cannot be found."

"What of the smuggler called the Laird? Is that you?"

"She is bold. I am laird of this glen," he said, jaw set, brows lowered.

"But you hid from the excise officers and your kinsmen lied. Why?"

"For your protection. Some revenue officers are worse scoundrels than the men they chase." He took her arm. "My kin and tenants will not harm you, I promise. But there are other rascals in these hills, so be wary. If word gets out that you are sister to an excise man, it could go badly for you and your brother. It is not in your best interest to speak of it here. And I must question whether you should be in this glen at all."

"I just arrived today, and I have been hauled about rudely, threatened with pistols, and—"

"And kissed. I know."

"—and my brother wanted me to leave—"

"You should have listened."

"—and now the laird of the glen wants me to leave too? I came here to do good work for the Edinburgh Ladies Society for the Education and Betterment of the Gaels. I agreed to teach here."

"The what?"

She repeated the name. "It is not amusing," she said as he chuckled. "I promised to teach until summer. School begins soon. There are children waiting. I will not leave."

He cupped a hand on her shoulder. Fiona felt some indefinable magic flow from him into her. The same feeling had overtaken her earlier and quite melted all reason and resistance. He bent his head toward her. For a moment she thought he might kiss her again. Her head tipped back, her body waited.

"Best go, lass," he murmured. "I will speak to the reverend. In the morning, I will send a gig and driver to take you to Auchnashee. If there are expenses for your return to Edinburgh, I will pay them. You may keep the rocks," he added.

"You have neither right nor cause to dismiss me."

"I do it for your welfare."

"Only Reverend MacIan can excuse me. He invited me." She stepped past him, feeling angry. She did not want to leave. Already the glen drew her, and so did its laird, though she did not want to admit that. Nor could she explain that she was here to satisfy her grandmother's last request—to find fairies and sketch them, and to find and marry a wealthy Highland laird. Clearly she would find neither here. But she would not go.

"I am no threat to your smuggling interests, if it worries you." She spun to walk to the house.

"Miss—Fiona! Wait." Her name, spoken in his deep, rich, lilting voice, sounded beautiful. Magical. She turned. He took her arm.

In the misty twilight, as he loomed over her, all else vanished. Wildly, impulsively, she felt enchanted, as if he were indeed one of the Sidhe. "Listen, lass," he said. "This is just not the time for you to be here. Trust me in that."

"I will not speak of what happened. We have a bargain. Let that satisfy you."

"Never bargain with the fairies."

"So you said. What do you mean? You are not one of them— are you?"

He bent toward her, and her head went back. She did not want a kiss, and yet it was all she wanted.

"Damn," he muttered, and straightened as a woman's voice cut through the fog.

"Is that you, Miss MacCarran? Who is with you?" Mary MacIan's voice broke the spell that rooted Fiona in place. She glanced toward the cottage, its door open, showing a woman and a glowing hearth behind her.

"It is me, Mrs. MacIan! I am just coming. The laird is with me."

"Mary MacIan!" he called. "I met your guest in the hills and brought her to you."

"Kinloch, you rascal! Come in, both of you." Mary MacIan beckoned. "Did you bring me a cask? Lovely lad! Is it the fairy sort this time? I hope not. I do not love it."

"Just the usual sort. I know what you like," he said with a smile.

Fiona looked up, curious. "The fairy sort of what?"

"Whisky. Secret brew. But we should not speak of it." He sounded amused.

"I want nothing to do with your whisky business," she said, and hurried ahead.

"Kinloch whisky is always welcome, and so is its bonny braw laird!" Mary MacIan reached up to kiss his cheek as he reached the doorstep. She was a small woman with a froth of silvery hair spilling out from a white cap. Her plain gown and tartan shawl hung loose on her small frame. Fiona stepped inside and the laird followed, bending his head to clear the lintel.

She set her knapsack on the floor, and MacGregor set the whisky cask on a table beneath a window. Standing in the simply furnished front room of the cottage, he looked large, imposing, handsome, and mysterious. He smiled at Mary MacIan.

"I am sorry, dearie, I cannot stay for long."

"Aye, there are gaugers about tonight," Mary said. "The lad was here earlier and told me of officers out on the road. Did you meet them?"

"All is well. Give my best to the lad." He stepped toward the door.

"The lad?" Fiona asked.

"The Reverend, my grandson," Mrs. MacIan said. "He promised to take you around the glen, and so he will be back tomorrow to do so."

"How wonderful," Fiona said, looking at Kinloch. "I am looking forward to it."

"A pity Miss MacCarran must leave the glen tomorrow," he said, gazing with equal intensity at her. She narrowed her eyes.

"Leave! She just arrived!" Mary MacIan looked astonished.

"And I am enjoying my stay here. I am not leaving." Fiona walked to the door and opened it wide. "Good night, Kinloch."

"Miss MacCarran." He inclined his head politely, leaned to kiss Mary MacIan on the cheek, and stepped out. Fiona shut the door firmly behind him.

"I wish he would stay," Mary MacIan said. "Such a lovely lad, is our Dougal."

Fiona willed her heart to slow, her hands to stop shaking. The attraction she felt toward him was surprisingly strong, but she told herself her reaction was just the result of an unexpected adventure in the romantic Highlands. He was a rogue, and she would do well to avoid him until it was time for her to leave Glen Kinloch.

"Och, hear the dog barking!" Mary said. "She comes running when the laird is here. She loves the lad fiercely and would follow wherever he goes if he let her. She has gone all the way to Kinloch House, she has, and he brings her back each time. Och, I must get her in for the night and out of the dark and mist." She opened the door. "Maggie! Come in!"

Hearing the dog barking in the yard, Fiona went to the door. "Maggie!" she called helpfully. Through the murk, she saw a black-and-white spaniel, tail wagging like quill feathers. The dog ignored them, busy jumping to greet the man walking away from the house.

Kinloch bent to pet the dog. The mist swirled around him, and as he straightened and shooed Maggie home again, he looked back at the house. Fiona felt his gaze burning over her. He lifted a hand, then strode away, whistling, to vanish.

She lifted her chin. She would not leave. The bond she felt with this place already had a place in her heart, despite its laird.

Maggie returned, jumping to the step and over the threshold, then leaping to her hind legs to greet Fiona. Stooping to rub her shoulders, Fiona then closed the door.

DAWN'S SILVERY SHEEN and the chill of morning woke her early. Soon she was pouring steaming cups of tea for Mrs. MacIan and herself while the woman cooked savory sausages over the hearth fire. Hearing hooves and wheels clatter in the yard, Fiona turned toward the window to see a carriage draw up.

"Is that my lad Hugh, come to take you round the glen?" Mary asked. Fiona went to the door while Maggie launched past her, barking. Fiona stepped outside and gasped.

A black carriage drawn by two bay horses had pulled into the yard from the dusty lochside road. Wheels creaking, heaving like a beast, it lumbered forward.

"A coach!" Mary hurried toward the door. "That is not my Hugh. It's the old coach from Kinloch House."

"Is it indeed." Fiona folded her arms, scowling as she recalled Kinloch's promise.

"That's Hamish MacGregor driving it. He is one of the laird's uncles. What does he want here? At least Kinloch is getting some use out of that old thing. His grandfather won it after a night of playing cards. But fine coaches are not meant for Highland roads," Mary added. "Perhaps they are carrying a load o' whisky. We could all make a profit. Oh!" She glanced at Fiona as if she had said too much.

"I believe Kinloch sent his coach for me," Fiona said. "He wants me to leave the glen. He says the school does not need a teacher at this time."

"Hah! He knows how much we do need a teacher," Mary muttered, and went into the yard. The coach shuddered to a stop, two stocky horses blowing and shaking their thick manes. The old vehicle swayed, creaked, quieted.

"Hamish MacGregor, you get down from there!" Mary called.

"Greetings, Mary MacIan. I prefer not to get down. I am in a hurry."

"Then I will pull your ears off when I see you next in kirk, for ruining my yard!"

The coachman sighed and climbed down. Maggie barked, running in circles as Fiona walked outside and lifted a hand against the morning sun.

"Good morning, Miss MacCarran." He was a solidly built man of middle age with a round, mild face and a wild mane of iron-gray hair. He wore the shabby, comfortable outfit common to many Highland men—old jacket and trousers, plaidie swathed across his chest, flat bonnet tilted on his head. "I am Hamish MacGregor, uncle to the Laird o' Kinloch. He sent me here for you." He doffed his cap briefly.

"How nice to meet you," she said. She wondered how many uncles the laird had.

"Why did Kinloch send you?" Mary asked.

"He said the lady wants to leave the glen. Pity, with her just arriving, and we needing a teacher, but if she wants to leave us, she shall go."

"I am staying," Fiona said.

"The laird said I should take you to Auchnashee. I will wait."

"Thank you, but you may go, Mr. MacGregor. Tell Kinloch I am content to stay."

"And tell him his coach is better used to carry whisky, not teachers," Mary said.

Hamish looked at Fiona. "Miss, are you certain?"

"I am."

"These are Kinloch's best packhorses," Mary said, walking over to pat their noses, two big handsome bays with long pale manes and creamy feathering around their ankles. "Groomed very fine, I see, all combed out."

"Andrew did that, and greased the carriage wheels so the lady would ride in comfort. I suspect this is far better than a plain cart and an old blanket."

Fiona hid a smile. So Hamish had heard about that.

"Well, take it back to Kinloch," Mary said. "And let those

horses out to graze. They are not used to harnessing. Just carrying pannier baskets full of barley bree," she added wickedly.

Hamish chuckled. "Och, aye then. But the laird will not like it."

"It is no fault of yours, Mr. MacGregor," Fiona said.

"Tell Kinloch he will see Miss MacCarran on the first day of school," Mary said. "My lad is out reminding glen folk to send their young ones to the school to meet the new dominie. Who will tell my lad his visits were in vain?"

"So be it. Miss MacCarran, I am sorry," Hamish said.

"Not at all. Will you have tea and sausages with us?"

"Oatcakes too, and fresh rowan jam," Mary added.

"I will then. If I may, I will bring some back to the laird. He loves Mary's cooking."

"He will not get fresh jam from me if he is rude to our teacher lass," Mary said. "Och, never mind. I want you to take some jam and cakes to Lucy," Mary said as she ushered Hamish into the cottage.

Following them, Fiona wondered if Lucy was the laird's wife. At the thought, her stomach wrenched. If he had a wife, she thought, the man was indeed a rascal.

She had been wrong to enjoy his kisses, and very wrong to dream of him last night, waking in a warm haze of pillows and plaid and memories of his arms around her.

"Come, Maggie!" She whistled the dog inside. Hearing a sound in the distance, Fiona paused to glance over her shoulder. Was that—bagpipes out in the hills?

The notes faded. She saw only the shabby coach, horses nuzzling at grass, and far blue hills beneath a bright blue sky. A few sheep ambled like pale dots high on the steep slopes. Perhaps their shepherd played for them, she thought.

Another tune began, far off. She stood listening, smiling, the sound filling her.

She wondered then if a tall, dark-haired man in a rumpled plaid stood on a far slope, listening to the same music and watching to make sure she boarded his coach.

She would not do his bidding. Let the infuriating Laird of Kinloch go about his day. No doubt he planned something illegal. Well, let him witness her form of disobedience.

Shutting the door firmly, she hurried to breakfast, hungry and eager to start another day in this beautiful glen, no matter what its laird expected of her.

Chapter Five

DRONE AND MELODY filled the air, cresting off the mountain and returning faint and rich, a quavering that soared over the glen. The sound filled him inside so that he need not think, nor watch for the coach rolling toward Auchnashee carrying the bright and lovely lass he would never see again.

The last haunting note faded. He set his pipes over his shoulder and walked higher on the hillside, wind sifting through his hair. Stopping along the slope, he drew a breath, set the pipes again, and propelled air through the blowstick to inflate the woolen bag and the stretchable sheep bladder inside. The bag with its four chanters had belonged to his grandfather, and its sound was rich and resonant. Tucking the full bag under his arm, he let fingertips fly over the holes along the main chant pipe. The tune was older than his bagpipe, played over so many generations that the echo sounded as if the hills themselves rang it out.

Dougal preferred playing in solitude, for his pleasure and for whatever sheep, cattle, goats, and wandering locals might hear. He did not play at weddings or funerals, nor at ceilidhs held in villages—Garloch to the west, Drumcairn to the east, with Kinloch House halfway between. The two villages at either end of the glen had a long rivalry that expressed itself at ceilidhs, kirks, ball games, and in distilling and free trading. Over generations, the lairds of Kinloch had been neutral. His father had played the bagpipes for social occasions, and his Uncle Fergus played for any and all. But Dougal kept the music to himself.

Keeping apart was protective, he knew, a habit developed by a lad who became a laird too soon, with the responsibility of tenants and estate on his young shoulders. Loyal in his bones to the people of his glen, he did not pipe for them, nor involve himself overmuch in their lives. Truth was, he knew he was not highly skilled at piping, not like his father or Uncle Fergus. He simply loved it.

He had learned much from his father, and after him, his father's brothers, Ranald, Hamish, Fergus, and great-uncle Hector. Those kinsmen had taught Dougal all he knew, guiding him, all of them acting as fathers as he grew. He had learned to make whisky from his father and old Hector; to play the pipes from Fergus, the red-headed blacksmith; learned herding and husbandry from stodgy, steady Ranald; and Uncle Hamish had shown him how to repair nearly anything.

Everything but that blasted old coach, he thought. Every time he and Hamish fixed it, the old thing would start to shimmy and creak once again.

But sometimes what was broken stayed broken. Like his heart. Once hurt, it had stayed that way. First with the loss of his mother, later his father, and years later the girl he would have married. She would have kept a neat house and a kind bed for him. But she had asked him to give up smuggling. When he refused, she left the glen to marry a shepherd.

And may she be happy with her four wee bairns and placid husband, he thought. Dougal had decided he was better off without a wife.

The last note he blew rang out like a lamb's bleat, slightly off pitch. He rested, looking down at the long loch and the pale ribbon of the lochside road. The old coach was nowhere to be seen.

After a while he saw Hamish walking along a ridge toward him, with two dogs at his heels, leggy gray beasts whose majestic, formidable forebears had ambled the halls of Kinloch House for generations. But this lazy pair, Dougal knew, wanted nothing more than to flop in doorways. Still, Sorcha and Mhor were fine guardians and amiable companions. And their presence meant that Hamish had returned to Kinloch House before following the sound in search of his nephew.

"So she refused," Dougal said as Hamish approached.

"She did." His uncle picked up a stick, tossed it. The dogs watched it fly, then settled at the man's feet. "Useless beasts," Hamish muttered.

"Fetching would make them seem obedient, and they cannot have that."

"That lass o' yours is not the least obedient either," Hamish said.

"My lass!" Dougal laughed. "I did not expect her to agree, to be honest. But on the chance she saw the wisdom in it, I sent you with the coach."

"That lass has more than a touch of stubborn in her. It was a waste of time and breath to tell her to leave. She intends to stay. And she had Mary to back her up."

"That could be a formidable pair. Her brother is a gauger," Dougal said. "He could bring men into our hills. She must go." He felt a twinge of regret as he spoke.

"She is determined to open the school, and the reverend is out telling the families so. Mary spoke of it while we ate sausages at her table."

"Sausages? Mary MacIan gave you breakfast?"

Hamish took a parchment bundle from his pocket. "For you and Lucy."

Setting the bagpipe on the grass, Dougal unwrapped the packet to find sausages and a stack of oatcakes. He ate a sausage, savory and still warm. The hounds stood, interested, and he tossed bits to them. "Mary is a fine cook." He licked his fingers.

"The Lowland lady made those for you," Hamish said. "She made oatcakes and good strong tea, too. We shared a fine breakfast. You should have been there, Kinloch. She cooks."

"She cooks?" He ate another sausage; it was seared, savory, perfect. He wrapped the rest to take home, wiping his fingers on his plaid. "A reason to keep her, then."

Hamish chortled. "Aye, now that your Aunt Jean has run home to her mother again, leaving us to fend for ourselves once more."

"Jeanie would come back if you were both less stubborn."

"Bah. Life is more peaceful. The Lowland lass can cook. That is good enough."

"It is not, and you know it. Though Lucy is near old enough to help," he allowed.

"That wee lassie has no interest in household matters. It comes of being raised by a pack of scoundrels."

"We are not so bad," Dougal said. "Aunt Jeanie taught her to make her bed and keep her clothes neat, sweep the floors, sew a seam, cook a little."

"She is not even seven years old. A bairn should not tend the fires and such. Besides, she makes salty porridge and weak tea. That wee bit needs a mother," Hamish said. "You should have married the one who ran off with the shepherd."

"She did not want me," Dougal said.

Hamish grunted. "Then marry this Lowland lady so we can have good sausages and cakes, and she will teach the school and tell her brother to keep his officers away from her husband. And we will all be content." He patted his belly.

"You have thought it all out," Dougal drawled.

"For the sake of our stomachs, one of us needs a wife in that big house."

"Jeanie will return." But Dougal feared that this time, Hamish and Jean might be done with their stormy, passionate, stubborn marriage. "Miss MacCarran would be out searching for wee rocks and letting us fend for ourselves, I guarantee. Nor would it help any of us if I brought a gauger's sister into our house."

"Blast all gaugers!" Hamish shrugged. "Well, send her away if you can. A pity the reverend brought her here just at this time. I wish he had waited a few weeks more."

"Aye." Dougal bent to pick up his bagpipes and walked beside Hamish, the dogs following. Aye, indeed, he did want the Lowland lass to stay, and he could not explain the strong feeling of it, the surge of craving inside him. He barely knew the woman. But he could not forget those kisses—or the fine way she stood up to him and expressed her thoughts and her own will. He admired that even more than sweet, earnest kisses.

He was not desperate for a wife, he told himself. He had dallied now and then with one girl and another, if they were willing, and lived beyond the glen. In truth, a long while had passed since the last time he had let his heart become even a little interested. By now he was resigned to bachelorhood. It suited him.

But this Lowland girl was different. He felt it throughout his body and heart. Scowling, he tossed another stick. The deer-hounds ignored it. "Lazy beasts."

"I know how to get the teacher to leave," Hamish said. "Let the fairies do it."

"What?" Dougal looked at his uncle. Hamish was tough as an old ram, like his brothers Ranald and Fergus. But Hamish was the skeptical one when fairy legends and such were told. "You do not believe the legends of Kinloch."

"I do not. But we have enough legends and haunts to frighten any Lowland lass away. Tell her about the fairies and haunts of Kinloch, and she will run home. And we will carry on. But without a cook," he muttered.

Dougal laughed. "If she ran off in a fright, her brothers would be here the very next day to ask what we are up to in Glen Kinloch."

"Brothers?"

"One of them is Lord Struan."

"Och," Hamish muttered. "We would also have to deal with the—what did the reverend call them? The Edinburgh Society for Ladies Who Fancy Themselves Better than Highlanders?"

"The Edinburgh Ladies' Society for the Betterment of the Gaels."

"The very ones. Whae's better than us?" Hamish said, quoting Robert Burns, as Dougal laughed. "And what might scare that lass away from this glen?"

"Very little. She breaks rocks for amusement."

"*Tcha*," Hamish said, shaking his head. "We will tell her about the sprites who haunt the caves, and the tall ancient race of fairies who live in the hills, and the ghosts who bother all at Kinloch House. Except they do not, but she does not know that."

"When she first saw me on the mountain, she thought I was one of the Sidhe. I only startled her for a moment. She was not frightened enough to leave, I can tell you that."

"Then warn her of women stolen away by the fairies."

"Scaring her is not the way. And do not take your wild scheme to the uncles."

"We cannot risk gaugers learning that we have a supply of whisky more valuable than any cargo yet moved out of this glen. And we do not need the sister of a gauger wandering the hills breaking rocks and seeing what we do."

"I do not want to sell that cache of whisky, Hamish," Dougal murmured.

"You have no choice. We all agreed. Selling that whisky will help you buy back the land that might be sold out from under us." His uncle looked hard at him. "Sell that cache once. Or you could sell fairy brew more often and earn a fortune. Some of us think you should."

"My father honored the old ways. I will do the same."

"Fairies do not exist, Kinloch," Hamish said. "Your father honored old legends, and that's fine. But he made a bad bargain that we only learned of recently. Protecting the fairy brew for tradition's sake will not benefit the glen. Selling fairy brew will."

"I will not sell the fairy whisky. Enough. We will find another way to save the glen."

"What if the wee teacher knew about the risk? She has a soft heart, that one. I could tell."

"We do not know if she can be trusted. There are too many secrets here, Hamish."

"Sometimes a man must give up something he values to gain something even more valuable."

"Tell that to Jean's stubborn old husband," Dougal said.

Hamish snorted, then whistled to the deerhounds that had bounded ahead.

Thoughtful as they returned to Kinloch House, Dougal could think of nothing important enough to convince him to give up Glen Kinloch's long-held secrets.

Then Lucy came running out the door to greet him, curls bouncing, sweet little voice calling, and he knew he had something of value beyond all else.

"GOOD EVENING, GRANDMOTHER. And Miss MacCarran, how nice to see you." Reverend Hugh MacIan entered the cottage as he spoke, then removed his black-brimmed hat and bowed a little.

"My bonny lad is here!" Mary MacIan smiled, setting plates on the table. "You are just in time for supper."

"So I hoped," he said, bending to kiss his grandmother's cheek.

"Mr. MacIan, greetings," Fiona said. He grasped her hand, dark eyes shining. Dressed in the old-fashioned black frock coat and white neckcloth worn by Free Church Highland ministers, he was a handsome and robust young man with thick sandy hair and a boyish grin. She smiled, enjoying his friendly attention. Yet it was nothing like the strong, passionate pull she had felt toward Dougal MacGregor the night before. And then she told herself to stop that, forget the laird, move on with the day.

"Did you ride far over the glen today, Hugh?" Mary asked.

"I did," he answered, "and visited the good folk to let them know that the school would begin again tomorrow. I rode here from Drumcairn to share supper with you." He turned to Fiona. "Miss MacCarran, I hold the living at the manse near Kinloch House, on this side of the glen. Garloch and Drumcairn are villages situated at either end of the glen, with Kinloch House closer to the middle, near the manse and the school. My father, Rob MacIan, keeps the Knockandoo Inn by Drumcairn Bridge. He would much enjoy it if you would visit his inn for a good meal at his blessing."

"I would love that," she said. "And I would love to see the whole of the glen. It is very beautiful, no doubt with a fascinating local history and legends."

"Aye. We do have some interesting legends, and we are proud of them. I wanted to take you about today to show you our glen and introduce you, but I got caught up in my visits, which took longer than I expected."

"Hugh is beloved here," Mary MacIan said proudly. "Miss MacCarran had an adventure last night," she went on. "Out walking the hills in the mist, she met Kinloch."

"Aye so? I am sure you came to no harm out in the hills, Miss MacCarran," the reverend said. "Though the laird is quite the fellow to meet of an evening. That must have been a shock."

She wondered why he would say so. "He was—courteous. I was not in danger."

He laughed. "Of course not. We have a brave lass in our glen teacher, Grandmother," he said with a wink.

Dougal MacGregor had been constantly in her thoughts. Certainly she understood that the smuggler might be danger-ous—he had all but kidnapped her, and then kissed her to distraction before she knew anything of him.

"I was collecting rock specimens up in the hills," Fiona said. "Mr. MacGregor, er, Kinloch, took me back in a cart when we met his kinsmen driving by, for it was foggy and getting dark. When I learned he was laird in this glen, naturally I felt safe." Though she knew he was a threat to her heart, this laird with his unexpected kisses in the dark, kisses she had dearly wanted. She glanced away.

"When Kinloch MacGregors are out and about in the hills, it is best not to know too much about their business," Mrs. MacIan said.

"We will not accuse anyone," the minister said carefully, "but Miss MacCarran, it is true these hills are not safe at night. Revenue officers and smugglers are sometimes about. A bit of free-trading traffic goes through here, which is common enough in the Highlands, and nothing to be concerned about. But do not go out alone at night."

"I appreciate the warning." Fiona turned away to stir another scoop of butter into the mashed turnips she and Mrs. MacIan had prepared for supper. The MacIans knew Patrick was an excise officer at the other end of the loch. Now the MacGregors knew too. She would need to say little about that now, and be wary for Patrick's sake.

"Good, since she will stay with us for a little while," Mrs. MacIan said.

The reverend looked puzzled. "She will be teaching at the school until summer."

"Kinloch sent Hamish with that wreck of a carriage this morning to take her back to Auchnashee, where her kinsmen could send her back to Edinburgh."

"Miss MacCarran, have you changed your mind?" MacIan asked.

"The Laird of Kinloch seems to think a teacher is not needed in the glen. We told Hamish MacGregor it was a misunderstanding," Fiona replied.

The reverend frowned. "I shall speak to Kinloch."

"It is already resolved," she said, as she moved dishes to the table.

"Will you share supper with us?" Mary asked her grandson. "There are mashed turnips and mutton stew, very tender. Fiona prepared it herself, and it is quite good."

He nodded and drew out the chairs for the women. When they were seated, they bowed their heads for the grace that Hugh MacIan murmured in a gentle voice that seemed more suited to sentimental love poems than insistent Biblical sermons. Fiona served the turnips and stew, and as they ate, she glanced at her new friends. She felt content in the cozy atmosphere, content to stay.

Mary's front room combined parlor, dining room, and a narrow kitchen, and a wide hearth wall, furnished simply with cupboards, a wooden table, and a few comfortable chairs. At the back of the small house, two snug bedrooms curtained off from the larger room held a box bed in each. A side door led out to a small garden.

The walls were whitewashed and smoke stained, the old, dark rafter beams overhead were hung with dried herbs that added a light, clean fragrance, which combined with the sweet, musty smell of the peat fire made the modest house seem very cozy. The table was set with very fine things—crisp bleached linens, blue-and-white porcelain, good silver pieces. The few furnishings were of excellent quality with polished wood and velvet cushions, the lanterns were of very good metalwork, and the window curtains were Belgian lace. Aware of the history of smugglers in the area, Fiona wondered if they had brought Mary such nice things—and if her late husband had engaged in transporting goods himself.

Hugh smiled. "Miss MacCarran, I am glad to know you cleared the, ah, misunderstanding with the laird. You will surely see him at the glen school."

"Oh? Will he be in class?" That puzzled her, as she had the impression Kinloch was an educated man. "You mentioned in your letter to the Ladies Society that there might be adult students in the school."

"There could be, since some here do not have much English." He smiled. "But Dougal MacGregor is hardly one of those. The schoolhouse is on his estate, and his young kinfolk will be in your class."

"I see. He did not mention that."

"He keeps to himself and says little. May I have more turnips? They are delicious."

Fiona passed the dish to him, not surprised that Kinloch had not said much about the school. He had been too determined for her to leave and abandon her obligation to the school and its students.

Later that night, as she drifted to sleep curled up in the box bed, which was deep and snug, quaint and comfortable, she could not forget the feeling of Kinloch's arms around her, and the sweet melding of their lips beneath the old plaid in the pony cart.

She knew why she had not protested when he kissed her, though he gave her the chance. She had been kissed before by suitors. But she had never known kisses could feel so tender, so loving, so perfect, so compelling. Swept away, she had wanted more.

Best forget that, she told herself. She must think only of her responsibilities. With her lessons prepared, she was ready to begin class. What she needed now was a good night's sleep. But her thoughts raced. Punching the pillow, she settled again.

If she met the Laird of Kinloch at the glen school, she would have to be cautious. He knew too much about her. And she was far too eager to see him again.

Chapter Six

S TANDING IN THE morning sunlight in the yard of Kinloch
House, Dougal watched the glen folk walking along hills and
paths, coming from various directions toward the hill where his
house—and the school—were perched. Kinloch House was
tucked in the lee of the pine-covered slopes that formed this side
of the glen's bowl, and the school was a short walk across the
shoulder of the same hill. Watching his tenants approach, he felt
keyed and nervous, his normally calm and stoic heart thumping
fast.

His glance strayed again to the place where the hills framing
the glen parted, leading to the cove by the loch. Fiona MacCarran
would be heading to the schoolhouse that morning too. Despite
himself, he kept looking in that direction.

Even from a distance, he easily recognized the people approaching. He knew each one, each family. For generations, their
kin had rented holdings from the lairds of Kinloch—and would
always have that right if he had any say in it, no matter the
clearings that were happening in other glens and regions.

Mothers carried small ones and guided older ones along,
some of the girls and boys running ahead. Fathers came too,
leaving their work for a bit, as it was an important day for the
families. The children leaped rocks and watery runnels while their
parents called, laughing or warning. Some walked through
clusters of sheep grazing on the slopes with flanks marked with

colored dye. Goats, too, scrabbled along steeper climes, while the children were reminded not to bother them.

The wind was cool, and bright sun crested the hill as Dougal lifted a hand to his brow. In late April, the slopes were greening up. Heather would not flower until late summer, its evergreen shrubs barely green at the tips; gorse bushes showed yellow buds; bluebells and buttery primroses spread blurs of soft color over the glen slopes, beside burns, and among trees.

The wild beauty of Glen Kinloch was more dear to him than he could ever express. He would do what he must to keep it safe and untouched.

"Kinloch!"

Turning, he saw Uncle Fergus coming near. The man hunched forward, walking in that rushing way he had, arms and fists swinging. His powerful torso and legs, and his thick black hair and beard reminded Dougal of a black bull, an image enhanced by the leather apron he often wore. Dougal waved and waited, gazing past his uncle toward the house.

Long ago, the structure had been a small, sturdy castle, an old tower house built generations earlier by a MacGregor whose cattle-reiving activities had warranted the protection of stout stone walls. After the strife and grief of Culloden had torn Scotland asunder seventy years earlier, when the Kinloch MacGregors and many thousands of others lost men and fortunes, the house had fallen into ill repair.

Resources were scant for keeping the old mortared stones together, but Glen Kinloch was populated with people of strong Highland stock who could live anywhere, under any conditions. Eventually, they recovered from those devastating days, and his kinsmen had done everything they could to support the glen folk, keep the old tower house upright and dry in the rain, and keep livestock grazing in the hills. Dougal was determined that his people and his kin would always flourish under his watchful eye, no matter what he must do, what risks he must take.

The greatest threat to the Highlands these days was no longer

English troops, but the steady infiltration of Lowlanders and Englishmen buying up huge tracts of Scottish land for sheep runs, hunting lodges, and holidaying sites.

Dougal would never let that affect his glen. He would protect it always. But he would not sell the fairy brew to do it, even if it could bring in enough to save them all. He kept a sizable cache of excellent Glen Kinloch whisky to sell instead. Aged to a rare degree, what sat in storage now would fetch a good price.

At that moment, he saw Fiona MacCarran crossing the glen. His heart leaped as if he were a hopeful boy rather than a man. He instantly remembered kissing her, but shook his head to clear the thought. There was no place for a woman in his life now, especially the sister of a gauger who could ruin all his plans.

She carried a packet, he saw, clutched against her, probably books or papers. Sunlight gleamed over her dark hair as the wind pushed back her straw bonnet. Her gown of deep blue accentuated her slim curves, and she wore a plaid shawl over her shoulders that whipped about in the breeze. Oddly, he thought of how the blue gown would match her eyes. *Stop,* he admonished himself again.

Whatever impulse had made him kiss her, he had apologized for it, and so it was over. Forgotten. The night and the mist, and the girl in his arms in a close, warm space—all of it had taken him over like a fool. The romance of it had taken her, too. But it was done.

Hugh MacIan, the kirk minister, hurried behind her and caught up to walk with her. She looked trim and small beside the reverend; he had the muscular build of a Highland warrior, though dressed in a somber black suit like a city man, and devoted, most of the time, to his Bible.

Even so, Reverend MacIan was a clever smuggler and a good help in that regard. Dougal smiled, wondering what the bonny Lowland teacher would think if she knew it.

Seeing her flashing smile as she walked and talked with Hugh, Dougal frowned. He knew that bright smile and the feel of that trim waist under his hands; knew the scent of her, lavender and fog, and the sweet warmth of her lips. He should keep aloof, he thought; let her decide that a handsome, educated kirk minister was more interesting than a Highland laird who had left university to distill and smuggle whisky.

No matter. Soon she would be gone. Just then, Hugh took her elbow as they walked, and Dougal felt a frisson of jealousy slip through him.

"Kinloch!" Fergus called as he came close. "The lass is ready."

"Lass?" Distracted, Dougal thought he meant the teacher.

"Lucy! She's ready and none too glad about it."

Glancing toward the house, Dougal saw a boy and a girl standing on the step. His heart tugged to see the small girl, his dark-haired niece Lucy. She was in a stormy humor, he saw, her hands fisted at her sides, her little brow glowering.

"She does not want to go to school. Jamie does," Fergus said of his grandson, the son of his daughter and her shepherd husband. The boy was tall for his age with blazing red hair, albeit contrasted by a sweet, peaceful nature. Young Jamie patted Lucy's shoulder. She shrugged it off.

"Lucy says smugglers do not go to school," Fergus said.

Dougal sighed. "I may have been wrong to raise my sister's daughter among kin who dabble in free trade. Kinloch is not the best place for a wee lass to grow up."

"It is! She is happy and cherished, though we be thieves and rogues. But good men for all that," Fergus said. "She is indulged, to be sure, and we could be more stern with her. But she is blessed with charm, and the wee lass knows it. You and Ellen were reared at Kinloch among whisky makers and traders, and you both did well enough," he pointed out. "Though Jeanie was a help, and Lucy needs to be raised by a woman. Good, until she left us," he muttered. "It is not so easy to raise a girl-child."

"Jeanie has left Hamish before," Dougal said. "She will be back, with luck." He saw Lucy push Jamie off the step. The boy climbed up again, smiling. Lucy glowered at him.

"That wee lad has a saint's patience," Fergus said. "She's a fiery sprite, a beauty like her mother, but a determined thing. When she is grown, there will be lads at your door and hell to pay."

Jamie tried to take Lucy's hand, but she picked up her slate and book and walked away. "We will be lucky if anyone knocks at the door to court her," Dougal drawled.

"School is about to start. Lucy! Jamie! Go on!" Fergus called.

The schoolyard was filling with a small crowd, Dougal noticed. The school, situated not far from the tower house, was a rectangular whitewashed building surrounded by an earthen yard, occupying a flat section of the hill where sheep and goats chewed the grass down neatly and regularly. Students and families were already gathering in the yard. Others without children had arrived too, curious to meet the new dominie.

"I hope she proves a fine teacher for the bairns," Fergus said. "She is not like the old dominie they sent from Edinburgh last year. She looks a bonny wee thing."

"She's a dangerous wee thing," Dougal remarked. "Remember the brother."

"True." Fergus nodded. "I saw Rob MacIan last evening at the tavern. He said Lord Eldin is interested in purchasing the best Highland whisky for his new hotel. He is willing to pay well, and he does not care if it is illicit stuff."

"Excellent. I hope Rob told him Glen Kinloch whisky is the best in the Highlands."

"In the whole of Scotland! But every distiller says that, aye?"

Dougal laughed. "Sometimes it is true. Glenbrae whisky, which my cousins in Perthshire make, is as good as ours too, I would say."

"But the fairy whisky is exceptional."

"Extraordinary. But we will not tell anyone that. Tell Rob MacIan he can go to Auchnashee and let the earl know we have kegs available." He named a sum.

"Eldin would pay more, I suspect. He would pay a very high

price for the fairy brew. He asked if it existed. He's heard about the tradition."

"You know my answer to that. We do not offer the fairy brew and we do not talk of the legend, though it is known about here. We can get a good price for Glen Kinloch brew. We have to deliver kegs and casks to the buyers we already have, but there will be some left for Lord Eldin. We may be able to move all of our store. A good thing."

"And then we brew more. Very good."

Lucy and Jamie walked across the yard now, and she reached out for the boy's hand. But when she saw Dougal, her little face became determined.

Understanding her reluctance, he pointed, firmly and silently, toward the school. She frowned but relented, walking with Jamie.

Fergus chuckled. "Lucy thinks smugglers need not learn letters and math, but devote their time to distilling whisky and moving kegs through the hills. Reminds me of a lad I knew once," he added.

"That lad was just thirteen when his Da died. Lucy is only seven. Her time should be devoted to playing with her friends, doing chores, and studying. I told her that even free traders need an education."

"She would make a fine smuggler, that lass. No harm in it when she's older."

"No," Dougal said firmly. "She will get an education and marry well, and stay safe. I promised my sister, and I will see to it. She will have naught to do with the free trade."

"You sound like your father."

"I never fulfilled what my father wanted me to do, and I regret it. I will see to it for my sister's child."

"But you had a fine education here at the glen school, and a couple of years at university before you left to come home. We could not convince you to go back. We did try."

"We could not afford it."

"We would have found a way."

Dougal huffed. "Funded by smuggling?"

His uncle shrugged. "Someday I hope you will return to your studies. Such an intelligent lad. That was your father's wish for you, not distilling and running the brew over the hills."

"I am needed here. Fergus, I am thinking—the school session could wait a bit while we find another dominie, one who is not kin to a customs officer." As he spoke, Dougal watched the teacher approach the school with the reverend.

"And one who will not distract the laird?" Fergus asked.

"Huh." Dougal saw Reverend MacIan sweep a wide gesture as he spoke to Fiona MacCarran, showing her the hills surrounding the glen. She turned and her gaze caught Dougal's. Even at a distance, he felt the tug between them.

"Hamish says we should scare her off with tales of bogles," Fergus said.

"We will not," Dougal said sternly.

"The last Edinburgh society teacher who came here thought we were all Highland savages. That one left quick enough. This one looks tougher. We may not frighten her off so easily."

"True."

"Though if she should meet a few rascals out in the hills, she might think better of staying," Fergus said. "I can send Arthur and Mungo to visit her."

"I would not trust those two near her."

"Then we will all have to behave like a flock of angels, so she has no tales to carry to her brother."

"We could try that," Dougal mused. "I had best go welcome her, being the laird."

"Aye. Och, I near forgot. The school roof needs work."

"Again? We repaired it last fall when it leaked after the rains." Fergus shrugged. "The place is old."

"We need new thatch and new beams," Dougal said.

"We need a new building," Fergus grumbled.

Dougal watched her cross the hill toward Kinloch House and the school. "We need much in this glen," he murmured.

"She is a bonny lass, I will say," Fergus mused as she came closer. "Perhaps we can let her enjoy our pretty glen for a bit, and then we will send her away."

"Just do not scare her," Dougal muttered.

"I AM SURE you will enjoy being in Glen Kinloch," Reverend MacIan was saying as he walked beside Fiona. "We are so delighted that you came up from Edinburgh."

"Thank you again," she said. "Though I suspect not everyone is glad I am here." She glanced across the hill, seeing the glen's laird standing on the ridge, arms folded, watching the stream of people heading for the school.

"Kinloch? He has pressing matters on his mind, I imagine."

"So I gather. Mr. MacIan, let me thank you and your grandmother again for such a nice welcome." She lifted her face to sunshine and the cool breeze. "It is a lovely morning, and I am looking forward to working with the students. So the school is near the castle. I did not realize. Is that Kinloch House?"

"Aye. It is an old tower house. A small castle. The schoolhouse is just there." He pointed toward a whitewashed building with a thatched roof a little distance past the stone tower. Both were nestled in the lee of a broad hillside, where the slope flattened out, protected at the back by a high sweep of forested hillside. Beyond the sandstone tower, the schoolyard was filling with people.

Now the laird of Kinloch was striding toward the yard. Earlier, she had seen him standing apart with an older man. Even from a distance, she had sensed MacGregor's gaze so keenly that she had stopped, transfixed, distracted. Seeing him now, she clutched the packet of papers and books close, as if to remind herself why she was here and what she should be doing, rather than let this man's mere presence make her heart tumble so.

"There's Kinloch, and one of his uncles," MacIan said.

"Another one?"

"They all live in the tower house, have done since the laird was a boy and inherited the estate after his father's passing. Your class is gathering. Come and meet your students. In Glen Kinloch, the school session begins when a teacher comes to the glen, and ends the day the teacher leaves." He smiled.

That would be tomorrow if Kinloch had his way, Fiona thought. "I understand most Highland schools are only in session six months out of the year."

"The students must take time off seasonally to help their families with planting and harvesting, and to help take the cattle into the hills in summer to graze. We cannot afford the yearly fee to retain a dominie permanently, so we must rely on the Highland societies to send teachers for a few months at a time."

"The last teacher sent by the charity stayed only two weeks, I heard."

"She changed her mind. The glen was too remote for her taste."

"Too much smuggling?" She glanced at him.

He shrugged. "Who knows? I heard she had a terror of ghosts and fairies."

"I am intrigued by such things and would not run from them."

"Then this is the place for you. We are happy to have a teacher again. For a long while, the laird's sister was our dominie."

She blinked in surprise. "His sister?"

"She died of a fever a few years ago. A dreadful time. The laird is the guardian for his niece, and has more interest in the school now that she is of learning age."

"His niece will be in my class?"

"Aye. Kinloch, good morning!" he called.

Fiona turned to see Dougal MacGregor coming toward them, his stride setting his kilt to swinging, and his dark hair wafting in the breeze. He scowled as he neared them and turned the glower on her. She smiled.

"Miss MacCarran. Reverend," he said. "I see you are ready to begin this morning."

"Despite attempts to the contrary." She brightened her smile. His frown deepened.

"Lucky to you, then. You have several scholars for your classroom."

"So I see." She turned to walk between the two men. "It is a pretty day. I had a nice walk across the glen with Mr. MacIan, who was kind enough to escort me."

"I could have sent the carriage for you," MacGregor said.

"No need. I enjoy walking. Your glen is so lovely and peaceful. No wonder the Highlands are growing so popular. There is such beauty here in the north."

"Aye." His sudden, crooked, charming smile was unexpected. "Glen Kinloch is a small and remote place, but it is like the romantic Highland glens that tourists go on about. It has a wild setting, majestic views, and good, hardworking souls living in it."

She wondered if he was teasing her for admiring the place like a tourist or warning her to remember that the outer world should leave the place in peace. Either way, he genuinely loved his glen. "It does have a wonderful quaint aspect," she agreed. "Coming here is like traveling back to an earlier time in Scotland."

"Back to the days of cattle thieves and rogues?" MacGregor drawled.

"I was thinking of something more idyllic."

"Ah, an idealist," he said softly. His eyes, in sunlight, were mossy green.

"At times. Are you, Mr. MacGregor?"

"Not any longer," he answered.

"By idyllic, I believe the lady means the Highlands as described in Sir Walter Scott's grand poetry,'" Hugh said.

"I do mean that. Do you know his work, either of you?" She smiled at both.

"I have read his work," MacIan said. "Some of his descriptions remind me of our glen." He drew a breath and began to recite in a sonorous voice.

The wanderer's eye could barely vie
The summer heaven's delicious blue;
So wondrous wild, the whole might seem
The scenery of a fairy dream.

"Perfect!" Fiona applauded. "I am just fascinated by fairy lore." She stopped, always wary of revealing how keen her interest was, and why.

"Kinloch knows much about local legends," MacIan said. "Quite the expert."

"No more than anyone else knows," MacGregor said curtly.

"I am interested to learn more," she said.

"He is the one to tell you," the reverend said. "I am inspired to read Sir Walter's magnificent epic, 'Lady of the Lake,' again, since it is about Loch Katrine, so near to us. We could discuss it, you and I." He swept an arm wide. "'On this bold brow, a lordly tower; in that soft vale, a lady's bower—'"

"Do not recite another blasted poem. The students are waiting," Kinloch said irritably.

Fiona glanced at him. "Do you dislike Sir Walter's poetry, sir?"

"I have read some of it. It did not enthrall me. I lacked patience for the length. Some verses did remind me of Glen Kinloch though." He tilted his head. "'But hosts may in these wilds abound, such as are better missed than found; to meet with Highland plunderers here—were worse than loss of steed or deer,'" he concluded, "or something to that effect."

MacIan smiled flatly. "We have no time for poetry, you said. Scholars are waiting."

"That was very nice, sir." Fiona loved the deep timbre of his voice, though he had mocked her, in the moment with his clear implication about smugglers in the hills.

As they reached the flat of the hill where the schoolhouse perched, Kinloch set a hand to her elbow to guide her up. His touch felt like gentle lightning. Even his polite, casual touch affected her. She had to avoid this man. Flustered, she held her chin high.

Near the school, the tower house loomed. She glanced up at its turrets and thick walls, and saw a shabbiness she had not noticed at a distance. Stone blocks crumbled in places, corners were coated in rusty ivy, stone trim was cracked, a window was broken, and the roof needed repair. She said nothing, turning her attention to the school.

"The schoolhouse was once a weaver's cottage," Hugh MacIan said. "So it is not large."

"It is old," Kinloch said. "We have kept it up best we can."

"It will do nicely," Fiona said. In the morning light, the whitewashed building and greening hills were picturesque, but now she saw that the schoolhouse, too, needed repair, with peeling plaster, old thatch, a sagging door, a chipped stone step. A goat and three sheep wandered through the yard. The folks gathered by the door moved aside when a large ram appeared and settled heavily near the entrance.

"It will do," she repeated rather too brightly.

"The roof leaks," MacGregor said.

"We will fetch buckets if it rains," she said.

"The walls are crumbling. Do not lean against the back wall during a heavy rainstorm."

"I never lean, nor would I allow my students to do so."

"There may be mice underfoot."

"I will get a cat," she said.

"I will find one for you," he answered. "You are determined, I see."

"I am." She smiled. He returned a heartwarming grin suddenly, and her heart gave a little fillip. Quickly she looked away. "The students are waiting."

"And some of their parents. Ah, there is Mrs. Beaton," the reverend said. "I must speak to her about her daughter's wedding service. Please excuse me." He smiled at Fiona. "Since the laird owns the school, he should introduce you."

"Thank you, Reverend." She smiled as he left. "Now that I know the way here, tomorrow I will arrive earlier. I did not know they would all be here before me."

"You would have to rise very early to be here first," Kinloch said, "since most of your students will be up before dawn to do the milking and chores before they head to school. Come meet them."

He touched her elbow, and again she felt that keen inner tug. She sensed the strength and calm in the man, though he was a smuggler and a scoundrel. She felt determined, as he had said— determined to let nothing, including this laird, distract her from her work.

Chapter Seven

DOUGAL NODDED, SATISFIED and oddly proud as he watched Fiona MacCarran greet each person in the schoolyard. She repeated their names as he introduced her and spoke to them in deft, good Gaelic, winning over even those suspicious of outsiders and Lowlanders. Everyone seemed more at ease after speaking with her.

"This is Pol MacDonald," Dougal continued as they made their way through the group, "and my young cousin Jamie MacGregor. And here is another MacGregor—Andrew, Ranald's son." He indicated the lads, tall and small, standing together. Knowing Miss MacCarran would recognize Andrew from their first encounter, he prayed she would not let on.

She smiled as if she had never seen Andrew before, while the boy blushed furiously. Jamie, just seven, his thatch of red-gold hair bright as a setting sun, straightened his narrow shoulders and shook his teacher's hand. And Pol MacDonald, with a trace of new blond whiskers along his jaw, was so nervous that his voice cracked as he spoke to the new teacher.

Dougal was pleased to see how Miss MacCarran took time for each person, pausing to chat with Pol's father, a farmer with a rough manner and a kind nature; and Ranald's sturdy wife, Effie; then Fergus's daughter Muriel, her hair as fiery as her son Jamie's. Shy Helen MacDonald, Pol's cousin, welcomed the new dominie quietly, pushing her twelve-year-old daughter, Annabel, forward, who was as timid as her mother, both of them delicate, blond, and fairy-like in appearance.

Then Pol's sister Mairi MacDonald and her friend Lilias Beaton came forward smiling. Both girls were among the older students in the class, and Dougal knew that Lilias was engaged to a young man in the next glen. Hugh MacIan had been discussing the upcoming wedding with the girl and her mother.

As they made their rounds through the small crowd clustered in front of the schoolhouse, Miss MacCarran glanced up at Dougal. "So boys and girls are together in this school? Genders are often separated in other glen schools, with classes on alternating days or scheduled for mornings and afternoons."

"We have so few students just now that Reverend MacIan thought it best to combine them in one class. It is not easy for them to find time for lessons, as they have chores at home. Many are kin, and used to being together." Seeing Lucy standing nearby with Jamie, Dougal beckoned her to come forward.

"And who is this?" Miss MacCarran smiled down at her.

"My niece, Lucy MacGregor. Lucy, this is your new teacher."

Lucy looked up at Miss MacCarran very sweetly, brown eyes sparkling, dark hair gleaming after a good brushing. He was pleased, and a bit relieved, to see that she had decided to comply nicely.

"Good morning, Miss MacCarran. Welcome to Glen Kinloch," Lucy said in English.

"Thank you, Lucy. Your English is very good."

"Aye, it is. So I do not need to go to school. I can speak Gaelic and English, and I can read a little. Uncle Dougal taught me."

"She is a quick study," Dougal explained, as Fiona MacCarran looked at him in surprise. "Away with you, lass—go inside with the others. A little reading is a fine thing, but you need schooling." Lucy scowled at him and then ran toward the schoolhouse.

"I expected more students this morning," Miss MacCarran said, looking about.

"Some families will wait to see what the others say. They

must be sure the lessons are worth the time the children are away from their chores. They might also wonder if you will stay. Previous dominies have not remained here for long."

"I will stay. I gave my word."

He nodded, silent, impressed by her steadiness. She was stubborn, this Lowland lass, but he was too. And he was still convinced that sending her away was in everyone's best interest, even if it proved difficult to accomplish.

"All Highlanders should learn to read and write in English and in Gaelic," she was saying. "I am glad that you have been tutoring your niece, and it is good to know you encourage your tenants to obtain an education."

"For all my sins, I do," he answered quietly.

She looked at him as if puzzled and intrigued, and once again Dougal felt an undeniable pull toward her. Despite common sense—the need to send her away—he was beginning to feel protective of the new teacher. He wanted to know more about her—wanted her to thrive here. Wanted her to stay.

He stepped forward to hold the door open as she entered the schoolroom, and her shoulder brushed his chest. The clean, womanly scent of her was enticing.

"I confess, sir, I am nervous," she whispered. "Would you come in for a bit?"

Nodding, he followed her inside.

FIONA SET HER packet of papers on the sturdy battered table that served as the teacher's desk, complete with a stiff, high stool. Standing at the front of the room, she folded her hands and tried to appear calm. While the students settled on long benches, she waited. She had taught in a few schools before this, but already she could see that this group—mixed ages, mixed genders, and a mix of interest in learning—might prove challenging. But suddenly she felt more distracted by the tall Highlander standing by the door than nervous about the class.

Kinloch leaned a broad shoulder against the doorjamb. Sunlight from the window spilled over his powerful torso and long limbs, haloing his dark hair, and brightening the tones of moss, earth, and cranberry in his tartan plaid. He was like sunlight and rock, warm, earthy, and handsome. She drew a breath, and a sense of calm from his solidity as well. He might be a dangerous sort, but there was something reliable and secure about this quiet laird.

She smiled at the class. The students, from small Lucy and Jamie to lanky Andrew and Pol to the older girls, sat on the plain benches looking awkward, expectant, a bit nervous as well.

"Good morning," she said in Gaelic. They murmured the same. Soon enough she planned to speak most often in English, requiring them to use that language so they could learn it naturally. "And good morning to MacGregor of Kinloch as well."

Again the children, big to small, murmured in unison. Lucy squirmed in her seat and waved to her uncle. He came to the front of the room.

"Good morning. Miss MacCarran is your teacher now," he said in Gaelic, "and will be in charge here. Remember the rules of the schoolroom. We do not want Miss MacCarran to think we are all savages, eh?" Some of the children giggled.

"Obey your teacher," he explained, and Fiona recognized the rules so often recited in Highland schools. "Do not run inside, or in the yard. And what else?"

"Neither shout nor stare at others," Jamie said, raising a hand, "nor quarrel while you are here."

"And?" Kinloch asked.

"Bow or curtsey when we enter and go quietly to our seats," Lilias said.

"Aye, thank you. Miss MacCarran may have rules of her own." He inclined his head toward her.

"Thank you, Mr. MacGregor." Fiona folded her hands. "Here

is what I expect from each of you. Treat others with respect. Wait your turn to speak, and raise your hand if you have something to say. And pay attention to your schoolwork and apply yourself to your books."

A hand rose at the back of the room. "Miss, we have no books," Andrew said.

Fiona raised her brows. "None?" Most schools had a few copies of certain texts.

"None in English, Miss, and only a couple in Gaelic," Andrew answered.

"I have a book," Lucy said. "So I brought it. But it may not be what you want." She waved it. "It has some poems in it."

"Thank you, Lucy. There are only seven students. I wonder, Mr. MacGregor." She turned toward him and spoke softly. "Translated texts for teaching English to Gaels are scarce. But I was told we would have some books."

"Few books have been translated into Gaelic, I am sure you know," he said, as she nodded. "I purchased several from a Glasgow bookseller, but the other teacher took them when she left. Your arrival was something of a surprise, but I will purchase more books for the schoolroom—if you are staying."

"You know I am," she told him under her breath. "The Bible and some religious texts have been translated—do you have those in your home? We could use them, if so."

"This is a school, not a kirk."

"I agree. But they are useful if they are all we have. Scholars need texts to read and to improve their English skills. Perhaps Reverend MacIan has some books in both languages that I can borrow for the class."

"I have a small library at Kinloch House. Lucy found her book there," he said. For an instant, Fiona wondered if he were jealous of her mention of the reverend, but she dismissed that. "You may borrow whatever texts you like." He tilted his head. "I recently acquired a copy of a book by the American Thomas Paine, which has been translated into Gaelic. I would be happy to lend it to you."

"I would find it quite interesting, though it is above the level of these students. Without proper texts to suit, they may as well stay home."

MacGregor smiled slowly. "Very true."

She leaned close, speaking in nearly a whisper. "That is not a reason to close the school and send the dominie away."

He raised his brows, looking amused and innocent. "Miss MacCarran, I am wounded," he murmured. "I am here to help, not plot your demise. The offer to borrow my books stands. Farewell for now, and I wish you luck of the day." He lifted a hand to the students, and left.

Fiona turned back to the class, aware that her heart was beating very fast. "Can anyone tell me what supplies we have here?" she asked.

Mairi MacDonald raised her hand. "We have slates and chalk in the cupboard."

"Thank you, Mairi. Please fetch them and pass them around. Andrew, will you help her?" The two students went to an old cupboard beneath a window, removed a stack of slates and a box of cut chalk sticks, and began handing them about.

"We also have quills and ink, but not very much paper," Lucy said. Fiona nodded, turning toward her. The girl's heart-shaped face, curling brown hair, and wide dark eyes would make her a beauty one day, Fiona thought.

"Thank you, Lucy. Now who speaks some English, and who can read a little in English or in Gaelic?"

Two or three hands went up. Fiona soon learned that while some could barely read, most could write their names and a few words. Lucy, the youngest, had the best grasp of both languages. "And I can write in English, too," the little girl said.

"Miss MacCarran," Andrew said, "if we can all sign our names, and the pastor reads the Bible to us at Sunday kirk sessions, why do we have to learn more?"

"Because you cannot always be a smuggler, Andrew Mac-

Gregor," Lucy said.

"Lucy," Fiona said sternly. "Please do not speak out of turn. Raise your hand before speaking in class, and be considerate of others in what you say."

"But Andrew is my cousin!"

"Here at school he is your fellow scholar," Fiona pointed out.

Lucy scowled. "When my mother was the dominie, we did not have to ask permission. Well, I did not," she added.

"I am the dominie now," Fiona said gently, aware the girl had lost her mother.

Lilias raised her hand. "My uncle says Highlanders need scholarly skills to do well in the future. The lads cannot be free traders for long, for soon the laws will not permit—*ow!*" This as Pol MacDonald elbowed her into silence.

"Class," Fiona warned. She then asked the students to write their names on their slates. While she listened to the scrape of chalk on slate, she went to the window beside the door and peered through the glass. The pane was old, thick and hazy, but she could see the yard and beyond.

Near the stone tower of Kinloch House, the laird stood talking with Ranald and Hamish MacGregor. They were soon joined by Fergus as well. For a moment, she saw Dougal MacGregor glance toward the school, while Fergus gestured insistently. As if in answer, Kinloch folded his arms and shook his head.

"MacGregor of Kinloch," she whispered to herself, "do not think to move me out of here. I mean to stay."

"HAVE YOU HAD news from the Glasgow solicitor?" Ranald asked Dougal. Various tasks usually occupied his uncles in the mornings, so as they gathered around him now, Dougal knew they had something on their minds.

"Glasgow? No more than we have heard already," he answered. "If we cannot produce the funds to buy back ten thousand acres of the old Drumcairn estate, the plot of land my father sold off, then the government can sell the deed. My father made that arrangement to save the glen. Now the payment has come due."

"We must sell all the kegs we have and get the best price," Hamish said.

"All of them, aye," Ranald said.

"Not all," Dougal said.

"The fairies will understand," Ranald said.

Dougal laughed bitterly. "Not according to the legend."

"You cannot bother with legends at a time like this," Hamish barked.

"I respect the traditions of the glen, as its laird. And I respect the Fey."

"Too much like his father," Hamish grumbled, shaking his head.

Dougal looked toward the hills where John MacGregor had once taken him to reveal the secret of the fairies of Kinloch. "We can sell our store of Glen Kinloch brew, and keep the fairy brew for special gifts, as we have always done. The price we ask will be paid. The quality of our whisky speaks for itself."

"Glen Kinloch malt whisky is without equal in the Highlands," Fergus said, "but your fairy brew is legendary. Some will pay far more for that than even the best Highland whisky. They will want to try a legendary brew. And the glen needs the money."

"Whisky is whisky," Hamish pointed out pragmatically. "Sell it. A fairy legend means little when we know we must save this glen. The government would sell this land out from under us, and they have the right—most of the land in Scotland belongs to king and crown, and we only rent in those deeds. In perpetuity, if we are fortunate," Hamish added. "But in this case, the government has full right to cancel that and sell the land. Forget the fairy ilk, lad!"

"The fairies do not concern me as much as the customs officers, if we are caught moving that much whisky to make a quick and large profit," Dougal said. It was a wrenching decision to sell the whole of their stash of excellent whisky—it could be years before they had enough to sell for profit again. "If we are seen transporting more casks than usual, they will triple the number of gaugers in the area. We could lose our cache. I will not risk our best whisky. And I will not move the fairy whisky—the risk is too great."

"True, it is worth a handsome sum. We must protect it for now," Hamish said, deliberately misunderstanding what Dougal meant. "And if the teacher would leave the glen, we would be safer."

"I cannot simply order the lass out of here."

"You can," Hamish said. "I like the lass well too, but you can."

"Surely there is some way," Fergus said.

"Frighten her off, as I have said," Ranald suggested. "She will run like the last teacher did. A bit of a mouse, that one was. Easy to—" He stopped. The other two uncles glanced around, looking innocent.

Dougal narrowed his eyes. "What did you do to make that one leave quickly?"

"Why would we do such a thing?" Ranald asked mildly.

"Me, I never even spoke to her," Fergus said.

"Tell me what you did," Dougal growled. He had always suspected, seeing how fast the other teacher had packed and left, that one or more of his uncles had influenced her decision.

Hamish made a face. "The lady knew there were thieves in these hills, and she did not like Highlanders to start. Then Ranald warned her about the wicked fairies who would steal her away as she slept. Just that."

"Just that?" Dougal looked from one to the next.

"I might have walked around her cottage a bit at night. I might have whistled some," Fergus said.

"You deliberately frightened the wee woman." Resisting the urge to laugh, Dougal made sure to scowl.

"Bah, she was a timid thing," Hamish said. "We did not like her much."

Dougal twisted his mouth awry. "Do not think to do that with Miss MacCarran. She is not timid, this one."

"Seems a bold lass with a curious mind and quick wit," Fergus said. "That gauger's sister will notice too much of what happens in the glen."

"We have a fortnight at least before we must move that whisky," Hamish said. "And a fortnight before the spring ball game in the glen. Which side will you join as a player, Dougal? Drumcairn or Garloch?"

"The laird of Kinloch keeps neutral for the ball game and takes no side in the long rivalry between the glen villages. I should not play," Dougal said.

"You, lad, are one the best at the ba'!" Ranald protested.

"Declare a side and just play," Fergus said. "With you there, everyone will come to watch. So that would be the time to move the whisky."

"That day?" Dougal asked. "I am not sure I like that."

"Fergus is right. It is a good plan," Hamish agreed.

"True, all will be distracted by the ba' game," Ranald said.

"Huh. It could work," Dougal admitted. "I suppose we could move some casks down to the loch."

"Otherwise, it would take us several trips over several nights," Fergus pointed out.

"You should send the teacher away before the game," Hamish said. "If she discovers this, she could alert her brother, who would bring gaugers into the glen."

"Though if she will not go, you could make her one of us instead," Ranald said.

Dougal laughed. "I doubt she would join us at midnight with a pistol and a pony."

"Ranald means that a woman of the glen will not speak of

what goes on in these hills," Fergus said. "Not even if her brother was a gauger."

"But she is not a woman of the glen—oh, no!" Dougal raised a hand, seeing his uncles' eyes brighten. "You want me to seduce the woman? I will not."

"Seduce? Just marry the lass," Fergus said. "That would do it."

Ranald smiled. "It is a good idea, lad."

"Marriage would be good for the lad, hey," Hamish told his brothers.

"Would help him recover from his lovesickness." Ranald grinned.

"You auld rascals," Dougal growled.

"The dominie came to our glen at the wrong time," Ranald said. "She is stubborn and will not leave easily. We can see that. Nor will you scare her off. But if she were bound to the glen and its laird, she would not talk."

"A wife would be good for you," Fergus said. "Hamish could use one too."

"I have one. We do not suit," Hamish growled.

"Lucy is growing fast, Kinloch," Fergus said. "She needs a mother."

"She has female relatives. And I do not need a wife just now. We must manage this lady for two weeks, not a lifetime. We only need to move that cargo through the glen soon without being seen."

Hamish clapped Dougal on the shoulder. "Gain her loyalty and swear her to secrecy. Do it however you can." The others chuckled.

Dougal folded his arms, shook his head. "You are mad, all of you."

"She will fall for your great charm," Ranald said. "Like she did the other night."

Dougal gave him a sour look, and his uncles chortled. Truly, he did not know how the lady regarded him. He only knew that he thought about her far too often. And he did not need his uncles pushing for more.

"They do say no lass can resist the bonny Laird of Kinloch. When that lad decides to take a wife, every lass in the glen will be knocking at his door," Ranald said. "More than one has pined for you, fortunate lad that you are."

"I doubt that. Besides, I am not looking for a wife."

Hamish frowned. "You should be. You need to marry."

"It would be foolish for me to marry now, with all the secrets in this glen." Dougal shook his head. "As for the lassies, they can easily find husbands and happiness without me. I am content to do as I please."

"What if we wait, then?" Fergus asked. "What if the Lowland teacher soon goes south? Then we need not worry about what she might see."

"You cannot frighten her off. I will not tolerate it," Dougal said.

"Well, we cannot wait until summer," Hamish said. "We need to move the cargo soon. We need to make a profit on it, and we can find buyers. Your land must be bought back, Kinloch, or else we will all have to leave this glen."

"The schoolhouse and tower house, bridges too, all need repairs. That could discourage any Lowland lass," Fergus said. Dougal shook his head, but was ignored.

"What if the teacher thinks the schoolhouse is haunted by the ghost of a scholar who failed? She might pack for home then," Ranald said. "Or what if the roof leaks on her head?"

Dougal frowned. "Interesting. The roof leaks, the walls are crumbling."

"Aye. If we must close the schoolhouse, that solves the problem," Fergus said.

"Perhaps," Dougal replied warily.

Hamish shrugged. "And we can find another teacher later."

Dougal nodded reluctantly, glancing toward the school, feeling guilt and regret. Behind those windows and that old door with its peeling paint, the teacher was helping the children of the glen. That included his niece.

He was a beast indeed, as Fiona MacCarran had called him once, to stand here scheming her departure. Yet he must consider his glen and kin over all, though he did not like the choice before him.

"But the children need a glen school and we have a teacher who wants to help," he said. He needed the teacher too—the thought came impulsively, as if his heart knew something he did not.

Despite the risks, he wanted her to stay. But a lifetime, as his uncles suggested, was out of the question. But he might be a better, stronger, finer man if she did stay. He shook his head against the thought.

"You have secrets to protect, lad, we know that," Ranald said. "There is a cache of whisky to be safely moved and sold. And there is fairy brew to be made soon. The time is coming when you must go up the mountain to start a new batch. It is your duty as laird."

"Aye, the fairy agreement," Dougal said quietly. Ranald and Fergus nodded. Hamish rolled his eyes.

Sighing, Dougal gazed at the broad flank of the mountain that loomed over the glen. "We cannot invite more interest to our glen just now. A Lowland teacher with a gauger brother and other kinsmen—a viscount, an earl setting up a tourist hotel. It is a predicament."

"Tourists. *Tcha!*" Hamish grimaced.

"They may come to our beautiful glen, looking for unspoiled, wild Scotland," Dougal said. "Loch Katrine is nearby, and has brought much attention to the Highlands, thanks to the Bard of the North and his poems."

"Bah, I will not read such stuff as that," Ranald said.

"I have. I did not like it much," Hamish said.

"I read a bit," Fergus said. "A lot of running about and rescues and fights. A fine story. But our glen will not remain protected and secret for long if tourists come here."

"I still say Kinloch could do worse than marry the teacher and keep her here. Get her promise to honor our secrets," Ranald said. "The glen needs a teacher, the laird needs a wife, and the lass is bonny. A wife as smart as that one will keep him interested and happy, hey."

"It is not that simple," Hamish grunted. "An educated Lowland lady will not want a poor Highland laird with a small estate and a taste for free trading."

"She could not find a finer lad or a finer home in Highlands or Lowlands," Fergus replied.

Listening, Dougal glanced at the schoolhouse door again and heard laughter coming from inside. The children were enjoying their day. He felt a surge of regret, and at the same time, resolve. This had to happen.

Decided, he turned to his uncles. "Tell her about the roof. Tell her the school must be closed until repairs are made. But first, we will give her a few days to enjoy our glen."

LEANING BACK AGAINST a sun-warmed boulder on the hill, Fiona studied her pencil rubbing to make sure she had captured the delicate imprint of an ancient arthropod, left in limestone eons ago. She slid the page into an envelope in her knapsack, then laid a fresh sheet of paper over another rock surface and rubbed it with graphite to capture an impression of another minuscule fossil.

Putting the things away, she walked across the brow of the hill, gazing out over glen and loch. The afternoon was cool and misty, and she had excused her students a little early, knowing that many had chores at home or in the fields. They had done good work that day, and she was willing to be flexible with lessons, as it would keep them content to return to school.

The extra time gave her a chance to do some hillwalking in daylight to search for fossil remains. She had promised her brother James to look for specific rock varieties, take notes, and sketch what she saw to help his research on the geological nature of the antediluvian earth in the Scottish Highlands. Her knowledge of fossils dovetailed nicely with his research, and she often supported his work by sketching finds for him.

Identifying rocks and fossils was enjoyable and no trouble, but finding any trace of fairies, as required by her grandmother's will, would be impossible. Still, armed with a notepad and Conte pencils, she hoped to find something that would meet the approval of the solicitor, Mr. Browne, and especially the scrutiny of Sir Walter Scott, her grandmother's old friend. The late Lady Struan's will had to be satisfied unless her brother could succeed in contesting it. That was doubtful too.

Heading across the breast of the hill, she kept the loch to her left as she went, allowing her to easily find her way back to Mary MacIan's house. Seeing an outcropping of greywacke, she climbed toward it and knelt to study it.

She examined it closely, particularly interested in finding clusters of fossils and varieties of rock and minerals that could mingle in greywacke. Boulders were easy enough to explore, thrusting out of grassy turf and heather.

One small rock, small enough to fit in her hand, preserved a tiny impression of a trilobite. An ancient sea had left its traces even as high as these hills, she thought, reaching for her notebook to record the thought and make a sketch.

"That is a devil of an insect you have there," said a voice behind her. Fiona jerked in surprise, turning to see Dougal MacGregor standing nearby. "Pardon, Miss MacCarran. I did not mean to startle you."

"Good afternoon, Kinloch. I nearly threw a rock at you, I was that surprised," she said with a half laugh.

"And I am glad you did not." He dropped to a knee beside her and glanced at the pages poking out of her knapsack. "Very nice drawings. Yours?"

"Yes. Some are drawings, and some are rubbings made over the stone. Those are arthropods," she explained, as he looked at some of the pages. "The one in your hand is a trilobite—the devil of an insect that you mentioned. They were not exactly insects, but rather like very tiny crabs, little creatures floating about in the ancient seas. When they died, their bodies left impressions in mud, which over time became rock, preserving them forever."

He nodded. "I have seen such things before, out in the hills. But I did not know what they were." He glanced up, his eyes a piercing green. "Ancient sea? Here?"

"Some geologists believe that much of the Earth was covered with water eons ago, including Scotland, since we can find fossils of marine creatures, fish, and shells to prove the theory. My brother is studying the geological part of the puzzle."

"Lord Struan is a scholar, then, not just of the peerage. A professor, you said?"

"Natural sciences, aye. When I find good examples like these, I make sketches and rubbings to help his research."

"You also haul away rocks to give him," he drawled, hefting her knapsack.

She laughed. "I hope the Laird of Kinloch does not mind if I take a few rocks."

"He does not care in the least. Steal as many as you like." His eyes sparkled with humor. "Fish on a Scottish mountain, how curious."

"This one is an ancient shrimp," she said, showing him another drawing. "There, at the bottom, is a row of tiny arthropods left in limestone."

He studied them carefully. "We call these fairy tracks."

Fiona tilted her head. "They do look like tiny footprints."

"When I was a lad, I was sure they were fairy footprints. I have read some about fossils since then, but I never thought they could be the fairy feet my father showed me when I was young."

"Few fossils are so complete that we can recognize them as

the tiny animals they once were. It takes a keen eye to find them impressed in the rock. You can see plants too, leaves and ferns and bark, if you look closely enough." She smiled. "But I rather like calling them fairy tracks."

"It is better than calling them Highland shrimp." He laughed, then stood and held out his hand. "Come up to me," he murmured.

Fiona paused, recalling the first time she had seen him on another hillside. She had taken him for one of the Fey then, and he had used that same odd, lilting phrase. Now he was smiling, affable—and yet still compelling and mysterious, as if he did indeed have a magical aura about him on this misty hillside.

She very much liked the man she saw now, already familiar to her, who smiled easily and did not insist that she leave this place. She set her gloved hand in his as he helped her to her feet.

Brushing dirt and grass from the skirt of her dark-blue gown, she adjusted the drape of the plaid shawl. It was a gift woven by weaver Elspeth MacArthur, Lady Struan, James's wife. She smiled up at MacGregor. "What brings you into the hills this afternoon? Surely not fossil collecting."

"Flowers, Miss MacCarran." He lifted her knapsack to his shoulder and began to walk beside her. "You roam the hills searching for rocks, and I look for wildflowers."

"For your lady love?" she asked. "You have not collected a bouquet."

"My lady love wants a different sort of bouquet. She is a great belching thing, pretty and shiny, but she is fussy and demanding when the steam begins to roll off her. But oh, she gives great comfort when she is ready."

She blinked. "A copper still?"

"Ah, she guessed the riddle and her rival." His hazel eyes twinkled. A tiny thrill ran through her at his gentle teasing.

"Why does she need flowers, then?"

"Spring flowers will grow along the course of the burn near here, and I need to know what is there. The water feeds the stills down the slope."

"I did not know flowers were part of illicit whisky distilling."

"Legal whisky, Miss. Am I always a criminal in your regard?" He set a hand to his heart in mock wounding, and she laughed. "All manner of things are taken into account when distilling pot-whisky."

"Why the flowers?"

"They flavor the water. Whatever grows by the burn makes the water taste sweeter, lighter, and gives the water, and so the whisky, a hint of fragrance. Some plants lend a tart or a bitter taste. Grass, wild onion, garlic, even your precious rocks, when the water flows over them, can affect the whisky. I come out now and then to check the burns and streams, so I know what goes into the batches. The quality of the barley, the peat, and the water," he went on, "help to determine the flavor and character of the whisky. We keep watch over all three."

"It sounds like an art."

"More art than crime." He glanced down at her.

"Ah," she murmured. His devotion to every detail of the whisky was a fascinating revelation. The making of whisky was a passion, not just a business.

"Alas, though I would be honored to escort you today, my search takes me in another direction. And I see my kinsmen waiting." He gestured with a thumb.

Fiona saw two men waiting on another slope, a young man she did not recognize and an older man who resembled Kinloch's uncles. "Please do not let me delay you. I am content to wander. It was very nice to chat with you."

"And with you, Fiona MacCarran." He leaned toward her. "Do not wander too far, lass. Stay near the road and the loch."

"I will."

"And safe home before dark. Promise me."

"I promise." Her heartbeat quickened.

"Just so." He handed her the knapsack, fingers grazing hers in the transfer. Even through her glove, she felt that casual contact, kept its memory in her hand.

As he walked away, long strides taking him over the slopes, kilt swinging, she watched him for a moment—then sighed and turned to examine some nearby rocks.

Safe home, he had said. Suddenly, she felt as if her life was too safe, dull and intellectual rather than exciting and filled with passion. She had taken a risk in coming to the Highlands, yet clung to the safety of her scholarly pursuits.

Some impulse made her want to run after Kinloch, walk with him beside the burn, searching for wildflowers to please his love, a belching old copper still. She wanted to taste the wild whisky and laugh about fish in the mountains and fairy tracks in the hills.

But he was already in the distance, walking with his kinsmen into the hills where he belonged. And she was a visitor, a Lowlander…an outsider.

Chapter Eight

THE SCRATCH OF nib over paper seemed loud in the quiet front room of Mary MacIan's home at such a late hour. By the light of a flickering lantern, Fiona dipped pen to ink and continued to write, while the peat fire crackled and Mary snored softly in the back bedroom. Done with writing out the week's lessons, verses in Gaelic translated to English to share with her students, Fiona now replied to a letter from James that had arrived by the mail coach just that day.

Outside, the wind rattled the windowpanes and pushed at the old door, but the house was peaceful. Since Mrs. MacIan had a habit of retiring early, Fiona used the quiet evening hours to prepare lessons, compose letters, and work on her drawings.

She still owed a letter to her great-aunt, Lady Rankin, but would leave that for later. Though she loved her aunt, who had raised the twins after their parents had been lost in a shipwreck, she knew the viscountess dismissed Fiona's charitable work, thinking most Highlanders little more than quaint savages. Lady Rankin would rather see her great-niece make a good marriage and stop pining for her lost love.

Fiona would far rather write to her twin brother, enjoying their exchange. She knew he wanted to hear about her work in Glen Kinloch, and she looked forward to having his thoughts in return.

I am delighted that dear Elspeth is feeling so well, she wrote to her brother, having already reported on the glen, the school, and her students. *I look forward to becoming an aunt, though my anticipation cannot match the joy of the babe's dear parents! How wonderful that Elspeth is weaving a new tartan blanket for the little one. The green plaid she made for me is very pretty and keeps me warm.*

She went on, telling him of the mail coach driven by Hamish, uncle to the Laird of Kinloch, and mentioned the distant kinship between Elspeth and her grandfather and Kinloch himself.

Then she wrote that she had no drawings for their grandmother's fairy book yet. She was at a loss how to illustrate that, for Lady Struan had requested drawings of fairies that her grandmother's friend Sir Walter Scott would judge for worthiness. Fiona did not want to disappoint him, and wanted to honor Grandmother's belief in fairies, even though she was uncertain of such things herself.

I hope we can all succeed in the tasks Grandmother gave us as beautifully as you have done. Finding your Elspeth with her family lore of fairy ancestors was a miracle. I do not expect such luck, but I am willing to try.

Next she wrote about the excellent trilobite specimens she had found in limestone, with evidence of a thick quartzite layer beneath Old Red Sandstone. She stopped, glancing up as the door banged in the wind. Startled, she smeared ink on the page, blew on it, and rose to secure the door, fearful its old latches might give way.

Outside, Mary's dog began barking, agitated and incessant. Mary had asked Fiona to let the dog in later that night, but those frenetic barks were concerning. Grabbing her shawl from a hook, she took the dog's rope lead and pulled open the door to step out into a whipping wind.

"Maggie!" She did not see the black-and-white spaniel, although the dog was usually nosing about and guarding nearby. "Maggie, come here!"

Fiona walked across the earthen yard, clutching the shawl against the chilly wind, which held a hint of rain. Wind tugged at the fat, unkempt knot of her hair, spilling it over her shoulders. She pulled the plaid over her head and walked on, calling repeatedly for the dog.

Clouds drifted across a nearly full moon. Across the meadow in the cove, the loch reflected the moonlight. Fiona stopped, turning to look for the dog, and took in the beauty of the dark, sparkling night: black mountains against an indigo sky, the pale wafer of the moon behind swift clouds. Someday if she found time to paint, she would want to capture the mysterious beauty of a night like this one. Lifting her face to the wind, she heard the sound of gusts layered with the lapping of water against the pebbled shore.

The dog barked again, and frantically; the sound seemed close to the cove, and Fiona went in that direction. Overhead, the moon peeked bright between the clouds, revealing the loch's rippled surface—and a boat far out on the water, its elegant black silhouette just visible in the darkness.

She paused. Wanting to fetch the dog inside, she did not want to be seen by anyone aboard a smuggling vessel. Surely it was one of those; there was no other good reason for a ship to sail along the shoreline that touched this remote glen, especially at night.

Half running, searching in earnest for the spaniel, she reached the path that led from the cove to the main road. She called out softly, not eager to be heard. Whatever went on in Glen Kinloch at night, it was safer not to know.

A flash of black and white ran over the meadow toward the main road. Fiona turned and hurried after it. Maggie barked again, a warning, protective sound.

Glancing warily around in the darkness, Fiona sensed a chill run down her spine. "Maggie," she called. "Maggie, come here, girl!"

When she came to the main road, the clouds parted overhead, bathing all in silvery moonlight for a few moments. Another bark, and this time she glimpsed a patchy white coat heading up a hillside. Fiona left the road to pursue her quarry.

Some urgency in the air made her want to hurry. She glanced around at the shimmering loch, the empty road, the dark, massive slopes rising up from the roadside. Higher on the nearest hill, Maggie barked again, and Fiona felt a sense of relief, seeing her within reach. She climbed upward in the unreliable moonlight, shawl clutched in one hand, dog's lead dangling in the other.

"Maggie! Here!"

The wind snapped at her plaid and blew her hair free. The clouds extinguished the moonlight like a candle flame, the darkness so complete that Fiona nearly stumbled on the slope. Here, the ground was thick with heather, juniper, and grass, and scattered with rocks. She dared not run too quickly for fear of falling.

Seeing a flash, she moved toward it—yet it was not the black-and-white dog. Starlight sparkled like bright bits of fire, as if the stars hung very close to the top of the hill. Fiona watched them sink and swirl—and then coalesce into something ghostly. She gasped, stepped back. The lights spun, whirled, vanished.

Ahead, she saw a cluster of standing stones cresting a low hillock, where the moving starlight seemed to have disappeared. Intrigued, she went slowly toward it. Somewhere higher on the slope, the dog barked crazily, excited.

As she went, she heard other sounds—thumps, footfalls, hooves, then the jingle of metal and harness. Her blood ran chill in her veins, and she stood motionless. The dog continued to bark, but Fiona dared not call out now.

Men and horses were approaching from somewhere. She could hear the breath and bluster of horses, the low murmurs of deep voices.

In a new burst of moonlight, she saw them.

They were not the Fey riding in a cavalcade, as legends claimed in the Highland hills, nor were they the ghosts of men lost in battle. These men were real, grim, determined, some mounted, others leading ponies.

Smugglers. And she stood out in the open, easily seen.

Clouds shifted again, casting a shadow over her. Taking a chance, she ran swiftly toward the standing stones to hide, slipping behind the tallest menhir. Standing stones were not uncommon on hillsides and in fields, abandoned ages ago, their meaning and purpose lost. Grateful for their shelter, she drew her dark plaid around her, hoping to blend with the shadows until the men went past.

Lanterns swung like golden drops of fire as they came closer. Fiona stood still, leaning against the stone, legs trembling. She peered out, fear and curiosity mingling. They neared the place where she had just been standing.

Not far away, Maggie continued to bark incessantly, untroubled, bold. Fiona cringed for the dog's sake. The smugglers could decide to silence the little dog to protect their secret. Suddenly, Fiona caught her breath, seeing a black-and-white blur chase down the slope toward the passing group.

Men and horses were visible now, glowing lanterns scattered among them. Cold fear slid through Fiona as she pressed against the tall stone. She could hear the thunk of hobnail boots over the rocky terrain, the clop of horses' hooves, even the slosh of liquid in the kegs strapped to the ponies' backs. She heard rumbling male voices: a question, a reply, a curt laugh. And the relentless barking.

Maggie bolted down the hill and came straight for her, circling the stone circle. Fiona hissed at her to stop, and Maggie, excited, wheeled and ran toward the men again. Clinging to the stone and the shadows, Fiona waited, heart pounding.

Beware the hills when the Laird is walking…we always keep clear…

Fiona would not have gone out at night but for the little dog. But now she was helpless to save Maggie from the passing smugglers.

Some of the men looked toward the standing stones, but moved on. A minute more and they would pass by; another few minutes and they would be gone entirely.

Her heart slammed, but some hint of courage and determination emerged, calming her, slowing her breath. She peered out just far enough to watch the men pass, hearing the rhythmic *chink* of harness fittings and steady footfalls.

One of the men walking along stepped away from the rest. Fiona pressed flat to the cool rock, peering around the side of the stone to see where the man had gone. From behind, a hand snatched her arm, and another hand covered her mouth as he turned her around quickly.

His eyes gleamed in the darkness—the eyes, the height of him, the width of his shoulders, the swing of his dark hair were familiar. She breathed out, felt a trembling relief as he bent closer.

"Fiona MacCarran," he whispered, "go home and lock the door." His breath caressed her cheek, melting her, buckling her knees. She reached out and gripped his jacket, and his hand came away from her mouth, thumb tracing her cheek.

"Dougal," she whispered.

"Hush, you. All is well here, but you need to go." His fingers took her chin, tilted it.

She leaned up, not moving, waiting. He hesitated.

Then his lips touched hers lightly. Drawing in a breath, she slid an arm around his neck and returned the kiss—and then he was kissing her full, deep, holding her close as they stood behind the stone, his body pressed hard against hers. A sudden, hot thrill sank through her, body and soul, fueled by the kiss, the darkness, the danger, and him.

"*A Dhia,*" he murmured, lips finding hers, separating. "What is it you do to me? You do not need this in your life—"

"What if I do?" She splayed her hands on his chest, surprised by a powerful craving. "Take me with you."

"No. Go now." He stepped back, turned away.

Her heart tumbled as she watched him return to the group, his strong rhythmic stride familiar now, almost dear to her. He rejoined the others without a word, and Maggie gamboled after him. He stooped, petted her, shooed her away. Someone murmured, and Dougal laughed low and pointed ahead, away from the stone where Fiona stood. The group moved onward, the sound of their passing eerie. Reaching the road, they merged into shadow.

Now Maggie ran toward her, and Fiona reached for the dog's collar, looping the rope to it. "Now I have you! Come here, my good lassie."

The dog pulled, trying to follow the smugglers and her beloved laird. Fiona realized that Maggie was not defending territory but greeting friends, men she knew and saw often out on the hills and moors at night. Fiona pulled, murmuring encouragement.

As the lanterns flashed and vanished like yellow stars, Fiona paused. She should cross the road quickly and return to the house. But like Maggie, she only wanted to turn the other way and follow the laird of Kinloch. The power of the urge took her breath away, muting the voice of common sense.

Her life felt dull and limited, but for her travels and work in the Highlands. She longed for a bold spark of adventure and passion. Longed for love again, for something wild, fierce. What she had felt in Dougal MacGregor's kisses hinted at passion and discovery far beyond what the safe circles of her life could offer.

But smuggling was criminal, and her new dream was simply a fantasy. Even Kinloch had urged her to go home, lock the door, keep safe, leave the glen. Yet his kisses said something different, tempting, hopeful.

Adventure was one thing—folly was another. She should not entertain such a foolish dream as this.

The clouds dispersed again, and in the pale moonlit glow, she saw lanterns flare, saw two men on horseback along the road. Their hoofbeats were rapid, and she could hear shouts in the distance. She watched, skirts whipping in the wind as she held tight to the leash while Maggie barked, strained for release.

"Customs and excise!" one of the riders bellowed. "You there! Stop!"

She recognized the voice of Tam MacIntyre, the officer who had stopped Ranald MacGregor's cart the first night she had come to the glen. Maggie pulled at the leash, growling low.

Fiona patted her. "Stay. Good girl," she murmured. She held the dog in place in the darkness near the standing stones. The dog continued to growl. "Hush, stay," Fiona said.

"Dougal MacGregor!" Tam called. The sound carried as the horsemen pulled up their reins. The group of men ahead stopped, and one man walked back toward the excise officers. "Kinloch. Why am I not surprised to find you out here tonight?"

"Ah, Tam!" Dougal said. "Who else is with you?"

"What is in those baskets, Kinloch? MacCarran, go look in those panniers. I wager this lot is smuggling something."

MacCarran! Patrick was here? Fiona gripped the dog's leash tightly and crouched beside Maggie, holding the dog's trembling body, her own limbs shaking in fear.

DOUGAL CROSSED HIS arms and surveyed the mounted gaugers. "Smuggling? You are mistaken," he said calmly.

"What else would bring you lot out here tonight, with pack-horses?"

"MacIntyre, what are you doing here in Glen Kinloch, on my land? It is outside your jurisdiction," Dougal countered.

"The stink of peat-reek whisky from Highland stills, carried in the panniers of those horses, brought us here," Tam said. "Your glen has no customs and excise man, so we must extend ourselves though we are overworked. But we have MacCarran now to help us. The one who held this post died a while back. Curious, that."

Now Fiona saw Fergus, his silhouette distinct and recognizable, leave the group to come toward them. "That one died in his bed months back, and you know it. He was not fit for chasing about these hills. Bred in the south, and too old."

"Even so," Tam said, "here we are. I would wager those baskets and kegs hold a cartload of illicit peat reek."

"Call it the best Highland brew, as it deserves," Dougal said. "You cannot prove it illegal, though. We pay taxes, we can transport a certain amount, and well you know it. Good night and be on your way."

He turned to return to the group, his heart pounding at the chance he had taken. Each basket carried by these dozen horses held whisky in bottles and kegs, from his stills and others. Yet no gauger could easily distinguish the product of different stills, not as well he could, and they would have a devil of a time knowing which kegs were carried legitimately and which were not. Their assumption—rightly so, he had to credit—was smuggling activities. But they had to be dissuaded.

Fergus leaned toward him. "What are you doing?"

"Taking a righteous path," Dougal murmured. "I learned it from the reverend."

"Ah. So we are insulted and carrying a legal amount, is that it?"

Dougal nodded subtly, glancing back toward the gaugers sitting their horses in the middle of the road. "Where did they learn about this run?"

Fergus shrugged. "Not from us."

"Kinloch!" Tam called. The sound of a cocking pistol broke the silence.

Dougal touched the gun hidden beneath the swath of plaid draped shoulder to waist. "Mr. MacIntyre, you are disturbing the peace of my glen."

"Bold lad," Tam growled. He and his deputy—MacCarran, Dougal realized—urged their horses forward. "So you are moving the peat reek to a ship on the loch," Tam said. "We spied a boat out there earlier."

"Did you now? I know nothing of a ship. When we move whisky, it is from one household to another in lawful amounts. Gifts, see. We share it regularly hereabouts."

"Am I to believe this is all innocent?"

"Believe the truth. We have a few bottles of the legal stuff here, and sacks of barley kept over the winter. We are taking it to those who need extra stores."

"Lawful amounts of whisky and barley to feed the poor?" Tam spat. "Saint Kinloch! MacCarran, I told you to check those panniers. Do it!"

The younger man dismounted, looking reluctant, and came toward Dougal. "Mr. MacGregor," he murmured.

"Mr. MacCarran." Fiona's brother, he noticed, was a tall, fine-looking young man with dark hair and features that, while longer and more angular, looked familiar.

"If I may, sir. Excuse me." MacCarran walked toward the group of men, and Dougal went with him. Fiona's brother reached toward the nearest horse, its back strapped with pannier baskets, and peered into the baskets.

Dougal waited as the young man shifted aside small sacks of barley placed to serve as packing to stifle the clink of stout glass bottles.

Dougal smiled. "Patrick MacCarran, good to meet you, sir."

Patrick looked around. "Have we met?"

"Your sister is the dominie in our glen school. Teaches the bairns."

MacCarran frowned. "We need not discuss my sister, sir."

"Of course not. I only want to say she is well thought of here."

The new gauger's hand stilled on the barley sacks, inches from detecting far too many bottles to pass as local supply. "Do you have more to say, sir?" he murmured.

"Just a warning."

"MacCarran! Hurry up there!" Tam shouted.

"Take your sister away from this glen," Dougal muttered. "There is danger in this glen for her. And you, sir."

"Danger from rogues like you?"

"I am keeping the rogues away from her, have no doubt. She

must leave, but she is as stubborn a lass as I have ever met in my life."

MacCarran huffed. "That is my sister."

"Does MacIntyre know she is here?"

"I have not mentioned it."

"Good. See he stays ignorant of it. Do not trust him."

"Why should I trust you?" MacCarran asked low.

"Trust me or not. Just get Fiona MacCarran out of here. It is not safe for her."

"I will think on it."

"Just so," Dougal murmured.

Patrick moved to the next horse and the next, checking each basket. Dougal knew the young man must have noted the quantity of bottles tucked among the small grain sacks that cushioned them. Finally he progressed to Fergus's pony, opened the panniers, and rooted around. He lifted a bottle, upended it to find it nearly empty, and took that and a small grain sack toward MacIntyre.

"What did you find?" Tam demanded.

"A few bottles," Patrick said. "Mostly barley sacks, as Kinloch said."

Fergus, standing with Dougal, huffed quietly. "That is a good lad."

"Transporting barley is no crime," MacIntyre growled. "But they will just make more whisky from it. How many bottles?"

"Not a lot. Most are like these." He handed the bottle up to his supervising officer, who took it, tugged out its wax plug, sniffed it, and upended it to his mouth to drain the rest of it.

"Bah, nearly empty!" Macintyre snarled, wiping his mouth. "Good stuff. I doubt they only share it locally. It would sell well, this, and earn good coin."

"They do seem to be transporting barley, which is fine." MacCarran handed up the grain sack. "If they carried more whisky than I found, it is in their bellies now. You can smell it everywhere on them. Some of them can hardly stand upright.

They are fou, sir. Drunk as can be."

"Fou," Tam growled, and looked at Dougal. "You devil, Kinloch."

Dougal grinned, crossing his arms. Fergus wobbled, just then, grabbing hold of his horse's bridle for good effect. One of his cronies leaned over and retched loudly.

"I will look at the damn panniers myself," Tam said, and began to dismount.

"Take my word, sir. I did a thorough search. I am doing my best to follow orders."

"So far," Tam sneered. "But you are an idiot if you think those sneakbaits are not transporting peat reek tonight. Dig deeper into those baskets."

"I did. I found these." MacCarran handed Tam two bottles that he had tucked under his arm—full bottles of Glen Kinloch's finest. Dougal had not seen him snatch them from the load. "Perhaps you will find a use for it."

Well done, lad, Dougal thought. Bribing MacIntyre was an impressive move.

"Hah! I do have a use for this. But perhaps I will look for more of the same." He glanced past the group at the road. Patrick MacCarran turned, and his mouth dropped open. "What the devil," MacIntyre growled.

Dougal turned, too, and swore under his breath.

A woman walked toward them along the road, leading a dog on a rope. The dark plaid draped over her head covered most of her, but for her skirt hiked high over bare feet. The dog trotted obediently beside her as she neared the men clustered on the road. She kept her head down.

Though she looked like a Highland housewife, Dougal knew Fiona immediately, and Maggie too. The lass had not gone home as he had advised. He took a step forward, but Fergus put up a hand to stop him.

Instead, Patrick MacCarran walked toward the woman, speaking quietly to her. She answered softly, then passed by him, approaching Dougal. The dog came with her.

"Ah, Kinloch, is it you?" she asked in a clear voice, in good Gaelic.

"You know damn well it is," he growled in that language, satisfied that MacIntyre, at least, could not understand the words. Maggie bounded around his legs, pleading for the petting he refused her, focusing on the lass. He did not know whether to feel furious, or relieved, or both. "What are you doing?"

"Speak English? I try," she said. "Is it you bringing the barley for the soup?"

"I am," he replied, scowling.

"*Tapadh leat,*" she said, "thank you. My grandmother is pleased, aye? We have so little. The laird is a blessing in this glen. I am bringing my wee dog with me to her house. *Oidhche mhath,* good night." She walked on, the dog pulling on the leash, wanting to stay with her favorite laird.

Watching, Dougal felt his heart leap into his throat when MacIntyre looked down at Fiona MacCarran.

"Miss," the officer said in a snide growl. "What is your name?"

"I am Fionnuala. Good evening, sir," she said in English. "A thousand wishes for your health and happiness."

Dougal lifted a brow to hear the girl murmur the traditional greeting so sweetly to such a scoundrel. As she smiled at MacIntyre, Dougal scowled again. He so wanted that smile for himself, luminous as the sun and the moon. Feeling increasing unease as she lingered, he moved toward her. She did not seem to need his protection, but he would be ready all the same.

"Mr. MacCarran," Fiona said, looking at her brother, "is that your name? Good night and a thousand wishes to you as well." Head high, she walked past them all, tugging the dog firmly along with her.

MacIntyre tightened the reins and turned his horse. He snapped something to MacCarran, who walked back toward Dougal.

"Tam says he has no more time for nonsense with you lot," MacCarran said.

"Good. What did your sister tell you?" he asked low.

"She wants to be sure you are safe tonight. She also said she will not leave the glen, if the laird should ask." Patrick looked hard at him. "Kinloch, keep care for my sister. And watch your back too."

Dougal nodded. "I will. She is safe with me. Do not doubt it."

"Take the barley to the young miss and her grandmother, and the others who need it," MacCarran said loudly then. "See to it done and return to your homes. From now on, move your goods in daylight. Do you hear?"

"Ah, but young sir," Fergus said, "we are that busy in the day with our flocks and herds. We do not have time then to carry the goods we promise to those in the glen."

"See that you make the time." MacCarran returned to his horse and mounted.

"You took too damn long with that," Tam snapped. He pointed at Dougal. "You, Kinloch! You will not come out in these hills by moonlight or darkness again, is it clear? Next time I will have more men. Mark that well."

"I do as I please in my glen," Dougal answered. "Mark that. Good night."

Tam muttered, but turned his horse, riding off with MacCarran following. Dougal let out a long breath, feeling spent for a moment.

Fergus came toward him. "I like your wee teacher. I think she should stay for the whole of her agreement with the reverend. The rest of the year, perhaps."

"I may throttle her before long," Dougal growled, as he watched Fiona and the wee dog walk over a rise and out of sight.

Chapter Nine

RAIN DRUMMED ON the windows of the schoolhouse, the soft squeak and scratch of the chalk in Fiona's hand adding layers of sound as she wrote on a large slate bolted to the wall. She glanced at the students. They sat quietly on benches, striving to copy her chalked words onto the small slates each of them held.

They were nicely focused now. All morning they had listened well and seemed happy to be in school. They had chatted and laughed, passing around slates and chalks and reminding each other to hush when she spoke.

Fiona added a few more words to the list she was making, and drew simple images to go with the words—cat, chair, cradle, and so on. The chalk squeaked and the children whispered, and she heard their chalks scraping on slate as well.

She had been surprised at how quickly the school was flourishing. Kinloch and his uncles had seemed eager for her to leave the glen, so she thought they might interfere with her work, though that had not happened yet. After the events in the moonlight the other evening, she understood more of the business in the glen. The nighttime wanderings could be hampered if a gauger's sister saw what they were doing. They did not trust her, and she could not blame them for that. She would never report what she saw, but they did not realize that yet.

Her brother had sent a message to Fiona the following day, carried by a man who beached a small boat in the cove below

Mary MacIan's house and knocked on the door with the sealed note.

Dear Fiona, Patrick wrote, *If you are ready to leave Glen Kinloch, send word with Mr. MacGrath, the bearer of this note. He is Eldin's man. I can send a carriage for you. If you intend to stay, tell MacGrath you are content.*

But if you do not feel safe, gather your things and go with MacGrath. He will bring you to Auchnashee today.

Fiona had read the note while the man drank a cup of Mary's good brown beer, brewed that week. Had Kinloch told her brother that she must leave the glen?

That was not going to happen. "Mr. MacGrath, please tell my brother I am content to stay. I will give you a note to deliver to him." He had nodded and soon left.

Now she frowned, standing at the slate board lost in thought. Wrong or right, smugglers or none, she would stay. Kinloch was a stubborn man, but she was stubborn too. She had agreed to teach, and she had to satisfy her grandmother's request, if that could ever be accomplished.

Sighing, she knew her situation was already complicated. She was losing her heart, quickly and unexpectedly, to the laird. But she could not meet her grandmother's conditions if she fell in love with a poor Highland smuggler.

Love. The chalk paused on the board. Did she feel that? She longed for it, wanted marriage, a family, a home of her own. After Archie's death, she had never expected to feel love, or loved, or happy again.

This was not love, only fancy, she assured herself. This was just the romantic notion of a Highland smuggler on a moonlit night, a man unlike any she had ever known. Her feelings sprang from an insubstantial daydream.

Besides, Kinloch did not share her feelings. His kisses and kindnesses were only meant to coerce her into leaving the glen so he could smuggle undisturbed.

Lifting her chin, resolve set, she wrote fiercely on the slate. The chalk cracked.

She only felt more determined to stay. She cared about her students, wanted to encourage them and help them learn. She wanted the glen school to succeed. The students needed a teacher who would stay and help them grow.

They were quick-witted young scholars and quick learners, and she had to be alert and diligent to keep pace with them. She spent evenings writing lessons by lantern light until her eyes stung from oil smoke and her fingers were ink-stained. Soon she planned to challenge them further, adding more mathematics, even some geography; she had found a dusty book of maps in a cupboard in the schoolhouse.

Her work was going well, for she was finding time in the afternoons to search for fossils and rock formations, and make sketches and rubbings. Of course she had found no trace of fairies and never would. But she would find some way to fulfill the request.

As for the stipulation that she marry a wealthy and titled Highlander—she could not easily find one let alone expect marriage. And her infatuation with Dougal MacGregor would soon pass, she told herself. She was too busy to think about him or look for chances to encounter him. The time would pass quickly until summer came.

If nothing else, she thought with a quick intake of breath, she would consider marrying Lord Eldin—he might be interested, for he seemed to have a fondness for her, a weakness for her, one of her brothers had said once. They were not close cousins. Marriage to the Earl of Eldin would certainly meet the requirement and solve a host of problems.

And stir up others, she thought. Eldin was a cold, mysterious, and selfish fellow, though he had been a good and friendly lad and youth in their childhood. Something had happened to change him. She did not know if she could bear life with a man who had closed off his heart so completely.

Kinloch MacGregor was much the opposite, and no matter how hard she tried, he was never far from her mind.

Still, though she walked by his tower house daily going back and forth to the school, she had not seen him for days. When she did next, he would just urge her to leave Glen Kinloch. He did not care about her, she reminded herself. He was only doing what he thought necessary to protect his secrets from a troublesome woman. However unfair his misconception, she should simply ignore it.

Hearing chatter rising behind her, she turned. "Lucy Mac-Gregor, that is enough," she said crisply. Lucy had been whispering to her cousin Jamie, and now the girl looked up with an innocent smile.

"Lucy, please fetch fresh chalks from the basket and give them to everyone," Fiona suggested. Lucy nodded and set to the task. The child had no malice, Fiona knew, just a strong spirit and an impish nature.

She glanced at the two new students who had arrived that morning. Duncan and Sorcha, a young brother and sister, sat quietly working on their slates. She smiled, nodding her approval, and they looked pleased. She was glad that the people of the glen were sending more students as word spread.

Returning to her desk, she took up quill and ink to record a few comments in a leather-covered notebook. *Duncan MacSimon, 10, Sorcha MacSimon, 8. Cousins of the laird,* she wrote; *father is the miller at Drumcairn. They speak a little English. Have a long walk to reach the school, accompanied by an older brother.* Starting a new line, she noted, *Lucy MacGregor needs more challenges to occupy her mind and energy. Should speak to her guardian.*

But the teacher was not quite ready to face Lucy's guardian.

Standing, Fiona folded her hands calmly. "Good work with the vocabulary, students. Now, let us try something new," she told them in Gaelic.

Soon she would speak English more often, though she was allowing them time to grow more accustomed to lessons. Picking up a sheaf of papers bound in string, she opened the pages, which she had painstakingly copied one night.

"When I was a girl, I loved the Gaelic songs my Highland nurse taught me. I translated some into English for you. Jamie, please hand the pages around."

The redheaded boy jumped up to pass the handwritten sheaves around the room. The students chatted as he did so, and Fiona raised her hand for silence.

"We will recite the verses. If you cannot read the English, just follow along, and place your finger on each word as we say it, to help you recognize the word again. First in Gaelic, then in English," she said, and continued:

"Dear Lord, shield the house, the fire, the kine, and everyone who dwells here tonight," she read, then went on in a soft sing-song.

Shield myself and my dear ones
Preserve us from harm
For the sake of the angels
Who watch over us this night...

Mairi MacDonald raised her hand. "Miss MacCarran, my grandmother says this verse every night. She calls it the prayer before resting."

"My mother says it, too," Lilias said. Others murmured agreement.

"I know this one," Lucy said. "My Aunt Jean taught it to me, and now that she is gone, my Uncle Kinloch says it with me at night before I sleep."

"Very good," Fiona said, feeling a quick twinge of sympathy to learn that small Lucy had lost her mother and, apparently, an aunt who had cared for her. Fiona felt touched to know that the laird of Kinloch took time to recite a Gaelic prayer with his little niece. "Let us say it in Gaelic and then in English."

Using a stick, she pointed to each phrase she had chalked on the large slate hung on the wall.

Air an oidhche nochd 's gach aon oidhche,
On this night and every night

The students recited in Gaelic, then in halting English, the sound rich and soft in the air. Fiona felt the thrill that sometimes came over her when she spoke Gaelic and heard its soft resonance and rhythms, as if magic were woven all through it.

"Excellent," she said. "Again, please, and follow the words with your finger. Sing if you know the melody." As a shy harmony swelled in the room, one voice, silver clear, rose above the rest.

Fiona saw Annabel sitting straight, chin lifted as she sang in a voice with astonishing purity and strength despite her youth. As the other students finished, Annabel sang the last note truly.

"That was lovely, Annabel," Fiona said.

The girl blushed, her silver-blond hair sliding down to hide her face. "Thank you, Miss MacCarran," she said softly, shoulders hunched. Someone laughed and whispered. Peering through the slanting sunlight coming in the small windows, Fiona frowned in that direction, and the laughter subsided quickly.

She went on with the lesson, reciting in English, the students following. Annabel did not sing this time, though Fiona wanted to hear that clear and haunting voice again.

For the rest of the morning, the students focused on learning English words until Fiona excused them for the midday meal. They ran outside, glad to see that the rain had stopped. While the children sat under trees or on boulders, unwrapping cheese and oatcakes and other foods brought from home, Fiona filled wooden cups with clear water from a nearby burn and handed them around.

Opening the packet of food that Mrs. MacIan had given her, she found barley cakes and cold bacon. She took it inside, thinking to finish a little work, leaving the door open so that she could see the students as she ate and worked at lessons.

"Miss MacCarran," a voice said. She looked up.

Ranald and Fergus MacGregor stood in the open doorway. Rising, she beckoned them inside and went to greet them. "Mr. MacGregor, and—Mr. MacGregor! How nice to see you. What can I do for you?"

"Please excuse us, Miss," Ranald said, "but we came to check the roof. With the bairns outside, this might be a good time."

"Of course. Is there a problem with the roof?"

"Och aye," Ranald said. "Are you done with school for the day?"

"Not yet. We will work for an hour or so after luncheon. Some of them have chores at home, so I give them afternoons free for those tasks."

"And some only have tasks when the laird asks them to help him," Fergus said, smiling politely, just as if he had not seen her only days ago facing smugglers and officers in the dark of night.

"Ah," she said. "So the older lads help the laird—at night, in the hills?"

"Hills?" Ranald looked very innocent. Then she saw a twinkle in his eyes. "We sometimes bring casks and supplies around to others in need."

"Of course. Though if the older lads will be occupied in the evenings, I would like to know about it."

"Why?" Fergus asked, glancing at Ranald.

Oh, dear, she thought. They might worry that she would take that information to her brother. "Only so that I can understand why they are especially weary some mornings, or unable to finish their homework. That is all."

"I see." Ranald nodded. "My son Andrew, is he a good scholar?"

"Very bright and a fast learner," she replied.

"And Jamie? He is my grandson," Fergus said proudly. "A good lad."

"He is a very smart lad, and quite willing to help others."

"Andrew has his mother's wit, not mine," Ranald said. "I do not read English."

"You speak it very well. And you are a clever man. Your son is like you."

"That is true," Ranald said, puffing proudly.

"Miss, you are a good teacher, I am thinking," Fergus said. "What of Lucy? We are all her uncles, you know. And the laird will also want to know how she does."

"She is extremely bright, though a bit spirited," she said tactfully, while they chuckled. "I—I have not seen Kinloch for a while."

"He has been busy with matters in the glen," Fergus said.

"I am sure of it," she answered, unable to keep the spice out of her tone.

Fergus huffed. "And wee Lucy, is she tormenting poor Jamie?"

"Sometimes, but I suspect it is a form of affection."

"Huh. She does not want to be in school, that one. Jamie likes the lessons, though," Ranald said.

"Sooner or later, they will all learn what they need to learn."

"Miss MacCarran is a good dominie," Fergus told Ranald. "Here, we must look at the roof."

Fiona glanced up. "I noticed dampness on the ceiling. I hope it is not a concern."

"We will see," Ranald said. "We have not always had a teacher here at the glen school, you know. Sometimes a traveling dominie came to the glen and stayed a season, going house to house so the bairns could learn letters and math at home. We learned that way, my brothers and I."

Fergus shrugged. "We did not learn much. And John—he was our youngest brother, Miss, the father of the young laird—was more interested in learning than we three. He studied on his own, had a great interest in books and learning, wanting education for his tenants and his son, too. He wanted Dougal to go to university."

"He attended for a bit," Ranald said. "The needs of the glen brought him back."

Fiona nodded, realizing why Kinloch seemed educated while claiming he was not. "A traveling dominie can be a good solution sometimes. If other children want to come to the Glen Kinloch school but are too far away, I will speak to Reverend MacIan about hiring a traveling dominie to tutor them at home."

"He will refuse. We cannot afford two teachers. We are a poor glen," Fergus said. "One teacher. You."

"The roof is leaking," Ranald affirmed, walking away to look up. "It is bad."

"Can you fix it, Mr. MacGregor?" Fiona asked as she and Fergus joined him.

"It will take time."

"Can the roof wait until I return to Edinburgh in a few weeks?"

The two men looked at each other, then walked away again to examine the back wall for signs of dampness. There, exposed roof beams angled lower beneath thick and visible thatching. Fergus reached up to tap at the rafters within his reach and murmured to his brother. Fiona went toward them.

"I hope it is nothing serious," she said.

"It shows the damp," Fergus said. "See there." He indicated stains and cracks.

"Could you patch it for now?"

"A patch will not do. It needs a new slate roof or at least new thatch," Ranald said. "And the rooftree needs replacing. There is some rot there, see." He pointed.

She was not sure what to look for. "Could you replace it properly later?"

"We cannot wait for long," Ranald said. "The roof could collapse."

"Oh dear! Is it so dangerous as that?"

"Could be," Ranald said.

"Could be," Fergus said.

"Oh my." Fiona glanced through the window. Most of the students had finished eating and had begun kicking a ball between them. She turned back. "The students are doing so well. It would be a shame to interrupt their studies now."

"It would not do for the roof to fall on their heads," Fergus pointed out.

"Perhaps you could come back to Glen Kinloch later to teach," Ranald said.

With sudden suspicion, she crossed her arms, tilted her head. "Did the laird send you here to tell me this?"

"Och, no, everyone knows the school roof is old," Ranald said.

"Then why were we permitted to hold school sessions here?"

Fergus shrugged. "You must ask the laird."

"I will," she said firmly. The shouts from the yard were growing louder. "It is time to call the children inside now. Thank you, sirs."

She went to the door, the MacGregors behind her, and saw near pandemonium taking hold in the yard as the children kicked the ball around. They had lost their earlier manners and decorum; now they shoved and shouted as they jammed together in a group, boys and girls both tussling over the ball.

Fiona had felt just such excitement in her childhood when she had played similar games with her brothers and friends. But as a teacher, she could not condone it. "Time for class," she called, stepping outside. "Time for this to end!"

Ranald and Fergus hurried past her, and she expected that they would quickly end the rough play. Instead, they joined in, laughing and calling out. "Here! Here to me!" Fergus shouted.

Just then, striding out from between the trees, the laird of Kinloch stepped into the group to huddle with the others, who cheered and welcomed him.

"Where is that ba'!" Ranald called. Dougal glanced toward his uncles, who were shouldering into the thick of the group.

"Watch the wee lasses," he told Ranald, putting up an arm to protect one of the girls as the group jostled and enlarged. He knew well that his uncles took any game of football a bit too seriously. "Fergus, mind the wee ones. Jamie! Lucy! Out with you now. The game is growing too rough." Ignoring him, the younger two scrambled on with the rest.

"Da, which side are you on?" Andrew called out. "We need more players!"

"What sides are we playing today?" Fergus asked.

"Kinnies and Glennies," Pol said. "Those related to Kinloch, and those not."

"We are all on the same side," Ranald called, amid laughter. He swept at the ball with his booted toe. "Nearly had it—damn!"

"What is this?"

Hearing a woman's voice, Dougal glanced up to see Fiona MacCarran at the outskirts of the circle. He had not seen her for several days, and so looked toward her longer than he should have, long enough for a child to stumble near him. He caught the lad easily.

"Watch out for the little ones, if you please!" she called.

He stretched out an arm to slow those nearest him. "Stop, now. Enough."

"But we only started—" Pol began.

"Time for class to resume," Fiona said. The children slowed but did not stop, still pushing the ball around. The teacher walked to the edge of the cluster. "Time for lessons," she repeated sternly.

"A bit longer, Miss," Fergus pleaded, while some of the students laughed. "Please," Fergus added, to more laughter.

Her frown only grew, Dougal noticed, and pretty as it was, it was quite stern. "We must begin lessons again, or the day will be very long," she said.

"Enough, lads, lasses." Dougal stepped back, shooing the students away to break up the circle of players. "Listen to your dominie." He looked at his uncles. "You big lads too."

"Och, so it's lessons for you lot," Fergus said, ruffling Jamie's red hair. "Good work at the football, laddie."

Jamie grinned and ran to join the students trudging past their teacher, who stood watching, her mouth set in a prim line that, to Dougal, still looked rosy sweet no matter her temper. He nodded as he approached.

"Good day, Miss MacCarran." He fisted a hand at his waist. "It is a fine day for a game of the ball."

"It is," she agreed, "but better done after school. Lessons to be learned first, and play comes after."

"In school as in life," he drawled. "Until later, then, Miss MacCarran."

"Kinloch." A smile touched her lips, that luscious mouth he had tasted and wanted to again. The feeling tugged at him.

The ball was at his foot. He kicked it with his toe and sent it toward her.

Quickly she raised her skirt hems and punted it back to him with ease, scooping the ball with the top of her foot and sending it upward to land softly at his feet. Dougal halted the ball with his toe and chuckled.

"I am impressed, Miss Dominie," he said.

"See, Kinloch, I can also play games here in the glen."

"So I see." He gave her a long look, and she returned an amused smile before turning toward the schoolhouse. Watching, Dougal smiled to himself. She was stern and lovely, and no doubt her scholars would have extra lessons today.

Picking up the ball, he bounced it in his hands and strolled away toward Kinloch House. In the yard, Ranald and Fergus waited for him.

"That's a good lass," Ranald grunted, jabbing a thumb toward the schoolhouse.

Dougal threw the ball at his uncle. "Keep this, we will need it," he told his uncles. "And spread the word. We are forming a game. A big one."

"When? And who will play?" Fergus asked.

"Soon enough, and everyone," Dougal called back as he went into the house.

"WE HAVE ANOTHER verse to try," Fiona told the class. "It is called a *fith-fath.*"

"Fith-faths! They are old charms," Mairi said. "My grandmother and my mother recite them. Why should we learn those in English, if the Southrons do not have such charms?"

"Because they use words that are easy to learn. Listen," she said, and began in Gaelic:

Fith-fath ni mi ort
Bho chire, bho ruta,
Bho mhise, bho bhuc...

"A fith-fath I make on you," she translated in English, "from sheep, from ram, from goat, from stag..." She had chosen the ancient household blessing for its common form—lists of animal names and plain nouns simple enough to learn in English. She was counting on her students to find the old verses familiar and easily absorbed.

Glancing up at the ceiling uneasily while the children recited, she wished she knew a blessing charm for a roof. She was not entirely sure if the roof was indeed precarious, or if Ranald and Fergus MacGregor were leading her on in a scheme to scare her away from the old building.

Hearing the thunk of boots on the front step, thinking Ranald and Fergus had returned, she looked up. Dougal MacGregor stood in the doorway, which was open to the fresh air. He folded his arms and leaned against the frame to listen.

Though her heart leaped in her chest to see him again, she calmly finished the verse. Then she reviewed the word list, keenly aware that he was watching.

While the students patiently copied words, she walked toward him. "Mr. MacGregor."

"Pardon the interruption, Miss MacCarran." He inclined his head. "I would like a word with you if you have a moment."

Her heart gave a little flip of excitement and dread, but she merely nodded. "Can you wait until after class?"

"Another day, then," he said, straightening. "I have some business to tend to."

"Aye, then," she murmured, disappointed, and wondering if his business involved more secret treks over the hills. "You can find me here tomorrow."

"I can find you," he murmured, "whenever I want. And when you want."

"Tomorrow," she suggested. "What do you wish to discuss? Do you need to look at the roof, too?"

"Not that. Another matter."

She leaned forward. "An illicit one?"

"You," he said, leaning and nearly whispering, "are far too eager for such."

"I rather enjoyed myself the other night." She blushed, smiled a bit.

"Did you now?" He pinched back an amused quirk of the lips. She yearned for more of that from him, wanting his wide, bright smile, his ready laugh. Wanting his strong arms to reach out, draw her close.

Enough. Her cheeks burned. "Did you? Enjoy the other night, I mean?"

"I did not. Watching you walk boldly between gaugers and smugglers? Indeed I did not."

"I only meant to help. I worried that my brother would have to arrest you."

"He would have had no choice if Tam had ordered it done. And there would have been a skirmish, with you in the middle. I know you meant to help, and you did. But I did not enjoy it," he said low. "But I did enjoy the other."

"The other? Oh!" She gasped, remembering the kiss.

"Aye," he whispered. "A wee taste of heaven, that was. Did you think so?"

She glanced down, breath quickening, and nodded.

"You should not be standing here with a scoundrel and a smuggler who only wants to kiss you again." He spoke low, leaned close, breath brushing her cheek. "He would bring no good to your life. Your brother and I agree you would be safer away from here."

"Does he," she said sourly.

"Aye. Until tomorrow, Miss Dominie," he replied lightly, tilting his head. "A *fith-fath* on you and yours."

"A blessing to you too, sir," she murmured. She stood too close, felt too drawn to him, and so she reminded herself where they stood, who he was. The laird. But not a scoundrel. Not at all. His green eyes reflected the mossy tones in the plaid draped over the shoulder of his old jacket, and his gaze was striking and unreadable. She could not look away.

Wildly, she felt as if he cast a spell over her with that hazel gaze, felt as if he truly could be a man of the Fey. Recalling their kiss by the standing stone, she drew in a quick breath.

"Go back to your scholars, miss," he murmured.

She straightened away from him. "If you only want to tell me to leave this glen, do not come by tomorrow, Kinloch. You will not easily be rid of me," she whispered.

"Och, Fiona," he murmured, sounding regretful, "I only want to show you something that is important to me. Go on, now, the young ones are waiting for you. And I will wait for you tomorrow."

Chapter Ten

DOUGAL SAT ALONE at a table in the front room of the small inn kept by Rob MacIan. The only other patrons were three of his own tenants gathered at another table, discussing when they would send their cattle into the higher slopes to graze on the sweet hill grass there. The winter had been harsher than usual, they were saying, and the cattle were thin still, though it was nearly May.

His own cattle were also in need of the better nutrition of the higher slopes, where sunlight and clear mountain streams fed the grasses and flowers, and livestock could grow healthy after a long winter and a wet spring. The Highlands of Scotland did not produce good hay for cattle, though toward harvest time there would be good oats and barley crops to feed them.

Soon enough, glen families would herd their cattle up the slopes to the shieling huts, simple cottages used in spring and summer by those tending the cattle for weeks at a time. Once the hills were more populated during the shieling time, moving whisky about without attracting attention would be more difficult.

When the tenants invited Dougal to join them, he declined with a smile. He was waiting to meet someone, sipping ale in silence, watching through the small window near his shadowed seat in a corner. Along the road, he saw a black coach—not the shabby beast Hamish drove, but a sleek barouche and four.

The coach drew up in front of the inn, and as the tenants craned to look out the window with curiosity, Rob MacIan strode through the room. Like his nephew, the reverend, the innkeeper was a tall, fair sort, gone big and ruddy with age and ale. He went to the door and stepped out into the yard to call to one of his sons to see to coach, horses, and driver. Rob then greeted the passenger.

Taking another sip of ale, Dougal appreciated the fine, fresh brew. He could usually tell by the flavor which household in the glen had produced it. Turning the pewter cup on the tabletop, he waited patiently.

A tall man, lean and dark haired in a black frock coat, neat gray trousers, and high black boots entered the tavern. He removed his black hat, ducking his head slightly beneath the lintel. Though he carried a cane, he seemed to have no real need of it, given the agility and athleticism in his form and motion.

The tenants glanced at each other, then at Dougal, frowning. Perhaps they assumed that the newcomer was a government officer. The handsome fellow was clearly privileged, Dougal noticed, which would not identify him as a government official at first sight. Most of the gaugers he had ever known, in fact, were a shabby lot. The man's piercing eyes seemed to assess everything and everyone in the room with a swift glance. Seeing Dougal raise a hand, he came toward him.

"MacGregor of Kinloch, I presume."

"Lord Eldin," Dougal said in greeting, rising to his feet, as Eldin seemed to expect a more formal greeting. He offered his bare hand, gripping the earl's gloved fingers and strong handshake.

Sitting on the opposite bench, Eldin set his hat gingerly on the table, sweeping the table surface first. Rob MacIan came toward them. "Sir, you must be thirsty after your journey," he said, setting down a tankard of ale.

"From Auchnashee to here is not far," Eldin said, looking at the tankard with mild disdain. "I will have a dram of whisky, if you please. That local brew you recommended once before to me—Kinloch whisky. Among the finest brews in the Highlands, so I hear."

Dougal tipped his head as Rob hurried away. "My thanks, sir."

"I am not flattering you. If your brew is that good, I am merely stating a fact."

"Indeed," Dougal said, and sipped his ale.

Eldin lifted his own tankard, tasted, set it down. "That is more than passable stuff for a local ale."

"A cousin of mine, Helen MacDonald, makes it."

The earl swallowed again. "Light and delicate for an ale. Refreshing. I have never had the like. What makes the difference in the brew?"

"Heather flowers, I believe. She uses an old recipe known to the family."

"Heather ale? I've heard of it. Excellent. Does she sell it?"

"She does not produce enough quantity for that. And of course her price would be high for a larger amount."

"I will seek out the woman and order her ale for my hotel."

"I will ask her," Dougal said firmly, "and send her answer to you."

Rob returned with a dark bottle and two glasses, which he poured out, the liquid golden, its familiar fragrance wafting to Dougal's nostrils.

"Sláinte," Dougal said, lifting his glass as Eldin lifted his. As the earl sipped, Dougal studied him: wealth and elegant lifestyle were apparent in the smallest immaculate details, from the man's snowy linen neckcloth and precisely cut woolen coat to the polished beaver hat set on the table, and the gold-headed cane leaned beside it.

Almost unconsciously, Dougal straightened his shoulders, his jacket the plain woolen one he wore often, his plaid old, in the MacGregor hues of burgundy and green, his linen shirt with a simple open collar and no neckcloth. His hair was unkempt, too long, his beard unshaven. Lord Eldin was a man of obvious means and sophistication, probably raised with luxury and ease, and Dougal felt the differences keenly.

He thought of Fiona MacCarran and knew she would be more used to men like Eldin. He wondered which sort she preferred.

Yet he felt no lack within himself. He was satisfied with his solid, reliable nature, good manners, and simple Highland gear. He suspected Eldin was not as content as the expensive garments and black barouche made him appear. He saw shadows beneath the man's eyes, a sour set to the mouth. Eldin downed the whisky quickly, reaching for the bottle to pour another inch into his glass, offering Dougal some. He declined with a shake of his head.

"Excellent stuff," Eldin said. "This is from your distillery?"

"It is."

"Legal or illicit?"

"Does it matter?"

"It might."

"You requested we meet. What is on your mind?"

Eldin turned the small, thick glass in his hand. "This is a small coaching inn," he said, glancing about. "Does it do much trade?"

"The MacIans have run this inn for generations. Most days the patrons are local men. Occasionally, a coach comes by with tourists who want to see Loch Katrine and the surrounding hills because of the poems they have read about it."

"And they are treated to this fine whisky?"

"Provided Rob MacIan has it in store, and provided the guests want something more than ale or the French wines he keeps in his stock," Dougal said. "Other local whiskies are available too. The MacDonald family in this region make a very fine whisky, as do the Lamonts. Rob MacIan produces a few hundred gallons of his own whisky per year, according to his allotment. An inn is permitted to produce more than a household."

"Everyone in this glen makes whisky, it seems. And most of it illicit?"

Dougal leaned back, regarded the earl. "And what is it you want of me?"

"You are the laird of this glen."

"I am."

"So you know all that goes on here."

"At times. Why?"

"I have a hotel at Auchnashee, ready to open to tourists and travelers. By summer I expect a good deal of patronage. I want to obtain the best whisky for my establishment."

"There is plenty of good whisky to be had here. If it is Glen Kinloch brew you want, made by the MacGregors, tell me what quantities you have in mind. We may be able to bargain."

Eldin sipped again, considered the glass, nodded. "What is the finest brew you have available? The very finest," he added.

Dougal tapped his fingers on the table. This gentleman was Fiona's cousin, he reminded himself. He narrowed his eyes, looking for a resemblance, seeing it in the finely cut features, the dark glossy hair, the direct and intelligent gaze, and the stubbornness in the lean, firm jaw. But what he saw in this fellow's eyes he had never seen in Fiona—cunning, calculating thought behind the polish of courtesy. Eldin might be a decent sort, yet Dougal did not trust him. He sensed a secretive nature that set his hackles to rise.

"The finest whisky we have," Dougal said, "depends on what price is offered."

"A handsome one," Eldin said. "Name it."

"I have a batch that has been stored three years in oak casks," Dougal said, and stated a price that was rather high. Eldin did not look surprised.

"Is it legal, this brew?"

"From a licensed still." His distillery had only recently obtained a license, a detail he did not bother to add.

Eldin waved his fingers dismissively. "What else do you have? I expected something more valuable. Something unique, otherwise unobtainable."

"Something illicit?" Dougal cocked one brow.

Eldin leaned forward. "Sir, understand me. I do not care a whit about the law. If the whisky is the very finest you have, its origins are unimportant," he said low.

"We do have something else," Dougal said, making a quick decision. "Twelve years if it is a day, made with barley grown in our own fields, and brewed with clear Highland water passed through heather blooms. Proofed to perfection, stored in sherry casks that have been turned regularly. The richness of the old Spanish shiraz that was in those casks, turned over the years, has mellowed the whisky to an exquisite degree. We have not bottled it, and so it continues to age."

"And?" Eldin waited.

"And it would be expensive." Dipping a finger in the whisky, Dougal wrote a considerable number on the table surface with a fingertip.

Eldin shrugged. "Is the revenue paid?"

"What do you think?"

"I see. Too good for the government, I think. Do they even know it exists? Ah, your silence answers that. How many casks?"

"Seven are available." Dougal had more, but would not let on.

Eldin sat back. "I will think about it."

"Think all you like," Dougal said. "Within the month, it will be gone."

"To England?" Eldin asked quickly.

"There are some lively markets for good Highland whisky."

"The blight in the French vineyards has reduced the amount of wine a man can obtain there," Eldin agreed. "Grain whiskies made in England and Lowland Scotland can be poor specimens indeed, compared to Highland malt whisky. But a Highland whisky that is hand nurtured and aged, stored twelve years and never found by the revenue—that is rare stuff."

"Thus the price," Dougal said.

Eldin nodded, played with the brim of his hat, looked at

Dougal. "And Miss MacCarran, my cousin? I assume you have met her? How does my fair Fiona?"

"Well enough." Dougal was startled. What the devil? "We have met on occasion." Indeed. "She is doing a fine job with her students."

"I trust she is busy with the teaching."

"Very dedicated to her work."

"When she is not teaching, does she wander the hills?"

An odd question. Dougal narrowed his eyes. "She collects rocks and stones, from what I understand. Sometimes, she walks the hills. It is safe," he added. He should tell the girl to lob a couple of rocks at her cousin if he came near.

"Has she asked you about fairies, Mr. MacGregor?"

Dougal did not blink. "She is interested in local legends, like many visitors to the Highlands." He wondered where these questions were going and why.

"Tell her nothing. If you know fairy legends, do not share them with her."

"There is no harm in the tales. We have many legends."

"Be wary, nonetheless," Eldin said. "Do you have a personal fortune, sir?"

Dougal bristled. "That is no concern of yours, Lord Eldin."

"Allow me to caution you. If you have any wealth, play the pauper should my cousin ask about it."

"What?" Dougal returned sharply.

"Fiona MacCarran has reasons beyond teaching to come to the glen. She has a particular interest in fairy matters, stories of fairy gold and such. I confide in you, sir, to warn you," he said low. "My cousin is determined to marry a wealthy Highland man."

A muscle pumped in his jaw. The man had outrageous nerve and was all but insulting the girl. Dougal fisted a hand under the table. "After the Clearances and Culloden, wealthy Scotsmen are rare enough," he drawled.

Eldin laughed. "Regardless, she has her mind set on this. Her family has little fortune of its own, and a wealthy husband is a solution for them."

He wanted to throttle the man. "You speak unkindly of your kinswoman."

Eldin shrugged. "A warning. Advice against a fortune hunter."

"I possess no fortune, and I do not think she is hunting. Nor am I interested."

"Is it so?" Eldin looked doubtful.

"None of this is your concern."

"She is my cousin."

"Then treat her with respect."

Eldin gave a flat smile. "Should we bargain further for your best whisky?"

"I may not sell it to you after all."

"No?" The earl leaned toward him. "How much do you want for the Kinloch twelve-year, all seven casks?"

"More than you can pay. Priceless, now." He was growing furious.

"I wonder if you have an even more priceless brew tucked away."

"Our whisky is rare and valuable."

"There is a legend of another sort of whisky. An ancient brew whose recipe was given to the MacGregors by the fairies themselves."

Dougal huffed. "Legends do not produce profitable whisky."

"They say the lairds of Kinloch have always produced this secret brew."

"I am not aware of it, if so," he drawled.

"If you have a brew of that sort, I am willing to pay whatever you ask."

Dougal shook his head in silence.

"Very well. Think on it, Kinloch." Eldin stood then, lifting his hat and snatching his cane. Inclining his head, he opened his gloved hand and deposited several coins on the table, including the glint of gold sovereigns and silver shillings, far more than was needed to pay for the drinks. The man left the inn quickly, shutting the door behind him.

Rob came to the table. "He wanted no supper? We have a fine roast ready."

"No supper," Dougal said, standing. Through the window, he saw the earl's barouche leaving the yard. "Serve the roast to all with the earl's compliments," he said, indicating the coins.

Glancing out the window again, Dougal frowned. What had Lord Eldin heard about fairy whisky—and why did he want it?

And what had he meant by those sly remarks about Fiona MacCarran?

The earl's warning had a different effect than intended. Dougal was even more interested, curiosity piqued, sympathy roused. Miss MacCarran had a devil for a cousin. A scheme to marry wealth, particularly in the Highlands? He almost laughed. If she wanted that, then she would be scheming to marry that blasted cousin of hers.

But if she should ever decide that a poor, plain, solid Highland laird was to her liking, there was one willing and waiting.

That thought, clear and certain, was more revelation to him than anything Eldin had said.

THE NEXT AFTERNOON, as the door to the schoolhouse opened and the students exited into the sunshine, Dougal walked toward the school. He came from an adjacent glen slope, where a distillery was hidden in a thicket of evergreen trees. Fergus had started a new batch of whisky there, and Hamish's sons, Will and John, were testing the proof on a previous batch. Dougal had stayed to help until the angle of the sun reminded him that he wanted to get to the schoolhouse before lessons ended.

Walking there now, he saw the door open and children

emerging. He waited, folding his arms, watching for her.

For days, he had wanted a private word with Fiona MacCarran, but he had let other matters interfere. Even the day before, he had not taken much time to speak to her. He did not feel ready, somehow, he needed his distance.

Besides, other matters needed his attention. The barley laid down to germinate for a new batch of brew required shoveling and turning. Then he had ridden down to Loch Lomond to meet with English clients interested in Kinloch whisky. That visit was worth a stay at an inn—their offer gave Lord Eldin's proposal some competition.

Upon his return to the glen, Ranald and Fergus told him of their attempt to convince the new dominie that the roof was bad and she should suspend school sessions. Dougal knew he must speak with her about that and other matters.

Though he had kept away, time and distance had not changed his feelings. Whenever he saw her, he near stopped in his tracks—glancing out a window in his tower, he had noticed her head toward the schoolhouse, moving gracefully, arms filled with books; looking across the glen hills, he had seen her far off, searching for rocks and fossils, her face lifted to sunlight or bonneted in rain.

Just yesterday, he had glanced up at the sound of her voice and nearly forgot that he was playing ball, where normally he never lost focus. Each time she caught his eye, his heart stirred, thumping as if he were a half-bearded youth.

As many excuses as he found to keep away, from tasks in a stillhouse to visiting tenants, counting herds, or leaving the glen altogether, he could not stop thinking about her. Whenever he saw her, his body responded, his heart craved, yet his resistance made his loneliness feel even more profound.

He was glad, now, that he had waited to speak with her until after his meeting with Lord Eldin. It was all too clear that the girl had to leave the glen, as much as he wanted her to stay. But the Laird of Kinloch had best manage the complications of his life alone.

Nodding a greeting to the children as they passed, he stood waiting. After a few minutes, Fiona MacCarran emerged from the schoolhouse, tying the ribbons of her bonnet. Seeing him, she paused, as if startled. Then she walked toward him.

His heart pounded hard. She was simply beautiful in the gray gown, jacket, and bonnet that she had worn the first time he had seen her on the hillside. The wind pushing the soft fabrics revealed her womanly form and the natural, alluring, confident way she moved. He could have watched her endlessly.

"Mr. MacGregor," she greeted him quietly. "You wish to speak to me about some matter on your mind?"

"I do," he said smoothly. "So my uncles told you about the roof?"

"They did. I asked if it could be patched until I am gone." She lifted her chin, her eyes snapping blue, bright and stubborn. "Unless you have your way and I leave soon."

"If I had my way with you, lass," he murmured, "we would not be talking about a roof just now."

Her cheeks glowed like pink fire, and she pinched back a smile. Tendrils of dark, glossy hair escaped her bonnet. He wanted to pull the hat away, loosen her hair, pull her close—

"About the repairs," she reminded him.

"Aye." He cleared his throat. "The thatch and some of the rafters need replacing. My uncles would rather install a slate roof, which would last longer and give better protection against the elements. But that would take time."

"Can it wait?"

"Some kind of repair must be done soon since it is leaking. One more good rainstorm and the old thatch will come down on your head."

"So your uncles said. If you knew the schoolhouse was in such condition, why were the repairs not made before sessions began again?"

"My uncles made a few repairs months ago. We did not expect you so soon."

"Or perhaps it is your way of saying I am not wanted in Glen Kinloch."

"You are wanted," he said, "in the glen."

She tilted her head. "But not by you."

He sighed. "This glen is not a safe place for the sister of a gauger. It can be dangerous, as you have seen."

"The greatest threat to me so far seems to be from you."

"And the roof."

"Please do not send me away. I do not want to go," she said bluntly.

Dougal glanced away from those earnest sky-blue eyes. "You are a fine teacher, and you are needed here. That is true."

"Thank you."

"Lucy tells us about school. She enjoys it very much."

"She is a bright child, and quite delightful."

"She has loathed lessons until now. I owe you a debt there."

"She was not content at first, but she seems eager to learn. I must find more challenges for her. She works quickly, then sets about bothering Jamie. He is such an easygoing lad that he puts up with pestering, but she must be diverted to better activities."

"I agree. I am afraid I have little idea how to manage a small girl, let alone one as bright and willful as wee Lucy. Though I will say, Jamie adores the lass."

"And she knows it, which only makes it worse. She adores him, you know."

"Does she?" He tipped his head, watching her steadily.

"Otherwise she would ignore him altogether."

He smiled. "Someday she will have her reckoning."

"Could be. What does she love best? If I knew, it might help."

"She claims she wants to be a smuggler when she grows up, and she is convinced they do not need studies."

"I do hope you discourage those notions."

"I try to set a good example," he answered wryly. "We read poetry in the evenings. So now she believes smugglers enjoy poetry but do not need math."

She laughed at that, and Dougal smiled at the enchanting sound. "You, sir, know better than I do what smugglers need."

"Oh, what they need," he mused, regarding her with half-lidded eyes. "Math, of course, to figure the number of gallons and ponies and ships needed. And to accurately count the gaugers sneaking about the hills."

"And they must be able to count coin to the last penny," she suggested.

"But poetry, alas, they have little use for that."

"Poor Lucy! Will you tell her so?"

"I do not have the heart for it. You tell her."

She laughed, and Dougal reached out, touched her elbow. "Come with me."

"Where are we going?" She did not protest as he led her along the path ribboning between gorse bushes and trees.

"This will be a pleasant surprise, I hope."

"Are we off to see a troupe of fairies, or a pack of smugglers?"

"Which would you rather?"

"Both," she said. "The fairies for me, the smugglers for—"

"Surely not me. They would be reward for your brother, hey."

She frowned. "He is much on your mind, my brother."

"You have been more on my mind than he has. You and your safety. But he seems a decent fellow, and that sort of work can corrupt a good lad."

"That will not happen to Patrick."

"It could, and it has, to many good men before him."

She stopped to look up at him. "You truly believe he is in danger?"

"Aye, and you as well." Pausing beside her in the shadow of a thicket of trees, Dougal wanted to fold her into his arms, dispel her worry, make her feel safe. "Fiona," he murmured impulsively.

Her gaze searched his. "Aye?" she whispered.

"Uncle Dougal!" A high-pitched voice sounded. "Uncle! Wait!"

"Lucy?" He turned, seeing her. "What is it?"

The little girl ran toward him, dark hair like a flag behind her, its ribbon lost as she came forward looking panicked, waving her arms, spilling to her knees on the path, scrambling up again. "Uncle!"

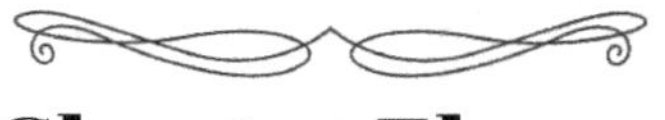

Chapter Eleven

"I WANT TO go over the glen with Annabel to her house," Lucy said, coming closer. She indicated the other little girl, waiting behind her.

"Is that all? You gave me a scare, lass."

"I am invited to have supper with Annabel and her mother, and to stay the night there."

"Are you asking me, or telling me? What about your studies?"

"Tomorrow is Saturday," Lucy said. "There is no school. We have no assignments. Isn't that so, Miss MacCarran?" Fiona nodded.

"Very well. Ask one of your great-uncles to walk you both there, and go straight to Annabel's house. Do not linger along the way," Dougal said sternly.

"Thank you! I will do that." Lucy smiled brightly, her dimpled expression reminding him keenly of his sister. "I told Annabel we would give her mother some of our fairy brew."

"Did you now," he drawled. "Then tell Maisie I said she can fetch you a small bottle and put it in a basket for you to take with you. Maisie is at the tower today, I think."

"Aye, she is cleaning and cooking. And I hope she has not put away my paper and pens to make things neat. I am writing a poem!"

"Go on, now." He waved Lucy onward, and she ran back to join Annabel. The little girls joined hands, chattering as they went up the hill.

"Lucy writes poems as well as reads them?" Fiona looked up at him.

"She loves poetry. She copies verses she fancies from the books, and writes her own too."

"You are a fine guardian, Kinloch. Some men would not have the patience for a child of that age."

"She is my ward, but I have come to think of her as my own. My sister has been gone three years." That said enough, to his thinking. The love and protectiveness he felt for his niece was strong, but it was not in his nature to talk about such things.

"Her father is gone too?"

"Aye," he said gruffly, without detailing the wooing and abandonment his sister Ellen had suffered. "My uncles and aunts lend a hand. There are many to care about her and watch out for her."

She nodded. "I can see that. What is fairy brew?"

He walked beside her. "A spirit traditionally brewed in the Highlands."

"Not made by fairies?"

He laughed, shook his head. "Not directly."

"My sister-in-law has a kinsman who makes a fairy whisky that has some kind of magic, so the family claims. They are secretive about it, though."

"You mentioned that Lord Struan married a MacArthur girl," he said casually.

"Elspeth MacArthur, aye. Her grandfather is Donal MacArthur, a weaver."

"Ah." Donal was a cousin on his mother's side, an older fellow than his uncles. That was yet another bond with Fiona MacCarran, but he was not about to reveal that he was the kinsman who delivered the fairy brew to the weaver.

"What is fairy whisky?" she asked again.

"Oh," he said, "simply a Highland whisky made in some households, according to very old recipes kept within families."

She tipped her head. "According to magical secrets handed down by fairies?"

He chuckled. "Not quite so special. A few flowers might be the difference."

"In whisky? You mentioned that another time, and I wondered about it."

"Flowers can flavor the water used in the brewing process— heather, primroses, buttercups, bluebells, and so on. The water has a certain character from the burn where it flows, and that can change and take on the flavors of its surroundings. Peat, flowers, grasses, wild garlic, and the kinds of rocks that the water flows over can affect the quality and taste of the water."

"I see. Is that what makes fairy brew, a certain flower or plant, or a kind of water? Is it illegal, this fairy brew, or just legendary?"

"Legendary, lass." He smiled. "Highland distillers pay careful attention to the many factors that influence the taste of the whisky. It is tradition and part of what sets Highland whiskies apart. We do not manufacture it merely for quantity but for quality. As for what is legal and what is not, that depends on the quantity produced. Every Highland household is permitted to distill up to five hundred gallons a year."

"That seems like quite a bit."

"Not when families consume it and share it, and store it to age it. Whisky can be kept in casks for years, and its flavor and quality will increase, unlike ale. Once it is bottled, the taste and quality are captured and held."

"The value increases with the aging as well," she said, nodding. "But fairy brew—such a romantic name! I might like to try some."

"And you such a practical lass, collecting rocks like a scientist," he teased.

She smiled. "Rocks fascinate me. They are so primeval and ancient, and they can have their own legendary character. I love hearing legends of fairies and such," she added. "I want to learn more about the tales of Glen Kinloch."

Dougal remembered Eldin's odd remarks about her, yet he sensed nothing unusual in her interest in local fairy stories, some of which involved Kinloch whisky and the fairy brew. He smiled, nodded, did not reply directly.

"Is that a clachan ahead?" She pointed toward the buildings visible beyond the bushes and trees where they walked. The path skirted a bend there and crossed a meadow to the cluster.

"It does look like a village," he agreed. "But it is the Kinloch distillery."

"I thought Highland stills were hidden away to keep them safe from revenue men."

"Some. This one is legitimate. There is no need to hide it."

"Are there many such stills in the area?"

Against his will, he thought of her gauger brother. "Why do you ask?"

"The night we met, the customs man said the laird of Kinloch could be held accountable for any illegal stills found on his lands if the owners were unknown."

"A new law, aye. And a devil of a thing it is."

"It seems unfair," she agreed.

"Along with that, the government lowered taxes on barley to discourage us from plying our trade."

"The free trade?"

"Not the free trade. The manufacture of it. Specifically, they are taxing the wort," he explained. "That is the mash created from boiling and steaming the barley. The wort, you see, is the heart of the whisky process. The steam from it simmers in a large copper pot and is channeled through copper coils to drip down and be caught. The distillation that is collected will become the whisky itself."

"So the wort is key to making the whisky? No wonder they tax that part of the process. But how does lowering it make a difference?"

"The boiled mash is taxed according to how much whisky

might be produced. We are obligated to report each time a wort is made from barley."

"I do not see how the government can expect that," she said, frowning.

"Just so," he replied. "It is part of the problem. Highlanders grow barley, use it for food, and sell it as grain. Only a portion of it is used to produce whisky, and not by all. Whatever we grow for our families and our livelihoods should be considered ours, with nothing owed to the government. Most Highlanders feel that way, I assure you. But lowering the wort tax means many more Highlanders can produce it, which eventually takes away the value of good Highland whisky. It is an underhanded way of making smuggling unnecessary."

"No wonder there is such tension between excise officers and smugglers."

"It goes even deeper. They do not show fair treatment to simple citizens or honor their rightful household production. Gaugers make a fee on each bottle they confiscate, so they are just as eager to take it as Highlanders are to hide it. Lower taxes on the wort makes whisky smuggling less profitable, and so the government assumes making it will no longer be worth the effort."

"Is it truly not worth making?"

"Do you want a Highlander's opinion?" He laughed. "At any rate, the king's men have the devil of a time enforcing any laws in the Highlands. Regulations that make sense in the city law courts are nearly impossible to enforce in the Highlands."

"And as the laird, you could be arrested for stills the revenuers find in Glen Kinloch, even if they are not your stills?"

"True. But Highland stills are well hidden. Many have been in place for generations. What my tenants produce is their concern, not mine. The law does not agree, so we make sure the stills are not found. Not all Highland whisky is illicit, I promise you," he added. "And more legal distilleries are opening every year, encouraged by the lower taxes. The new laws will help many to make a living from producing and selling legal Highland whisky."

"And if the laws decrease smuggling," she said, "those ventures will die out."

"Someday. So you see why we opened our Kinloch distillery, to make our very fine *uisge-beatha ghleann ceann loch.*" He touched her elbow. "Have you never seen whisky in the making? Come, let me show you."

AS THEY ENTERED a shady little glade, Fiona saw a tidy cluster of whitewashed buildings with neat slate roofs and doors painted in different colors. It looked more like a picturesque village than a busy enterprise. The path led to a wooden footbridge that crossed a burbling stream. All seemed quaint and peaceful.

"I thought Highland whisky was made in small copper stills," she said, looking up at Dougal MacGregor as he walked beside her. "The equipment here must be much larger than that. Surely you produce quite a bit here."

"We needed more buildings for a legal distillery and enterprise." He strolled with her over the wooden bridge. "Originally these were outbuildings for Kinloch Castle. Two hundred years ago, an old castle stood on the hill before the tower house was built," he explained. "That largest building was the stable, and the others were byre, granary, and bakehouse. They were abandoned once the tower came into use. My grandfather and father reclaimed them for the whisky."

On the bridge, Fiona paused beside Dougal and looked down over the railing. Water rushed over rocks to channel away, the sound swift, the moisture in the air refreshing. Two young men exited the largest building and waved at Dougal. They glanced curiously at Fiona and went on their way.

"It looks a flourishing place," she said.

"Busy enough." He seemed pleased and proud, Fiona

thought, his smile slight but genuine. Her brother had mentioned that there were hundreds of secret stills to be found in the Highlands, and casks moved by smugglers bold enough to manufacture and move whisky rather openly. The laird of Kinloch must be one of the bolder ones, she thought, to oversee such an organized business that included both smuggled and legitimate whisky.

She thought of the moonlit night when she had stood on a hillside watching Kinloch and a band of smugglers walk past with their ponies. *Fiona, go home,* he had said, *and lock your door.* A shiver went through her at the memory.

"What a rogue you are, Kinloch," she said quietly.

"Am I?" He tilted his head to look at her.

"Making whisky without apology, and smuggling it out of Scotland when you could make it legitimately."

He paused. "I brought you here to show you that I am not just a smuggler and a rogue. That I have dreams."

Revelation struck. She had been wrong. "Oh! I apologize. I thought you were combining your ventures to make large quantities here in the open, while smuggling it out. This is a licensed venture."

"Fully licensed." He chuckled. "But what a bold ambition—an enormous smuggling enterprise that we pretend is legal. We could plant more trees to hide the place."

She laughed ruefully. "The revenue officers would notice too much chimney smoke and activity here. You would have to show them the documents."

"Rest assured, every square inch here has been examined and approved. King George himself might be served Glen Kinloch whisky at court one day."

"The king asked for his favorite whisky when he visited Edinburgh last summer. There was quite a kerfuffle over it—he did not even realize he was asking for illegal spirits, and he seemed unaware his favorite brew came to London through smuggling. Some people were outraged. Others were amused."

"I heard about that. My cousin, Ronan MacGregor, is responsible for Glenbrae whisky, the king's favorite brew. A very fine whisky, I admit. It was originally delivered to the king in London, and he asked to meet Ronan in Edinburgh. There were—curious circumstances, from what we heard, but Ronan is a good man and it worked out well."

"Ronan MacGregor is Viscount Darrach now—he is your cousin? I saw him at one of the royal assemblies in Edinburgh. A very handsome fellow, all done up in Highland kit, looking like a true warrior. He put some of the other Highlanders to shame. Tartan peacocks, some said, but he was called handsome and beautiful."

He grinned. "We are a handsome lot, we MacGregors."

She smiled. "You are."

"And I have no doubt he looked the perfect Highlander, tall and strong and notable. But outshining others is never his intent. He is a quiet sort, is Ronan. A lawyer, bent on defending others in trouble. Then he was put upon himself. Arrested for smuggling, and nearly hanged for it."

"I heard some rumor of that. I do hope he came away unscathed. He was with a very pretty young lady, the daughter of a government official, they said."

"Truly! I wish them well. I must send word to say I am thinking of him. He suggested that I send some Kinloch brew to King Geordie in London for a gift. The king loves Highland whisky, which gives the Scots a good laugh. He does not seem to realize that every drop of his Highland whisky may have been smuggled to London."

"Do let me know if you have news of your cousin. I would like to know he fared well after the king's visit. As for your whisky, we have a family friend who could convey a bottle to the king if you like. He meets with him now and then."

"It would be difficult for anyone to reach King George with a new bottle of whisky, I would imagine."

"Not for Sir Walter Scott. I would be glad to ask for you."

"Indeed?" He cocked a brow. "You have impressive friends and kinsmen, Miss MacCarran. I am surprised you agreed to come to our wee Highland glen. You must be very busy in Edinburgh."

"I would rather be in this wee glen than anywhere, I think." She smiled, took in a breath. "Such fresh air, beautiful hills, and welcoming people." She waved toward the distillery buildings. "My brother told me to beware the laird of Kinloch, but perhaps he did not know you have a legal enterprise." And perhaps she was wrong about his other activities.

"My distillery was only recently approved by the government. It is possible he did not know about it."

"If your tenants also obtain licenses, that would put an end to smuggling." She would like to see danger removed for Kinloch and his glen. Not long ago, she had not known or cared. Now she did, very much.

"That would not happen quickly. Highland whisky is more expensive than Lowland whiskies and takes longer to make, as we produce it from malted barley, a longer and more careful process. It is superior to the cheaper grain whisky made in the south, which is more easily made. We must move our whisky out of Scotland to earn enough income to sustain the folk who make it. Many are losing their other means of livelihood, thanks to the clearings in the glens, when land is bought up and people dispossessed."

"I know. It is very sad." She shook her head. "And since Highlanders use the best ingredients in a careful process, the price will always be higher than the grain stuff."

"Aye. And it will come even dearer with more excise officers being sent up to the Highlands to find and destroy small stills and enterprises."

"And my brother among them. I feel I should apologize." She sighed. The more she knew about Kinloch, the glen, and the whisky enterprise, the more she understood his dedication. And the more he cared, the more she cared, too, now.

He looked at her for a long moment. "No need."

"Patrick worked in Edinburgh as a lawyer," she explained, "but he wanted adventure. So he accepted a post as an excise officer."

"He will find enough adventure here, and may he survive it. Why did you both come to this part of the Highlands?"

"My brother and I need to—" She stopped. She could hardly explain her grandmother's will and her true reason for coming here. "My brother James owns the Struan estate now, and we thought it would be nice to be close by."

"I wish someone had told Patrick he would do better in Edinburgh as an advocate. His adventure could come at a heavy price."

"It is dangerous, I know. And it worries me."

"I am sorry, lass. But these men can be a sorry bunch. The government pays them poorly but pays extra coin for every bottle and keg a gauger captures. So they scheme to betray Highlanders even when we follow the law, so long as they can confiscate bottles and barrels to put coin in their own pockets."

"You do not care much for revenuers."

"Gaugers killed my father," he said curtly. "He died for the price of the small kegs he carried on two ponies."

"I am sorry. Truly I am," she murmured, setting a hand to her chest, sensing in his quiet but brusque tone a hint of the sorrow and bitterness he must feel.

"The whisky he carried was legally made, not smuggled. They did not care."

She shook her head sadly. "Was it recently?"

"I was thirteen."

"Just a boy!" She saw his guarded expression alter for a moment, saw the vulnerable boy—then it shuttered closed. He wanted no sympathy or fuss, she realized. But she wanted him to know that she understood. "I lost my parents when I was young. I know how that feels."

He nodded. "I became laird of Kinloch that day. Since then, I have learned much. Most of it outside the schoolroom," he added wryly.

"You left schooling behind because of so many responsibilities," she said.

"I went to the glen school, and then to university for two years. My father wanted that. But I was needed here and came home. Come this way, Miss MacCarran." He took her arm to guide her over the bridge, their footsteps thudding over the planking. "We've lingered too long. The sun will set soon."

"I should like to see the distillery, if you will show me."

He gestured for her to precede him. "We spent last year repairing and expanding the place. We planned to rebuild the schoolhouse this spring as well. But the Lowland teacher arrived sooner than expected."

"So she did. I have not fit your plans from the start."

"You have not," he murmured.

She lifted her head as she detected a sharp, strong odor in the air, wafting from one of the nearby buildings. "That smell! It reminds me of the beer the servants made when we lived in Perthshire when I was a girl." The odor was distinct, like wet hay. She wrinkled her nose.

"The processes of making whisky and beer are the same, to a point," Kinloch answered. "What you smell now is the hot barley mash, being boiled down to produce the wort, from which the whisky will be distilled. It's not a pleasant smell. First the barley must sprout, so it is turned for days with shovels, then dried over peat fires, which will give the whisky a smoky flavor. Then the sprouted barley is boiled down to the wort, distilled and collected, and mixed with water from burns and streams. Finally it is set in casks to age. I will show you if you have time."

"I do. I mean to stay in Glen Kinloch a long while."

"So I gather." He tilted a brow, smiled. To one side as they walked, the water of the burn rushed and frothed, setting up a screen of sound. Fiona felt so drawn to the man, and so entranced by the place, that she sighed, wishing she could stay for a very long while.

But that reverie was broken when she heard a man shouting. She spun to look, as did Kinloch. Hamish MacGregor ran toward them, waving his arms.

"What is it?" Kinloch called.

"Fire!" Hamish shouted. "At Tom MacDonald's!"

Dougal MacGregor began to run. Fiona picked up her skirts and followed.

Chapter Twelve

FEET POUNDING, SKIRT hems lifted, Fiona ran behind Kinloch along the earthen lane leading between the distillery buildings. Seeing Hamish running toward them, Fiona hurried beside the laird, glad he had not tried to send her back—she would have come regardless.

"Hamish! What is it?" Kinloch asked as they reached him.

Hamish halted, catching his breath. "Fire," he repeated. "The black pot."

"Is anyone hurt?" the laird asked.

"None. But the smoke and flames can be seen far and wide. The gaugers might see it and come soon."

"Black pot?" Fiona asked, phrasing it in Gaelic, *poit dubh,* as Hamish had.

"A still," Kinloch answered quickly. Then he gestured. "You should go back."

"But I want to help," she replied.

"No need. Better you leave." He spoke curtly, taking her shoulder to turn her. "Please, go home now, back to the MacIans."

"She cannot go alone, Kinloch," Hamish said. "The gaugers will see the smoke and come up here to find an illegal still. The girl must not meet them on her own."

The laird glanced at Fiona. "You could go back to Kinloch House and wait there."

"I will not. I want to stay. Let me help. I can carry buckets of water."

"Fiona, *mo gràdh*," he murmured in soft Gaelic. *My dear.* She felt a thrill slip through her. "I want you to be safe."

"I am safe here," she replied, returning his steady gaze.

"Och, bring the lass and come along," Hamish said impatiently.

"Very well." Kinloch took her arm, his grip strong yet gentle. "But see you keep out of the way and safe. And promise you will not speak of this to anyone."

She frowned. "Still you do not trust me."

"Caution is best."

"And this from a man who likes a risk himself?"

"Some risks are safer than others," he said, turning with her as they hurried along after Hamish.

"Do you still think me a threat because of my kinsmen? None of us would bring harm to you or yours, Kinloch. I can speak for all of us."

"It is just that I do not trust easily."

"I pose no danger to you, Kinloch."

He did not look at her, walking quickly while she kept pace. "You are a danger to me all on your own, lass. I dare not trust myself near you. Do you know it?"

Fiona glanced toward him, seeing the profile, the sweep of dark hair, the guarded expression. What he said had a simple honesty that made her heart beat faster. "You need not be wary of me."

"*Tinneas-an-gradh-dubh,*" he said after a moment. "The black lovesickness is not easily cured. Hurry now. Hamish is well ahead of us."

Lovesickness. Her heart leaped. Rushing along with little time to think, she knew she had a touch of the same ailment. No easy cure indeed.

Where the path narrowed and wound through trees and up a slope, the laird of Kinloch touched her arm to guide her. The light was dim where the way cut up and then down the hill's angle, studded with roots and tangles of bracken. Stumbling, Fiona reached out to keep her balance. He took her hand, fingers warm and sure, and kept it in his. The clasping felt so good that she did not want to let go. He did not release her hand as he stretched out his free hand to push away overhanging branches as they passed through together.

"Hamish is far away now," she said. "Do you know where he is headed?"

"I do. Promise me you will not tell anyone what you may see." They left the shelter of trees for the open sweep of the glen floor.

He meant her brother, she realized. "You have my word. Why do we go this way? Crossing along the shoulder of the hill would be faster."

"Too open. We cannot risk being seen and leading gaugers to this place."

They reached the valley floor and stepped out into the glen. Approaching a narrow stream that cut through the valley floor, they crossed its rushing waters by stepping rock to rock. Dougal MacGregor took her hand again.

Beside them, the massive, rounded hills rose upward. Perched on the sturdy, rounded shoulders of the hills were a few cottages. Sheep scattered, grazing, along the slopes—herders and dogs had not yet brought them in, perhaps summoned away by the fire. Ahead, another stream rushed down through a rocky passage on the hill. Beyond the cluster of homes, pine groves thrust skyward in rich dark patches all along the hillside.

Above the trees, she saw the smoke, curling thick and dark, too much so for a home's chimney. It rose up from a great thicket of pines that crested one of the lower hills. A little below the pine grove, she saw Hamish in the distance, hastening upward and between the trees.

"There," Dougal said, pointing. He lengthened his stride, and Fiona hurried to keep up. Overhead, smoke billowed. She could smell its pungency growing stronger. As she ran, her bonnet ribbons loosened and her hat dropped to her shoulders, then blew away, skittering down toward the meadow. Gasping, she spun, but could not catch it.

Lifting her skirts to hurry after Dougal, who strode far ahead, she noticed small lights flitting over the glen and hillsides, like dust motes glimmering in sunlight, even as dusk gathered and firelight bloomed hot and bright. She ran on.

Ahead, she saw Hamish MacGregor with two other men. The laird joined them, then turned to wait for Fiona. The others, she saw as she approached, were her student, Pol MacDonald, and his father, Thomas.

"It is Neill's *poit dubh* on fire," MacDonald was saying.

"Is the lad hurt?" Kinloch asked.

"He is fine, and the fire is lessening now, thanking the Lord. But the hut is destroyed, and a good copper still has blown apart. We moved the casks away, but until the rest burns off, we can do nothing."

Dougal nodded. "Gaugers about?"

"Not yet, but there is a risk," Hamish said. "Thomas sent his older sons out to look around. We are off to examine what is left of the still."

They walked onward, Fiona hastening after, unsure she was welcome. Dougal slowed to fall into step beside her.

"Neill was testing the proof?" He directed this to Thomas MacDonald.

"He lit the sample, but it blew. Too strong," Thomas grunted.

"Your proofs are never too strong," Dougal said.

"It was Neill's own batch," Thomas said.

"Neill?" Fiona asked.

"My oldest brother," Pol said.

"Neill is safe," Thomas said, "and has learned the power of the whisky brew."

Hearing shouts ahead, the men hurried, Fiona with them.

Smoke rose anew above the pine trees. Something flashed among the trees, and she saw a narrow trail of flame snaking down the slope.

"Look!" she said, pointing. Dougal put out an arm to hold her back.

"The stream," he called to the others. "It's burning!"

Fiona cried out as she saw yellow flames licking furiously along the surface of the stream, the brightness whipping down the hillside like a dragon's tail.

Above that stream of fire, tiny round lights swirled in the air. Sparks, Fiona thought—but they were pale in color, not the hot gold of the fiery stream.

The men surged forward, and she followed.

FIRE DANCED UPON the flowing water in bright ribbons. Dougal slowed, seeing its downward course, awed for a moment by its fierce beauty and danger. Sparks flew all about, snapping in the air. He glanced up, concerned the trees might catch the flame too. So far the fire was staying close to the stream, but he had seen this sort of thing burst out of control before.

Men shouted, running down the hill toward them. He put out his arm again to keep Fiona at a safe distance. She stayed back, staring as they all did at the burning water. Others gathered along the banks as well.

"There is little we can do now," Dougal said. "It will extinguish on its own." Others murmured agreement. Beside him, Fiona coughed a little in the smoky atmosphere.

He touched her shoulder in silent concern. Soot darkened her cheek, she had lost her pretty bonnet, and the flames, far too close, reflected gold in the sheen of her dark hair. He wanted to send her away, but knew she would refuse. He liked that in her, a stranger yet to this community; he was glad to see the ease with which the others had accepted her presence here on this hill.

Hamish came near, waving a hand toward the flames. "Gaugers will arrive soon for sure. That light can be seen for miles."

"Neill must have dumped a fair amount of brew into the water," Dougal said.

"Is it whisky that burns there?" Fiona asked. She coughed again, waving her hand in front of her face, blinking as the smoky air stung her eyes. The odor of the burning was strong, and the air was hazy with smoke. Dougal coughed too.

"Aye. When whisky is poured into a stream," he told her, "it can catch a spark and burst into flame, and the stream will be covered in flames until the spirit burns out. In shallow water, like this stream, the fire can burn the length of the spill as it pours downward."

"A terrible and beautiful sight. Like the end of the world," Thomas said.

"It just looks like a waste of good whisky to me," Hamish said pragmatically.

"You have seen this before?" Fiona asked. Dougal and the other men nodded.

"Most distillers will make a mistake at least once that sets a stream burning like hellfire," Thomas said. "It is part of the risk. But do not be afraid, Miss MacCarran. You are safe with us. Just stay back."

"I am not afraid. Just—amazed to see this." Her gaze lingered on the bright dragon's tail of the burning stream.

Dougal glanced around while they spoke, taking account of those along the banks and the others among the trees. He knew each one—kinsmen, tenants, comrades, young Neill MacDonald, too. The lad stood alone at the top of the stream near the smoldering remains of the hut and his black pot still.

"I will have a word with Neill," he said quietly, stepping away, then turned back on a sudden thought. "Miss MacCarran, come with me, if you will." He wanted to keep her near him.

This night was fraught with too much risk.

She came with him, plucking her skirts free of the ground, neat boots and ankles, a quick and fit step, a strong and lovely woman—but he could not think about that now. Possibly he should never think on it again.

"Can I help in some way?" she asked, walking beside him.

"Just stay close while I talk to Neill," he replied. "You have seen more of our enterprise than you should have. I am sorry." He pushed his fingers through his hair, hoping he could rely on her silence. Hoping he truly could trust her. Certainly he wanted to—but the girl's brothers included a gauger and a viscount, and the lass was prone to taking notes as she wandered hills where smugglers roamed. He should not trust too soon but rather remain vigilant to protect his friends and the glen. His frown deepened.

"Why would Neill MacDonald pour whisky into the stream?" Fiona asked.

"He may have been testing a sample, and it poured out. Accidents happen too easily at that stage, since we use black powder and flame."

"Gunpowder?" She sounded surprised.

"Commonly used for proofing spirits, but it must be handled carefully. If the whisky is weak, the gunpowder will not ignite. If the whisky is the proper strength, it will burn clean and go out. But if the brew is too strong, it explodes."

"And if whisky is in the stream, it catches a spark."

"Aye. But Neill MacDonald is young and inexperienced as yet. Something similar happened to me when I was near his age." Dougal held up his left hand, splaying the fingers where a patch of small scars crisscrossed his palm. "I was lucky not to be blinded or killed outright."

"Oh, Dougal!" She touched his hand, smoothed her fingers over his palm. The feeling plummeted through him. He drew back his hand even as she spoke. "That must have been painful. Neill is fortunate, then."

"He is. If all goes well, the batch is proofed and sealed up in kegs to age. Sometimes it will be aged for years." He waved to Neill, who raised a hand. "But accidents can happen when proofing a strong new whisky."

"I wonder if he saw excise men coming, and poured it out into the stream."

"That can happen too. He might have poured out the proof in haste to avoid being caught with too much of it. Stay here, if you please, Miss MacCarran. I will be back shortly." *Fiona, mo gràdh,* he had said before, and nearly said more. Now he felt the need for caution. He stood too close to the edge, heart in hand, and must step back.

She coughed, setting a hand to her mouth against the smoke. He turned away.

As he approached Neill, the lad watched him, eyes wide in distress. Ash smeared his face, hair, shirt. The stream burned less fiercely here, sluicing past the charred hut, while thick smoke drifted on the breeze.

"I am so sorry, Kinloch," Neill said. "I am so sorry!"

Dougal patted his shoulder. "We all know the risks, lad. I am only sorry that you lost your whisky stores, and glad no one was hurt."

"I saw MacIntyre," Neill explained. "I was proofing, and the spark caught, and the fire began. I poured the brew into the stream quick as I could, but it caught flame and spread through the water."

"It is burning off now and will go out soon. Where did you see the gauger?"

"Coming from that direction." He pointed south. "When I ran to get water for the fire, I saw the signals out in the hills. The washing was spread out on the hillsides between here and the south end of the glen. I had not seen them earlier."

"Ah. The linens." Dougal knew, as they all did, of the simple system long used in the glen to alert others that excise men were in the area. Bedsheets would be spread hastily along the slopes as if drying and bleaching in the sun, a signal method that gaugers often overlooked. "How many customs men?"

"Three along the ridge of a far hill. Big Tam MacIntyre was with them. I could not mistake his size," he added.

"They may be nearby. If they come this way, there is no evidence of a still, hey. Just a fire in a storage building. Barley and other grains. Understand?"

"Aye. And our good copper still was destroyed," Neill said glumly. "Blew up. My father paid a good deal for that fine still and copper coil."

"It can be rebuilt and a new coil purchased. For now, hide away any pieces that survived the fire."

"Geordie has gone off to do that," Neill said, referring to one of his brothers. "I am sorry, Kinloch."

"I blew up my still when I was a lad. You will make more whisky."

Neill laughed ruefully and peered past him. "Is that the schoolteacher? Pol and Mairi like her very much. They talk about lessons at supper. They have never been interested in schooling before." He seemed relieved to talk about something else.

"Aye. She is a fine dominie for this glen." Dougal glanced over his shoulder and beckoned to Fiona, who walked toward them.

"Da says he hopes this one will stay for a while," Neill said. "He wants me to go to school too. But I am a man now, with no use for schooling."

"Age makes no difference in education, lad. Take what learning you can get, and you will be a better man for it." Neill nodded.

Fiona joined them, eyes red rimmed from the smoke. She held out her hand as Dougal introduced her to Neill. "I am sorry for your troubles," she said.

The lad shrugged. "As the laird says, we will build another still and make more whisky, and soon have a new batch."

"Good," she said. Dougal cocked a brow and smiled a little.

"My uncles and I will stay and help clear the debris as soon as it cools enough," he told Neill. "Miss MacCarran, the smoke is making you cough. You should go down the hill and home."

"I am fine. Neill, you should rest. Come away from here, lad." Fiona spoke calmly, touching the boy's arm. Neill seemed to relax.

The woman had a serenity about her, Dougal thought appreciatively, and a quiet, capable air that could bring peace to others. He felt that influence himself, he realized. When he was with her he felt good, solid, focused. He had seen her quiet strength the night she had approached the excise men, and saw it again tonight when she had not flinched or crumbled amid chaos and disaster. He was glad she had come with him.

"Miss MacCarran," Neill said, "it is not the time to ask, but perhaps I could attend your school? It will be a while before I have a still again. And it would please my father."

"You are more than welcome, Neill. Come to school whenever you like."

In that moment, Dougal realized how deep his dilemma had just become. He and his uncles agreed that the teacher must go. But each moment with her showed that it would be better for many if she stayed. Her pupils needed her.

He needed her.

Scowling against the thought, he quickly changed to a flat smile just as Fiona looked up. Tilting her head, she gave him a puzzled expression.

"I had best go to school," Neill said. "I am not much of a brewer."

"Everyone makes mistakes," Dougal said. "It will all come right again. Here is your father—we will leave you two to talk." He turned as Thomas came toward them. Saying his farewells, he took Fiona's arm as they left.

Although the stream had absorbed most of the burning fumes, sizzle and smoke lingered in the air and patches of flame still burned on the water and along the bank. Hamish, Pol, and others were stamping out small flames on the turf as Dougal and Fiona walked toward them.

She began coughing in earnest. Dougal rubbed her back, thumping gently, then dropped his hand away. "You need better air than this."

"The wind is clearing the smoke away—oh!" She gazed up, eyes wide. "Look!"

"What is it?" He peered upward, expecting to see smoke or flame.

"Those tiny lights, just there! I saw them earlier and thought they were sparks or a reflection. Do you see them?"

He saw them, but would not say so. He knew very well what they were. "I am not sure," he said carefully, astonished. Could she see them too?

"Could they be fireflies?" Her shoulder pressed his arm. "So lovely!"

Lovely indeed, he thought, but he was staring at her. She saw them, the fairy lights he had seen as a boy. She saw them too. His mind whirled. He had believed that he alone could see them, as his father had seen them too.

Glancing toward the lights that swirled and glittered like dabs of sunlight, he tilted his head. He had noticed them earlier in the glen, sparkling and spinning among the trees. Whether a warning or a lure, he did not know, but he had thought he was the only one aware of them, magical and mysterious, in the air tonight.

To be sure, he had not seen them often in his life. First with his father, who had explained that the tiny lights were visible only to a special few who could perceive them. They marked the presence of fairies, John MacGregor had said. They were not the fairies themselves, somehow, but signified they were close by, like guardians to that sort. The Fey themselves kept hidden, so legend claimed, and so his father had said. Dougal had seen them only a few times since then. Until now.

Yet Fiona could see them too. Dougal watched her, wondering. She smiled up at him. "Do you see them, there? What are they?" she asked.

"Sparks, or reflections from the fire or the sunset. It is growing late, Miss MacCarran. We should not linger here. Pol can walk you back to Mary MacIan's."

He took her elbow to guide her away from there, away from the Fey. They were calling to him after a long absence—and calling the schoolteacher as well.

What that was about, he could not begin to guess.

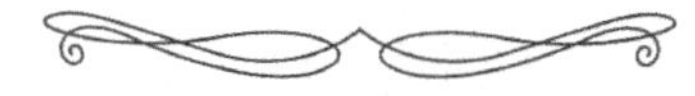

Chapter Thirteen

"P OL CANNOT WALK the lass home, he has gone with his brother to hide parts of the copper still," Hamish told Dougal. "And Miss MacCarran cannot walk the glen alone, with Tam MacIntyre out and about."

Dougal sighed, glancing at Fiona, who had insisted she was fine. Now she stood at the stream bank watching the last of the flames flickering into darkness. She was coughing, holding a kerchief to her mouth. "The smoke is affecting her poorly," Dougal said. "I will take her up to Kinloch House myself."

"I wonder if she could cook some supper," Hamish said.

"She is our guest, Hamish. If Maisie is there, we will ask her to stay and cook a meal, or we will fend for ourselves again. Lucy has gone to Helen MacDonald's for the evening, and we cannot have it said that the teacher stayed at Kinloch House with only the laird and his kinsmen there. Nor that they treated her like a servant and had her do the cooking."

"Then see if Maisie is about. But hurry back. We have much work to do here."

Dougal nodded. "Miss MacCarran," he called, walking toward her. The sunset poured golden light over her face and hair, and illuminated the gentle curves of her body. She was a vision of grace and beauty, so much so at that moment that Dougal stopped, forgetting his resolve to keep his heart distant.

"Mr. MacGregor?" She turned. "All is well?"

"For now. Come to Kinloch House for a bit to rest and re-cover from the smoke. I will take you. It is not wise for you to cross the glen alone just now."

"I thought you were needed here to help the MacDonalds."

"I will return here. A local girl helps us in the house. I will see if she can stay there the night. You and I would not be alone, if that worries you. My uncles and I will be away much of the night dealing with the damage from the fire. You are welcome to stay the night and we will be sure you have a companion."

"I would like to rest a bit. But I cannot stay. Mrs. MacIan would worry about me, especially when she hears about the fire."

"I will send someone to tell her you are safe at Kinloch House."

"I will go back to her cottage later this evening."

"Not on your own. Gaugers will be about."

"I am not afraid of them."

"You should be. They are unlikely to treat you with respect even if your brother is one of them. That would cause a problem for all of us, I promise."

She coughed again. "Very well. I will stay for a bit, and we shall see."

"Aye then. Come with me." Dougal escorted her out of the smoky woodland and down into the open glen. Taking that route was dangerous enough, he thought as he walked beside her. Though she coughed and sniffled, she kept pace. Glancing over his shoulder, he saw smoke rising and drifting above the tree line. Tam MacIntyre and his men would surely investigate it.

"This way." He walked with Fiona past the trees that hid the distillery and toward the broad path leading to Kinloch House. As they crossed a terrain rough with rocks and uneven ground, they came to a narrow burn. He took her hand to aid her over the water, stepping stone to stone. When they reached the other side, he did not let go of her hand, nor did she pull away. She accepted the support and comfort of clasped hands even once it was unnecessary.

She glanced up. "The lights," she said. "I see them again, there. How odd."

"Just the sunset." He did not look, only tightened his fingers over hers.

THE MOMENT SHE entered Kinloch House, climbing the few steps to its worn oak entry door, Fiona felt at home. Until now she had seen only the crumbling exterior of the tall peel tower, formed by two rectangular sections constructed to form an L-shape. The entrance opened into a stone-floored foyer, with a curving stone stair to the left and to the right, several doors along a corridor.

Sunset light spilled into the hall from windows along the turning stair, turning whitewash and wood to a rosy gold. Once inside, she saw small rooms along the corridor furnished with old, shabby pieces, worn patterned rugs, scarred wood floors. The entry walls were paneled wood, with other walls whitewashed or painted in earthy tones. All seemed simple, worn, comfortable, and inviting.

"It's lovely," she told Kinloch. Just then two large hounds careened around a corner and loped forward so fast that Fiona stepped back. Kinloch took her arm.

"Steady," he said, and she was not sure if he spoke to her or to the dogs—tall and gray, the sort of noble beasts she had seen in old portraits. Despite their majestic appearance, they were clumsy gluttons for their master's affection as he rubbed their heads and shoulders vigorously. She did, too, laughing when the dogs butted against her seeking more petting and licking her hands.

She coughed again, for the irritation in her throat had not yet cleared. Kinloch reached out to pat her back and rub her shoulder. Warmth flowed through her, wonderful and indulgent. She sighed, rolling her head, feeling a little like one of the dogs begging for his touch and affection. As his hand briefly comforted her shoulders and neck, Fiona wanted very much to turn into his arms.

But he dropped his hand away and gave the dogs his attention again. "This is Sorcha and Mhor," he said. "They are useless creatures, but we love them. Let me show you the house. There is not much to it. A simple place, and very old."

She followed him, the dogs bumping between them as they turned a corner, and looked around. "This is a lovely place!"

"Do you think so? It is just two upright towers with a turning stair between them, and a few rooms off to the sides. Here is the parlor." He gestured.

Fiona peered inside the small room, with its pale walls, bare planked floor, a worn Oriental rug. It looked well-used, with a settee covered in faded-green damask, a red wing chair, an old table with two wooden chairs, and a stout Jacobean cupboard under a window. The fireplace crackled with flames and the musky scent of peat bricks. The table held a stack of books, and a child's toys occupied the floor in a corner of the room. A modest chamber by many standards, but so cozy and inviting in its simplicity that Fiona longed to sink onto the threadbare settee, pick up a book, and relax. She turned away with Dougal as he crossed the hall.

"The dining room," he said. Here, a long table and several chairs sat on a shabby rug and corner cupboards were crammed with mismatched porcelain. A fire flickered in the hearth and the room filled with golden sunset light—another cozy, shabby, inviting room, and she longed to sit and rest there. But Kinloch beckoned her along the corridor.

The kitchen had whitewashed stone walls, an arched fireplace, a jumble of cupboards, and a long, heavy worktable. On the hob, a kettle of soup simmered, savory and enticing. Fiona felt so hungry that she licked her lips and hoped her guide would invite her to eat.

"You may like to see the study," he said. He seemed so eager to show her the house that Fiona followed, glad to see the love and pride he had in his home. Up a few stone steps to a snug room with a low ceiling, its walls lined with shelves crammed with an untidy, extensive collection of books. Books and papers were piled on the central table and on a narrow desk in a corner by a window. Two wing chairs held stacks of large ledger books.

"I do accounts here," he explained. "Rents, livestock, the distillery, and so on."

She nodded. "It is a wonderful room. I would like to look at the books in your collection someday, if I may."

"Anytime. I believe Maisie, the girl who helps, is still here, and I smell supper in the kettle downstairs. She usually cleans rather than cooks, so we are in luck. You should get something in you." He led her down the steps to the foyer again. "It is not a large castle," he explained as they went, sounding apologetic. "Above this level, there are bedrooms and a wee room Lucy calls her parlor. The place is very old, in places falling to bits. I am sure you are used to finer."

"Not at all. I like it very much." Fiona smiled. The place felt warm and welcoming and somehow just familiar. As they reached the foyer again, one of the deerhounds trotted toward her, nudging at her hand to be petted, and she obliged.

"Kinloch House began as a castle. A peel tower," Dougal explained. "Two block towers placed to form an L or a Z—the design provided good protection centuries ago, defense against cattle reivers or enemy clans, and sometimes king's men. We also have a priest's hole, which my father converted to a storage room."

"How fascinating to grow up in a place like this."

"I suppose. We even have a ghost or two, and visits by the fairies as well, so they say." He shrugged, smiled.

She lifted her brows, pleased. "Fairies? Has anyone seen them?"

He shrugged. "As a boy, I thought I saw them now and then. Imagination," he added with a laugh. "The house is over three hundred years old now, and things always need repair. Some days

I think the whole thing will fall down around our heads. But it has always been a good home for our family," he finished.

"I can tell," she said, smiling. Sighing, rubbing her arms, she felt relaxed, reassured, wholly welcome in the house he loved. "I feel at home, and I have only just arrived."

"They say the fairies of Kinloch decide who is welcome, and who is not." He tilted his head, looking at her. "They seem to approve of you."

She smiled widely, brightened, forgetting the discomfort in her throat and chest. "I would love to know more about Kinloch's fairy legends. My grandmother wrote books about Highland lore and loved fairies especially. My brothers and I heard many tales."

"Then you know more fairy legends than I could tell you."

"I think there are more in this glen than you let on," she murmured.

"Aye so?" His gentle smile hid his thoughts. "You are here to rest, so let us see to that. Warm yourself by the hearth in the parlor now, and of course, you may use the library if you like. The collection is modest but excellent. And you are certainly welcome to stay the night in a guest room. And I will ask Maisie to stay tonight as well."

"Thank you. But I do not want to be any trouble."

"None at all. You should not be out in the glen until the customs officers have gone, and should not walk back to Mary MacIan's just yet. Even if your brother is with the excise officers, lass," he added quietly, "I will feel better knowing you are safe here."

She caught her breath, wondering suddenly if she were safe near this man. The danger he presented was a different sort, and she felt too willing, too tempted, to be near him. "I know you must go back to the hill, but will you be here tonight?"

"Perhaps not until morning. It depends on the work to be done. Off to the parlor with you, Miss MacCarran. I will find Maisie." He gestured toward the room and turned away, boots echoing on stone as he went up the steps in search of the housemaid.

In the parlor, Fiona wandered about, studying the portraits hung on the walls, including a beautiful red-haired woman, and a handsome, dark-eyed man with a striking resemblance to Dougal. She peered closely at a cluster of small, enchanting landscapes and lake scenes in gilt frames. Then she sat, adjusting pillows to lean back on the settee. The fire burning low in the grate gave off warmth and the sweet musky smell of peat. Coughing again, she felt the tickle of it beginning to ease. Kinloch House had a curiously healing influence, as if it were her own home. Closing her eyes, she sighed.

Soon, hearing footsteps, she looked up to see a young woman carrying a silver tray holding a teapot and porcelain dishes. She was plump and pink cheeked, with soft coppery hair spiraling out from under a white cap. Her apron was wrinkled and stained, her blue gown patched at the hem, and she did not curtsey or defer, as a Lowland serving girl would have done. She smiled, her expression so friendly that Fiona instantly smiled in response.

"I am Maisie MacDonald. The laird said to fetch you some tea. Here it is, with oatcakes, butter, and rowanberry jam, all we had this day. Not expecting guests," she added, and Fiona heard a slight reproach in it. "There is soup in the kettle, should you wish that too."

"Thank you, Maisie. I am Fiona MacCarran, the schoolteacher."

"Oh aye, Miss, everyone in the glen knows who you are!"

Fiona smiled. "Are you kin to the MacDonalds who live up the hill?"

"Thomas and his? Aye. They had much trouble tonight. All in the glen will work together to help them."

"Good." Fiona looked toward the door. "Is the laird still here?"

"He left to help my cousins. Oh, what a terrible night!"

Fiona agreed, ignoring the pang of disappointment she felt knowing Kinloch was gone, even though she had expected it.

Maisie filled a blue china cup with steaming tea and handed it to her. "Thankfully no one was hurt in the blaze."

"Aye, though losing the building and so much whisky is a hardship for them. But they have a good store of it." Maisie frowned as Fiona coughed again. "Your breathing is still irritated from the smoke, I think."

"It was very thick on the hillside, and bothered me, but it will clear soon."

"My mother had a good remedy for coughs—whisky with honey and hot water. Will you take a wee dram of it? Some ladies think it improper, but whisky is very good for the health of the body. Many Highland ladies take *uisge beatha* every evening—and some more often than that." She grinned.

"Thank you," Fiona said, feeling another tickling cough. Her voice was growing hoarse when she spoke again. "Sometimes my nurse gave me a whisky and honey remedy when I was a child in Perthshire."

"Perthshire, is it? Very good, Miss. You are part Highlander, for all that you came up from the Lowlands. Will you be staying the night, then?"

"Perhaps I will." She made up her mind as a glance out the window showed that the sky was already dark. "Kinloch extended the invitation, and I am a bit tired. Can someone bring word to Mrs. MacIan, so she will not worry?"

"The laird said he would send a lad to do that."

Fiona nodded and sipped, the tea soothing her throat. Noticing that her garments still smelled of smoke, she brushed at her skirts. "I wonder if I could wash up," she said.

"I will prepare a bath for you, with a good soap that my mother makes from lavender and heather bells. If you do not mind me saying so, you do smell badly of the char." Maisie wrinkled her nose.

Fiona laughed, not used to such frankness in serving girls; her great-aunt Lady Rankin would never have tolerated an opinionated maid in the household. But Fiona found Maisie charming, friendly, and not at all rude. When the girl left the room, Fiona heard one of the dogs barking elsewhere in the house. She set down her teacup to walk to the window to peer out.

In the gloaming, looking across the fields surrounding Kinloch House, she saw a man running, and recognized Dougal MacGregor—the rhythm of his stride, the set of his shoulders, the dark banner of hair were etched in her mind. Then she realized he was not heading for the slope that led to the burned-out still.

Instead, he was going in the opposite direction, taking a slope that would take him to the mountainside where she had first met him.

She frowned, watching, wondering where he was going.

LATER, MAISIE LED her upstairs to the guest room on the uppermost floor, following the stone turning stair up to the fourth level, past wide landings that opened on to other chambers. The uppermost bedchamber, small and snug, had a beautiful, aged simplicity in its sturdy poster bed hung with pale brocade curtains, a highly polished table, an ancient ironbound trunk, a threadbare patterned carpet, and a narrow-arched window set with stained glass above the lower casement. The furnishings hinted at generations of past wealth come to the genteel poverty common to so many Highland aristocratic families after the years of rebellion had changed life in Scotland in so many ways.

That sense of better days long past seemed everywhere in Glen Kinloch, she thought. Thanking Maisie, she shut the door and turned, brushing a hand over the bedcover, going to the window to gaze out at the lowering night sky.

And she shook her head in silence, wondering how she could ever satisfy her grandmother's request to marry a wealthy Highland laird. That was an ironic expectation—many Highlanders had suffered in the past few generations, with fortunes lost. Nor would she consider wealth when contemplating marriage. She would far rather have a caring husband and the comfort of a loving home. A home very much like this one, she thought.

But Lady Struan's demands interfered with her dreams. The inheritance would not come to the MacCarran siblings unless they met outlandish terms. James had been lucky. Chance had brought him exactly what Grandmother had wanted for him.

Fiona doubted she could ever be that fortunate. She would rather marry a proud, humble man like Kinloch, wealthy or not. Despite that he was a rogue and a smuggler, she knew at heart he was a good man—and charismatic, mysterious, fascinating, at times simply infuriating. And she only longed to be in his arms, craved the searing, unexpected passion she had tasted too briefly with him.

If Lady Struan had asked her, Fiona would have said she wanted love and adventure more than wealth and social status and a staid, safe existence. She wanted honesty, vibrancy, passion for life.

Sighing, she turned away from the gathering darkness and went to the door. Not tired yet, keyed from the evening's events, she decided to go to Kinloch's little library to read for a while. Heading back down the stairs, she found the door on the second level that Kinloch had shown her earlier. It stood open and waiting.

Had she not already been smitten with Kinloch House and its laird, she would have fallen in love the moment she had seen his library. A few good books, he had said. She laughed softly as she strolled past the full bookshelves. Glad to find a glowing lantern there, and three blazing candles in pewter holders on the table, she turned to look more closely at the books.

The room was fitted with bookshelves, floor to ceiling around the walls and the window opposite the door. The low ceiling had painted wooden beams, peeling and quite old. The shelves were crammed with books—a thousand or more on the shelves, interspersed with small treasures—paintings, figurines, colored glass bottles and silver flasks, even a delicately painted world globe. An oak table took up the center of the room, its surface scattered with papers and books. A wing chair in faded red was angled by a window, the table beside it piled with another untidy stack of books.

The room seemed to echo the presence of a man who was highly intelligent and curious, and not particular about orderliness. Fiona smiled to herself, dragging her fingers along the shelves, delighted with what she found: Ovid, Boccaccio, Chaucer, Shakespeare, Milton; an encyclopedia series; scores of books on science, agriculture, practical farming, and domestic matters; handwritten journals bound in leather and tied with ribbon, marked with dates along the spines, likely household accounts. There were works of poetry, too, including Spenser's *Faerie Queene* and Percy's *Reliques of Ancient Poetry*, tucked alongside novels, nature studies, and travel narratives.

He had said the collection was modest; it was also excellent. Works by native Scottish writers filled a few shelves, including Burns, Hogg, MacPherson, even an old edition of Blind Harry— and several of Sir Walter Scott's works as well, poetry and novels. The author had not yet publicly admitted to writing those anonymous books, although Fiona and her family, being good acquaintances, knew the authorship. Yet *Ivanhoe* and others were grouped with Scott's well-known poetry as if the library's owner either knew or suspected what else Scott had written.

One end of the table had a stack of paper with pens and inkpots, along with a slim red leather volume of *The Lady of the Lake*, several of its pages marked with torn slips of paper. Fiona flipped through the pages, noticing pencil lead underlining phrases: the quiet tracks of a thoughtful man who claimed disinterest in his education, yet cared about writing, books, and poetry.

So MacGregor of Kinloch, smuggler and rogue, very much favored books, poetry, fiction, and book knowledge of every sort. Smiling to herself, bemused, Fiona noticed writing on one of the pages, and picked it up.

A fat, childish hand script had earnestly copied some lines from one of Scott's collections of old Scottish verse:

O hush thee, my babie, thy sire was a knight,
Thy mother a lady, both lovely and bright;
The woods and the glens, from the towers which we see,
They are all belonging, dear babie, to thee.

This was Lucy's handwriting, she realized, as intent and stubborn as the girl. Also on the table was an open wooden box with a half-finished piece of embroidery showing stubby trees, brown hills, a gray castle all rendered in threads, and a few words partially stitched. This had to be Lucy's work too.

Something stirred inside of her, touched her heart, as she looked at the things, seeing more than a jumble of books, papers, inks, embroidery and needles. She saw love, sensed patience, companionship, and dedication. The uncle and niece spent time here quietly, peacefully learning, reading, sharing.

No wonder Lucy was convinced that she did not need school. She had a caring and competent tutor in her uncle. Realizing curiosity had taken over, Fiona stepped back. Comfortable as she felt here, this was their home, not hers. And she wished, suddenly and keenly, she was part of it.

Choosing a book from a shelf, she settled in the chair by the window and opened Ramsay's *Tea Table Miscellany*. The collection of songs and poems was interesting, but after the long day, she soon felt drowsy. Closing her eyes, she sighed, imagining herself sitting at the library table with Dougal MacGregor, leaning on his shoulder as he read aloud to her.

And she imagined touching his hair, feeling his kiss on her brow. She daydreamed that Lucy was there too, seated nearby, stitching on her little sampler and listening while her uncle read.

Smiling, eyes closed, Fiona felt such love and contentment that she let it spin onward, onward, into sleep.

INSIDE THE CAVE, seated on a rounded boulder, Dougal wiped sweat from his brow with his forearm and surveyed the interior. Lantern light flickered over irregular rock walls, and shadows angled from stacked whisky kegs that had been produced over many years. Some held whisky his father had made years back. Those, the most valuable, were set apart from the others.

Not long ago, over a hundred casks had been stacked together in this cave, carried in groups and batches over two decades to add to the store. Twenty-seven kegs remained, with twelve more outside, waiting to be brought in and added to the rest. For now, Dougal sat to catch his breath and contemplate his plan.

Tonight, he and his kinsmen had moved casks from the burned-out MacDonald still to the cave for safe storage. He had sent men and ponies down the mountain three times that night. His comrades had descended the hills like ghosts, silent, rhythmic, grim, and wary. Unlike ghosts, they carried glowing lanterns ready to be shuttered along with loaded pistols.

Swiftly they had moved some of the MacDonald whisky to the upper cave, while also moving some of the older Kinloch whisky to caves closer to the loch. Those secret recesses were known only to a few residents of the glen.

He went to the entrance and stood looking out over the night-dark hills. Here he overlooked the same slope where he had first seen Fiona MacCarran strolling with her brother while she collected rocks for her studies. Dougal was still uncertain if she and her brother had been innocently exploring or spying out the area that day. If the excise men were to learn the location of this cave and its hidden cache, let alone find the lower caves, there would be hell to pay.

Thinking of Fiona, he crossed his arms as if to shore himself against the temptation of her, and fixed his gaze on the dark and sparkling loch visible below a fringe of trees. From west-facing windows in Kinloch House, one could also see the loch and the hill where he stood. If Fiona were awake, if she looked out a window just as he looked out of this cave, they would be watching each other without realizing it. He wondered if she thought of him now, as he thought of her.

A rush of desire sank through him, hot and heavy, as he thought of her in his house tonight. Part of him hoped she was waiting up for him. What a rare joy it would be to have a woman at home who waited for him, prayed for him when he went out at night, who loved him. What a delight and a privilege if she were there to talk to him, to listen and care. And what a deep comfort and passionate reward if she willingly opened her arms to him, to his love.

Sighing, he rubbed a hand over his face. What the devil had happened to him since Fiona MacCarran had come to his glen? He did not need a woman in his life just now. He had chosen loyalty to kin and friends over personal happiness, and he was content. He had the affection of his kinsmen, the friendship of his tenants, and the honor of raising a wee girl who loved to share stories and drawings with him.

Content enough for any man, yet lately he wanted more. He had always wanted a family of his own, and being around Fiona had only made that longing more clear. He felt a tumult of desires and dreams, but by the time he sorted them in his mind and heart, the girl would be gone from the glen, and it would be too late for him.

Footsteps crunched on rocks nearby, and Dougal straightened, whirled to see a tall man approaching.

"Kinloch!" Reverend Hugh MacIan smiled a greeting as he came closer, and gestured to the kegs stacked outside the cave. "Nearly done with the storing and stacking, then?"

"Almost. Those are the last of Thomas's casks."

"Aye, good. What of the rest of your cache?"

"Some of the lads have taken a number of kegs down to the lochside. Once Thomas's kegs are inside here, it is enough work for one night, I think."

"More than enough. And too much movement in the hills can catch attention we do not want, hey. We cannot risk having the lower caves discovered. How much have you left of what was here?"

"A good bit has gone down to the loch," he said vaguely.

"Ready for shipping when the time comes. I see," Hugh said.

Dougal nodded, but did not want to share detail. He trusted Hugh, but was reluctant to share accurate numbers with anyone but his uncles. He kept count of his whisky in his head and in journals tucked in his library. And, unknown even to his closest kinsmen, he never kept his whisky all in one place. On his father's example, he stored it here and there, moving it around from caves high in the hills to down by the loch, and kept some of it hidden under the floors of his house. *It does not do,* John MacGregor had told his son, *to trust everyone, lad.*

"Sounds efficient. Good," Hugh murmured. "The sale will be made soon, and the glen will benefit." He took a leather flask from his pocket and offered a drink to Dougal, who swallowed and handed it back with a grimace for a burn and a smile for the rest.

"MacDonald whisky," Dougal said. "Not bad, but newer stuff."

"It tastes of smoky peat. I like it," Hugh replied.

"Thomas and Neill add peat from the north glenside when they toast sprouted barley over the fires," Dougal said. "It gives it a fine flavor, though this batch has not aged long enough."

"Glen Kinloch whisky is more elegant, I think," Hugh decided, then took another swig from the flask.

"Kinloch brew has a hint of flowers," Dougal agreed. "This year, the burnside was thick with primroses before we filtered it through. In three years' time it will be an excellent whisky, and better the longer we keep it. When we can, I like to take the water from higher up the burn in late summer when the heather blooms. It lends a honey flavor. But the spring primroses give the brew a light and subtle taste."

"Heather whisky—that reminds me," Hugh said. "The twelve-year batch. Have you set aside casks for Lord Eldin?"

"I have not yet decided if I will sell to him."

"The fellow can be cold and unpleasant to deal with, aye, though he has basic decency, I suppose. The money he offers could rescue the whole glen from the devastation that has plagued too many other regions."

"Aye, it might be enough to buy back the deed, but even that is not enough to save Glen Kinloch in the future. I want a better guarantee. I want all the deeds back, signed in perpetuity to me and my heirs. That will take more than Eldin offers."

"A fine dream, Kinloch. Do not let it go."

"Just so," Dougal said.

FIONA WOKE FROM a dream that felt so dear and intimate that she clung to it—the sense of Dougal's arms around her, his hands on her like heaven, playing over her body like a harper caressing strings. The heat of it lingered as she woke and swiftly vanished as she moved. Sighing, seeing the room had gone dim, she reached to the table beside her, looking for flint and candle.

Hearing footsteps on the stone stair, she glanced up. Maisie entered, holding a glass in one hand and a lantern in the other.

"I brought you whisky and honey," the girl said, setting the glass on a table. She set the lantern down, lit a candle, and turned. "Miss MacCarran, the laird asked me to stay with you, but my brother just arrived. He says our Da is doing poorly."

"Oh dear," Fiona said, sitting up as the girl spoke. "Was he hurt?"

"He was helping to fight the fire but was overtaken by smoke, like you. I want to go to him, but I promised Kinloch I would stay with you. Try the warmed whisky, do."

"Thank you. But Maisie, you must go to your father." Fiona picked up the glass to sip the concoction. The warm remedy slid down her throat with sudden, spreading heat that made her cough at first. Then she felt her chest begin to clear as her breathing opened.

"Helps the lungs and throat, see," Maisie said approvingly. "My father needs it too, but my brother is a dimwit and may not think to make it for him. My mother is no longer with us, you see, so I do for both of them."

"Please do not stay on my account, I am fine!" One of the dogs came through the open door, padding to her side to nudge at her hand. Fiona stroked the gray head. "I have Sorcha and Mhor to protect me."

"Mhor here is a great coward," Maisie said wryly. "Sorcha is the braver one. Fine then, if you feel better, I will leave. Your bath is filled and hot. I set a blanket over it to keep the heat until you are ready."

"Thank you. I could use a bath."

"Your room is ready, as you saw. I keep a clean house, though the laird and his uncles are a wretched lot to tidy after sometimes. The tub is in the kitchen, Miss. I would not drag buckets of hot water up those wicked steps for anyone, meaning no offense."

Fiona smiled. "Is the kitchen private enough for a bath?"

"It is. They are all gone and away 'til morning, I think. So much to be done out there." Maisie sighed. "Set the dogs outside the door to guard if you like. There's soup and porridge in the kettles," she went on. "I do not always cook an evening meal, and the lads are way to the fire tonight. They are often out on other nights making runs until dawn. But I thought tonight you might like something, and they can eat in the morning when they return—" She stopped, shrugged. "I will go, if you truly sure you are fine."

"I am, thank you." Fiona stood. If Dougal MacGregor and his kinsmen were making runs of a night, surely that meant smuggling. "Will I see you tomorrow?"

"I will stay with Da for a bit. I left some clean garments for you in your bedchamber." At the door, she turned. "Miss, please stay inside tonight. It is always wise to stay inside when the moon is out, and the sky is light, and wise to stay inside when the laird is out as well." She turned and left, footsteps light on the stairs.

Fiona looked down at Mhor, curled at her feet, resting his head on his paws. "What shall we do, sir? I wonder what your master is up in the evenings. Such secrecy," she murmured. "I wish he trusted me better. I would not tell."

The dog thumped his tail as if in agreement.

While she sipped the rest of the whisky, she picked up a book on the side table and read a bit little by candlelight. James MacPherson's *Ossian* was a stirring but controversial collection of ancient Celtic tales; she remembered her brother William talking about it once. Though a pragmatic physician, William was fascinated by ancient myths and legends.

And she was intrigued to find the book and so many others in the keeping of a whisky smuggler who claimed little interest in such things.

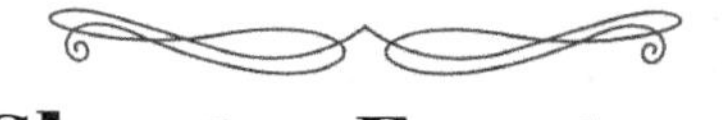

Chapter Fourteen

FTER A WARM, soothing bath while the dogs slept by the door, Fiona dried herself with a linen towel and then pulled on the things Maisie had left for her—a man's large, loose shirt for a nightgown, and a long dressing gown of dark-red brocade. Her own things needed a good airing, still smelling strongly of smoke. But she was glad to have washed the cling of smoke from her hair and skin with the lavender soap Maisie had provided.

The brocade robe carried the scent of the man who had worn it before her, a drift of pine, spice, a hint of woodsmoke that reminded her of Dougal MacGregor. She drew it snug about her, comforted by the faint aroma. Rubbing her wet hair with the towel, she was reluctant to leave the bathwater for someone to empty in the morning, but she saw no bucket with which to do it herself.

After a quick meal of soup and porridge, she noticed that the simmering kettles had cooked down a bit. Aware that the MacGregors might be hungry when they returned later, she searched and found root vegetables, barley, and seasonings in the pantry, and took a little time to chop and add vegetables to the soup with a bit of water. As the kettle simmered anew, she noticed that the night sky through the window showed inky black now. The hour was quite late, but the bath and her brief nap earlier had revived her. Instead of going upstairs to sleep, she carried a candle to light the way to the small library as the deerhounds trailed behind her.

Exploring the shelves, she found a volume on natural physics and geological sciences, and settled down to look for information about ancient strata and fossils. Though she was not the dedicated geological scholar that her brother James was, the subject fascinated her. She was looking forward to another chance to walk the hills in search of more discoveries.

Besides, she reminded herself, walking about the hills was essential just now. Lady Struan's will required that she make sketches of fairies for her grandmother's book, which James had been asked to edit. Unsure how to supply such drawings, Fiona hoped that sketches of Highland hills, flora and fauna, would do. Without a doubt, the lady's eccentric will was causing a kerfuffle for her grandchildren, but they would each find a way to meet its demands; there was no other choice.

Stepping over the dogs curled snoring at her feet, she re-placed the book on the shelf and searched through other titles. With a delighted gasp, she recognized a slim volume as one of her grandmother's own books, *Fairy Tales of Scotland and Ireland*. Remembering the book from childhood, she sat in the red wing chair to read.

She had brought the glass with a little whisky and honey left, and swallowed its comforting liquid heat as she read about fairies and pookahs. As she set the glass down, the dogs woke, leaping to their feet, woofing loudly.

Startled, Fiona missed the table, and the glass tilted and crashed to the floor. As the dogs tumbled eagerly out of the room, loping down the stone step, she heard booted footsteps somewhere below and a deep voice greeting the animals. Heart hammering, she stood and went to the library door to hear a deep, resonant male voice calmly addressing the dogs.

Dougal MacGregor.

His voice faded as he walked away with the dogs, perhaps to the kitchen. Not eager to be caught improperly dressed, raiding the library, with broken glass and whisky on the carpet, she hastened to pick up the shards and mop the spill, picking up the glass bits. But she had nothing to contain them, and had to set them down again. Looking for something to help clean up the mess, she pulled open drawers in a side cupboard, finding only paper, ink, and brass seals. Turning, she gasped.

Dougal MacGregor stood in the doorway, bowl in one hand, spoon in the other, leaning a shoulder against the doorjamb. He regarded her silently as he ate a spoonful. His hair was damp, curling along his brow and framing the strong column of his neck. He wore shirtsleeves and a wrapped plaid with knee stockings, without shoes. He smiled.

"You changed your clothes," she blurted.

"So did you," he said, lifting a brow.

Fiona pulled the robe closer. "I bathed and changed to be rid of the smoke."

"As did I. Thank you for leaving the bathwater. You look very nice in my things, Miss MacCarran." He took another spoonful of soup. "This is excellent," he went on. "Too good to be Maisie's work. Most of her soups are mush by the time we eat. She tries, bless the lass, and but for her, we are left to our own attempts. Did you make this?"

"I added some to what she prepared just to extend it. I am glad you like it."

"Cooking is a rare and welcome skill here at Kinloch House. Ever since Hamish's wife Jean stormed off and left, we have longed for good food."

"Stormed off?"

He shrugged. "Now and then she and Hamish go round about his smuggling. She wants him safe at home making legitimate whisky. I cannot blame her for it." He smiled. "But Hamish loves the free trade as much as he loves Jeanie. She will be back, so we hope. I thought you would be asleep by now," he added.

"I could not sleep and came in here to read. But I must apologize for breaking a glass." She pointed toward the shards on the floor, and pulled the robe tighter when it gapped open. "Maisie gave me some whisky. I hope the glass is not an irreplaceable piece. I could not find a cloth to clean the carpet—"

"It is a small thing and no matter," he murmured, coming into the room. He set down the bowl and unfolded a cloth that he held beneath it. "Let me help."

"I can do it. Thank you." Fiona took the cloth and knelt to wipe the carpet and pick up the shards. She realized her hands were shaking—his unexpected arrival, his nearness, whatever magic radiated from him, flustered her. When a sharp point of glass stuck her fingertip, she winced.

Dougal reached down for her hand, turning it in his to examine her bleeding finger. "That needs a bandage."

"It will heal," she said, rising to her feet, her hand in his. As he bent and she stood, their heads knocked audibly. "Oh!" She touched her forehead, embarrassed.

"Let me see." He brushed his thumb over her brow, sending shivers through her that erased the ache and caused other sensations. His fingers slid down to cup her cheek, lingered, traced to her shoulder.

Slowly, Fiona touched his forehead where he had bumped it against her. His dark hair felt cool and silken under her fingers, still damp. He smelled clean, she thought, a warm mingling of soap and his own natural masculine scent. She closed her eyes, sighed, opened them. He stood watching her, silent.

She reached up to trace her fingers gently over his brow and down to his jaw, its lean shape roughened by beard growth. The texture was bristly yet soft, his skin warm beneath the prickle, so masculine and intimate. She thrilled to touch him with such freedom, while he watched her in silence as she cupped his bearded cheek, surprised by her own boldness.

In the candlelight, his eyes were green and beautiful, edged in black lashes under black brows. She leaned close to the breathing warmth of his body, and he bent down, leaning with her in a shared and natural curve.

She longed for the heart-melting kiss he could give her, the chance of that drawing her nearer still. Logic fell away. He was a scoundrel, and she was a guest in his house, only partially clothed, and should not be here, doing this.

Yet the blood in her veins pulsed, and the urge in her body was subtle, then stronger. She caught her breath against it, summoned resistance. But it would not come. He inclined toward her, his gaze dropping to her mouth, his breath soft upon her lips. When his nose nudged at hers, she tilted her head back, desire swirling deep in her body. She forgot the sting of the cut finger, her aching head, forgot embarrassment and uncertainty. She forgot who she was, why she was here, lost awareness of her scant garments, or that she was inviting this man in a tender way, her hand lingering along his jaw, her gaze locked in his.

But he drew a breath and pulled back. "Your finger must need tending."

Gathering her wits, she nodded, glancing down at her clenched fist to see her wounded finger still bleeding a little. "I suppose it does," she admitted.

Dougal went to a narrow cupboard that was held a few small bottles of whisky and some glasses, and opened a drawer to remove a folded napkin from a stack of linens. He tore a strip of fabric. "Give me your hand, lass."

She might have given him anything just then, he'd need only ask. Sighing, she opened her hand in his offered palm and he wrapped her finger gently with the cloth. Simple enough and soon done, but even that touch sent shivers through her.

"I am sorry about the glass," she said. "I should not have had it in here."

"It is nothing to fret over. Dishes break and are replaced. We are not fussy here—a houseful of rogues." He gave her a smiling glance as he bent over her finger. "We eat where we like, and take a dram or a meat pie in the parlor or the library or bedroom as much as the dining room or kitchen. My uncles and I have all broken more glasses and dishes than we could count."

She laughed. "What does Lucy think of her rogue uncles?"

"Och, she tells us to behave," he drawled. "And sounds like a wee Jeanie MacGregor when she does it, too. But we are a parcel o' rogues and bachelors with no woman to guide us in better ways. Maisie comes in once or twice a week to cook and clean and does her best. Jeanie was a godsend too, for Lucy needed a woman about. But she left us. Hamish, rather. Perhaps she was done with all of us." He shook his head.

"As you say, she will return. Lucy does need a woman in her life, and so do her uncles. As her teacher, I think the lass would benefit," she added hastily.

"Aye." He wrapped his hand around her finger, pressing it, and looked at her, his eyes twinkling in the golden candlelight. "Your recovery is certain, I think. What was in your wee glass?"

"Whisky and honey for the cough."

"Good. Did it help?"

"Help?" Were his eyes truly that green, or was it a trick of the candlelight? His thick black lashes encircling moss-green eyes were simply beautiful. "Oh! It did. I drank some but spilled the rest."

"You should take another wee dram. The smoke of that fire was very thick. A number of us were overcome and coughing. I should not have let you come along."

"I came of my own accord."

He nodded. "So you did. Another dram, then? I do not know Maisie's recipe, but a bit of the whisky should do on its own. What is that commotion?" He turned as the dogs began barking downstairs. "I will go see what is bothering them. Pour yourself a dram, and one for me, if you will. That is Kinloch whisky, just there." He pointed toward the bottles on the low cupboard, and left the room.

Fiona went to the cupboard, not quite sure which bottle he meant. There were several, some of them with handwritten labels, paper strips glued to the glass. *Brandy*, said one; *MacDonald's Whisky*, another; *A Good Port*; *A Claret*; *A Shiraz*, read the other labels. One brown bottle said Glen Kinloch. Three small silver flasks and two green bottles were all labeled *uisge-beatha an ceann loch*. Kinloch whisky, in Gaelic. Surely that was what Maisie had given her, mixed with honey and hot water. Or was it Glen Kinloch? They must be the same, likely different batches. Lifting one of the silver flasks, she took a small glass from a cluster arranged with the bottles. Pouring out a little liquid, she sipped.

The whisky, by itself without honey or hot water, was wonderful. Strong and yet delicate, slightly sweet, it had a seductive simplicity unlike any whisky she had tasted before. Its natural heat spread quickly through her, the first small sip sinking gently, a stream of mellow fire building inside. Her tickly throat cleared almost immediately, and her chest felt better. Already she breathed more deeply. She sipped again, and a wonderful warmth filled her.

On the third sip, she sought its elusive sweetness and some undefinable spicy flavor. Sipping again, she chased after its delicate flavor, trying to define it. Kinloch's whisky was alluring, with both wildness and charm in the smallest sip. She carried the glass to the wing chair and sank into it, enjoying the mellow warmth that radiated inside of her. The little annoying cough had all but vanished. The stinging pain in her finger was gone as well.

Waiting, she picked up her grandmother's book and skimmed the pages, wondering at the strange assignment Lady Struan had given her. So far, Glen Kinloch had no real fairies, and few local stories.

Hearing noises below and then footsteps hurrying up the stone stairs, she glanced up as the dogs bounded into the room and Dougal followed.

"Have your uncles returned? I should go," she said.

"The noise was only the wind. My uncles are still out in the glen. It is a busy night and they may not be back before dawn."

"The fire, aye." She tipped her head. "Or is it busy because of the gaugers?"

"We have been busy trying to avoid them, true."

She appreciated his frankness and the trust he showed by admitting it. "They will find nothing. You are always careful, I think."

"We are." He went to the cupboard, picked up a fat brown bottle, and poured a little whisky into a small glass.

"I do apologize, I meant to pour you a dram as well." When he shrugged and sipped, showing it was no matter, she settled back. "You came home sooner than I expected. I thought you would be out the whole of the night."

"Maisie's brother told me she had gone to help their father. With the gaugers about, I was concerned that you were here alone."

"No need for concern. I have been safe here, and quite cozy."

"So I see." He lifted his glass in a lighthearted salute and sipped. "I know you are a stubborn lass, and I thought you might head back to Mary MacIan's."

"I heeded your advice to stay. I did not expect anyone back so soon, or I would have dressed." She pulled the robe around her and tucked her legs up under her in the chair to hide her bare feet, draping the dressing gown best she could. "This is so improper. I have never been in such a situation before. I am sorry."

"No need. In the city, I am sure you rarely meet smugglers at midnight, and in your dressing gown." He gave her a crooked smile.

"I believe it is your robe, actually." She smoothed the fabric draped over her legs. "Life in the city is dull by comparison to your glen."

He huffed a laugh. "So you live with your great-aunt there?"

"Lady Rankin, aye. She is a dear, though can be stiff in her attitudes. She prefers that I behave primly and properly, but sometimes—" She stopped.

"You want a little more freedom?" he asked quietly.

She shrugged. "I suppose that is why I accept teaching assignments in the Highlands, to get away from city life, and away from my aunt's very proper social circles." Fiona lifted her head. "My lady aunt is not happy about what I do, but it is charity work, after all, so she can say little against it. And I rather like the adventure. I am not quite as dull as people think," she added defensively.

"I do not think you are dull at all. Serene, I would say. Calm and capable. But never dull, Miss MacCarran." He regarded her with a relaxed, amused expression.

"I fear everyone thinks me the capable one." She frowned.

"And that is not what you prefer?"

Impulsively, she flung a hand outward. "I prefer a wee bit of wildness."

He laughed outright. "You have found a wee bit here."

"But I do not have a truly wild nature," she said. Her cheeks were heating up, her breath expanding. She felt open and expressive, and a little tipsy. "Oh, dear Fiona MacCarran, so capable, so calm, always does what she should and what she must. Though dear Fiona longs to be more adventurous. To be a more interesting person. Well," she said, "here she sits in a man's dressing gown, alone with the man who owns it. I suppose that is adventurous."

He quirked a smile. "Dear Fiona. I would not change a thing about her."

She felt her heart thumping hard. She sipped whisky, licked her lips, sipped again. "This is sweet," she said. "Light. It's very good."

"I am glad you like our Glen Kinloch brew." He came closer, leaned against the library table, crossing his feet as he rested there. The kilt he wore was in the MacGregor pattern, and he had added a dark jacket over it when he had returned. But the shirt beneath it was open at the throat, without the fussiness of a knotted neckcloth. Fiona admired the strong column of his throat, and liked, too, the breadth of his shoulders in jacket and shirt, and the sight of his long muscled legs, strong, flat knees, taut calves covered by the woven patterned socks. She liked every aspect of his earthy strength. It was reassuring. Warm. Protective.

"The Highland costume gives a man an air of masculinity that is very solid. Like a warrior of old. Very attractive," she said, speaking her thoughts before she could stop them as they tumbled forth. "The muscular limbs and the hard beauty of the male form is so enjoyable to see. Strong and elegant. The kilt shows the confidence and ease of its wearer. The natural attractive character of a strong male—is quite—oh, do forgive me!" She felt embarrassed—and yet a bit wanton. She was talking too much. And oh, how her head spun.

"Forgiven," he acknowledged. "And thank you, Miss MacCarran."

"Fiona," she corrected. "Feeeeeona."

"Fionn," he said softly in Gaelic. "Pale, fair one." A shiver went through her at his low, breathy words. He inclined his head. "And no more of this Kinloch and Mr. MacGregor. I am Dougal."

"Dubhgall," she whispered the Gaelic. "Dark stranger."

"Strangers no more," he murmured, lifting his glass slightly. "May I say you look fetching tonight. That rich wine color suits your dark hair and the blush in your fair cheek. Very bonny."

"Thank you," she said, tilting her head. Were her cheeks so hot, or was it the whisky? "So you prefer the plaid? My brothers wear it sometimes, particularly when in the Highlands and going hunting and hiking. Though Patrick prefers the more modern Southern fashion and usually wears trousers and coat."

"The plaid is a point of pride for many, especially in these times. And it is an easy thing to wear, well suited to Highland life." He took another swallow from the glass and set it down. Then he looked at her for a moment, tilting his head, folding his hands. "I think you have had enough, my lass," he commented.

Fiona sipped once more. Just once more. "I suppose I have. It is a lovely whisky. *Uisge-beatha an ceann loch*," she murmured in Gaelic. "Oh dear," she said then, setting a hand to her head. She felt dizzy and flushed, her face burning with a blush that spread to her throat and chest. "It is strong. But I like it."

"A wee bit is more than enough," he said. "This batch is nicely mellow, with a bit of spice from the flowers that grew by the burn that year." He looked at her and frowned. "How much have you had?"

"I had some earlier with honey and hot water. And about half this glass now. My cough seems to be gone now. But I feel, uh, lightheaded." She blinked.

"Aye, enough, lass. An Edinburgh lady will not have the head for Highland drink. I apologize. I should not have suggested another dram for you after Maisie's dose. May I?" He stretched his hand out for her glass.

"I am fine," she insisted, and set the glass on the small table. A strange sense of well-being, even joyfulness, filled her in tandem with the heated flush in her face and chest. She smiled, feeling content. Then she stood, wobbling a little, grabbing the chair for support. Looking up, she saw tiny lights flitting high up in the room. Reflections of the lamplight, she thought. Her head felt very spinny now.

"How do you feel?" Dougal asked. He was standing beside her chair. When had he stepped so close?

She smiled up at him. "Marvelously well."

"Indeed," he drawled. "So along with us being improperly alone here, and you in a state of undress, I am now responsible for your becoming fou."

"I am not fou," she said. "And if I am, I did that myself. And willingly."

"'We are nae fou, well, nae that fou,'" he quoted softly.

"Just so," she said, laughing, glad to hear a man quote Robert Burns so readily. His intellect, she realized, was equally as attractive as his kindness, his strength of will, his handsomeness. "You do make a lovely whisky, sir, if I may say. And if I am in a state of undress, well, that is my own doing."

He regarded her for a moment. "I think you should go upstairs now, lass."

"Not just yet. I like your company." She really did, she

thought, and stood, tipping her head. But the movement made her dizzy again.

"I like your company too. But your brothers would surely come after me if they knew we were together here, with you dressed like that."

"Only if I tell them. It also depends on what you decide to do this night." She reached for the glass again, but Dougal took it neatly away and set it aside.

"Decide to do about what?" he asked quietly.

She felt wicked. "About your black lovesickness."

"Best we leave that be for now."

"Perhaps we could cure it."

Dougal was silent for a moment, standing so close that Fiona tilted her head to look up at him. He lifted a hand, brushed her hair from her brow, while she closed her eyes, waiting, hoping. Dizzy. But he did not kiss her.

"What cure do you suggest?" he murmured.

"Mmm," she said. "Maisie's potion cures all, so she said."

"You have had enough cure, I think. More remedy is best not pursued just now."

"For a rascally smuggler, you are a true gentleman." She smiled.

"Just so." He took her arm to steady her as she wobbled against him. Glad for the support, she set a hand to his shoulder. Thought of dancing. Hummed a little.

Dougal stepped back, his hand encircling her wrist. "Here we go, my girl, off to bed with you." He began to turn her toward the door.

"I am not your girl," she said. "Am I?"

"Not so far, unless you want to be."

She looked up, slightly dizzy, yet finding steadiness in his quiet gaze. "I think I have a touch of the black lovesickness myself."

"Do you? I am glad I am not alone in that."

"We are in this together, sir." She leaned toward him, and he caught her by the shoulders quickly so that she would not tilt and fall.

"Oh aye, upstairs for you, my dear."

"With you?"

"Good Lord," he murmured. "Can you make it up the stairs to your room?"

"Aye—oh! I was reading a book. Let me fetch it." She turned impulsively, dragging him with her toward the table where the book lay upturned and open.

Dougal picked it up and looked at the cover. "*Fairy Tales of Scotland and Ireland*. I have read this. An excellent collection by—Lady Struan," he read on the spine. "Would she be related to you?"

"My grandmother was the author."

"Truly," he murmured. "How interesting."

"She wrote several books about fairies and fairy lore."

"A talented lady. So you became interested in such things because of her?"

"Quite." She glanced away. Spying the whisky glass on the table, she picked it up again and sipped the last bit quickly. The heat sank through her, soothing her nervousness. He stood so close—and she wanted him too much just then.

"Lass, that whisky has done its work on you. Up the steps and goodnight, sweet Fiona."

"What a stern laddie you are," she admonished. Her head spun. She did not feel quite herself. She felt strangely free, keen to say whatever came to her. Felt happy in his company, too, and knew clearly that was not due to whisky.

"Upstairs? But I want to stay here longer. I have been admiring your library. It is a handsome collection. You said you had only a few books."

"A few certainly, compared to other collections I have seen," he replied. "I enjoy books, but I am not a scholar. When I was younger, I disliked studying. I wanted to—well," he said, "no matter. Later I realized the value of education and how much I enjoyed it. So I read and learned what I could on my own. I was unable to complete my years at university, but I have benefitted from this fine library, reading whatever and whenever I can." He spread a hand wide to encompass the shelves.

"You have read all these books?"

"Many of them. I have acquired hundreds of volumes, but the library was begun by my grandfather. And my father felt so strongly about my education that he insisted that I complete a university degree and become a lawyer. But then he was gone, and I was forced to make other decisions. Education was simply beyond my reach, and it was no longer what I wanted."

"What did you want, Dougal MacGregor?" She leaned toward him as if he were a lodestone.

"I wanted to be a smuggler."

"Ah. You got your wish."

He watched her in silence. She realized he had never outright admitted to her that he was a smuggler, though the implication was there. Perhaps foolishly, part of her had hoped there was no real truth in it. But his silence spoke clearly.

Something caught her eye and she looked up, seeing the tiny lights again, swirling and floating in the dimness near the ceiling rafters. Some came down to encircle Dougal's head, even touch his shoulders. "Oh my!" She giggled, put a hand to her head. "That is a very fine whisky. I am seeing the lights again. Wee dancing lights all about."

Dougal frowned, taking her glass to sniff it. "Fiona," he murmured, "which bottle did you use for your dram?"

"That one." She pointed. The room spun. "The pretty silver flask."

"Silver flask." His voice went low, with a touch of thunder in it. "Not the bottle?"

"Flask, aye. Look at the wee lights—there, do you see? What are those?" She blinked as dazzling rainbow glimmers spun faster and faster. They came together, taking on shape, sparkling like colored stars, forming a column of light. The contours coalesced into a head, shoulders, body—

"Oh, look!" she breathed.

The lights began to form the shape of a small woman who came into clearer detail, as if a ghost. She was exquisitely beautiful. Fiona moved close to Dougal, grasped his arm. "Ghost!" she whispered, and felt as if she were trembling all over.

"What?" He glanced that way.

The woman made of light smiled kindly at Fiona. Her hair was a golden spill of light, her eyes glittered like diamonds, her gown was a starlight mist. She reached out a hand, fingers sparkling with rings. She nearly touched Dougal's arm. Then she looked at Fiona, smiled again, and floated away, dissolving in the shadows of the room. Dougal had turned his head and seemed to watch her too.

Heart pounding, Fiona pressed close to Dougal. "There—she is by the bookshelves now. Do you see her?"

He glanced at her. "What are you talking about? I see nothing."

"The ghost."

"We have no ghosts that I know of, old as this place is."

"Or was it a fairy?" she whispered to herself. The woman had been a sparkling luminosity, a mystical form that could have been other than ghostly.

"Fiona," Dougal murmured. "Come—"

"I need paper and ink," she whispered. He turned his head to listen. "I must make a drawing of the—the fairy."

"Good God. You are seeing things."

"It is just what I hoped to see in Glen Kinloch. A fairy."

"What?" He frowned. "I thought you came here to teach."

"I did, and also to—oh, she is gone." The beautiful woman in gold and gossamer had vanished. Fiona sighed. "It was not my imagination. I did see her just there. But I suppose you will say me wrong."

He was staring at the spot where the woman had stood. "No one is there."

"I saw her, I swear. A ghost or a fairy woman. I hoped—" She stopped, bit her lip.

He narrowed his eyes. "Was there another reason you came to Glen Kinloch, other than to teach?"

"I must find fairies, in order to get the inheritance," she blurted. She did not feel herself at all. She felt expansive, excited, feeling an urge to be honest, to be bold. "And I came to the Highlands to find—well, perhaps to find you. But you are not what my grandmother wanted. Or Sir Walter Scott either. My brothers will like you, though. That is, if you will have me."

"Inheritance? What about Sir Walter Scott? And your brothers? What are you going on about?" His eyes blazed green fire as he frowned at her.

She was blathering on, she realized, and ought to stop. The whisky had loosened her tongue, made her thoughts and her words race too quickly away from her. No dram or drink had ever affected her like this. She put a hand to her head. "I had little more than a glass of whisky. What was in that silver flask?"

"A particular brew that I should have locked away. Fiona, tell me what you are talking about. Why did you come to the glen? What inheritance?"

She looked up into his green and scowling gaze. "Do you know, sir, you are a beautiful man, and I think I want to kiss you."

"What—" He caught her by the arms as she lifted on her toes and leaned forward, stumbling against him. She kissed him, a smack as he leaned hard away when her mouth pressed against his. He resisted for an instant—then gave a soft growl under his breath, and took command of the kiss. Now it turned sure and fierce, lips seeking, finding hers, tender and delving.

Sighing, she felt her knees melt, felt as if she tumbled from a height, as if her heart bloomed like a flower. And she knew then, fou or sober, bold or shy, capable or wild, that she was falling in love, tumbling so hard with it that she sighed against his lips.

She wrapped her arms around his neck, pressed close,

stunned by her feelings. Safe, welcomed, partnered. *Loved.* Though she could not know for sure, it felt so.

Then he was kissing her again, gently now, soothing his mouth over hers, kissing her into breathlessness. His lips caressed, his hands cradled her head in a warm, luscious chain of kisses that made her knees tremble, her body ripple with desire. Joy sparked inside her like a candle. Love took flame, filled her. She slipped her fingers through his hair, the dark silk of it, as he traced his lips along her jaw and throat. She moaned softly, wanting more desperately, her heart pounding.

"Dougal," she whispered, savoring his name as he gathered her closer. She faltered a little, her legs unsteady. She felt overtaken by the whisky and overwhelmed by the emotions emerging within.

He pulled away, brows drawn tight. "Lass," he murmured. "I did not mean to—"

"But I am glad you did." She closed her eyes, tipped her head against his shoulder. "Oh. I feel so dizzy."

"We had best get you upstairs. First, tell me what you saw in this room." He kept a hand on her arm, and she was grateful for the steadying.

"Moments ago? A lovely creature, like a sparkling mist. At first I thought she was a ghost, but I think now she was a fairy, so beautiful and delicate."

"I see. And how much did you pour from the silver flask?"

"Not that much," she defended. "The flask said *Uisge-beatha an ceann loch*—Kinloch whisky. You said I should try it. Did I take the wrong bottle? I am sorry if so."

"My fault. I did not make the difference clear. Glen Kinloch whisky is in a brown bottle. The silver flask holds more properly what we call *Uisge-beatha sìthiche ceann loch*—Kinloch fairy whisky. I must change that label," he muttered to himself.

"Fairy whisky?" She blinked up at him, startled. "But you said there is no such thing, that the fairy brew is just a legend."

"We make different whiskies here. One is made from a very

old family recipe that traditionally we call fairy whisky. The MacGregors of Kinloch have distilled it for generations. We do not make much, just enough to share with kin and friends."

She was delighted. "I drank fairy whisky, truly? How marvelous!"

"Not always. It can be potent stuff, far more than the other."

"My brother once tasted fairy brew. It is rare stuff, he told me. His wife is Elspeth MacArthur—her cousin makes it and brings it to her and her grandfather. Are you the one who makes the fairy brew?"

He sighed. "That would be me, aye. I give some to Donal MacArthur every year. They are among the few of my kin who can feel the special power of the brew. Not everyone does. There is a magical spell about it, they say, and some have the ability to sense it. We treat it with care because of the legend."

"Legend?"

"The origin of the stuff. That is all," he said simply.

"But I felt something too. How odd." She shook her head a little, trying to clear the fog away. Had the whisky given her the ability to see the dazzling woman in the library? "I did see her, the fairy woman. I am sure of it. She stood just there. She reached out to touch you, but you did not notice."

"I knew she was there." He smiled. "I have seen her, and her ilk, before."

Chapter Fifteen

"Y OU SAW HER just now?" Fiona stared up at him.

"Not this time. But I felt her presence." He had revealed too much, which was unlike him. The ease he felt with Fiona MacCarran, the trust building there, continually surprised him. "I have seen such before."

"So you have seen the woman?" Her blue eyes were wide in her pale, lovely face, with a flush to her cheeks—brought on by kissing, and perhaps the drink, and he should have been more careful with her—but she was beautiful, alluring, creamy skin, sparkling eyes, hair like dark silk. He did not want to talk. He only wanted to kiss her again. He only nodded.

"Not her, perhaps, but others like her. When I was young," he said firmly, straightening away as if to distance himself from the truth he was about to tell her, "I sometimes saw—unusual lights, and people that others did not see. A small beautiful woman, and other strangers. Just now, I sensed one of them was near," he confessed.

"You did not say so."

"I keep such things to myself. Some Highlanders have the ability to see the Fey, with or without the whisky. It is a natural ability among some of the MacGregors of Kinloch and their kin—like the MacArthurs. Other clans too." He felt he was admitting too much—felt foolish about it as well—yet he wanted her to know.

She was not merely intrigued and curious. Fiona MacCarran had responded to the fairy brew in an extraordinary way that said something important about her, something she might not know herself. *Fairy blood*, he thought. That was said to be what gave some Highland folk the ability to see the Fey. She might not know it, but she must have the ancestry. Reaching out, he brushed his fingers over her hair. "I am very careful about who drinks the fairy brew. It has a strange effect on a very few people."

She tipped her head. "What does it do?"

"It opens the veil between worlds so that some can see the Otherworld of the Fey."

"Belladonna can do the same, but the visions are not real. It is a drug, then."

"Not a drug. It has to do with Highland ancestry. If the bloodline includes the fairy ilk—the ability may appear."

"It did seem very real. Do you add something to the drink?" She did not look pleased. "You ought to label it if so."

"There is nothing special or harmful added to the brew. It is a simple recipe." He thought of the morning dew gathered from the flowers up on the mountain, in the little glade that his father had shown him years before. "Legend says fairy ancestry grants the power to only a few who taste their ancient whisky recipe. For anyone else, it is just a very good whisky."

"I do not understand."

"If your ancestry includes fairies, you may have the ability. So they say," he added.

He saw her go a little pale. "Fairy ancestry," she echoed, and nodded. "Tell me, do the Fey make the brew themselves? But if they do not exist, how could that be? Wait. You make it yourself, you said so."

"I make it, just like the lairds of Kinloch before me. By tradition, only the laird himself can make it according to an old and secret family recipe. The fairies made that condition long ago, so the legend says. I suppose it seems quite mad."

"Not to me. My grandmother wrote about fairies, and now my brother, a scientist, does as well. And I know a little about the power of conditions," she added, sounding wry. "Are there more secret legends of fairies among your kin?"

"Every clan has its legends, and we have ours. Some are known, some we keep to ourselves. This particular tradition claims that the fairies require secrecy from Kinloch in exchange for the recipe of fairy brew. That secret is passed down from the laird to his heir, and only the closest kin may learn it. A grandfather. A father. A son, a daughter. A wife," he added. He felt the urge to tell her more. Suddenly, keenly, he wanted Fiona to be part of that circle. He pressed his mouth tight, folded his arms against the feeling.

"We have legends in our family too that might seem odd to some. And my grandmother's will is certainly—" She paused, shook her head, drawing the brocade robe snugly about her. "Well," she went on, "can you tell me more, or is it not permitted to speak of it? After all, I did see the fairy of the whisky just now," she pointed out.

"The fairy of the whisky! Perhaps that is who you saw." He smiled at her description. "Very well, since she appeared to you. According to the old legend, long ago a laird of Kinloch did the fairies a favor, and in return they gave him a recipe known only to the fairy ilk. We must make it a certain way, and can only give it away, and only to a few. We must never sell it or profit from it."

He was telling her more than he should. It felt like a promise for the future.

"Then you cannot make much quantity," she replied with a half laugh. "It is not economical."

"Not very. It is blessing from the fairies, not a means to an income."

"They must have given it to your kin for a very special reason."

He leaned a hip against the table, folded his arms. "One of my ancestors saved the life of a fairy woman one night during a blizzard. He brought her to his house and revived her with a dram of whisky to warm her." No harm in telling her the legend, he told himself. But each revelation, each secret, brought him closer to—to some commitment he dared not pursue. He trusted her—that was all, he told himself.

"So you can make it but must never sell it, only give it away. A lovely tradition."

He nodded. "One must never profit from a gift the fairies bestow freely. The recipe is known only to the laird and his wife, and passed down to a son or a daughter, though so far it has only gone to sons and sons, and thus stays with the MacGregors of Kinloch."

"I see. It is a potent drink, more so than the usual whisky." She set a hand to her head. A high blush colored her cheeks, and her throat was pink at the open neck of the dressing gown. "I do feel it. Oh, my."

"Sit down," he said, though she did not. "Word about Kinloch fairy whisky got out eventually, over generations. It is known to be extraordinarily good stuff. We gift it here and there. My cousin Donal, for one." He smiled ruefully. "If it was better known, there could be a clamor for it, and we cannot make it in quantity. And if word got about and brought tourists here, it would make a spectacle of our glen. We do not want that."

She sighed. "Highland romantic legends are very popular now."

"I intend to keep my beautiful glen from becoming an attraction."

"You are right to be careful. This glen would no longer be a remote and private place. People would come to explore, and would want fairy whisky."

He nodded. "They already come in droves to Loch Katrine, wanting to experience the Highlands of the Bard of the North, as they call Scott."

"Although," she ventured, "your glen might be rescued from

poverty if tourists were allowed here, and paid a fee to visit and stay at an inn, and so on."

"I refuse to encourage the traffic of strangers in the glen. But I will tolerate one Lowland teacher." He smiled, slight but sincerely, hinting at more than he dared tell her.

"Will you now," she said wryly. "I thought you were anxious to be rid of her."

"I am reconsidering." He settled back against the table. "Tell me about your family legend. Sit, Miss MacCarran," he urged, seeing her sway and set her hand to the chair.

She did, demurely adjusting the overlarge robe around her lithe and slender form. "I have heard there is an old family seat at Duncrieff, and inside the castle there is a cup. A band of gold set with jewels encircles the cup, engraved with a motto. It was gifted to an ancestor long ago, and tradition claims the MacCar-rans of Duncrieff are obliged to follow that decree. If we do not—" Her blush deepened. "You will think it very silly."

"I make whisky according to an old fairy recipe. Nothing you could say would seem foolish after that, lass. Who was this special and wise ancestor?"

"An ancestress, actually. A fairy. So they say," she added quickly.

"Ah. Fairy blood somewhere in you, then. Go on."

"The jeweled cup was the gift of a fairy bride who married a MacCarran long ago."

"And she proclaimed a motto that you are all obliged to fol-low? Is it secret?"

"Not secret," she said. "Love makes its own magic, the cup says."

He caught his breath, then nodded. "Nothing silly about that. What is the obligation? Be kind to others? You do well in that regard, I think."

"We are obliged to honor her gift by finding true love," she said quietly. "It does not always happen."

"Not an easy thing to find. What is the consequence of not

finding true love?"

"Poor luck for the family. And we have surely had some."

"That is often the way of it, with fairies. They bless and curse freely, without thinking about the effects of their ultimatums."

"Sometimes, so the tradition says, members of our line must marry those with fairy blood. If we can find someone to meet that condition!"

"Difficult, that." He looked at her steadily, marveling at her family's tradition, understanding completely, for his kinfolk had met conditions for generations. "Even to me it seems impossible, and at the least would not help generations continue."

"Indeed." She stared up at him, her graceful fingers folded together, her beautiful eyes gray blue in the shadows. "Very hard to manage."

"It might interest you to know," he murmured, heart pounding, "that I have a bit of fairy blood."

"Do you?" She blushed deeply. He watched it flow into her cheeks.

"So they say."

"Not surprising, though." She cleared her throat.

"My guess is you have more than a trace of fairy blood, lass, judging by the way the fairy whisky took you."

She lifted her brows. "Because I claim to see lights, and—the woman?"

"Because you did see the lights and the lady. I believe you. They say fairy whisky only affects those with fairy blood in their veins. So you have the wildness of the Fey in your blood. Otherwise, you would think it just a very good whisky."

"These are all just legends," she said quickly, shrugging.

"How can we say for sure what is truth and what is legend?" he asked softly. "What if your reaction to the whisky proves the claim? You knew nothing of the legend, yet you saw something extraordinary. They do say the fairies choose who sees them and who does not. They chose you, lass," he murmured.

"Perhaps there is another reason they chose me," she whispered, glancing down. "Well, no matter. Your excellent whisky has worn off. If I drink it again will the lady return? I would so love to see her again."

"Why?" He smiled, touched by her earnestness and her interest.

"I want to make a drawing of her."

"You will have to draw her from memory. Even if you drank your fill she might not return. She allowed you to see her, but the Fey are a fickle lot."

"But you have seen the same lady before?"

"When I was a boy, aye. Or I thought I did."

"Where do the fairy ilk live in Glen Kinloch? Is there a place we could find?"

"They are everywhere," he said, straightening. He reached out his hand to her, and she stood. He drew her toward him as he spoke and she moved gently closer. "It is said they dwell peacefully here, but we cannot seek them out. They choose the when and the where of it."

"Perhaps I came to the right glen after all."

"Why do you say that? Was it fairies that drew you here, or teaching?" *Or this,* he nearly said, as he pulled her toward him. The keen awareness that they were alone attuned him further to the desire he felt, and the bond that he sensed growing between them. The impulsive kisses earlier had taken him by storm, and his body pulsed easily and naturally when he was near her. She was damnably distracting and he wanted to be close to her for more than physical reasons. He was growing certain that his feelings for her were real and worthy, and would not easily be dismissed. It puzzled and drew him.

"Tell me about the fairy woman." She rested a hand on his arm. "Does she help you make the fairy brew?"

"Fiona." Setting his hands around her waist, he drew her even closer. She did not resist. "I do not want to talk about fairies."

"But I want to know. I need to know."

"I wonder," he murmured, touching her cheek lightly, "why

you are so keen on the fairies of Glen Kinloch."

"I cannot say, not yet. I am sorry." She pulled back. "We both have secrets."

"We should talk of this later. You ought to go upstairs to rest."

"My head is still spinning a bit, I admit."

He turned to pick up a candle in its brass holder, then waved her ahead of him to the door, then began to lead her up the turning stone steps.

"I will go first," he said. "The way is steep and dark."

At the upper landing, she reached for the door latch and glanced up at him. Dougal hesitated. A cool, mere good night would abandon the promise of what was happening between them. Perhaps that was best.

One more kiss, he thought, one more moment to hold her. Morning and his kinfolk would arrive all too fast. They would not have this chance to be close, alone, honest.

But they were unchaperoned, and already he should take the full blame for it. Already he knew he ought to offer marriage for the situation she was in at his home. She and her Lowland family would surely expect it. *Marriage.*

Suddenly the state he had resisted for so long—the yoke of marriage—did not seem such an ill fit. Here she was, standing so close, alone with him in his very house, in front of a bedchamber, wearing his very dressing gown. Here she was, a girl he could love, a girl special enough to sip the fairy brew and see the fairy of the whisky—he liked the name she gave it—and she had come into his arms willingly and sweetly. And he had already confided secrets to her that he would never have shared with another.

Trusting her felt good. Right. Marriage. The word had a soft insistence. Even his uncles had suggested it not long ago. He tilted his head, watching her.

"Good night," she whispered, pressing the door handle.

"Fiona," he murmured. He set the candle in a niche in the wall. "Wait."

"Aye?" She turned, and in that instant, she moved, he moved, opened his arms. She went into his embrace silently, smoothly, looked up.

He touched his lips to hers, and she complied, gave back. Sweet as honey, hot as the burn of whisky, a new kiss, another, blending together in a chain of kisses, tentative, then deeper. She opened her lips beneath his, curved her body snug to his. He cradled her head in his hand, fingers sliding through her silken hair, tumbling loose its curling softness.

"Fiona," he said, "this is madness—"

"It is magic," she murmured, touching her lips to his again.

"It is the whisky," he answered, drawing back, "and I will not—"

"It is not all the whisky," she whispered, sliding closer, the brocade robe slipping open, her body in a plain lawn shirt—his own—pressed intimately against him, warmth through fabric.

"More than you know, lass," he said firmly. Though he knew he should let go, he pulled her closer, kissed her deeply. His hand skimmed down to her waist, to her hip. Sighing, he straightened, then released her.

"Into your room, now," he said quietly.

"If you think I am fou, I am not. Not any longer." She touched his shoulder. "Would you stay with me?"

"If you were sober, you would not ask that. Go on, now. Later for it, when we both are clear, and in agreement. Then we shall see, and we shall discuss what obligation the laird owes the lady."

"Obligation?"

"Hush. Enough for now. It is rest you need, and no more talk." He brushed his knuckle over her cheek, and kissed her again, could not help it, lips dragging hungrily over hers, his body pounding in its need for satisfaction. Mustering his will, he pushed her gently away. "Go, my girl."

Opening the door, she stepped backward over the threshold, watching him. "What if I see fairies again tonight, when I am all alone?"

"That may happen, for the whisky is still upon you. I thought you wanted to see them."

"Not alone, in the dark."

"Then go to sleep quick as you can," he suggested.

"Tell me more about the fairies of Kinloch."

"A fairy story before sleeping?" He quirked a brow, amused.

"It is important that I know. I wish I could explain. Later." She put a hand to her head. "I am dizzy. So tired."

"Go on, now, and good night."

"But I do not—oh!" She looked past him. "Oh!"

"What is it?"

"The wee colored lights, just there, on the stair behind you."

He turned and saw them, the ones who flitted in that form. Sometimes they appeared at dawn or dusk, other times when something of significance was about to happen. Why were they here again, so often lately? He shook his head to clear his vision. They did not vanish. He turned back. "They mean no harm."

"You do see them! I thought you did, earlier tonight. Are they the fairy ilk?"

"So my father used to say. I have seen the lights many times. There, now, I have told you another secret of mine."

"You have many secrets." She stood very still, watching him.

"As do you. When the wee lights appear, they only mean to protect us."

"From what, here in this place?"

"You, from the laird. Or perhaps the laird, from you," he mused.

She smiled, radiant, the smile he craved to see, impish and lovely. He savored it, returned it. "Are you and I the only ones who see them?"

"My father saw them. You have a fine bit of fairy blood, to see the lights of Kinloch. That long-ago fairy of that bejeweled cup—she has blessed you, lass."

"I wonder," she said slowly, "if something special happens

between us whenever we are together, since we can both see this phenomenon."

"You are a scientific and practical thinker, my girl, even with something magical. And I think you could be right." His heart, his breath, quickened.

"Kinloch," she said, holding out her hand. "I do not want to be alone tonight."

He watched her for a moment. Then he took her fingers in his.

THE ROOM WAS small and cozy, with the humble elegance that permeated the house. A four-poster bed filled the space, carved wooden posts, dark green curtains, a mattress draped with a pale coverlet. Near a window stood a small table and two stiff carved chairs on a patterned rug thin with age, and nearby, a large chest bound with leather straps.

Fiona turned, seeing that Dougal leaned against the door as if he was not certain he should enter. He held the candle and watched her. Shadows and light sculpted the planes of his face, highlighting the green eyes, the strong jaw, the sensuous lips that had met hers so sweetly. Her heart thudded, and she felt shy. Yet she had invited this boldly. He had not forced it on her; indeed he seemed wary.

She felt as if a sort of spell had been cast over her, for the decision was made in her mind, and did not trouble her. Instead, it seemed the open path, the way she must go, wanted to go.

"You are safe here," he said then. "I want you to know that."

"I know."

"Well, then. Good night, lass." He set the candle on a table and stepped back.

"Dougal," she said. "Do not send me away from the glen. I want to be here. I want to be with you."

He began to answer—then crossed to her in two long strides, took her face in his hands, touched his mouth to hers. The kiss was tender and fierce all at once; she felt her knees weaken, moaned, grasped hold of his shoulders as his lips caressed hers. He turned to bring her to the bed, sitting with her on its edge, the mattress sinking gently beneath them.

She cupped his cheek, the angle of his jaw, his beard's texture like soft sand. Sliding her hand to the open throat of his linen shirt, she touched warm skin, sensed the hard beat of his pulse. Groaning low, he sank back with her, pulling her to him. Even through layers of linen and wool, she felt the hard urgency of his body against hers.

As she trailed her hands over his shirt and plaid, he traced kisses along her cheek, her throat, small, exquisite, cherishing kisses, and then she found his mouth with her own and opened to his gentle tongue. She pressed against him, her hand flat over his chest, feeling his pounding heart. He stretched out with her on the coverlet now, mattress sinking, as she felt his solid strength, her body fitting easily to his as he kissed her again, his breath warming down along her arched throat.

She shaped her hands over his wide shoulders, needing more, wanting more from him, and as he kissed her she urged him to fierceness, catching her breath as his hand slipped over her breast, caging softly over her shirt, then tracing downward. She arched in anticipation, his fingers exquisite, his lips pliant. Trembling slightly, she gave in to the bliss of touch. She did not want to think, did not want to reason what should and should not be. She only wanted his hands upon her, his lips on hers, his body hard against hers, warm curves and hollows finding their seductive fit.

He explored delicately over her, and her body pulsed, ready, though she knew she should stop him, she let this continue, aching for secret touches now, arching and inviting, compelled by the wildness he was rousing in her.

Then he drew back, even as her heart slammed. He rested his brow against her own, went still, his body hard with a keen tension, his embrace tightening.

"Not this way," he rasped. "Not with the whisky in you and with too many questions and no agreement between us. I want you—dear God, I do—but not this way." Pushing up on an elbow, he got up, stood in the shadows. "Rest," he said, stepping back. "You need to rest."

"I do not want to be alone," she whispered.

He sighed, sat again, took her hand. Warm, solid, firm. She sensed a fine tremor there, like contained passion. "Sleep, then. I will be just here."

She began to protest, but curled away, not quite certain if she was rejected or protected. But she felt safe. And soon slept, falling faster than she expected.

In the night, she woke, her thoughts foggy, to find Dougal lying beside her in the darkness. His breathing was deep and even. Asleep, then. She curled against him, and he looped his arm around her. As she slid back into sleep, she felt his lips touch her hair.

Much later, she woke to gray light dissolving the darkness. The air was cool, and she shivered, turning. Dougal was gone, the bed cool where he had rested. She looked around the room.

He stood in shadow by the window, parting the curtain to stare out through the old glass. Quietly, Fiona slid from the bed, drawing the robe around her, and went to him. He held out an arm silently, drawing her to him. She stood beside him looking out over the silvery fog that blurred the hills in the moments before dawn.

"The day I met you," she whispered, "those very hills were misted over. I thought you were one of the Fey, come for me."

He laughed softly, kissed her hair. At that moment, she felt a powerful magic stir between them, a spell she could not resist. She turned to him, set her hands on his shoulders for a kiss. Her head no longer spun, but her heart turned within, moved by a depth of emotion—of love. Caught between sleeping and waking, like the veiled and misty world outside, time suspended, she knew what she wanted.

"My head is clear now," she whispered.

"Is it?" he murmured against her lips. "So is mine."

"I know what I want." She framed his face in her hands, his whiskers rough under her fingers.

"And what is that?" He leaned down, lips tracing her brow, her cheek.

"Not to think. Not to talk," she whispered. "Not to wonder what we should do or should not do, or what is proper or not."

"This is not entirely proper," he murmured against her hair. "Highland or Lowland, you know this obliges us to marry."

She sucked in a breath. But she could not marry MacGregor of Kinloch. This fine, strong, wonderful man did not satisfy the conditions of her grandmother's will. A wealthy Highlander he was not, nor did she care about that in the least.

But marriage to him would jeopardize her brothers' inheritance. She could not do that. Then it struck her. If she gave up her share, withdrew from the will—that might do. She ducked her head against Dougal's shoulder for a moment, thoughtful, heart racing.

It might indeed do to withdraw her interest in the will. Then she would not be bound by its legal conditions. Then she could do what she wanted. Marry whom she wanted, have the life, the love, she craved, not dictated by others.

"Fiona?" His voice was a deep thrill against her ear.

She looked up, smiled. "This feels good to me. Proper. It feels right, and I do not want to talk of obligations."

"But lass, if we—"

"Hush," she said, pressing tightly against him. His big hands warmed her waist and back, pulled her against him. She could feel the hard shape of him. "Hush, Kinloch."

Her heart was beating a strong rhythm now, her body taking on a deep, irresistible, undeniable need. When he kissed her next, sweeping his hand down over the hem of the long shirt she wore, she grabbed the hem on impulse and lifted it for him.

She gasped as the cool air hit her skin, gasped at her own boldness as she raised up the shirt and tossed it aside. She caught her breath again, hearing his own breath catch, hearing his low growl as his hands warmed over her back, her hips. He was kissing her deeply now, hard and passionately as she tugged wildly at his shirt, wanting to feel his skin against hers, wanting to feed the urges that now made her heart pound, her body throb under every grazing touch.

Under her hands now, the breadth of his back and shoulders were velvet smooth and muscled hard, and as her hand met the woolen edge of his wrapped kilt, more boldness came over her, so that she pulled at it, so that his own hand met hers, slid it aside as he tugged at his kilt, unwrapped it. She touched his taut stomach, his hip, slid further. His hand met hers again, moved it aside.

"Not yet, love," he murmured, and his lips found hers again, sudden and swift and hungry. All the while his hands shaped, teased, discovered softness and delicacy and warm readiness. Her knees faltered, and suddenly he swept her into his arms and carried her back to the bed, to the still-warm tumble of linens there. Stretching out with him in the cozy, curtained shadows, she waited as he tugged away what he wore, the cloth a muddle on the bed. She fell back into his arms, delighted, wanton, willing. All doubt had washed away as if by magic—she had hardly thought about it and now it was gone, her desire and conviction certain.

She arched, caught her breath as hands and lips touched and traced, as fingers slipped downward, he finding her ready, delving to touch, so that a swift wave of blissful sensation rippled through her. She explored him, curious and keen, shaping him, finding warm velvet sheathed over iron. Her kisses took his groan into her lips. And then he half lifted her, turned her full to her back, pausing. Not hesitation, she realized, but a question. He waited in silence, breathing hard.

"Aye," she whispered, and she shifted to open to him, while

he pressed and moved, like hand into glove. The feeling was stunning, sharp for a moment, and she surged toward him, feeling a rhythm growing, subtle and then greater, a rocking, a swirl of joy. Without words, she felt loved. She felt loving, wanting him to feel the same wild heat and deep comfort that filled her.

Then he rolled with her, parted, lay beside her, held her warmly, silently, in his arms. Nestled against him, his breath gentle on her cheek, his body solid and safe, hers now as she was his, she closed her eyes.

"Fiona," he whispered, "we—"

"Hush." She set her fingers to his lips. "Or the magic will be gone."

"Ah, but love makes its own magic, so I have heard." He kissed her brow and murmured something under his breath that made her heart soar.

"ARE YOU GOING past the laird's tower this early morning? I will walk with you," Mary MacIan said. "Perhaps we will see the Laird of Kinloch when we go by." The old woman smiled mischievously-ly.

Blushing, turning away, Fiona picked up her books and papers, ready to walk to the glen school for morning lessons. Two days had passed since she had lain in Dougal's arms, two days of dreaming and remembering so that her cheeks still heated pink at the thought of him, the mention of his name. "I am in a hurry to get to school this morning."

"Ah," Mary said knowingly.

Glancing away, Fiona felt sure Mary had guessed something had happened between the teacher and the laird. She had acted cool and detached, and had deliberately avoided seeing Dougal MacGregor, afraid that her feelings might shine in her eyes, and some might realize that she loved the glen's laird.

Because of her grandmother's will, there could be no future with him unless she gave up her share in favor of her brothers, and even that was not certain. MacGregor was not the wealthy Highlander she had been directed to find in order to receive the inheritance and he never would be. She did not mind. But she should explain it, should be truthful with Dougal. But for now, perhaps his mention of marriage was past and done. It was unlikely for a Lowland girl to expect a marriage offer from a Highland smuggler. She had done what she had done, and would not regret it.

For now, she only wanted to treasure what was in her heart. Too soon she would more than likely lose him to circumstances. She had lost her first love, dear Archie, and never wanted to endure that pain again. But that sweet, young affection had been nothing like the passionate, soul-deep feeling that had overtaken her so recently.

Truly, she did not know what to do, what to say to Mac-Gregor, what to expect.

"I will come with you. I must pay my rent to the laird," Mary was saying. "It is odd that he has not come to collect it and give me a bottle of his finest stuff, which is his habit each month. I have earned enough from selling my cheeses and beer to the innkeeper, and I think I will bring my fee to the laird this day. It is a good day for a walk. Maggie, come!" Mary called to the dog trotting behind them. "She needs a good walk, too, on such a fine morning."

"She gets plenty of exercise at night, roaming about," Fiona said. "Which sort of whisky does the Laird give you?"

"His very best, the Glen Kinloch brew," Mary said. "And he gives me an even better brew once a year, at Yuletide."

"Is that what they call the fairy whisky?" Fiona asked.

"*Och,* no! That stuff is not so good. I have tried it and do not see the fuss. Too sweet, and flat. No strength to it, despite what they say of it in the glen." She wrinkled her nose. "I like the Glen

Kinloch sort, and the more it is aged, the better. The laird is saving the oldest stuff for—" She stopped.

"Saving it?"

"They all keep some back, of course. How did you hear about the fairy brew?"

"Kinloch told me about it."

"Did he! Interesting. Did you taste it when you stayed the night at Kinloch House? Perhaps Maisie gave you some. She might mix them up, silly lass that she is. I suppose the laird was not there, with the fire that night."

"I tasted it when I was there by myself," Fiona said vaguely, willing to let Mary believe Dougal had been away with his kinsmen all night. "It was quite nice."

"If you enjoyed it, then the fairies favored you. I hear some see the fairies when they drink it, a sign that the fairies give their blessing to that person. Did you see them? They never blessed me, I can tell you."

"See them?" Fiona laughed.

"Then you saw nothing much, like me?"

"I thought it was lovely." Fiona looked across the meadow that filled the bowl of the glen, scattered with wildflowers in the morning sunlight. On the other side of the valley, a league's walk across the meadow, a hill rose toward the mountains behind it. There, the tower of Kinloch House stood tall, its stone walls catching golden light.

She wondered if Dougal was there, or already out at this hour. Two days ago she had been alone with him there, gloriously and privately; she would never forget it. She had returned to Mary's house the next morning as if nothing had gone on at the laird's tower. But the night, the whisky, and the man had taken her over, heart and soul.

She had seen him at the kirk session later that day when she had attended with Mary to hear Hugh MacIan's sermon on responsibility toward one's neighbors. Restless, she had looked around and had seen Dougal, had caught his gaze. Her heart had near leaped into her throat. She had looked away calmly, but that spark between them, gazes touching across the church, had been filled with yearning.

Outside in the kirkyard, although she did not see Dougal, she felt welcomed by the locals. Perhaps it was the reverend's sermon about helpful neighbors; perhaps her presence at the fire had assured the glen residents that the teacher could be trusted.

Grateful, wanting their acceptance as well as the laird's, she knew she should keep her distance. Both of them needed time to think. She had much to explain to him about her grandmother's will, her need to comply to allow her brothers to inherit—and the requirement that she marry a Highlander of means. That alone would give him pause.

She would wait and keep silent. His status as laird, poor or not, did not matter to her, but if he regretted what they had done, if he were uninterested in marriage, the dilemma would be solved. She wanted to be with him, and that would not change. Her thoughts tumbled with possibilities, her heart with feelings. She felt in a tangle.

Maggie barked and launched past them, racing toward the glen slopes. "She has found something to chase," Mary remarked.

Fiona nodded, then noticed people moving over the slope higher up, running quickly. She heard distant shouts and laughter. "What are they doing there?"

Mary shielded her brow and watched for a moment. "Playing at the ba'."

"Oh, the ball game—they played it in the schoolyard. Why are they at it so early this morning?" As she and Mary walked closer, she recognized some of her students and their kinsmen.

"They are practicing," Mary said. "There will be a game soon, for all the glen."

Fiona raised her brows in surprise. "The whole glen?"

"It is a tradition in Glen Kinloch to play on New Year's, and also in the spring on the first of May. It is nearing May now, so the laird has called for a game."

"I heard nothing of it." She watched the players as they ran in a cluster that seemed characteristic of the ball game they favored in Glen Kinloch.

"Word went round with the men. The women do not generally play."

"I played at the football with my brothers when I was young."

"You may have, but this sort of game is different. They play from the east side of the glen to the west. All the men and boys, a hundred and more, with the one ball." Mary gestured wide to indicate the whole of the glen. "They form two packs, those from the north glen and those from the south, and they start in the center—there, where the burn crosses past those rocks," she said, pointing.

"They play over the whole glen?" Fiona asked, incredulous. "All of them?"

"Aye, from the fieldstone wall below Kinloch House, across the glen floor, and down near the lochside road, where the standing stones are."

Fiona knew the place. "That's about two miles."

"Not far for this game." Mary nodded as if it was nothing much.

Astonished, Fiona watched the players on the hillside. "And one ball?"

"Just the one. 'Tis sturdy leather stuffed with goose feathers, and hardly survives the day, let me tell you, with two enormous teams playing the length and breadth of the glen. It goes on all day and into the night, sometimes the next day."

"Does the laird play too? His tower is in the middle. Which side does he take?"

"The previous lairds did not always play, but our Dougal does—no one could keep him out of it. He is strong and good at the ba' and both sides want him. So each year he plays a different side. He will play for the North this year. The South has more players."

"Are they not even, the two teams?"

"Oh no, it is decided by where a person is born. All but the Laird."

As they crossed the glen and began to climb the slope toward Kinloch House and the school, Fiona saw the spaniel chasing back and forth, and the men and boys hooting and pushing. Somewhere in the middle of the pack she saw the ball thrust upward triumphantly, only to sink into the cluster of players again. "When will they play the game?"

"The laird called for it on the coming Thursday."

"But the lads have school!"

"Oh, there will be no school that day. All the glen will either be playing the game or watching it. The laird did not tell you?"

"He did not." Again Fiona felt that tiny, sharp pull of separation, and with it a tug of sadness and hurt. Despite feeling more accepted by the glen folk, she sighed, knowing she was still very much the outsider. Yet it felt more important to be included now.

"It sounds like good fun. I know you will have a wonderful time." She forced a smile.

"You will be there, too," Mary said. "We will go watch and cheer them on. We could not miss a game of the ba'!"

"I would like to see it. Thank you."

"The laird will want you there, no doubt. *Tcha*," Mary said. "Himself thinks very kindly of you, anyone can see it."

Fiona slowed, staring at Mary in wonder, then hurried along.

IN THE DIM blue light of dusk, Dougal stood on the steep hillside that tipped to the clouds above Kinloch House, bagpipes tucked under his arm. He lifted the chanter to coax out plaintive, haunting notes. Most of that day, he had wandered the hills, and earlier had noticed Fiona with Mary MacIan as the women crossed the glen toward Kinloch House. He had guessed that

Mary might be bringing her rent, but he did not go to meet her. Some urge, perhaps the preservation of heart and hope, told him to keep distant from Fiona for a while yet. He needed to think.

And his heart needed to cool from its ember stage before he could be certain what he felt for her. The passion that had blazed between them was the sort that would burn steadily for a very long time. But he had to know for sure.

Lifting the chanter again, taking a breath that filled the rounded bag under his arm, he set his mouth to the reed and exhaled, long and steady. The sound grew, rising and lingering, echoing outward.

He played the tune, marshaling his breath, listening as it flowed across hills and glen, he realized that he wanted freedom—the sort of freedom that only love could bring to one's life. A solid foundation of partnership and support that grew from a love that would last forever. He could find that with Fiona MacCarran.

Lovesick or not, he was a cautious man. He would wait, not yet ready to rush headlong. He took risks in smuggling more easily than in this matter of love and marriage. It needed to be just right for him, for her, and for the people of the glen too.

But his heart was sure and decided. The fairies had shown the way from the first. He realized that now. Fiona could see them. They had chosen her.

That was the best proof he could have.

Chapter Sixteen

"W HEN WE PLAY the ba'," Dougal told Ranald and Fergus later that evening, while Hamish stood by the cave entrance, listening while he watched the hills, "we must work all the details carefully. We all know our parts."

"Aye, we each join the game, play a bit, then get out and set off to the caves," Fergus said. "With so many playing and all the rest watching, no one will notice who is in and who is out. But what of the gaugers?"

Hamish huffed, arms folded. "They have been in the glen too often lately, with the gauger's sister being here, and after the fire as well. I wonder if they have heard some rumor about our plans. Do you suppose the lass might have told her brother what she has seen here?"

"She would not do that," Dougal said.

"We cannot be sure," Hamish said. "You must admit there are more gaugers about now than before."

"True, but there are other reasons for that. They say that the government has hired more gaugers than ever these days, sending them to every region where there has been smuggling. And those in the Loch Katrine area know we have been active in these hills," Dougal said.

He refrained from saying that he trusted Fiona. His uncles knew that he rarely felt secure of anyone's loyalty beyond their own support. Ever since the day his father had been killed, quick and cruel and without justice, Dougal had not allowed himself to believe that life could turn out for the better.

Now he wanted very much to trust Fiona. He loved her and yearned for dreams he had never dared to claim—a wife, a family of his own. He was ready, yet he hesitated.

As if he stood on a precipice, he knew life could be joyful on the other side of the gap, and realized that the jump was not so far after all. But he still felt unsure of the leap, and made no move.

Clearly, he was obligated to the girl now and should marry her. Clearly he loved her and wanted to spend his life with her. Yet he waited. He had devoted his life to the glen and its people, and to the production and the trading of whisky in order to protect the glen. He was just a Highland laird, a farmer, a smuggler, a distiller. He had little to offer a Lowland lady of fine family—a bit of a university education, but no fortune, no high title or accomplishments. Only the glen, a simple life, an earnest enterprise, and his heart. Those were his to give, and he would freely offer them to her.

But he did not know if she would accept him. Perhaps she would prefer to return to her fine life in the city. Perhaps all of this had happened too quickly for both of them. He had been so determined to send her away from the glen, but then he had succumbed to some indefinable magic that had spun him about, heart and soul. Now he could not imagine life in Glen Kinloch without her.

But unanswered questions remained, unsettling him. What had Fiona meant by her remarks about fairy drawings, money, even Sir Walter Scott? Had she simply babbled nonsense due to the whisky, or was it more substantial than that? Lord Eldin said that his cousin had come to the glen for a purpose other than teaching, and she had hinted at something too. Did it have to do with her brother the customs officer, or her brother the viscount, or Eldin himself?

Right now, Dougal dared not risk the imminent transport of a very valuable cache of whisky. But that would be resolved soon, once the ba' game was in progress and the expected cutter sailed up the loch to fetch the cargo and depart.

"Hugh is down the glen," Hamish announced from the cave entrance, looking back at Dougal. "And he is not alone."

"Who is with him?" Dougal joined Hamish to stand looking out.

"Eldin."

The high vantage point provided a clear view down the slopes toward the road and the loch beyond. Along the road, two men walked toward the glen meadow. Dougal huffed, shook his head.

"Why is Hugh with Eldin?" Fergus asked.

"Hunting," Ranald said. "Eldin is carrying a gun. And look, a young lad is following them, see, leading a horse. There is a brace of game on it, looks like."

"So he's come up the glen for a wee bit of sport," Dougal growled. He left the cave entrance to make his way down the slope, soon striding toward the road to hail the men with a raised arm.

Eldin and Hugh saw him, waving, stopping to wait while the lad with the horse caught up to them. Slung over the saddle was a brace of hares and another of birds. Two hounds trotted along beside the horse. Dougal walked briskly toward them.

"Kinloch! Nearly shot you, man." Eldin propped the butt of his long gun against the ground. He was dressed as a Lowlander might for hillwalking and hunting, in a brown coat, trousers and waistcoat of fine wool, neat neckcloth, high black boots. Even Lowland men who came into the Highlands for hunting most often wore the kilted plaid—yet Scottish as Eldin was, he did not. Hat in hand, gun in the other, Eldin waited.

"Greetings," Dougal said, shoving back his long windblown hair, his plaid rippling about his knees, his sturdy tweed coat practical yet rumpled. If Eldin was the sort Fiona MacCarran was accustomed to knowing, he was no match for that. Enough, he told himself. "What is your business in my glen today, Lord Eldin?"

"Greetings, Kinloch. Reverend MacIan and I came out for a bit of hunting. I thought you would not mind."

Hugh, dressed as usual in a plain black suit, looked uncomfortable, neck reddening above his collar. "Eldin took down a couple of hares and some birds, but that is all," he explained. "The curlew are flying today, returning for the summer, nesting in the hills. He got two already. A wicked shot, is the earl." Hugh's frown and sidelong glance seemed to convey distrust.

Nodding slowly, Dougal thought perhaps Hugh only disliked the earl, not in itself surprising. "Here on my land, in my glen," he told Eldin, low and fierce, "my permission is needed for hunting."

"Is it? The lower section of the glen is mine now," Eldin said. "I am purchasing the government deed to the southern end of Glen Kinloch. As you must know, it is now available."

"Not yours yet. The deed will not be released until next month, to be exact," Dougal said tightly. "This Kinloch is a peaceful glen, sir, and we do not condone hunting for sport. The glen folk are going about their daily work, and no warning was given that there might be shooting in the hills."

"I explained that to Lord Eldin, and suggested we ask your permission," Hugh said.

Dougal was familiar with Eldin's arrogance, and knew the haughty barrier Hugh must have faced. "I have to deny it today."

"A pity. I have enjoyed the day so far. Glen Kinloch has such an idyllic atmosphere," Eldin drawled. "It will be so pleasing to tourists who come up to see the famous loch. Though I understand that in the dead of night," he continued, "it is not so peaceful here as one might hope."

"Tourists will not be about in this glen, day or night, if I have anything to say about it," Dougal replied.

"Is it so? By the way, I applied for the full deed rights. Since there has been no offer made from any other quarter, they will certainly come to me. I assume you have not yet applied to buy back your own deed?"

"There is time yet," Dougal growled. Truth was, he needed to wait for funds from a profitable source once the ship picked up threescore and ten kegs of whisky to be sold at a generous price.

"I offered to buy a portion of your excellent whisky for a good sum," Eldin said, as if he had read Dougal's thoughts. "Had you accepted, you might have bought the deed back already. So I can now lay claim to it. You were to send word about selling some valuable casks to me, but as I did not hear, I presumed your refusal."

"You will hear my decision soon enough," Dougal said, drawing a breath to cool his temper. "Here and now, this is still my land. And there will be no hunting today. Good day, gentleman." He turned and walked away.

MARY'S HOUSE WAS quiet at night, the little mantel clock ticking, fire crackling, soft rain falling outside. Fiona enjoyed the peacefulness as she sat at the table, leaning forward, pencil to paper. Her braid slid loose over her shoulder as she tapped the pencil thoughtfully against the table, studying her work. Rubbing at the drawing with a fingertip, smudging here, adding a light, airy line and then darker line, she made small changes.

The image looked nearly like the fairy she had seen in Kinloch House. Yet something was missing. She was drawing from memory, trying to capture in pencil tones that sparkling, delicate, translucent lady she had seen in Kinloch's library.

She sighed, setting the page aside for a fresh sheet, sketching loosely, quickly, coaxing the image out with strokes of the pencil. Still, it was not quite right. Over a few days she had made several sketches, drawing the fairy lights as bright bits in pale watercolor and pencil, dabs of gentle color floating over flowers and streams.

And she had attempted to create the beautiful, ethereal creature from the library.

Thoughtful, she set her pencil down and picked up the folded letter that lay on the table. Opening Patrick's letter, she read it again.

Her brother was glad to know that life in Glen Kinloch agreed with her; she chuckled at that. He was reassured that she had not reported untoward activities in the glen, which told him she was safe there. *The laird of the glen seems sincere in his desire to protect you,* he wrote. *He is a good fellow from what I hear, despite wandering the hills at night in ways that raise suspicion. Nor is he alone in that activity.*

Fiona read on as her brother explained that he and Mr. Mac-Intyre would patrol the north end of the loch, including Glen Kinloch. *Tell the laird the only evening star he should view is through a window.*

A clear warning. Frowning, she read on as Patrick mentioned little success so far in contesting Lady Struan's will. That meant they all must meet her odd conditions somehow. *As for the husband you are tasked to find, Kinloch is a poor glen—your chances are better elsewhere. You should come home.*

Fiona set the letter down, shaking her head. "Not yet, Patrick," she murmured.

Maggie, sleeping by the fireside, lifted her head suddenly and woofed, then stood just as tapping sounded at the door. Startled, Fiona went to the door. So did Maggie, head and tail alert.

The knocking sounded again. Fiona leaned forward. "Who's there?"

"Kinloch." Hearing his quiet voice, her heart bounded. She released the latch to open the door.

Dougal stepped inside, rain blowing in with him. The dog leaped to greet him, and he rubbed her head, praising her, before looking at Fiona.

"Good evening," he murmured. "I hope I am welcome."

She folded her hands. "Of course. Mary is sleeping, if you

wish to see her."

"I came to see you." He glanced past her at the table. "Schoolwork?"

"Just doing some drawing." She hastened to the table to tuck the pages into a leather notebook. When she turned, Dougal was just there, pulling out a chair.

"Sit, please," he said. "We must talk."

"Would you like tea? Or ale, or whisky?"

"Nothing. Please sit, Fiona." He touched her elbow. "I have something to say."

"Say it, then," she said, standing, ignoring the chair he pulled out for her.

Several days had gone by and she had heard no word from him, despite their night together. She had felt hurt at the silence. Now that he was here, the tension emanating from him made her nervous. She lifted her chin, mustered dignity, expecting to hear his regret, apology, and renewed suggestion to leave the glen.

Whatever he was about to say, she could endure it. Perhaps she did not belong here after all—but her yearning heart told her otherwise. Love is no reason to stay, she reminded herself, if it is not returned.

"I owe you something," he said.

"No explanation is necessary," she said stiffly.

Sighing, he indicated again that she should sit. When she did, he placed a chair beside her, and leaned forward in silence, taking her hand in his. For a moment he stroked her hand with his thumb. Fiona could not seem to look at him.

"I owe you something. Marriage," he said simply. "I have disgraced you."

Surprised, she stared at him. "You did not disgrace me. I wanted what happened. I thought you did too. Marriage is not owed to me. I suppose I should leave the glen soon. But I would like to finish teaching first."

"Fiona—"

"I will always remember that evening with great fondness

and thankfulness. It is true," she said, as he began to protest. "I do not need a marriage proposal."

He kept her hand in his and did not look at her. "When I was a lad," he said, while he seemed to study their joined hands, "my father taught me the way of making the fairy brew, which is somewhat different than the usual. He said that the lairds of Kinloch must keep the process secret, sharing it only with close kin."

Fiona listened, waited, not sure of the track of his thoughts. Dougal entwined his fingers in hers, sending delicious shivers through her. She closed her eyes against the longing, aware she might never feel such tenderness again. She did not want an obligation of marriage. She wanted love. She did not want a wealthy Highland nobleman, as her grandmother dictated. She wanted Kinloch—and could not explain adequately to him why she must refuse.

"My father never told his brothers, my uncles, the recipe of the fairy whisky. I have shared a little of the process over the years. Not all," he said, "but I wanted them to know, as it was better to work together. Now I find it burning in me to tell you the recipe. The truth. Not this moment," he said, "but someday I want you to know. And I want—" He stopped, turned her hand in his.

She leaned closer. "What?"

"You asked me once what I truly wanted. I know exactly what I want, now." He glanced at her, eyes green and sincere. "You."

"Me," she repeated, heart pounding faster.

"One day, I hope we will bring our children to the place in the glen where my father brought me when he showed me the secret of the fairy whisky of Kinloch."

"Oh," she whispered. "Oh!" She had no words for the moment. This was not what she had expected—yet it was what she had yearned for from him. She had longed to know that he wanted a future with her, wanted her to stay in the glen. Her heart filled with love then, soft and strong, expansive and hopeful, love for him and all he had to share—the glen, its secrets and fairy legends, kinship with those he loved, all that was deeply important to him.

But she could not find the words to accept. First, she owed him honesty. She sat silent, and he did not look up, still studying their entwined fingers.

"It is not obligation that brings me here," he murmured, "but love. Love, you see, and I will say it. And so I leave the decision to you." He let go of her hand and stood.

Fiona caught her breath, wanting desperately to jump up, loop her arms around his neck, return the joy he offered her. Yet she sat still, fisting the hand that felt lonely now that his fingers had withdrawn. "There is something I must tell you." It had to be said. She could hardly meet his eyes.

"I know you have secrets, Fiona. I know some reason beyond teaching brought you here. But if it does not concern me or my glen, you need not tell me."

She reached for the notebook and opened it, revealing the drawings of the fairy. "I have been trying to get this just so. It is drawn from memory."

"She is beautiful," Dougal said.

"But it is not quite right. I have not truly captured her," she said. "Dougal, I do have obligations of my own. Promises I am expected to keep."

"What sort of promises?"

"My grandmother's will specifies conditions that my brothers and I must meet if we are to inherit. I am bound by those conditions too, unless I break my word and break my bond with my brothers."

"That would not be easy." He watched her, waited.

"And yet I may have to do it." Quickly, quietly, she told him about Lady Struan's will, how it made unique requests of Fiona and her brothers regarding fairies and other conditions to release the inherited funds. "I am to make drawings of fairies for the book my brother is finishing, which our grandmother began. I came to the glen for that."

"Drawings? That is not so bad. Why this glen in particular?"

She shook her head. "No reason. The Edinburgh Ladies' Society sent me here to Glen Kinloch, so I thought being here might help me meet—some of the obligations."

"I see. There are other conditions?" His voice was graveled, wary.

"My drawings are to be judged for their genuineness by Sir Walter Scott."

"Your drawings would please anyone, including such a fine gentleman as that." There was a new wariness in him as he watched her.

"There is one more condition for me." She looked away. "I am instructed, and expected, to find a Highland husband."

"We could solve that," he murmured.

She twisted her hands together. "The clause stipulates that I am to marry a wealthy, titled Highlander."

"Ah." He stepped back.

Her heart sank at his caution and coolness. "Wealth takes all forms," she said.

"The will refers to only one form, I think." He took another step back.

"You offer so much—this beautiful glen, the loyalty of kin and friends, even the rare secret of fairy whisky. What you offer is a different kind of wealth. The best sort, and it has far more meaning than material wealth." She glanced up then, hopeful. But his eyes were dark green. Stormy.

"Regardless, whatever I offer will not win you your inheritance."

She sighed. "I cannot meet all of the conditions. It is impossible."

"You can if you marry someone else," he said. Fiona lowered her head, but felt his gaze upon her. "Marry another, and make a few wee drawings."

He leaned over the table and picked up the pencil. A stroke here, there, and as Fiona watched the drawing sparked to life under his deft hand. Whatever was missing, he provided before her eyes. "There," he said softly. "Now she looks a little like you. Beautiful. That was what you needed to add. The resemblance. Your own magic." He set the pencil down. Stepped back again.

"Dougal, wait." Fiona stood, stretched out her hand, met air.

He went to the door, turned back. "Decide what you want for yourself and your family. I will not tell you what to do. I know what I want, lass. You must sort this out for yourself."

"Please, Dougal," she said, hands trembling.

"Lass," he said, gripping the door handle, "whatever happens, my life will not change. Life in the glen goes on as it always has. Hearts endure somehow. I learned that years ago." He opened the door, stepped out, shut it.

She ran to the door and opened it, but he had vanished in the shadows. She leaned her head against the oak planking. *Hearts endure somehow*. He must have discovered that years ago. She had felt the same after Archie's death, when she had learned to endure and move on somehow.

But she wanted to be happy now, wanted it desperately with Dougal; she wanted him to feel that happiness too. Yet if she chose to live in the glen to claim what could be a peaceful, fulfilling life, her choice could set her brothers up for ruin.

In Glen Kinloch, the impossible had happened for her, and she could not overlook that. She had fallen in love with a Highland laird whose wealth lay in his offer of love and a good life. But he might not want her now that he had learned the truth of why she was here. Falling in love with him was all she wanted, but it would not satisfy the will.

And so the inheritance would go to Nicholas MacCarran, Lord Eldin.

Hearing a whimper, Fiona looked down to see Maggie beside the door, pawing to go outside. Fiona opened it again. "Go on, go after him, he will speak to you!"

She watched the dog dash through the shadows. Fiona longed to follow and find the laird, too. Instead, she shut the door and went to the table, sitting, chin in hand.

Her drawing was beautiful, improved by the delicate touches Dougal had made. But as she sat and looked at it, a tear dropped on the paper, smudging the pencil lead.

Her choice was clear, though she did not want it. Her siblings depended on her to fulfill her part of the agreement. And now the Laird of Kinloch had let her know that he could, and would, be fine without her.

She would not be so fine—but she knew she must leave Glen Kinloch.

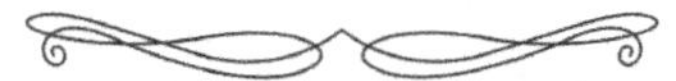

Chapter Seventeen

"THE GAME IS going well," Fergus said, even as someone shoved hard against him. He shoved back, his face reddening. "Very well!"

"Aye," Dougal grunted, pushing a shoulder into the huddle, watching his feet as the players kicked and shuffled. Like the rest, Dougal was looking for the elusive feather-stuffed leather ball that darted and rolled amid a forest of legs—like any of them, if he found it, he would kick it away and try to take possession.

He and Fergus hovered at the outer edge of the great press of men and boys. Dozens crammed together in a great, wicked beast of a crowd, grunting, shoving, and sweating as they vied to find, snatch, and direct the ball between one goal and the next. North and South were huge teams both, the north glen claiming an old, crumbling stone wall on the hill below Kinloch House for a goal, while the south glen claimed the standing stones near the lochside road. No quarter was given. Each time the ball was sighted, every man went after it.

All were here, Dougal thought, glancing around. By now they were gathered in the middle of the glen floor toward the end of a very long day. The huge group of players had gone up the glenside and down the lochside, taking the slopes, moving in great herds through villages, splashing through burns and leaping over and around rocks, even darting in and out of houses and byres. Now they were back in the broad meadow near a long stretch of muddy bog.

To a man, they were exhausted after hours of shoving, push-ing, running the ball in packs from one point to the next. They had endured pummelings and hardships for the sake of the ball, and were bruised, aching, and thirsty. But each player called up the energy to carry on, following up and down the glen. The ball, muddy and torn, had been stolen countless times from gripping hands, hidden under shirts, crammed under wads of turf, or sunk in a stream while others searched for it. Countless times it had been found, claimed, kicked, caught, and zigzagged around the glen with players in endless pursuit.

The day had begun in a civilized way, the two teams assem-bling at the midpoint of the glen. Dougal had opened the game by playing a tune on his bagpipes, and rousing cheers rose from the crowd assembled ready to watch and follow the players. Rob MacIan had brought carts loaded with ale and cheese and other food from his inn, and claimed the privilege of tossing the leather ball high up to begin the game.

No particular rules existed beyond a tacit agreement to do no deliberate harm. The only certainty was the presence of the two goals at opposite ends of the glen, and the willingness of every man there to do his damnedest to make a goal. The winning team would be decided either by nightfall or exhaustion, or both.

Scores of men—near a hundred this year, Dougal guessed—now clustered around the ball, chasing it along, not always certain where it was, simply going along in the wake of the shouts and scrambles. They pursued it through houses and byres, some even rushing through the schoolhouse after the renegade ball. They went shouting and shoving past and through houses and illicit stills too, pausing for a quick sip of peat reek or ale from casks opened for the purpose. By tradition, everything but direct harm was considered fair play, so whatever stood in the ball's path was at the mercy of the game.

Stepping back from the press of players, Dougal watched as the ball popped free of the crowd. One fellow went fast after it and another hopped on his back, spinning together while yet another man snatched the ball away, only to be chased by a hooting pack of players.

Already that afternoon they had crossed the glen floor and reached the lochside road following the ball's wayward path. Men had even thundered through Mary MacIan's little house after the ball, tumbling over furniture and knocking her clock from the mantel. While Maggie barked wildly, Dougal had prevented both dog and mistress from being trampled, even as the players pounded onward.

Several men fell into one or another of the flowing burns that crisscrossed the glen. All knew that if the ball reached the cove it could be lost in the loch, while men might go splashing and swimming and nearly drown to find the thing. To avoid calamity, they drove their leathery prize inland again toward the central moor and played on.

Despite exhaustion, near calamities, and even danger, Dougal knew that all were enjoying the day. For a moment, he grinned at Fergus, then shouldered his way back into the shoving, shouting band of men. Lunatic and joyful, they were all brothers in the game of the ba' when they played across the glen and back.

Soon enough, he would have to ease out of the crush and slip away with his uncles. Ducking to avoid a thrusting elbow, he saw the ball slip unnoticed between the feet of the men in front of him.

Bending, scooping it up, he crammed it under the muddy hem of his shirt and was away. The others turned in swift pursuit, but for a moment, with that bit of leather clutched cold against his skin, he felt the elation of possessing the prize. But logic prevailed—he needed to be elsewhere.

He approached the outskirts of the fray with men pulling at him, and tossed the ball high overhead to surrender it. Arms reached, shouts burst out, men leaped like salmon. The prize disappeared into the cluster, the players rounding after it.

Breath heaving, Dougal stood still for a moment, wiping his

face. Turning, he saw Ranald and Hamish. "Let's away," he rasped.

As they slipped free of the ragged edge of the frenzied crowd, Dougal glancing back. Fergus was in the thick of the play, swearing like a savage, not ready to give up the game no matter the plan.

"Have you seen the gaugers?" Dougal asked Hamish.

"Aye, they are here, just as we thought. Some are watching, but a few have joined the game now." He tilted his head toward the throng. "Patrick MacCarran is in there, and Tam MacIntyre's son too. Tam and of others are following the scramble with the crowd. They will be too busy to worry what free traders might do tonight."

"And they will think we are in the thick of it with the rest," Ranald said.

"Just so. Come ahead." Dougal pointed away from the crowd.

The hour was later than he had thought, with late twilight thickening to purple as Dougal and his uncles went down to the lochside road. With so many players and spectators scattered about the moor and hills, they did not look out of place. They might be catching their breath, or going down to the loch for some cool water.

The air felt fresh and cool beyond the close, sweaty throng. Dougal breathed deep, felt the relief of clean air fluttering his tattered, dirty shirt and kilt and damp hair. He paused to tuck his shirt in best he could, straightening the swath of the plaid around him and over his shoulder.

For a moment he glanced about, hoping to see Fiona before he was off on the night's mission. Here and there, he had seen her watching the game together with some of the other women. She had been standing with Mary MacIan and Lucy. Seeing the three together, each one so special to him, renewed his strength and resolve when he had been all but exhausted.

He had not seen her since then, and wondered if she had

gone with Mary MacIan to the house to help right the mess here. He would offer to repair the damage and would bring the old woman a cask of her favorite whisky. But he could never make up to Fiona what fate, and his own misjudgment, had wrought.

No doubt she had decided to be done with the laird of Glen Kinloch, who preferred to muck about in a rough game, smuggle whisky, tend sheep, play the bagpipes, work in his distillery, and roam the hills rather than don a frock coat and complete his university education to become a true gentleman laird. Privately he savored more book learning, but he was not like the aristocratic gentlemen that Fiona MacCarran knew. He lacked the polish of men like Eldin. No matter the circumstance, the laird of Glen Kinloch would always be more suited to a plain existence in the Highlands. Could Fiona accept that, and leave her sophisticated life to live rustically? Deeply, desperately, he hoped so, and yet doubted it.

Tonight, though, he had more immediate matters to hand. Running down the hill to the lochside road in the purple gloaming, he sat on an old stone wall to wait for his uncles.

TUCKING HER SHAWL around her shoulders against a cool breeze, Fiona stood on a slope a little apart from the others, watching the ruckus of the game continue. Not far away, Lucy gathered flowers in the lowering light, humming as she went. Fiona smiled to see the girl happily occupied making a bouquet of yellow primroses and the bluebells that covered the hills in a blur of vivid color.

She had spent most of the day with the women of the glen, as well as the girls who attended her school. Lucy had been with them too, along with Maisie and Annabel, Jamie too. Walking the hills as the game ranged across the glen, Fiona had enjoyed watching. She had never seen anything quite like the game of the ba'—nor had she laughed this much in a long time. The quick glimpses of Dougal MacGregor in the thick of the game, sometimes controlling the ball, sometimes leaping after it with others, were exciting too, more wonderful than she would ever admit.

As they moved along the glenside with the game, she had found moments to explore the foothills, searching for rock samples, the children eager to help. The afternoon was sunny and warm and she had removed her straw bonnet, enjoying the fresh Highland breezes. Jamie had collected rocks and scouted for fossils, while the girls had gathered flowers. Lucy had a surprising knowledge of flowers useful in the whisky-making process—Fiona, impressed, realized the wee girl was learning from her uncles. Annabel, whose mother was known for her fine ale, had good knowledge too. Shy Annabel had walked with them, singing a little in her sweet, beautiful voice. Fiona had smiled to herself, listening.

She realized that she truly loved Glen Kinloch—the place, the people. The laird.

In one spot, she discovered an outcrop of limestone containing some rare fossil remains, including fat swirled ammonites that she showed the children. She had brought her knapsack and tools, and broke away some of the stone with a small hammer. Lucy took rubbings of the tiny shell impressions, and Jamie had been thrilled to find traces of a beastie—a fat little trilobite petrified in stone. Fiona had split away that chunk of stone so the boy could keep his treasure in a pocket.

While walking the hills, Fiona and the children stopped now and then to watch the game as the men edged closer to the lochside goal.

"The Southies will win," Jamie predicted. "They have more players. And the gaugers are watching and will not pay heed to what the laird is doing."

Fiona lifted a brow. "What else is Kinloch doing but playing at the ball today?"

"Smuggling," Lucy said blithely.

"What?" Fiona asked.

The child held out a little posy of flowers to her. "Here. I heard the uncles say they would go trading tonight when it was all dark. They will meet a great ship from France, I think they said. It is coming up the loch to take the whisky and will pay good coin. We will be rich!"

"A cutter, not a ship," Jamie said. "Only fast boats make the whisky runs."

"Is it so?" Fiona asked mildly. "Only fast boats on the loch?"

"Aye, they sail up the loch and then down, and then they move the whisky to a bigger ship and go all the way down the River Clyde to the sea," Jamie said. "My grandfather took me to see a cutter coming up the loch once and told me how the whisky runs go over the water."

Fiona had seen a cutter as well, she remembered, when she had first come to the glen. Frowning, she glanced toward the ongoing game. A great clog of men gathered in the meadow, while spectators stood watching. The tenacity of the glen players was remarkable, she thought—Mary MacIan had said these sorts of games could go on for days, even as much as a week. Men came and went in shifts, taking a little time to eat and rest before joining the ruckus again.

Women, being sensible creatures, so Mary had said, watched for a while and then returned to their work and their homes and children. Now and then a woman might dive into the throng too, welcome to play and giving as good as she got.

"Not me," Mary laughed, "but I have seen some do so over the years of this mad glen game. I expect when Lucy grows up," she had said, "she might join the fray."

Laughing at the thought, Fiona felt a fleeting temptation to join the fun herself. But the urge quickly turned practical as she watched the rough game continue. Looking around, she noticed something far off in the glen, away from the commotion in the center.

A few men walked across the moorland away from the great cluster of players and spectators. One of the men captured her attention. She knew the set of those shoulders, that rhythmic walk, the dark-sheened hair. Her heart thumped quick and fast. Had Dougal seen her on the slope with the children—was he coming up to meet them?

But he was heading away from the game, away from the meadow toward the loch. And he was with two of his uncles. She could see that now.

Smuggling, Lucy had said. The raucous game provided a perfect distraction, Fiona realized. Dougal had arranged the game today, which was being held earlier than usual. Did he intend the distraction to cover a night of smuggling and a rush to meet a boat?

Hearing a shout and Lucy's quick answer, she saw Hugh MacIan climbing the hill toward them. The reverend waved, smiled, and as the children ran toward him, he stooped to admire their collections of stones and flowers. Then he joined Fiona on the slope, standing beside her as they watched the riotous game down in the glen.

"The Southies look to win," he said. "They are pushing the game toward the loch and have the advantage just now. Shall we walk that way with the wee ones?"

Crowing with delight, Jamie and the children began to race along the shoulder of the hill, while Fiona called after them to slow down and come closer. Gathering up her bag with the little hammer and tools, she walked beside Hugh MacIan.

"Will the game end soon, then?" she asked. "It is coming on twilight."

"Some light will linger this time of year. And they will play regardless of the time until there is resolution. I see we have attracted some outsiders." He gestured toward the road.

"Customs officers!" She noticed the men on horseback, and a few on foot, and saw the weapons they carried.

"Aye, your brother included. I had the chance to speak with

them before I came over to you. He promised to meet us down by the loch. Lord Eldin is here too. He heard about the game. Dougal MacGregor best be careful," he added low.

Fiona sent him a quick, concerned glance. "What do you mean?"

"The cutter," Hugh said. "He arranged to meet a boat on the loch tonight. Did he not tell you? I rather thought he might have confided in you, since he seems keen to court you."

"Does he?" she asked casually, though her heart took up a tripping beat.

"It seems so. In fact, I was sent to find you and bring you to the laird and your brother. I thought you might welcome that news."

"Kinloch asked you to find me?" She frowned. "Has he been hurt in the game?" She could not think of any other reason that Dougal might send Hugh to fetch her, but his uncles were clearly busy. She felt a little frisson of hope that Dougal had thought of her even in the midst of the fray.

"He is fine. He just wants to see you, I think, and Lucy as well. He is too tired and too involved to come up here for you himself. I offered to take you down to meet him."

"Of course."

"But do be warned," Hugh said, "he may have a dangerous thing planned. I am worried, I will tell you."

Danger? She felt a chill run down her spine. She had only hoped that Dougal sent for her to be near him, perhaps to talk to her when he had the chance, just as she longed to talk to him, explain as honestly as she could and convince him to listen.

But perhaps he sent for them to protect them if smuggling was going forward tonight. She felt a small twist in her gut, a warning knell. Risk, danger. Fear.

"Miss Fiona, forgive me if I am being familiar," Hugh said, "but I hope we are friends. And as the kirk minister, I am concerned for every soul here in the glen. The night of the fire, when you stayed over at Kinloch House, I hope all was well between you and the laird. If I may ask—"

"There were unusual circumstances that night, but there is no need for concern, I assure you," she said.

"Then I trust you were safe and it was not—an awkward situation for you."

She frowned. "The laird was very respectful, Reverend. Do not fret on my account."

"Good. Maisie said she found whisky glasses about, and broken glass, and a bit of a mess. She is not a gossip, I promise. We two are fond of one another, if I may say, and so she often confides in me."

The whisky glasses, Fiona thought, stomach sinking. She had forgotten to go back to the library and clean it completely, so Maisie had seen them the next day. "I was coughing from the smoke and took a whisky remedy for it. I dropped the glass, and it broke."

"Was it fairy whisky?" He glanced at her. "Maisie said that bottle was open, which puzzled her. The laird does not normally drink that sort, nor does he take much whisky at all, though he makes the best around. Forgive my curiosity, but did you sample it? It is legendary stuff, and they say it can have an odd effect if too much is taken."

Startled, she shrugged. "I did taste it. A very nice whisky. The laird came home, and we visited briefly. It was a lovely evening. I was tired and went to bed early." She turned her head to look up the slope and hide her deepening blush.

They walked downward in near silence, approaching the road that cut through the glen, and so walked among the crowd. The chaotic center of the game hurtled and rumbled along, approaching the standing stones at the base of one of the slopes. Fiona remembered hiding behind one of those very stones one night, encountering the smugglers—and their laird.

She called to the children to come closer, anxious to keep them away from the crowd and the rough game. Hugh called too, then took Fiona's arm.

"This way," he said, drawing her away from the horde. "Dougal will be waiting nearby. He left the game a little while ago. Lucy, Jamie, Annabel! Come along!"

"Aye, sir," Jamie said, running toward them, making sure the girls came too.

Feeling the pressure of the reverend's grip, Fiona frowned. He was deeply concerned, which increased her fear for Dougal and his uncles if they were indeed planning a risky venture that night.

MacIan led her and the children toward the shore of the loch and around a curve of the hill, the spread of the glen fading behind them. Ahead, a massive cluster of limestone and red sandstone rose up near the edge of the loch, partly blocking the view of the winding, pebbled shoreline. A thicket of bushes and trees further screened the area, but soon Fiona spotted a narrow path that paralleled the shore. The water slapped rhythmically against the base of a gigantic rock that thrust upward like a chunk of the cliffs above.

"Reverend, where are we going?" Fiona asked. "Children, hold hands and stay by the rock wall. The way through here is narrow. Be careful as you walk. Sir, are you sure Dougal is waiting for us here?"

"Aye, he said he would meet us up there." Hugh led the way, again taking her arm.

Fiona glanced up at the rock walls. Dark crevices split the rock face, and she could see more gaps hidden by bushes. Caves likely honeycombed the rock, she thought, caves that smugglers would use. Dougal might indeed wait up there. Reassured, she followed MacIan and reached back to take Lucy's hand, the others coming along behind.

"Here," Hugh said, shepherding them up the rocky slope.

Fiona felt a deep misgiving. She paused, looking around, feeling that something was not right. Why would Dougal want them to come up here? She hung back, but MacIan smiled encouragement, gestured upward, and took her hand this time.

He guided her to walk just ahead of them and gestured toward a triangular crevice in the rock face. Urging her inside the niche, he ushered the children in with her, and then ducked his head to step inside too. The entrance was low enough that Fiona had to dip her head a bit too, but once past the overhang of the entrance, she could easily stand upright inside the cavern. Jamie and Lucy jumped around and hooted with delight to be inside the cavity in the rock, while Annabel turned around in silent awe.

Lucy looked up. "It is not very big! Why are we here, Reverend?"

"Where is Kinloch?" Fiona pulled away from Hugh's grasp. "Kinloch! Dougal MacGregor!" Her voice echoed. The cave was narrow yet seemed quite deep, and she soon noticed footprints in the scattering of dust on the floor. "Who is here?"

"Kinloch was here, further in with his whisky stock. If he is not here, he will return soon." MacIan pointed into the shadows formed by the rough creviced walls. The back of the cave ran into deeper darkness, where Fiona could see a sharp downward slope.

"I do not want to be here. I want to the ba'!" Jamie protested. MacIan took the boy's shoulder and turned him firmly toward a second opening at the back of the cave. Reaching up to a natural shelf, he produced a lantern, which he lit quickly with a flint.

"Go on," he told them. "It is safe."

Something was wrong. Fiona reached for Lucy and gathered the three children toward her, backing away, her hands moving along their shoulders, prodding them. But as she rounded with them toward the light-filled entrance, MacIan stepped in her way. Tall and broad, he blocked the exit, so that she had to turn sideways, shuffling along with the children. MacIan turned up the lantern wick to show a rough, descending path.

"This way. You know Kinloch is smuggling cargo out tonight," he said. "He wants you kept safe should there be trouble. I know more about this than others, so he trusted me to bring you here. Come on."

Fiona hesitated, looking around, realizing that there were

multiple caves connected here in a complex of rock like a honeycomb. The cells must have formed as bubbles in the intensely hot ancient liquid material that had hardened over eons to form the limestone cave and cavelets where they stood now.

Intrigued by the formations despite her growing wariness, she noticed various strata, sandstone and greywacke sparkling with thousands of crystal particles. The lantern light caught them, turning common stone to glittering surfaces. Crystals were embedded beside veins of metal that could, she realized, be mined. Something else caught her attention then.

"This is astonishing," she breathed. "Some of these crevices and caves go downward—under the loch!"

"They do. Very good. The caves go deep into the earth, and the loch is above these spaces," MacIan agreed as they continued downward.

"Under the loch! Woo-hoo!" Jamie hooted, and Lucy echoed him, voices bouncing.

"Hush!" the reverend said sharply.

"I do not want to go under the loch! We will drown!" Annabel said nervously. Fiona took her hand.

"It is perfectly safe," she assured the girl. "The rock is very, very thick and solid, and it has been here for a very long time."

"This way," MacIan said. "Dougal keeps a cave down here. Come on."

Fiona went forward, keeping the children close. Peering at the cavelets and niches along the natural corridor, she realized Dougal did indeed use this space. The lantern light that MacIan carried showed kegs piled inside various spaces, stacked within the smaller caves. Many were small enough to ride on a man's shoulder. Some were larger, the sort that would be rolled along.

The containers stored here could be moved quickly to other caves or out to rowboats that would take the cargo to a cutter on the loch—and away over the water before they could be spotted and followed.

"Where is Kinloch?" she asked.

"He will meet us here, if he is not here already. Kinloch!" MacIan called.

"All of this is whisky to be smuggled? Is that why the game is going on today, to cover this enterprise?"

"I believe so." MacIan shrugged. "I am only here to help you meet Kinloch. I am not a smuggler."

"Smugglers' caves!" Jamie said, as he and Lucy ran ahead with Annabel.

"Quiet," Hugh said. "Miss MacCarran, I regret bringing the bairns with us. But it was best, since they were with you and would tell others where we went."

Fear spiked through her. "Why did you bring us here?" Fiona rounded on him.

"I told you. To meet Dougal."

"But he is not here, is he." Her voice trembled, her heart raced as dread mounted. She called to the children to come back, reaching out again to gather them close. "I should never have trusted you."

"Of course you can trust me," MacIan said. "I also thought you might like to see this place because of your interest in fossils and ancient rocks. The walls are thick with ancient imprints, see." He gestured. "Tiny shells and such, is that not so?"

She was not distracted. "Kinloch did not send you after us, did he?"

He sighed. "Miss MacCarran, I confess. I wanted you to see this cargo stored here. I thought it was important for you to know what a rogue he is. A true smuggler."

She laughed bitterly. "Rogue and a smuggler! That is no surprise. I know what he does. I also know he cares deeply about the glen and the people here. I know he smuggles cargo to protect his tenants from poverty and unfair taxation. I also know he makes legitimate whisky. Is this legal or illicit stock?" She gestured, fingers shaking.

Even so, she glanced furtively about, wondering how she could get the children out of here quickly and safely. MacIan was convincing, and might be telling her the truth. But her gut sank, twisted, warning her that something was very wrong. She should have paid attention. She should never have followed him, especially with the bairns.

"The spirits produced in his legal still are not aged enough to compete with this lot. These kegs hold nicely aged whisky. Very good and costly stuff. He will make a fortune on the shipment."

"Where is he?" she demanded. "Why is no one here guarding this?"

"They will be here soon. Come this way." He turned along another natural path between uneven stone walls. Feeling truly unsettled now, Fiona gathered the children close and whispered to them to turn and run toward the outer entrance as fast as they could go. They whirled without question to pound up the slope toward the outer cave and the glow of the twilight sky.

Spinning, she followed. But Hugh MacIan whirled, shouting, grabbing for her, taking her wrist in a tight grip. Fiona urged the children ahead, and they ran, sliding, rushing. Stumbling on the uneven path, she regained her balance.

Just then, a tall man stepped out of the shadows. He reached out to snatch Lucy first, then Annabel, one under each arm. As the girls flailed and screamed, Jamie ran ahead up the rough, narrow path. Fiona lunged to help the girls, but MacIan had her by the arm, and then grabbed her by the waist, dragging her back toward him.

MacIan barked at Jamie to stop, and the boy ran on, but stumbled, rising to his feet. Fiona saw him fist his small hands and glance around, gauging his chances.

Writhing, she punched at MacIan. The tall, dark man, a lean and looming shadow, dropped Lucy and Annabel in two tumbles, snarling at them to stay. Lucy got to her feet and he pushed her down. Fiona twisted in MacIan's hold to look up, and gasped, startled.

"Eldin! What are you doing here? Leave the children alone—"

"Get in there, all of you," Eldin growled, pushing the girls into a small cave. He took Fiona by the upper arm and shoved her in with them. She saw Jamie run for the entrance, but the reverend lunged for him with long strides, snatching him up and shoving them into the crevice with Fiona and the girls.

Then Eldin moved into the shadows to pull an iron grate across the entrance, securing it.

A cage—but not intended as a jail, Fiona realized. The space was nearly full of kegs. The bars secured the cargo from thieves. But it could serve as a jail—and did now.

"Let us out!" Fiona cried, pulling on the rusted bars. The little cave was low enough that she could not stand upright, and had to kneel. She reached out to keep the children behind her, but Jamie and Lucy stepped forward, pulling on the bars beside her. Annabel stayed behind, whimpering. "They are only children— you must let them go. I will stay. What do you want?"

"You are insurance, Cousin Fiona," Eldin growled.

"Aye? Insurance against what?"

The newcomer spoke casually, his deep voice echoing. Footsteps grated over stone as two men approached from the entrance slope. Golden light bloomed along the stone passage as Fiona looked up.

Dougal walked toward them, his face a fiery glow in lantern light. Behind him came Patrick holding two pistols that he aimed at Eldin and MacIan.

Chapter Eighteen

"ELDIN—AND HUGH TOO," Dougal said. "I should have suspected sooner than this."

In the flickering light, he and Patrick stood wary and watchful. Behind Eldin and MacIan, he saw Fiona and the children trapped behind the iron grate that had only guarded good whisky. Now it guarded those who had his very heart. His glance flickered to meet Fiona's, then away. He could not allow anger or his fear for her and the bairns to weaken him. He fisted a hand, and merely tilted his head. "So. What is this about?"

"Kinloch," Eldin said smoothly. "And Cousin Patrick. Are you here for Fiona or the whisky?"

"Both," Dougal said.

"I saw my sister across the meadow," Patrick said. "I thought it odd that she was walking toward the loch with the children and with you, Reverend. So I found Kinloch and we came along."

"It did seem odd," Dougal agreed.

Fiona watched him, silent and pale as she knelt holding the children close. She was beautiful, the strength of her will shining in her, and he felt as if his heart turned in his very chest to see her in danger. The urge to protect them was raw and powerful. He wanted to tear open the iron bars, hurl Eldin and the reverend against the rock and into that prison, and do worse than that. He only clenched his fist, flared his nostrils, waited.

"Explain," he said.

But he suspected what this was about. Eldin wanted the whisky Dougal had refused him earlier. Hugh's involvement was puzzling. For now, Dougal was glad that Patrick MacCarran stood at his shoulder, a stalwart comrade, his hands steady on two pistols. The lad had backbone and heart. So did his sister.

"The other customs men are coming," Patrick said.

Dougal waited for an answer from the two who faced them. He knew the excise men were still in the glen and so they were on their own here, at least for now.

"Is the ba' game over? Who won?" Jamie asked suddenly.

"Southies," Patrick said.

"They had more players." Jamie nodded wisely.

"Be quiet, boy," Eldin barked.

"Eldin," Dougal said, "why take bairns and a woman? You are just proving your cowardice. Or do you have another purpose?" He stepped closer, easing his hand to the butt of the pistol hidden under the drape of his plaid.

With a quick move, Eldin produced a pistol of his own, drawn from inside his coat. He cocked the thing. At its echo, Fiona jumped, and the children shrieked. "Stand where you are, Kinloch," the earl snapped. "Patrick too. Move, and regret it."

"Cousin Nick," Patrick said quietly. "What is it you want?"

"Kinloch knows," Eldin said.

"I doubt all this kerfuffle is for my excellent twelve-year whisky," Dougal said.

"True," Eldin confirmed. "I want the other sort."

"What other sort?" Patrick asked.

"Nicholas, please listen," Fiona implored. "We admired you so when we were all young. You were such a kind boy, and a fine young man. But something changed. I know that, but I do not know what it was. Still, you have always been good to me and my brothers. So this, today, I do not understand."

"Perhaps he is eager to inherit Grandmother's fortune," Patrick said.

"Ah. Eldin, the cousin who could claim it all," Dougal said, remembering what Fiona had explained days ago.

"She told you about that?" Patrick asked. "She trusts you."

"I hope so." Dougal did not look at her. Could not, or in the next moment he might go after Eldin and Hugh both in an ugly way.

"So you know Eldin inherits if we do not find fairies and such," Patrick went on.

"Then by all means, you must find fairies," Dougal murmured.

"Quiet, both of you," Eldin snapped.

"Nicholas, I never thought you capable of real harm," Fiona said. "It borders on evil, what you are doing."

"My dear, so harsh!" Eldin said. "I have good reason to do this. Kinloch refuses to sell his whisky to me. I have little time, and little choice but to act thus."

"You are just a wicked man!" Lucy stood by the grate, staring up at him.

"Shut up, child," Eldin hissed.

"Do not," Dougal growled in warning, raising his palm to Eldin.

"I have no interest in harming children," Eldin said. "Once I have what I want, you are free to go. With some exceptions." He stared, flat and cold, at Dougal. "It depends on what you want to do."

Dougal looked at Hugh. "Reverend, what is your part in this?"

"I did not know all of this. Sell the whisky to Eldin and be done with it," Hugh said. "Do not take it to the ship."

"It is a cutter, not a ship," Jamie corrected.

"Shh," Fiona said. She huddled with the children. "Hugh MacIan, I hope your grandmother does not know about this."

"She does not," MacIan answered. "Though she might agree if she did. Kinloch could make a great profit if he would sell his whisky to Eldin. I tried to tell him so. He could gain more, and faster, than by selling to the French or Irish by shipping it out.

Those funds could save this glen. That is my concern—the glen and its people."

"Then you had better save the glen from me, Reverend," Eldin snarled. "I hold the deeds to Glen Kinloch now. I do not have all the documents yet, but enough to control the glen—and its whisky distilleries.

"There will be tourists and hotels here," Eldin said, "and barges going up and down the loch taking them to Glen Kinloch. But you could stop that, sir," he told Dougal. "With the profit you make from selling that whisky to me, I will allow you to buy back some of the deeds. You could keep part of the glen."

"So generous," Dougal drawled. "After this assault is reported—you will not walk away free from this, I guarantee it—we shall see how the Court of Session views your claim on the deeds to the properties in Glen Kinloch. Land in Scotland belongs primarily to the Crown, so the decision ultimately lies there."

"We shall see," Eldin muttered, holding his pistol steady.

Under his plaid, Dougal rested his hand on the butt of his own gun. He could only pray Eldin would not fire his weapon in this confined space, with a woman and children nearby and the threat of rockfall very real in this ancient cavern. Yet if he had to fire his own weapon, he would risk it to save the ones he loved.

"Dougal, listen," Hugh said. "We can all profit from this. Sell him the whisky."

"Hugh, did you not hear? Eldin does not want the cache of aged whisky," Dougal said. "If he did, I would have sold it to him and made the profit already. He wants something more valuable, more rare even than Highland gold."

"That is so," Eldin said. "I want what no one else can have."

"If you did not want this whisky supply, why did you bring us here?" Hugh rounded on Eldin. "I agreed to your scheme because buying this stock would benefit the glen more immediately than other means. You never mentioned another whisky. What is it?"

"The fairy whisky," Dougal said quietly.

"That is just a legend," Hugh sputtered. "I tasted it myself.

Nothing to it. Good but rather bland whisky. It lacks the quality of the aged casks. You do not want that stuff, Lord Eldin."

"I do," Eldin replied. "And I will pay any price for it."

"It is a disappointing brew. You are making a mistake."

"The fairy ilk themselves make that brew," Eldin said.

"Not exactly," Dougal said. "We make it. Hugh is correct. It is just a legend."

"I doubt it!" Eldin snapped. "I have investigated the legends thoroughly. I have searched up and down the Highlands to find something indisputably part of the fairy realm. And Kinloch fairy brew is it."

"You are truly mad to believe that." Hugh gaped at him.

"Why do you care about the fairy brew?" Dougal asked.

"I am a collector of fairy lore and magical things," Eldin said. "I have heard of the fairy brew, and I must have it. Sell me whatever you have. I offer you a high price, one you should accept. Sell me the recipe, and make even more profit. I am sure you only wish your loved ones to be safe, and would do anything for them. Anything." He waved his small pistol toward Fiona.

"And if I will not sell?" Dougal growled.

"Then I can take all you have, the glen, the ones you love. Your life too if I must. Otherwise I can make sure you are jailed for smuggling. I will hold the rights to any brew produced in Glen Kinloch. And," Eldin said, "you will not see any of these dear folk again." He looked at Fiona and the children. Taking a backward step, he lifted his pistol to point it at Hugh, standing nearest him. "Or the good reverend either."

"The fairy brew is just an ordinary whisky," Dougal said. "Made from a family recipe. The legends are only stories told by the fireside."

"I will soon know for myself. I am among the few who will recognize the difference once I taste it," Eldin said. "When I have the rights to the glen and any goods produced in it, I will have the exclusive privilege of the water source used to make whisky here."

"No one can claim full rights to water that flows from one glen to another. Nick, truly, this is madness," Patrick said.

"Madness to one man is genius to another," Eldin responded.

"Even you cannot bring this about, cousin," Patrick said.

"Others are coming. Excise men quite like my money, I have found."

"Water source?" Fiona asked. "Does that matter?"

"Aye, the water quality is essential to the quality of the whisky," Dougal said.

"True, and there is a certain spring in the hills of Glen Kinloch that supplies water for Kinloch whisky," Eldin said. "I have pieced that much together from asking around, and learning about the local legends. The lairds of Kinloch will not reveal it, but others know something of the traditions. I want the rights to that spring, and I want to know exactly where it is."

"It is protected," Dougal said.

"Cooperate, and all will go well. You can have the rest of the glen if you will accept my money. You will be a rich man. Fiona would like that, would you not, cousin?" He smirked, glancing toward her. "She is desperate to find a wealthy Highland man."

"I have found the one I want," she said quietly, her gaze meeting Dougal's.

"A penniless Highland laird? Go ahead," Eldin said. "Break the conditions of the will, and the bulk of Lady Struan's accounts will come to me. I can only benefit."

"The laird of Kinloch has more wealth than you can ever imagine or appreciate," she said. "The wealth of a good heart, and the good fortune of loyalty, respect—and love." She looked at Dougal, her eyes wide and sheened with tears.

He caught her gaze, held it, felt his heart open wide, full to the brim. But he glanced away, fingers flexing on the hidden pistol. He must not allow distraction now.

"Sentimental nonsense," Eldin answered. "What have you done to the girl, Kinloch? She was a sensible lass until she came up here. I offer you a good bargain, sir. I advise you to accept, or all will go to hell in this glen."

"I do not accept," Dougal said. "You know that."

"Listen, fool! It is not difficult!" Eldin waved the pistol. "Just give over the fairy whisky you hold now, with the rights to the spring and the recipe to produce it. Do that, and Fiona and the children go free. I will pay handsomely, as I said."

"Do you truly expect to get out of this cave alive?" Dougal asked.

"I do. You will lose your glen without the funds I am offering you."

"If you had my whisky stock and the rights to the spring," Dougal went on, "what then? You do not know how to produce whisky. Little good the rest would do you."

"Glen Kinloch distillery would produce it for me."

"I sincerely doubt the glen folk who do the work would co-operate." Dougal kept his voice low, controlled, though he vibrated with anger. "There is one problem with your scheme. If the fairy brew is ever sold, that will undo its magic, so the legend says. Oh, but it is just a legend," he drawled. "What does it matter?"

"What do you mean?" Eldin leveled the pistol at him. "You lie. The stuff is powerful, and the magic of the Fey is what gives it potency."

"If I take money for it—if any money changes hands—that will render the product to just a modest peat reek. The spring would cease to flow, would never again produce water for the fairy brew. According to tradition, that is. It might be all nonsense."

"Not true. I heard none of that said in my inquiries," Eldin said.

"Because it is a secret, you nasty man!" Lucy said. "Only our kin know. Not you!"

Quickly Fiona covered the child's mouth, leaning to whisper to her.

"What do you mean, girl?" Eldin demanded.

"She is just a child speaking out of turn," Fiona said, and sent the three children to the back of the cave into shadows. As she turned, Dougal saw her motion surreptiously to him, tipping her head and pointing to the back of the cave. No one saw but himself.

Frowning, he nodded slightly to tell her to stay back with the children. He wanted them out of harm's way if it came to violence. She inclined her head again, and he understood she meant to go to the back of the cave for safety. Good, then.

"Child, what do you know?" Eldin barked. "What is the secret?"

"She is a bairn, and can be ill-mannered," Dougal said. Lucy opened her mouth indignantly to speak, but Fiona clapped a hand over her lips again. "Enough, Lord Eldin," Dougal continued. "Your so-called bargain would ruin the value of the fairy whisky forever. It would cease to be special, so legend claims."

"You would say anything to protect that brew," Eldin said.

"Put down the gun." Dougal drew his pistol then, cocked and ready.

"Kinloch is an excellent shot," Hugh said. "I would beware, sir."

"Patrick has a good aim too," Dougal said calmly. "He has not wavered a bit."

"You would be guilty of shooting a revenue officer if you try," Eldin said. He lifted the pistol once more. "You forget I am also a customs officer appointed to this region. MacGregor of Kinloch, I now arrest you in the name of the king for smuggling, and for a treasonous plot to steal revenue from the Crown."

"Nicholas, please stop this!" Fiona said.

Eldin ignored her. "Put down the gun, Kinloch, or be shot— and others with you. I call it a good bargain indeed to catch such a scoundrel with his supply of whisky."

"You are named an officer by title only," Patrick said. "You paid for the position. He never rides out," he added. "But he has some authority. Blast it all, Nick."

"Eldin, do not be a fool," Dougal said. "There is too much at risk here."

"I ceased to care long ago, when my heart was taken from me. I need fairy magic to replace what I have lost in life," he said in a low and dangerous voice. "Fairy magic of great strength, if I am ever to reclaim my heart and soul." He glanced toward Fiona. "You wanted to know what happened to me? What I want? I want to feel again."

Dougal looked toward Fiona. And stared. The back of the cave was dark. Empty. She was gone, and the children with her. Eldin noticed too.

"Fiona!" Eldin stepped toward the cave. As he turned, MacIan picked up the lantern and threw it toward Eldin, striking him on the shoulder, spilling sparks. It tumbled to the floor, but miraculously the light still glowed.

Eldin turned and fired the pistol toward Dougal and Patrick. The reverberation blasted through his ears, his skull, and the ball buzzed past like a metal bee, hitting the rock wall with an explosive crack. Moments later, a great rumbling shook the walls and grew to a trembling underfoot.

Part of the sheer rock wall cracked, then split, and the thunderous noise grew, peppered now with the hiss and sifting of dirt and smaller rocks.

"Fiona!" Dougal shouted, just as Patrick and Hugh threw themselves toward him in a heavy tackle that tossed all three backward to the upper slope of the walkway. Nearby, Eldin tumbled too, as limestone walls began to collapse around them, spewing rocks, dust, and shards of stone.

"HURRY, THIS WAY," Fiona said frantically, leading the children ahead of her. "Quickly!" She glanced over her shoulder as she pushed them into the narrow crevice she had spotted in the back wall of the cave. The golden star of light from the lantern Hugh had set aside was still visible, and she could hear the men arguing.

Rushing the children along, helping them pick their way through a slim channel in the rock that led onward, she was glad to see that the narrow corridor angled upward, just as she had hoped from a quick glance behind the kegs. The rock walls were damp stone, the uneven floor of the snaking, narrow passageway so wet in places that she stepped ankle-deep in water twice and had to make sure the children did not stumble. She could hear water trickling, then rushing, somewhere up ahead, though she could not yet tell what that might mean.

"Walk carefully," she whispered to the three young ones. "Let me go ahead now. We will all hold hands—there," she said, when they had formed a chain.

A little further on, she felt fresh air and increasing moisture. Seeing a glaze of bluish light on the dark, glossy stone walls, she felt sure there must be an opening ahead if they just kept going. The passage seemed a bit of a maze, sloping up, then down, up again, cantered right and then left. She prayed the exit, when they found it, would be large enough, for there could be small crevices and fissures throughout the rock that might not allow even a child to pass through.

When she had knelt with the children in the iron-barred cavelet, she noticed the sound of water, felt a drift of moist air, and saw that the ground slanted upward. Caves like these could be honeycombed with cells and passages, with water trickling here and there and openings to the air naturally occurring. The water seepage might come from the loch overhead, yet there was a good chance that it might indicate a larger opening in the earth, with a passage to freedom. It was worth exploring. If the passage proved worthless, she would bring the children back to the storage cave.

But she hoped past hope to get the children far away from here, no longer bargaining chips for Eldin. As for Dougal, Patrick, and Hugh, she prayed they would take control of the situation and stay safe. She knew they would all want the children removed from danger.

As they edged along, she heard a deep rumbling growl and felt the rock floor tremble beneath her feet. Pausing, reaching out to touch the bairns' shoulders and stop them, she waited. The tremors grew stronger. Lucy cried out, and Jamie and Annabel looked up at her, wide-eyed and frightened.

Something had caused a rockfall—she was sure of that, but unsure what had caused it so suddenly. Dear God, she thought, had someone fired a gun after all? Her heart leapt to her throat. As much as she wanted to go back and make sure Dougal and the others were unharmed, she could not risk the children's safety.

They could not go back now. They had to go forward. She prayed her instincts about the cave formation were correct.

After a few more twists and turns, Annabel pointed ahead. "There is light ahead, Miss MacCarran!"

"I see," she said. "Good! Keep going, my dearies!"

They were walking sideways now, the passage that narrow as they edged along with their backs to the wall, their feet constantly wet. Looking ahead, she saw a pale-blue light filtering over the walls. The surrounding rock was darker now, mottled and glossy. She paused, running her fingers over it. Granite deposits, mingled with quartz and shale and other igneous sorts. Fascinating, she thought.

"Miss MacCarran! This way!" Jamie called. "I can feel some fresh air. I think we can all get through!"

The channel he indicated was very narrow, but they turned sideways, sliding and pushing their way, passing through step by step until it opened wider and the going was easier. The highlights on the rock glistened and grew brighter, and now Fiona noticed other glittering elements threading and weaving through the dark stone.

Veins of gold, she realized, here and there, and there again. Catching her breath as she studied the wavering lines cutting through the stone, she said nothing, smiling to herself as she urged her charges on.

The watery trickle grew stronger, dripping down the walls, puddling on the floor. "The loch will crash down on us!" Jamie cried.

The girls whimpered, but Fiona shook her head. "He is only joking, lassies."

Jamie thrust back his shoulders. "I will go first and protect you!"

She smiled, seeing increasing courage in the wee lad who had let Lucy best him more often than not. He was enjoying the adventure.

"I think we are past the loch in this section," Fiona told them. "The passage through the rock continues upward, see. We are at the level of the loch or above it now. Climb with me, dears, and go carefully."

"We are walking through a stream," Lucy said. "My feet are wet."

"Mine too. You will be fine," Jamie said. "I will take care of you. And then I will come back and mine all this gold—it is gold, is it not, Miss Fiona?"

So he had seen. She nodded. "I think so. The stream rushes right through where the ore is located. The water might even carry the flavor of gold." And that would bring gold to the laird, and bless his whisky, and bless the glen as well, she thought.

"Gold would make excellent whisky," Lucy said. "We must tell Uncle Dougal."

"We will." Fiona said, sending up a little prayer that they would see him very soon indeed. Then she paused again, realizing that they were very close to an exit now.

"Look!" Lucy said, pointing. "A pool of water!"

"And a hole in the roof of the cave!" Annabel cried, as Jamie ran ahead, and Fiona reached out to slow and caution him.

Ahead on the upward slope, she saw the gleam of water, the surface of a shining pool that whirled at its center, bubbling riotously enough to propel upward to the rock ceiling above it, where a hole of rock and earth—and grass and flowers and sky, she saw now—allowed the water to surge upward.

"A well!" Fiona said. "A natural well with a fountain—the water comes up from an underground source."

"Water does not flow upward," Annabel said pragmatically.

"The fairies make it do that," Lucy said, nodding.

"It is an artesian well," Fiona said as they approached. "It bubbles up from below, and bursts out like a fountain. There must be a heated spring beneath it for it to bubble like that, and push up into the hillside above. Come on, and watch your step. We will have to go through the water to get out."

Closer now to the natural exit, she peered through the fountain's opening. Bright sunset colors glowed purple and red and amber. Thick grass edged the opening in the rock.

"Step into the pool—carefully, let me see how deep it is," she said, setting foot in it first. The water was warm indeed, the water swirling about her ankles and calves and the hem of her skirts, the bubbling frothing water wetting and splashing all of them as she assisted each child to step into the water.

The opening in the rock overhead was so close overhead, a wide, raw oval shape, that she could easily reach up and grasp its turfed edge. Boosting one child after another, she made sure each one was firmly out, kneeling on the grassy layers overhead. Then she took hold of the edge herself, and setting her feet on the rise of rock that formed a bowl around the small bubbling pool, she pulled herself upward, the children laughing and tugging and helping her, until she half kneeled, half lay on the grass, laughing with the awkward effort and sheer relief.

Soaked, laughing with the children, for a moment Fiona felt as if they had all been birthed into a new life and a magical place. They had entered a place of beauty and peace. As she stood, she knew with stunning certainty that she wanted to stay forever in Glen Kinloch.

They stood together in a grove of birches, with the beautiful fountain bubbling at their feet, a sunset of lavender and pink beyond the trees, and a thick carpet of bluebells underfoot. She smoothed her drenched skirts and laughed as she helped the children straighten their wet clothing and damp hair. Gathering them close as they shivered and giggled, she smiled with them and rubbed their backs and shoulders for warmth.

"Look at the bluebells!" Lucy said. "They are so beautiful!"

Fiona looked around in earnest then, enchanted by the sight of the flowers—thousands of bluebells in full bloom, covering the ground in a haze of purple blue that poured through the trees in a liquid wave of color—perhaps the most beautiful sight she had ever seen.

"This fountain will make good whisky, flavored with gold in the rock and the bluebells too," Lucy said.

"You will be an excellent distiller when you grow up, Lucy MacGregor," Fiona said. "And this place makes the very finest fairy brew, I suspect," she mused.

This must be the secret protected place, she thought, as she spun slowly around.

"Aye," Lucy said. "This is the place where my uncle goes. He does not talk of it much, but I have heard what the uncles say. This is the place that holds the fairy magic, you see."

"Ah," Fiona said, understanding. Here was the place where Dougal and his father and grandfathers before him collected water for the fairy whisky. He had told her only a little, but she cherished that he had shared even that much with her. And she hoped that someday he would tell her, and their children, the whole secret of the fairy whisky of Glen Kinloch.

"We must keep this secret always," she told the children, setting a finger to her lips, waiting as they did the same. Then she led them through the deep bluebells to find the way out to the bowl of the glen, and home.

Then she heard a rumble grow beneath their feet, a sound like low thunder and a shaking underfoot. The well burst upward in a high spike of rushing water.

Dougal, she thought. Oh, God. He and the others could be

trapped. She had to find help, bring men to the caves—

"Hold hands!" she called. "This way!" She hurried the bairns through the grove.

RUNNING OUT OF the cave with Patrick and Hugh, Dougal turned to dash back and drag Eldin, who had collapsed to his knees, free of the rubble and falling stones and into the air. They were all stunned, filthy, exhausted, and Eldin, hampered by a limp, struggled to make his way up the hill. Shocked and silent, Dougal stood in the sunset light, coated in limestone dust, looking around as the cave entrance shook, cluttered with rocks, and the thundering continued underground.

"Fiona," Patrick said, turning to him. "And the children—they will be trapped!"

"They might have made it through," Dougal replied. "Fiona took the bairns to the back of the cave even before the rockfall began. There is an old water channel in the back of the cave—I think she saw it, and took the chance that the passage would lead out and away. I believe it does, though I have never followed it all the way through. So there is a chance. Either way, we will make sure they get out."

"She knows rocks, that lass," Patrick said. "If anyone could find a way through the caves, she could."

"What if the walls collapsed on them?" Hugh came toward them, assisting Eldin, who limped heavily, looking exhausted. "We must search for them."

"We will. But if they got out, I think I know where they will be," Dougal said. "I will go there first. If I do not find them, we will gather the lads and go into the caves."

"The whisky!" Eldin rasped. "All of it—gone—"

"Not all," Dougal said. "The collapse was lower, among the smaller caves. Most of the kegs are stored near the upper entrance. But we are more concerned about Fiona and the children now."

"Fiona is fine. I know it," Eldin said. "I would feel it if she were not safe."

Dougal frowned at that, and met Patrick's gaze. "Cousins," Patrick explained. "Fairy blood and such. I do not seem to have much of it, myself. But those two do."

"Ah." Dougal nodded his understanding. He had seen it in Fiona. So Eldin had the manifestation of the MacCarran fairy ancestry too; interesting, he thought.

"Where do you keep the fairy brew?" Eldin asked. "Is it ruined now?"

"That lot is stored elsewhere," Dougal answered. "But I will not sell it. Patrick, stay with Hugh and Eldin. I will go look for Fiona and the bairns."

He hurried through the gap between two hills, following upward along the ridge of the glen. Feeling as weary and as anxious as he had ever felt in his life, somehow his legs found the strength and his heart found the will. He could not rest until he found Fiona and the children safe.

Yet he felt heartened that Eldin, albeit a scoundrel, sensed the lass was unharmed. Dougal wished he felt so sure himself. He only knew his heart slammed with worry and exhaustion, only knew he must find her, and Lucy, Jamie, and Annabel.

Hearing shouts behind him, he turned to see men on horseback coming along the loch road. Patrick and the others, standing on the hillside above the loch, waved and waited as the riders went toward them.

Recognizing Tam MacIntyre with a few gaugers, Dougal gave a grim nod and continued on his way. So the law had found them—and soon would discover that the men of Glen Kinloch had done nothing amiss following the wild ball game. But they had been caught in a rock collapse caused by Lord Eldin's pistol shot as he tried to demand a fairy whisky that only went by that name, an ordinary brew attached to a legend.

He was sure that Patrick MacCarran would keep the focus on Eldin and away from any smuggling in the glen. As for Hugh MacIan, the reverend was not a bad fellow by nature, just grievously misled by the earl. Dougal guessed Hugh would feel remorseful. And Mary MacIan would not let her grandson hear the end of it anytime soon.

Dougal walked onward. He would find them soon—he had to. Following that, he hoped that Patrick would be his brother-by-law, nor could he ask for a more trustworthy fellow. He hoped the rest of Fiona's brothers would accept him—a poor Highland laird, wealthy only in his heart. And indeed fortunate in that, if Fiona would agree to marry him. For now, all he wanted was to see her safe and unharmed and tucked in his arms.

With a fresh burst of strength, he climbed, breathing hard as he went up the steep slope. He moved steadily, as if he had not played to utter exhaustion in the glen's wild ball game, then somehow escaped a cave-in and averted a disaster of worse events. He ran now as if his life, and those he loved, depended on his muscle and will.

If Fiona had found the way out of the caves, as he suspected she might, then she would have emerged nearby, along a path hidden in a grove of birch trees. Reaching the crest of that hill and the meadowland edging the birchwood, he stopped to look around, seeing the thick cluster of birches with their roots deep in a frothy skirt of bluebells.

"Fiona!" he shouted. No answer. "Fiona! Lucy!"

Spinning again, he saw them coming out of the birchwood, wading through the blue-violet haze of flowers. Fiona held hands with Lucy and Annabel, Jamie following. Rosy golden sunset light poured its gleam over them. They were drenched, Dougal saw then, hair and skirts and jackets wet. The bubbling spring, he realized. They were laughing, the girls skipping. Lucy and Annabel clutched bouquets of bluebells, and Jamie chattered excitedly, holding a chunk of rock for Fiona to see.

Bluebells. They had found the bluebell wood. Fiona had discovered the very tunnel that led to the spring, just as he had hoped. The fairies, he felt sure now, had watched over his loved ones, guiding them to safety.

Laughing outright with relief and a burst of love, he ran toward them. Fiona's smile brightened to see him, and she left the children to hurry toward him. Reaching out, he took her in his arms, lifted her, spun her about. She circled her arms around his neck, laughing in sweet relief too, her cheek soft, his prickly with a day's beard. Around them, the children danced and jumped, giggling.

He set her down then and kissed her, tasting heaven on her lips in a slow, gentle kiss that he never wanted to end.

"Stop kissing!" Lucy said. "Come look what we found, Uncle Dougal!"

Fiona laughed, her lips to his, and he chuckled too, knowing she was as thrilled to see him, as thrilled and committed to their love, as he was. He kissed her brow, her damp, dark, beautiful hair. Then he winked at Lucy.

"My wee lass," he murmured, touching his niece's hair. "I feel a rich man, indeed."

"So rich, Uncle Dougal!" Lucy held up the bluebells clutched in her hand. "We found these, and the pool and fairy fountain. And we found gold too!"

"Gold?" He saw all of them nod.

"Aye, in the caves," Jamie said. "Lots of it!"

"Gold in the caves?" He was astonished.

Fiona smiled. "There is granite under the earth over there, veined with gold. Even if you never tap all of it, you can count yourself very fortunate."

"I am fortunate already, to have all of you." He swept his arms wide to encompass all of them, ruffled the children's heads, and then kissed Fiona again. The bairns whooped around them in a circle.

"Enough! We need supper," Lucy said, "and baths!"

"That, my wee lass, can be arranged. Come this way."

Dougal shepherded them along, snugging his arm around Fiona as they walked.

"I am hungry! But who will make supper?" Lucy asked. "Uncle Fergus is a terrible cook, and Maisie might be at her Da's house."

"I can make supper," Fiona said.

"We would be most grateful," Dougal said. "Will you stay in the glen, my love?"

She smiled up at him. "I might."

They descended the hill together, and Dougal raised a hand to wave as he saw Fiona's brother climbing the slope toward them, waving and hallooing.

Epilogue

FIONA READ ANOTHER rhyme aloud for her students, then listened as they recited it back to her—Gaelic to English, English to Gaelic. Hearing a commotion outside, she glanced at the window and saw people gathering there. It was yet morning, and lessons were hardly over, but she could hear the pleasant rumble of voices. Excusing herself, she went to the door and opened it.

Two dozen or more people stood in the yard, men and women and a few adolescents who worked the farms and herds rather than attended school. She saw Neill MacDonald and his father, along with Helen MacDonald, Annabel's mother, as well as Mary MacIan and others. Many names she knew now, though some she did not.

"Good morning," she said, heart thumping anxiously. She had no idea why so many would gather outside the schoolhouse now. She wondered, with a sudden ache, if they had come to bid her farewell. Her teaching agreement would end soon. "What can I do for you?"

Mary MacIan came toward her. The old woman had been saddened to learn of Hugh's involvement with Lord Eldin, resulting in the cave collapse, and she had fair blistered her grandson with her opinion. Hugh had apologized profusely to her, and to Dougal and Fiona too. Since then, he had kept to his side of the glen and his kirk and parishioners. Few outside a small group knew the truth of what had happened that day. Dougal was willing to forgive Hugh, but his uncles had taken the poor reverend to task more than once. The fellow was fair mortified, Fiona knew.

Just then, Dougal stepped out of the crowd to stand a little apart from Mary MacIan. Fiona's heart bounded to see him, just as it did each time he was near. If a day went past when they did not meet, she missed him keenly. In that moment, their eyes met, and he was the only one she saw. The others all faded to mist.

She did not want to leave the glen, if that were why they gathered here. Perhaps it did not matter that the laird seemed fond of the teacher; perhaps they had decided she must go, being kin to Lord Eldin, the man who would have brought tourists and ruin to their beautiful glen. But Eldin had sailed for the Continent, and would not return for a long time, if ever, so her brother said.

Nearly a month had passed since the ba' game and the cave collapse, and even longer had passed since she had spent a night at Kinloch House. Time went by too quickly while she taught daily and answered questions about everything from the cave collapse to geology, and took what chances she had to roam the hills looking for fossils and stones—and any sign of more gold to help the community of the glen. But the rest of what they had discovered that day in the birchwood remained a dear secret.

She knew Dougal had been occupied with the work of digging out the rubble-filled caves to rescue and relocate scores of whisky casks and kegs. Crossing paths with him on the meadow between Kinloch House and the school, or other paths in the glen, she learned that he had sold the promised amounts to merchants when the cutters arrived on another night. Just as agreed, he had met his part as distiller and seller. Smuggled or not, his honor and his word were of utmost importance, and she was glad to know he had met the quota he had promised, even if it involved some smuggling.

He had sold some of the whisky to Eldin for an exorbitant fee, meant for new hotel that soon would welcome tourists. Eldin, leaving for a holiday abroad and leaving his hotel in other hands, knew that his reputation teetered on rumors of what had happened in the Kinloch caves. He had asked that his disgraceful behavior never be mentioned or gossiped about. Dougal and the MacCarrans had quietly agreed.

Her cousin might come back and try to make amends, Fiona knew, but she would never trust him again. Eldin was like a hawk, an untamed bird of prey, cooperative only so long as it was convenient, unpredictable otherwise, and prone to quick, vicious action if provoked.

Watching Dougal now, with the crowd clustered behind him, she waited, wondering. Her students came to the door behind her. Her heart fluttered—did they truly mean to send her on her way so soon? She had longed for an invitation to stay here forever. But she had not found a chance to answer Dougal's question about marriage.

And to her disappointment, he had not asked again. Had he decided it was best she return to Edinburgh, while he returned to smuggling and a bachelor life? Or was he still waiting for her decision? She had not wanted to push the matter, glad that they had some time lately to come to know one another better. But had she been mistaken?

Now she walked through the dusty yard, brushing chalk dust from her hands, then clasping them. Her students followed her into the clearing. Silence and birdsong filled the summer air.

Mary MacIan murmured to Dougal, who leaned down to listen. He nodded.

"Fiona MacCarran, teacher in the glen," Mary said in Gaelic, for some of those here, Fiona knew, did not have much English, "the glen folk want a word with you."

She nodded, tightening her hands. "Aye, what is it?"

"We want to know if you will teach us," Mary said.

She blinked in surprise. "Teach you?"

"Some of us want to learn to speak and read English," Mary

said. "Some must learn to talk to others outside our glen. Some must learn to sign our names. And some of these rascals may want to read their own arrest warrants." A ripple of laughter sounded. "And so we want to join your class."

Stunned, Fiona glanced at Dougal, who nodded slowly.

"I would be honored to teach you," she answered in Gaelic. Several of those gathered nodded, pleased, murmuring to one another. "But just now the schoolhouse is full, with twelve scholars and no more seats. And the roof leaks. It must be replaced soon or it will fall down on our heads. And—my teaching agreement will end soon. I will have to leave the glen." She dared not glance at Dougal then.

"You could stay," Mary MacIan said.

"You could, aye," Dougal said mildly. Fiona flicked a glance toward him.

"Stay and teach?" Now her gaze was fastened to his.

He tipped his head. "If it is what you want."

She nodded, afraid to speak for the catch in her breath.

Mary MacIan looked up at Dougal. Fiona noticed the others turning to look at him too, as if expectant. "What else would you like, Miss MacCarran?" Dougal asked.

"I want to stay in Glen Kinloch and teach," she said, addressing only him.

"You could do that," Dougal said. "You could teach what some need to learn."

"What would that be, Kinloch?" she asked softly.

He shrugged, smiled. "Oh, I can think of a few lessons."

"Will you join the class, too, Kinloch?" Mary MacIan asked.

"Perhaps. I may need to read a warrant one of these days," he drawled, amid a burst of laughter behind him.

"Och, that lad reads well enough!" Fergus boomed. "He could write warrants if he wanted, with the university schooling he has had, and a library to rival any city man's collection." Fergus looked at Fiona. "Miss MacCarran, we will repair the schoolhouse roof, if that will keep you here."

"That would be good, aye." She could hardly speak, her throat tightening.

"One thing more might keep you here," Fergus said. "You could marry the laird and stay with us always."

Her heart soared, her breath caught. She heard gasps, saw beaming smiles. She heard her students behind her clapping and laughing. But she could not take her gaze from the man who moved toward her, then paused, his gaze green and deep.

"I could do that," she said. "I could marry the laird, if he would have me."

"The laird would marry the teacher, if she would have him," he said.

"Oh, she would indeed," she breathed.

He strode toward her, set his hands to her waist, and lifted her up a little, turning her around and setting her down again. Then he kissed her, gentle and slow and deeper than others would see. She felt herself melt, heard laughter and applause. But the truest sound was his steady heartbeat in time with her own, gone to wildness within her.

"Good, then," he murmured in her ear. "We will do that."

"They will do that!" Mary announced, for she had heard it.

Amid cheers, Dougal laughed and kissed her cheek. "Soon," he said.

"Soon," Fiona echoed, smiling up at him, seeing no one else.

He bent toward her. "It is nearly time to go up into the hills to the place where the bluebells grow, my love. I will take you there and tell you the whole of the legend of Glen Kinloch, and how to make the fairy whisky that brings the lights to your eyes, and the lights to our life, aye?"

"Aye." She gazed up at him. "And I promise to keep that secret all my life."

"I know you will," he whispered. "We will keep the fairies' promise all our lives."

"All that, and longer," she whispered.

Among all my books and my heroes and heroines from first to most recent, *A Rogue in Moonlight* (originally published by Avon as *The Highland Groom*) is one of my very favorites. Whatever it is about Dougal MacGregor and Fiona MacCarran, whether it is their ability to love, their banter and humor, their willingness to learn something new from each other and grow—start to finish, I loved writing this book. It was a pleasure to revisit it for this new Dragonblade edition, reading the story again and tweaking it here and there (for example, gold veins through igneous rock such as granite, duh! The little things we catch on another pass through!).

A recent trip to Scotland gave me the chance to visit the National Museum of Scotland in Edinburgh again, where I saw fascinating examples of fossils found in the Scottish Highlands, including ammonites, trilobites, leaf impressions, and other little critters and crawlers embedded in various rock formations—just the sort of thing that would fascinate Fiona MacCarran. I had almost forgotten what they looked like, and I took that new impression into account in giving this book a fresh edit. And of course other stories popped into my head, so there may be more coming from heroes and heroines who like rocks and fossils and very ancient Scottish things!

This book concludes the previously published series called the Whisky Rogues. I'm currently working on brand new stories connected to this world of Scottish Regency heroes and heroines involved in the whisky trade (and many other interests!). New this year, look for related stories set during the Regency and just after in Scotland, including *Lyon of Scotland*, a Lyon's Den novel, and *Dance Under a Highland Moon*, featuring one of the Whisky Rogues from *A Rogue in Firelight*. There's much more to come!

I hope you enjoyed Dougal and Fiona's story, and I hope you'll look for my other books as well. Check out my website at www.susanfraserking.com, and look for me on the Word Wenches blog—www.wordwenches.com—with some of my author friends!

Happy Reading!
Susan

About the Author

Susan King is the bestselling, award-winning author of (so far) 28 historical novels and novellas, a hefty nonfiction history, and dozens of magazine and web articles on education and the craft of writing. Her books, including mainstream historicals Lady Macbeth: A Novel and Queen Hereafter: A Novel of Margaret of Scotland, have been published by Penguin, Random House, HarperCollins, Kensington, ePublishingWorks, and Dragonblade. Praised for historical accuracy, lyrical writing, and storytelling quality, she is a USA Today bestselling author with numerous awards, nominations, and career achievement awards as well as starred reviews from Publisher's Weekly, Booklist, and Library Journal. Most of her books are set in Scotland ranging from the 11th to the 19th centuries.

Susan is a former university lecturer in art history, a private school teacher, and a founding member of one of the longest-running author blogs, "Word Wenches" (wordwenches.com). She holds a Bachelor's in studio art and English literature, a Master's in art history, and completed most of her Ph.D./ABD in medieval art history. Raised in Upstate New York, she lives in Maryland with her husband and three sons in an ever-growing family.

Website – www.susanfraserking.com

www.ingramcontent.com/pod-product-compliance
Lightning Source LLC
Chambersburg PA
CBHW071248300726
48975CB00002B/590